"More action than season two of *The Walking Dead*."
HORROR TALK

"A diverting, entertaining zombie siege novel—complete with all the delicious, bone-crunching, blood-gushing awesomeness a zombie lover could ever want."
BOOK SMUGGLERS

"While *Plague Town* is a really fun and action-packed ride, one cannot dismiss the darkness at the center of it all. There are sections laced throughout written from the perspective of the innocent people as they are turning into zombies… an emotional core that grounds the novel and keeps it from being just a shallow action/horror romp."
STRANGE AMUSEMENTS

"Read it—I zombie dare you. Fun, fast, read."
AFFAIRS MAGAZINE

"If you love zombies, strong, sarcastic heroines with heart, and fight scenes that will knock your socks off, you'll devour *Plague Town*!"
MY BOOKISH WAYS

"Delightfully gruesome."
NERDS IN BABELAND

"It's funny, scary, gory, sexy and goes a mile a minute."
CULTURE BRATS

"If you like butt-kicking heroines with a fair dose of snark and humor, then you're going to love Ashley."
GEEK MOM

BOOKS BY
DANA FREDSTI

Praise for PLAGUE NATION

"Fast, furious, and fun: *Plague Nation* takes the promise of *Plague Town* and builds upon it, delivering bigger and better zombie mayhem."
    MIRA GRANT, author of the NEWSFLESH TRILOGY

"If you like your heroines smart and sassy and kick ass capable, Ashley Parker has what you need. And *Plague Nation* is exactly what the zombie genre needed."
    JOE MCKINNEY, Stoker Award–winning author of FLESH EATERS and INHERITANCE

"*Plague Nation* is a rollicking zombie thriller packed with action, chills, and biting humor. Brava!"
    JONATHAN MABERRY, *New York Times* bestselling author of PATIENT ZERO, FIRE AND ASH, and DEAD OF NIGHT

"Snarky humor, lots of zombies (gore and all), and plenty of edge-of-your-seat action."
    LONG AND SHORT REVIEWS

Praise for PLAGUE TOWN

One of the Top Ten Zombie Releases of 2012
    BARNESANDNOBLE.COM

"A gruesomely good read that has me panting for the next book in the series. As hard to put down as a swarm of zombies.

    KAT RICHARDSON, bestselling author of the GREYWALKER novels

"In *Plague Town*, Dana Fredsti has created something truly unique in the world of horror fiction—a cool, hip zombie apocalypse novel. With crisp writing, a cast of memorable characters, and tons of undead combat action, it's a zombie lover's literary dream. When the dead rise, I'll want the wild cards by my side."

ROGER MA. author of THE ZOMBIE COMBAT MANUAL

"Fredsti's writing is razor sharp as her heroes fight off the horde while fighting their attraction for each other."

STACEY GRAHAM. author of THE ZOMBIE DATING GUIDE

"*Plague Town* is a fast-moving zombie tale that reads like a blast of energy. If you like zombie apocalypse stories, this is a must read!"

LOIS GRESH. *New York Times* bestselling author of BLOOD AND ICE and ELDRITCH EVOLUTIONS

"Chills and thrills for that season when you're looking for—chills and thrills!"

HEATHER GRAHAM. author of HALLOWED GROUND and the FLYNN BROTHERS TRILOGY

"Dana Fredsti has created a world as familiar as our own back yard and populated it with recognizable people we care about... and zombies. *Plague Town* will have you turning pages fast... and checking the locks on all the doors."

RAY GARTON. author of LIVE GIRLS and SEX AND VIOLENCE IN HOLLYWOOD

"As adorable an end of the world as you're liable to get... a brisk, witty ultraviolent romantic gurlventure..."

GINA MCQUEEN. author of OPPOSITE SEX and APOCALYPSE AS FOREPLAY

AN ASHLEY PARKER NOVEL

PLAGUE WORLD

DANA FREDSTI

TITAN BOOKS

PLAGUE WORLD
Print edition ISBN: 9780857686374
E-book edition ISBN: 9780857686404

Published by Titan Books
A division of Titan Publishing Group Ltd
144 Southwark St, London SE1 0UP

First edition: July 2013
10 9 8 7 6 5 4 3 2 1

Visit our website: www.titanbooks.com

Did you enjoy this book? We love to hear from our readers.
Please email us at readerfeedback@titanemail.com or write to us at Reader
Feedback at the above address.

To receive advance information, news, competitions, and exclusive offers
online, please sign up for the Titan newsletter on our website: www.
titanbooks.com

To my Three Muses
Brian Thomas, T. Chris Martindale,
and David Fitzgerald

PROLOGUE

"Son of a bitch must pay."

Jack Burton—*Big Trouble in Little China*

LONDON, ENGLAND

Stavros tried to tune out the hacking coughs, snuffles, snorts and other unpleasant sounds coming from the four passengers he'd picked up at Chelsea Physic Garden. Two women and two men, all wearing power suits and sharing what seemed to be a nasty cold.

Blow your nose, mate, *he thought as one of the men gave a snorting inhalation that sounded like a walrus.*

He thought about raising the window that separated the driver and passenger portions of the town car, but it seemed a bit rude. It might be taken the wrong way, and one of these corporate types would no doubt complain. So he contented himself with surreptitiously pressing the pump on his ever-present hand sanitizer, tucked into one of the cup holders under the control panel.

There was something about these wankers in their suits, fresh out of their oh-so-important meetings, and the self-importance that pumped them up. It just set Stavros's hackles on end. All the little slights and the condescension in their voices when they spoke to him… if they bothered to speak to him at all.

He didn't regret skipping university. He didn't have any desire to do more than he was doing, but every now and then he wished he had a degree that would allow him to slap one of these posers across their over-educated faces.

Another twenty minutes on the road and he'd be rid of them at Heathrow, so they could spread their germs in their own countries and not make an honest working man too sick to do his job.

Danny sat in the furthest seat in the back of the town car, huddled against the door in a ball of misery. He'd been sick before, but nothing compared to this—not even the four-day salmonella marathon he'd had in 2005. His body hurt inside and out; even his eyeballs felt as if they were going to crack in half if he blinked.

A line from the Haunted Mansion ride was stuck in his brain, something about hot and cold running chills... He had those, along with the sensation of boiling poison running through his veins and in his forehead.

"You okay, Danny?"

He opened his eyes to see Jan from Digital Media, Holland Division, eying him with superficial concern. Jan was one of those uber-competitive guys who equated the failure of his peers with personal gain. He also made it more than obvious that he lusted after Nita from R&D Sweden, whom Danny had been seeing on the sly for the last year. Jan had made a few comments at the LP meeting, hinting that he knew about the relationship.

"I'm fine." A wet cough contradicted Danny's words almost immediately.

Jan smirked with an unattractive twist of his lips that he imagined made him look wry and sexy.

"Too many late nights sampling Swedish meatballs, eh?"

If he hadn't felt so shitty, Danny would have flipped the asshole off. He closed his eyes instead, and drifted away on a wave of pain that faded into blackness.

Jan raised an eyebrow and smirked. Danny looked like shit. And he'd been the first to come down with the flu at the annual LP meeting, spreading it around quickly, judging from the coughs and sniffles of many fellow attendees. This was a flu bug that would get to see the world. Maybe Jan should start calling him Typhoid Danny, so no one forgot where it started.

Oh yes, the kind of thing that could dog a person throughout their career… and perhaps even shorten it.

Jan chuckled to himself, only to have the laugh cut off by a sudden tickling in the back of his throat and nose. He sneezed violently, barely catching it behind one hand. His smugness evaporated at the sight of blood mixed in with the spray of spittle on his palm.

And then Danny went into convulsions.

Stavros frowned as he heard yet more coughing from the back of the town car. Had they never heard of Hall's?

"Danny?"

The sharp note of concern in the man's voice caught Stavros's attention. He glanced back to see the lanky Dutch fellow in the back shaking his seatmate by one shoulder. Blood dribbled out of the man's eyes, nose, and mouth, his features slack and lifeless.

Shit. He looked dead. A nasty smell hit Stavros's nose.

The Dutchman recoiled, coughing as he hunkered back against the other side of the car, as far from his seatmate as possible. The two women in the middle seat, also coughing, turned around to see what the fuss was.

"Jan, what is wrong?" A thick South American accent matched the brunette's exotic Salma Hayek good looks.

"It's Danny. I think—" the Dutchman coughed again, a wracking, rattling sound like marbles in a can filled with phlegm.

The pneumatic blonde opened her eyes and Stavros winced as he caught sight of her in the rearview mirror. The whites of her eyes were yellow and streaked with red, a counterpoint for *the almost startling blue of her corneas.*

"Danny?" Her voice was weak and gravelly after all the coughing.

The man in the back gave a sudden convulsion, more foul-smelling fluid leaking from his eyes, mouth, and nose.

The Dutchman next to him vomited.

"I'll get to hospital," Stavros said to no one in particular, hitting the "open" button on the driver's side window in an attempt to cut the thick smell of sickness—a mixture of blood, shit, and rot—which filled the car. He fought the urge to vomit, concentrating instead on finding an exit off the M4 and to some medical attention.

The nearest exit was for Brentford. Stavros didn't know if there was a hospital, but at the very least they'd have a police station, someone who could help. He didn't care. He just wanted these people out of his car so he could take it to a car wash and get it detailed, vacuumed, aired out, fumigated, for Christ's sake, and maybe snort some bleach to get the smell and possible infection out of his nostrils.

Then the bloke Danny opened his eyes. The corneas were now bluish-white, the color of fat-free milk and all the more eerie set against the red-tinged yellow of the his whites. More black fluid dribbled from his mouth, the smell thick and vile in the enclosed car.

"Danny?" The blonde leaned over the seat, relief obvious in her voice. He reached for her, grabbed her head, and pulled her over the seat back on top of his lap, teeth sinking into the soft flesh of her neck before anyone could react. Blood sprayed over the leather seats, splashing all of the passengers.

The Dutchman recoiled in horror, only to go into his own convulsions, the same black viscous liquid spewing out of his mouth.

Stavros stared in horror as the sick bloke ripped chunks of flesh from the blonde's neck, the other passengers recoiling in horror, fingers scrabbling for the door handles. His only thought was to get the hell off the road, out of the car, and away from whatever was wrong with his passengers. So he didn't bother looking in his rearview mirror when he swerved into the right lane over—directly into the path of an oncoming tanker.

CHAPTER ONE

Bad things happen to good people. Never forget that. The world is not always a fair place. And the dead really do walk the earth. And let me tell you—
That part really sucks.

"How many do you think there are?"

I glanced over at Nathan as I tried to count the rotting corpses shambling toward us on the rooftop of a University of California, San Francisco medical building. Most of the figures heading our way had been octogenarians—and some septuagenarians—when they'd died, which wasn't surprising, since the building held the geriatric ward. But damn, they were spry for their age.

"No idea." Nathan took a shot with his M4 and one of the zombies collapsed onto the roof. "But now there's one less rotting geezer."

I snorted. "You know, that's like something Tony would say. I expect better of you. I mean, aren't you too old for that?"

"You're never too old for sarcasm." Nathan nailed another zombie in the head with a well-placed shot. "Ah, make that *two* less."

Okay, Nathan wasn't all that old. Somewhere in his late forties, early fifties, with one of those lined faces that made it hard to guess his actual age. He also had a "screw you" attitude toward authority that made me predisposed to like him. Well, that, and the fact he'd pulled my ass out of the fire a couple of weeks back, saving me, Lil, and two cats from becoming zombie chow. So I tended to forgive his "hermit with shitty manners" attitude.

This particular building had the only rooftop in the facility with the room to accommodate a helicopter. There were two access doors, one each on the east and west sides of the building. One of them accessed the glass-covered catwalk that led to the Center for Regenerative Medicine. The catwalk also held the James Bondian elevator that went down to the super-secret lab.

We were there to secure the roof and its makeshift helipad with a sloppy red H painted on the concrete, so incoming helicopters carrying the core personnel from Redwood Grove could land safely.

Besides, when it came time to clear zombie infestations, who you gonna call? That's right. The few, the proud... complete with enhanced strength, agility and senses.

The wild cards.

Although the enhanced sense of smell wasn't necessarily a gift when dealing with decomposing cannibals.

"Man, this is *boring*."

Tony looked at the incoming zombies with dissatisfaction. A nineteen-year-old punk-ass gamer with multiple piercings—most of them empty now due to a particularly painful close encounter with a handsy zombie—he had an attitude that often screamed "Slap me, I'm a jerk."

Nathan and I both looked at him.

"Boring?" I raised an eyebrow. "Seriously?"

"Seriously," Tony said. "If this were a video game, it'd be all like 'Plug a Granny' and totally made for five-year-olds."

"Plug a Granny?"

Nathan snorted, although whether from disgust or amusement I couldn't tell.

Me? I had to smother a laugh. I mean, it *was* funny—kind of, in a sick and twisted kind of way, and these days I needed to take humor where I found it. Considering the truly fucked-up state of pretty much everything.

I mean, the Zombie Apocalypse. Who'da thunk it?

How many survivalist types were creaming their jeans at the chance to put their years of anal-retentive planning into practice, all those zombie preppers who'd had their brief moments of fame on reality TV. Most likely they were cowering in their reinforced bunkers, listening to their loved ones pounding on the door with rotting fists…

Okay, brain, that's enough of that, thank you very much.

I gave myself a mental shake. The horror show in front of me was more than enough. I didn't need to create another one in my imagination. Drawing a bead on a target, I pulled the trigger.

At least the movies hadn't lied about how to perma-kill zombies. Shoot 'em in the head. Destroy the brain. Or the stem, or the whatever-the-heck portion controlled the reptile functions. It would have totally sucked if that had turned out to be bullshit, while the rest of the zombocalypse proved to be true.

But it *did* work, and if you were creative, there were many ways and many weapons you could use to put them back in the grave, once and for all. Luckily for us, the more zombies we killed, the more creative we tended to get.

Thus ended the upside to the zombie outbreak.

"Why are there so many of them up here on the roof?" I wondered aloud. As soon as I spoke, I shot Tony a look and said, "If you say 'because this was once a very important place to them,' I will hit you."

Tony smirked, but kept his mouth shut.

"They were probably attracted to the sound of the helicopter when it took off yesterday morning," Nathan said as he put a round through the head of a Ruth Gordon look-alike. "Guess nothing better came along to distract them."

My jaw tightened.

We'd survived a chopper crash, fought our way through a zombie-infested San Francisco to UCSF, and found the hidden DZN lab. We'd lost five people along the way, but we'd made it—only to be ambushed upon our arrival. Gabriel had been hustled off at gunpoint by the proverbial men in black, and I was pretty sure they were the same bastards who'd sabotaged our helicopters, plus raided and burned down our lab at Big Red.

Whoever it was, they didn't see a problem with the spreading plague—and if our suspicions were correct, they were spreading it deliberately.

Why anyone would do that was beyond my comprehension... but then again, I have difficulty with the concept of fracking and GMOs in the food supply, so I probably wasn't the best person to analyze the motives of psychopaths.

What really bugged me was that someone involved had a personal grudge against yours truly. When someone points a gun at you and says they, "have a present for you from a old friend," you can bet your ass it's not a candygram. Plus they knew my name.

That's never a good sign.

More senior zombies stumbled through the door across the rooftop. I heard shots coming from the interior of the building, the comforting sound of the rest of our team doing their jobs. The bastards who'd ambushed us had wedged as many stairwell doors open as they could on both sides, making sure we'd have plenty of walking dead to play with.

Bastards. Did I mention that?

Luckily we had plenty of ammo. We couldn't clear the entire medical center—it would be suicide to try—but a few floors? Piece o' cake.

At least that's what I kept telling myself, because my spirits couldn't afford to sink any lower. Losing Kai had been bad enough, but when Mack died, it had ripped the heart out of our team—especially Lil, who was conspicuously absent from the current bout of zombie carnage. It was the sort of thing that typically made her dance with glee.

And Gabriel… it'd been like a punch in the gut when that helicopter took off, and when we were told we weren't going after him, well, I hadn't exactly handled it gracefully. Having to cool my heels was a special circle of hell.

Right now, though, I had a job to do. A messy, smelly, and totally cathartic job.

"Um, Ash?"

Tony's voice brought me back to the present—which included a frail-looking octogenarian in a hospital gown, pieces of flesh caught in its dentures and bite marks oozing black fluid from its arms. I capped it right away, the barrel of my M4 only a foot or so away from its head. It dropped in its tracks, falling forward. The hospital gown flapped open to reveal a naked, withered, greenish zombie butt with a chunk taken out of one cheek.

I could have gone my entire life without seeing that.

Nathan eyed me sternly.

"Keep your head in the game, kiddo," he said. "We can't afford to lose anyone else."

I nodded. "Yeah… sorry."

He gave me a rare, comforting pat on the shoulder.

"Don't worry—we'll get him back," he said. "Both Gabriel *and* Dr. Caligari."

Nathan's obscure but accurate film reference made me smile, but it only lasted for a moment. The same creeps who'd taken Gabriel also snatched Dr. Albert, our pet mad scientist. His vaccine for Walker's Flu was supposed to be the next big thing for pharma. Yet because he'd ordered his ego super-sized, he hadn't bothered with trivial details like clinical trials.

Unfortunately, his vaccine came with one whopper of a side effect. In laboratory lingo, it "reacted to a dormant variant of a retrovirus in about ten percent of the population, causing a mutation in the DNA." At least that's how Simone had explained it. In plain English, it turned its victims into the walking dead.

If only Dr. Albert had just stuck with prostate exams and yearly physicals. To think as a kid I'd accepted lollipops from that man. Now, however, he was our best hope for figuring out a cure. Otherwise I'd have been happy letting the megalomaniacal bastard rot wherever he'd been taken.

A new influx of zombies came shuffling through the far door, doing their best Moe, Larry, and Curly.

"What the hell?" I said. "Is Gentry herding them up here on purpose? Does he *want* us to get eaten?"

"It's 'cause you smell so tasty, Ash," Tony said.

I flipped him the bird.

"Where are Davis and Jones when we need 'em?" I grumbled, even though I already knew the answer.

The Gunsy Twins were two out of the original four snipers who'd survived the trip from Redwood Grove. Their shooting skills bordered on mystical, but they weren't wild cards, and unsuited to close-quarter encounters with extremely infectious enemy. So they were perched safely above the loading docks, picking off zombies with carefully placed headshots. Once that area was sealed off and we'd finished on the roof, all entrances to the DZN lab would be secured.

While I was a decent shot, thanks to my oxymoron of a liberal gun-nut father, I wasn't good enough to keep up with the numbers pouring out the roof access. At this point, I'd infinitely prefer close-quarter fighting. I could slice and dice faster than I could aim, fire, and reload.

"Let's conserve ammo," Nathan said, as if he was reading my mind.

Tony grinned, slung his M4 over one shoulder, and pulled a small but effective sledgehammer out of the loop on his belt. I followed suit, drawing my modified katana from its scabbard with what was now a fluid motion, almost as if I practiced in front of a mirror.

Okay fine, I totally do.

My faithful tanto—see what I did there?—remained patiently in its crossover sheath over the left side of my chest.

Cool accessories? I haz them.

"Go play, children." Nathan waved us toward the zombies. "I'll stay here on cleanup duty."

Tony and I exchanged a quick fist bump and dove in with enthusiasm. Blood, viscera, brain matter, and black goo flew with abandon as Tony swung Thor's Wee Hammer into zombie skulls, with deadly results. He might be an annoying punk-ass kid at times, but he was a kick-ass zombie-killing machine.

Myself, I practiced the fine art of decapitation, mixing it up with sweeping cuts and sharp thrusts through the eye sockets. We didn't have to worry about becoming infected. Hell, Tony, Nathan and I could swallow all manner of zombie crap, and be just fine.

Blerg. Why my brain consistently came up with mental images like that, I knew not.

Oh, well, I'd wait until after I'd finished my job to page Dr. Freud.

Our kills were punctuated with the sound of Nathan's rifle. He had some sort of fancy-ass firearm from his private collection. It could be dismantled and stored in its own plastic butt. With it he calmly and efficiently took out the incoming zeds without wasting a single round. If anything rattled Nathan, I had yet to see it.

Well, except Simone.

With every cut, every thrust, every kill, I pictured the asshole who had tried to shoot me, the one who "had a present for me." He'd missed, thanks to Lil's intervention, but the resulting ricochet damaged our team in a way that could never be repaired. He deserved the business end of my blade far more than the poor blue-rinse elder tottering in front of me.

Snick. Sword point in.

Schlorp. Sword withdrawn.

Sorry, Zombie Granny.

It didn't take long for Tony and me to respectively smash, slice, and dice our way across the roof. Meanwhile, the number of zombies coming through the door on the far side trickled down to a slow stagger. Tony gave a war-whoop as he put down a zombie in scrubs, half of its face already missing before the rest of it was obliterated.

I took out a male zom wearing blood-crusted jeans and a blood-spattered white shirt that screamed GAP. It had several chunks of flesh missing from its neck and face. Maybe a son, visiting his sick father in the geriatric ward when the shit hit the fan.

I really needed to stop looking at their faces, and just do my job.

With this thought in my head, I heard footsteps behind me and spun around with my katana, using hip torque to generate enough momentum to do the job with one blow, just like any good executioner.

Instead of chopping through flesh and bone, the edge of my blade connected with a barrel of an M4, the impact sending painful shockwaves up my arms.

"Careful now," an amused voice said. "I like my head where it is now."

Crap. Normally I would've been delighted that it was a living, breathing human being, but in this case, I think I'd have preferred another zombie.

Griffin—or Griff, as he liked to be called—had been one of the people already at the DZN lab when our group had arrived, bloodied and battered. The people at the lab had viewed our struggles on video, like some sort of sick reality show, yet done nothing to help. Including the guy standing in front of me. I resented him, even if he was another wild card. He wasn't one of *our* group. And more importantly, he hadn't helped when we needed it.

If not for the fact we'd been losing wild cards like Spinal Tap drummers, I'd have refused to work with him.

"Sorry," I said, sounding anything but. "Next time you might want to announce yourself."

He grinned down at me, his hazel eyes amused under ridiculously long lashes the same dark brown as his hair. He typified the whole gender unfairness bullshit illustrated best by peacocks. The males get the brilliant jewel-toned feathers, while the peahens get the drab brown colors. And for some reason, this particular peacock had been trailing his tail feathers in front of me ever since we'd been introduced.

"No worries," Griff replied with an indefinable accent that spoke of foreign lands, but was probably just pretentious. "Worth it to see you in action."

I stifled an undignified snort; *so* not buying what this dude was selling. Don't get me wrong. Griff was definitely what most people would consider hot. Angular cheekbones, strong straight nose, and firm lips, the guy looked as if he should be gracing the cover of *Esquire* or *Details*.

Then again, Kai had been just as hot, and he knew it, but his hotness had been more... well, innocent, for lack of a better word. Irritating at times, but never predatory. Griff had a self-awareness that saturated every gesture, every expression. His internal theme song was probably "Magic Man," throbbing drumbeat and all.

I trusted him as much as I did rattlesnakes and frat boys.

"You actually do anything down there," I asked, "or did you just watch the action on video?"

Griff held up his M4.

"Barrel's hot." He dropped it down low and added,

"You're welcome to touch it and see for yourself."

"No thanks," I said. "Not interested."

"Afraid of getting burned?"

"Oh, *please*." I snorted. I couldn't help it. Then I gave him a quick once-over, noting the lack of gore and goo on his clothes and armor. "Awfully clean for a zombie killer, aren't you?"

"Hey, I get the job done," he said with a shrug. "I'm not interested in getting up close and personal with dead people." Then he repaid my once-over with one of his own, albeit a slow, lingering travel up my body to my face. "Guess you don't mind getting down and dirty."

"Not with the zombies."

Griff's eyes narrowed just enough to tell me I'd scored. Gotta love a cheap and easy shot, right?

Tony joined me, Thor's Wee Hammer dripping with zombie goo. I could feel the dislike for Griff emanating from him with the uncomplicated black-and-white emotional range of youth. He started to say something, then paused as what could have been the corpse of the Oldest Confederate Widow emerged from the roof access door. About six feet away, it didn't moan, and its slipper-clad feet barely made a sound on the cement. Its mouth opened and closed, blackened tongue wriggling in the confines of its toothless gums.

"There's a zombie behind you," Tony said casually.

Griff rolled his eyes.

"Sure there is."

His eyes stopped in mid-roll as a rotting hand clutched at his Kevlar-clad shoulder. The zombie's gaping maw dripped black drool next to his face. To give him credit, though, Griff didn't yell or jump in surprise. He just rammed the stock of his weapon into the zombie's midsection, then spun around and delivered a blow to its head with enough force to smash the skull in.

"Guess you didn't get the job done as good as you thought," I observed.

"Better watch it next time, or you might get gummed to death." Tony delivered the line totally deadpan, something I couldn't have done if my life had depended on it.

"Funny," Griff replied, unamused.

"Dude," Tony said, "I tried to warn you."

"Dude," I echoed, "He totally did."

Tony grinned. Then I jerked a thumb toward the open door as a zombie MD lurched into view, looking like it'd been used as a chew toy.

"Incoming."

Griff looked at me with an odd little half-smile, and nodded as if reaching a conclusion. Then he turned and dispatched the zom with the same move as before. He made it look easy, almost balletic in its grace.

A blob of decaying brain matter landed on his sleeve. He eyed it with distaste, flicking it off with one finger. I fully expected him to start grooming himself like a cat. Instead he stepped into the roof access shed and peered down the stairs, turning back with a smile of satisfaction.

"*Now* it's clear."

Footsteps sounded on the stairs below.

"You sure about that, dude?" Tony asked.

The top of a helmeted head appeared and Gentry—one of *our* wild cards—appeared at the top of the stairs. He'd originally been a member of the ZTS (Zombie Tactical Squad), one of the more obscure branches of the military's Special Forces. A lucky reaction to an *unlucky* encounter with a zombie in Redwood Grove had upgraded his status to that of a wild card.

Gentry grinned and gave us a thumbs up, his babyface making him look like a teenager playing soldier, instead of a sergeant in his twenties. I had to restrain myself from pinching his cheeks like my grandma used to do to me, when I was a dumpling-faced toddler. Somehow I didn't think he'd appreciate it.

"Looking good, people!"

Griff smirked.

"Like I said… all clear."

SHEFFIELD, ENGLAND

"So," Indiana said. "What do you want to do first?" Brushing back his shoulder-length hair, he smiled suggestively at Hannah, who gave him a coy look from heavily lashed brown eyes as they walked away from the platform at Sheffield railway station.

In a red ruffled skirt, cream-colored peasant blouse and thick leather belt, Hannah looked like a fair-skinned steampunk gypsy. The leather belt had bits of brass thingees on it, gears and such. She wore a matching black leather collar similarly embellished, and black motorcycle boots. A cozy fleece shawl in a rich red completed the outfit.

The entire effect was guaranteed to turn him on.

"I thought I'd let you decide," she said demurely, brushing a heavy lock of black hair out of her face.

"I have some ideas." He noticed her struggling a bit with her overnight bag, and held out his hand. "Here, let me take that for you."

She handed it over with a grateful smile. Once he hefted it, he understood why.

"Christ, this is heavy. What do you have in it, barbells?"

"You'll find out." She smiled again, only this time there was nothing coy about it.

Oooh, boy.

He'd met her at a mate's fetish night a few weeks ago—the kind of party where most of the attendees were there to play. Hannah hadn't played, but she'd watched with avid interest. Upon meeting Indiana, her first question hadn't been the obvious, "Were your parents fans of the film then?" but rather, "Are you good with a whip?"

"Oh, yes," he'd replied, and he'd asked for her email. She'd given it to him without hesitation. Over the next few days, as they'd gotten to know one another online, she'd shared her mobile number and several social media handles. Certain photos she'd posted on Facebook and her Twitter ID "kinkykitten1313" prompted him to invite her to Sheffield for the weekend.

He still wasn't sure if she was a top or a bottom, but while Indiana tended to lean toward the submissive side of things— he did so love to be spanked—he wasn't averse to administering a good paddling, as well.

Either way, the weekend promised to be a good one.

They reached the covered bridge over the tracks and headed toward the stairs that led from the station itself, sparsely populated at this relatively late hour. The few people who were there all seemed to be hoisting tissues, some of them looking like they'd be better off in hospital than thinking of traveling. A particularly ill-looking fellow about Indiana's age erupted in a coughing fit as they passed him. Indiana winced as the man spat up a wad of black phlegm onto the station floor. He hoped Hannah hadn't seen it.

Talk about a mood killer.

Indiana had seen postings from his American and Canadian pals about the severity of Walker's Flu over there. He'd also read a recent article and seen some tweets about cases springing up in the UK, along with the usual crap about it being the next Black Death. He didn't buy it, of course. Look what happened with H1N1 and SARS, after all. He hadn't even bothered to get one of the flu shots that were being offered for free by Sheffield Hallam University.

But still, the amount of coughing and hacking going on made him anxious to get Hannah to relatively fresh air.

"I hope you don't mind a bit of a walk," he said, adjusting his pea coat as they reached the main exit. He held the door open for her. "I wanted to show you the glory that is Sheffield."

"And your car's in the garage." She gave him a playful poke in the ribs. "I can see your Facebook wall."

Indiana willed himself not to blush.

"So you can."

"Never mind, I love walking." She looped her arm through his. "And this is nice."

They headed up the slope toward town, passing what Indiana's mother liked to refer to as a "water feature" on their right, as well as a fountain and a series of waterfalls on their left.

"This is pretty." Hannah looked around with a pleased smile, and gave his arm a little squeeze.

"It gets even prettier when we get into town," Indiana assured her. Their current surroundings were modern and stark in the gray November weather.

They kept walking past the station parking lots to Sheaf Street, up the hill toward Sheffield City Centre.

"On our left," Indiana intoned in his best poncy tour guide voice, "is the excellent independent Showcase Cinema. And that lovely grassy area contains the Sheffield Hallam University buildings, with the Engineering block in the background, as well as my old stomping grounds, back when I was a student."

"Did you do a lot of stomping then?" Hannah asked innocently. "Or did you prefer to be stomped?"

"I could go either way," Indiana answered with a straight face.

"Nice." She smiled up at him.

Yeah, this is going to be a stellar weekend. Hell, maybe even more than that. Indiana hoped so. He liked this girl. And while he wasn't quite ready to settle down, he wasn't averse to settling in to a relationship that could lead that way.

As long as the path was decorated with paddles and leather restraints.

Ahem.

They continued walking.

"And here you see the Mansfield, one of the oldest pubs in Sheffield—the oldest being the Old Queens Head."

"That almost sounds naughty."

Indiana grinned. "Did you want to stop in for a pint?" The offer wasn't entirely altruistic. He could use a break from lugging her overnight bag.

"Could we?" Hannah's voice was eager. "I'd kill for a pint."

"Your wish, m'lady, is my command."

They headed toward the pub's entrance, only to stop short as the door burst open and two women—a bleached blonde and a redhead—staggered out. Both were in their mid-twenties and dressed for a night out on the town in heels too high to be safe after a pint, let alone as many as they'd probably had. The redhead was bleeding copiously from a wound on her forearm and crying in great gulping sobs, while her friend patted her drunkenly on the shoulder.

"There there… you'll be fine."

She immediately tripped, clutching her friend on the arm for balance, right on the bleeding wound. The redhead screamed in pain, slapping the blonde's hand furiously.

Indiana stepped forward.

"Do you need some help there?"

The blonde shook her head, regaining her balance.

"Thanks, pet, but we'll be fine. One of our friends had a bit too much and got a bit bitey." She punctuated her words with a strident belch, then covered her mouth with one hand, smearing blood from her friend's wound across her lips without realizing it. Between that and her southward-bound eye makeup, she looked like a sad, gory clown.

"I'm gonna kill the bastard," the redhead muttered between gulping sobs.

"There there," the blonde intoned again. Indiana couldn't believe anyone actually said "there there." "Let's get you home now, and put some hydrogen peroxide on this. You'll be fine."

They staggered off down the road. Hannah looked up at him uncertainly.

"Do you think we ought to go in?"

"Depends on how you feel about biting." Indiana was proud of himself for that. He thought it had just the right amount of nonchalance mixed with innuendo.

"That depends entirely on the circumstances," she replied. The slight smile playing around her lips contradicted her prim tone. Muffled shrieks of laughter sounded from inside. "It does sound like they're having fun." A particularly strident scream rang out. Her smile grew wider. "Maybe even our type of fun."

"Want to risk it then?"

"Oh yes. Just make sure you don't let anyone bite me." She paused. "Except you." She gave his shoulder-length hair a tug, just hard enough to send a definite message.

Indiana reached for the door handle, pulling it open and holding it for her, giving a "you go first" gesture with his free hand. Hannah dipped a little curtsey and went inside with a very appealing and deliberate sashay of her hips.

Before they'd taken more than two steps inside, someone grabbed Hannah and dragged her to the side. Warm liquid sprayed across Indiana's face, momentarily blinding him. Hands seized his shoulders, so he swung out blindly with Hannah's overnight bag, connecting solidly and knocking his assailant away from him. Frantically Indiana scrubbed at his face with his coat sleeve, trying to get the viscous fluid out of his eyes so he could see.

He fell against a nearby table, hand flailing against a pint glass. He couldn't see if the contents were alcoholic or water. A quick taste test confirmed that it was water, so he dashed the liquid into his eyes, swabbing them with a napkin and clearing his vision enough for him to see the chaos around him.

At least half the furniture had been overturned, lager and stout spilled over the floor to mix with what looked like blood. The pub was full—nothing unusual for a Friday night—but nothing was normal about the crazy fuckers attacking other pub-goers with their teeth and hands. It looked like at least a quarter of the customers had gone totally mental. They needed to get the hell out of there.

He looked around for Hannah.

He wouldn't have spotted her if he hadn't caught a glimpse of one black leather motorcycle boot and a swatch of red fabric on the ground. Most of her was covered by a hefty-sized man hunched over her, teeth worrying at her already savaged neck hard enough to spray chunks of flesh about.

Indiana's heart broke a little.

"Oh, Hannah."

The man looked up from his snack. Indiana recognized the hulking git as a security guard at the university. The bloke had never been handsome, but now he was downright hideous, yellowed teeth stained with blood. Black slime coated his upper lip and chin, blood drizzled out of his ears, and his eyes had gone wrong, all milky in the middle and red-streaked jaundiced where the whites should be.

Fucking zombies.

Indiana looked at the bag still looped over one wrist. Without stopping to think, he swung it around his head, letting momentum do the work for him as he clocked the erstwhile security guard in the side of the face, knocking him off Hannah's body. She didn't move. The bloody mess of her throat and her wide, staring eyes told him all he needed to know.

"I'm sorry, Hannah," he whispered.

He ran out of the pub without waiting to see if she came back.

CHAPTER TWO

I'd kill for a pair of jeans and a colored T-shirt.

Okay, maybe not kill, but definitely commit a minor felony like, say, jaywalking, if it meant some wardrobe options that didn't include forest camo or basic black. Would it really be so wrong to kill zombies while wearing some nice jeans and a brightly colored T-shirt?

I stared with loathing at two pairs of black BDUs and matching black shirts in light thermal or short-sleeved tees. I'd worn the same thing every day for the last month, ever since I'd found out I was a wild card, and I really wanted a change about now. While Kevlar had its uses, and even looked cool, it got old when you had to wear it every day, weeks on end.

Catholic schoolgirls had more variety in their closets.

Scrubs were my only other wardrobe option while housed at the *Dolofonoitou Zontanous Nekrous* lab. So my fashion choices came down to Linda Hamilton's wardrobe from *Terminator 2*—mental ward chic, or "gonna kick me some cyborg ass" paramilitary.

Sigh.

Well then, BDUs and a black thermal it is.

As if the clothing wasn't bad enough, I reeked of the ever-present smell of bleach, a by-product of the disinfection process. All of the vanilla spice body butter in the world wouldn't cover that stench.

I consoled myself with a touch of lip gloss and some mascara, trying to pretend I still lived a halfway normal life, and that Gabriel—my sort-of-kind-of-boyfriend— hadn't been taken away at gunpoint in a textbook example of really shitty timing.

Seriously, Gabriel and I had just reached a new equilibrium in our relationship, if you could call it that. Sure, the antiserum gave him a bad case of 'roid rage. Without it, though, he faced the irony-laden choice between eating human flesh in order to retain his humanity, or succumbing to the virus and becoming a mindless zombie.

Then there was his basic personality, which included a certain amount of stubborn self-righteousness that sometimes flipped him into douche mode. Even so, we'd worked through it, and I'd begun to have some hope for our future together.

And then he was gone. There was a real chance that I wouldn't see him again.

No, screw that.

I couldn't and wouldn't believe it. I wouldn't even *think* about it. Instead I focused on my favorite mantra. WWRD or…

What would Ripley do?

One, she'd go back for the cat.

Check.

Two, she'd kill as many of the monsters as she could.

In progress.

Three, kick the ass of a sleazy corporate bastard.

On my to-do list.

Four, rescue the hero. Well, crap, Dallas had died. Although she *did* rescue Hicks.

But then he died in the third movie.

Crap.

Grabbing a black hairband from the utilitarian dresser stacked next to my smaller-than-twin-sized bed, I gathered my mass of tawny brown hair into a thick ponytail, and gave myself a cursory once-over in the mirror to make sure I was fit for public consumption.

Ha-hah, very funny.

I shook my head in disgust. There was nothing to laugh about right now, but my mind couldn't stop its wise-cracking. Then again, without my sense of humor, as inappropriate as it was at times, I think I would have gone quietly around the bend, back when my husband dumped me for one of his eighteen-year-old students, ten years my junior. Nothing busts your self-esteem like being replaced by the younger model.

With that gloomy—and yes, shallow—thought lodged in my mind, I took a second, closer look in the mirror, noting the circles under my dark green eyes and the hollows beneath the planes of my cheekbones. I wasn't anywhere near the heroin chic level of gaunt, but I could stand to gain a few pounds, and have at least a week's worth of sleep uninterrupted by nightmares. I gave a mental shrug.

It's not like I was trying to impress anyone.

Looking around my temporary living quarters, I was amazed how much the place resembled the DZN facility at Big Red. The same sterile white hallways, faux wood doors, and lack of any personality whatsoever in the rooms themselves. *Ugh.* The place depressed me. I'd seen Motel Sixes with more charm. Plus I was hungry, almost to the point of light-headedness. So I decided to go find food.

But first, I needed to check in on Lil.

I'd met her at the beginning of the clusterfuck in Redwood Grove. Since then she'd turned from an incredibly sheltered eighteen-year-old college student into a disturbingly gleeful zombie-killing wild card. Her mother had gone missing during the initial outbreak, and Lil's already fragile emotional state slipped a little more every day she wasn't found. The fact Lil was on psychotropic drugs for some sort of bipolar disorder didn't help.

Especially since, to my best guess, she'd been off the drugs for several days now. She needed more meds, if I could only remember what it was she'd been taking. Dr. Albert knew, but he wasn't much good about now. I'd tried to talk to Dr. Arkin, the head physician here at UCSF, to see if she could help, but I'd been stonewalled by her assistant, Josh.

"Dr. Arkin is busy," he'd said. *"I'll let her know of your concern."*

Officious jerk.

Oh, well, now that we'd cleared the rooftop, Simone would be arriving soon, and she'd know what to do.

I stepped out into the hallway, closing the door behind me without bothering to lock it, and promptly collided with someone.

CHAPTER THREE

While I didn't do anything as girly as shriek with surprise, I did give a little gasp as strong hands gripped my shoulders, steadying me, and I looked up to see Griff smiling down at me.

There was a hint of smug in his smile. Subtle, but definitely there. I realized our little collision hadn't entirely been an accident. Which meant he'd been waiting for me to come out of my room. Which could either be construed as flattering or creepy and kind of stalkery.

I went with creepy and stalkery.

"You want something?" My tone was less than welcoming, the sort of tone usually reserved for Jehovah's Witnesses and AT&T salesmen.

Griff continued to smile.

"Always."

I rolled my eyes, not even trying to hide it.

"Seriously. Is there a reason you're lurking outside my room?"

His smile widened. A very sexy smile… if you liked crocodiles.

"Just thought I'd see if you wanted company."

"No thanks," I said brusquely.

Griff raised an eyebrow and crossed his arms, leaning casually against the wall.

"Why not?"

I thought fast.

"I'm going to check on Lil, and I don't think extra company would be a good idea."

"Lil." Griff stared off into the distance as if flipping through a mental Rolodex. "Little round gal with big eyes and lots of hair, right? Slightly off?"

I glared at him. "You'd be slightly off too if you'd lost—" Then I stopped, not wanting to get into it with this man.

"Sorry, not trying to offend," Griff said without a hint of apology in his voice. "But maybe more company is exactly what she needs."

What could I say to that that wasn't totally rude?

Probably plenty of things, but then I'd have to care about what he thought.

"Since you just met us two days ago," I said, "I don't think you're the best judge of what Lil needs." I smiled up at him. "Now if you'll excuse me…"

I started to move past him, but in a move so subtle I wasn't entirely sure how he pulled it off, Griff managed to take up enough of the space in front of me to block my path.

"You don't like me, do you?"

Why did I suddenly feel as if I'd wandered into a *Twilight* movie?

"I don't even know you."

"We can change that." Griff moved closer, one corner of his mouth going up in a seductive expression that had undoubtedly loosened the thighs of many a female.

"We could," I said levelly, staring him straight in the eyes. "But I'm not interested. So let's just part as—"

"As friends?" He grinned at me. "We can start with that."

He moved in closer, just shy of invading my personal space, his body heat palpable, along with a faint scent of something rich and spicy, like Mexican hot chocolate. The man smelled good, but then so did those carnivorous plants that attracted prey with deceptively sweet scents.

Griff's internal thermostat appeared to be set perpetually high, to generate pheromones and attract unwary females with his bad boy looks and cocky mien. His confidence smacked a little too much of arrogance, something I didn't find attractive, not even in Gabriel. And I was kind of sort of in love with him. Griff just came across as arrogant dipped in superiority sauce with a side order of "I'm all that and a bag of chips."

It made me want to slap him.

"On second thought," I said, "Forget friendship. Let's just part."

Set phasers on sarcasm, Captain.

I began to step around him when he blocked my path again, quite obviously this time, backing me up against the corridor wall. His body language, while not quite threatening, was definitely meant to intimidate.

So not in the mood for this shit.

"Who the hell do you think you are?" I glared at him.

"Just a fellow wild card trying to make…" He paused, stepping in closer until only an inch or two of air space remained between our bodies. "…friends."

I'd had enough.

"You're not a 'fellow' wild card," I said with real venom. "You didn't go through fire and hell to get here. You didn't fight the swarm with us or hack your way through a zombie-infested city, watching your friends die along the way." Mack's face flashed through my mind and I immediately clamped down on the memory. I wasn't going down that path. It was too easy to cry, and I sure as hell didn't want to show any weakness in front of this guy.

Griff was a predator, the sort who would go in for the kill as soon as he sensed any weakness. I wasn't about to play gazelle to his lion.

He frowned, the expression looking oddly out of place, as if he didn't wear it often. I got the impression he was used to being in control at all times, and didn't much like it when things didn't go according to his internal script.

"You don't know what I've been through," he said.

"You're right," I agreed. "I don't. For all I know you ran into a zombie toddler, lost a pinky tip, and won the wild card lotto. I do know that you were safe down here, watching us on video while we all nearly died up on the walkway." I glared up at him. "You're not one of us. Now if you don't mind—"

I tried shoving past him, but he refused to move.

"Fine," I growled. I brought my hands up between us and gave him a two-handed, open-palmed shove in the middle of his chest. I didn't have a lot of leverage, but what with my wild card strength, it still had enough force behind it to send a normal man reeling backward. Griff rocked back on his heels slightly, a flash of something dark and dangerous in his eyes before it vanished...

And then he stepped in even closer.

Narrowing my eyes, I raised my hands for another shove but found myself suddenly slammed against the wall, hands held down at my sides as he pressed up against me, holding me there with his body. His long fingers encircled my wrists like handcuffs and I found myself unable to pull free—an unwelcome reminder that I wasn't the only wild card in the immediate vicinity. He had the advantage of more upper body strength and a couple inches of height, too. I tried turning both wrists toward his thumbs to break his grip, but he easily countered by tightening his fingers and pinning my arms to the wall.

He grinned down at me, the expression in his dark green eyes a disturbing combination of anger and enjoyment, along with something not quite... sane, dancing in the background. I'd be lying if I said he didn't kind of scare me.

That *really* pissed me off.

"You're gonna want to let go about now." My voice implied a threat we both knew was empty.

"You don't know me very well if you think that's true." He pressed against me even harder, taking away the micro-millimeter of space that had still been between us. His body temperature seemed to increase, as did the smell of spice and chocolate. The only way our bodies could be closer would be if our clothes were gone, and that *so* wasn't going to happen.

I looked up at him, keeping my voice as level as possible.

"You don't know *me* very well," I said, "if you think I'm interested in what you want." He started to speak, and I added, "And do *not* tell me I don't know what I want. You say it, and I will put a world of hurt on you."

Once I get my hands free.

"I wasn't going to say that," Griff replied softly.

"Good."

"I was going to say I don't *care* what you want." He kept smiling, the hint of instability now clearly visible in those eyes.

My stomach clenched and I swallowed, hard.

I'd gotten used to the feeling of never being quite safe, ever since the zombie shit had hit the fan. But this was different. There'd been a soldier back at Patterson Hall who'd tried to put the moves on me, and I'd slammed him into the ground. He'd been a normal person, though, not a wild card. Judging from the unwanted feel of toned muscles under his clothes, I suspected Griff had been pretty damned strong, even before he turned. I might be able to whomp his ass in a fair fight, but right now he had the advantage of leverage.

"Have you ever considered trying flowers and chocolates?"

Both Griff and I jumped as a male voice spoke from a few feet away, where the hallway made a sharp left turn.

A young man somewhere in his twenties leaned up

against the wall in a deceptively casual pose, brown hair flopping over a red paisley bandana tied around his head. Well-muscled arms folded across a white sleeveless T-shirt with a black Darwin fish on the front. Loose-fitting black pants made him look like he was ready to kick-box the shit out of someone. His brown eyes gleamed with manic goodwill as he continued.

"I mean, I'm all in favor of forced assault and—" He stopped, shaking his head. "No, wait a sec. I'm really not. You need help, Ash?"

I took advantage of the distraction and found a weakness in Griff's grip, breaking free. I followed up by grabbing his right wrist with one hand, simultaneously stepping to the opposite side and yanking hard on his arm while sweeping one foot out from underneath him.

The thud Griff made when he hit the ground?

Priceless.

Gotta love leverage.

I dusted my hands together and stepped away from my would-be suitor-slash-assailant, and smiled at the newcomer.

"Thanks, JT, but I'm good. Were you looking for me?" I added, mouthing a silent "yes, you were."

JT nodded, not missing a beat.

"Yup. Tall, dark and grouchy—" He had to mean Nathan. "—asked me to find you. Figured you'd be down here."

JT wasn't a wild card, but he had mad physical skills involving the sport of free running, otherwise known as parkour. As acrobatic and nimble as a spider monkey, he could scale walls that for most people would require ladders, ropes, and pitons. We'd picked him up on our trek through San Francisco—or more accurately, he'd attached himself to our group, clearing a path through a swarm of zombies by creating what had to be the most irritating and effective diversion in history. He crackled with manic energy, was consistently entertaining and annoying, and right now, I couldn't have been happier to see him.

Griff, meanwhile, got to his feet in one smooth, angry move, as graceful as a cat and just as conscious of his own dignity. He shot JT a look that promised future pain. JT grinned back, unperturbed.

Then Griff turned back to me, eyes smoldering with a veritable cocktail of dark promises.

"You and I are not finished yet."

Wowza. Cliché much?

I could do better than that.

"Can't finish what wasn't started."

Okay, that wasn't *quite* as immature as "you're rubber and I'm glue…" but it was close.

We stared at each other, the theme to *The Good, the Bad and the Ugly* wafting through my head. My mind and body were still on high alert, fight or flight adrenaline coursing through me, and I really wanted a violent outlet. Specifically my fist colliding with Griff's face.

Instead, trying to ignore the rapid hammer-like beat of my heart, I turned my back on Griff in a deliberately dismissive—and potentially dangerous—gesture, and joined JT at the far end of the hall.

"Lead on."

JT linked an arm through mine, and we left Griff glowering at us in the hall where he stood.

SAN DIEGO, CALIFORNIA, USA

He stood on the small bluff overlooking the ocean next to the battery below the lighthouse. Took a deep breath, enjoying the cold air with a slight tang of salt water as the mist swirled around him. His eyes were less light sensitive than they'd been for the first few days after he'd changed, but direct sunlight still gave him a headache, even with sunglasses. He wasn't sure why—it didn't seem to bother

Captain Drake, Typhoid Mary, or the nut job.

When he'd first realized he would survive the contagion, he'd assumed he would be one of the wild cards. And oh, yes, he hoped for a chance to deal some old-fashioned military justice to the little bitch who'd caused his infection in the first place.

Then, when the cravings began, he realized he shared more in common with Captain Drake, and had been given an antiserum to keep him stable. It hadn't worked, and he'd railed against the arbitrary nature of genetics.

Then he'd been recruited, and had accepted his new diet. It wasn't really that difficult. Like his father, he'd always been a meat and potatoes man.

Besides, humanity fell into two categories, as far as he was concerned. There were wolves and there were sheep. Predators and prey.

No, he had no moral quandary. After all, the alternative—letting the contagion take control, his body and mind rotting as he became another mindless shambling corpse—that was unacceptable.

He'd been chosen for a reason, by his colleagues and by the Almighty, to help lead the world out of chaos. He hoped Gabriel would eventually come to the same realization. Right now, Drake still fought against the changes. Dr. Albert had instructions to give him just enough of the remaining antiserum to keep him from going past the point of no return, but Drake would have to make the choice soon.

The good lord willing, it would be the right one. A good soldier like Drake would be of far more use than a loose cannon like Typhoid Mary, although the latter's lack of special dietary requirements were admittedly an advantage.

He shook his head. Typhoid Mary was a disappointment, although the name fit perfectly. He could—and had—spread the disease in his own special way. Why he'd suddenly chosen to clean up after himself was still a source of mystery and irritation. Still, if he did what he was told on his current assignment, he'd be worth the time and money invested in his creation.

The same couldn't be said for the nut job.

What was the man's name? John... or Jack? He dismissed it as unimportant. "Nut job" would do. A fascinating case, mind you, but only a civilian, and a weak-minded one at that.

The man had been bitten, and then trapped in a cabin with his wife and kid. The wife had nursed him through the fever, like any good helpmate would, and been repaid by becoming her husband's next meal. He wondered briefly if the nut job—Jake, that was his name—if Jake had retained enough of his own humanity to kill them first. He hoped so. No parent should watch her child die, and no child should witness such violence against his mother.

He couldn't imagine giving into his cravings with that kind of single-minded lunacy. Still, if not for his own strength of will, and the grace of God, that could have been him.

He shrugged. No time for such pointless musings. He had a job to do, and new concerns had been brought to his attention. The vector was no longer contained to Walker's vaccine, or contact with the carriers' saliva or blood. It had mutated and, according to Dr. Albert, gone airborne. Quarantine efforts were laughable in the major cities. How could you enforce something that drifted on the wind?

It didn't trouble him as much as it would have before his own change. Watching the video feeds from around the world gave him a strange sense of satisfaction. Looking at all the sheep running around bleating as they were slaughtered. He felt no sympathy for them now. He was different.

Better.

But still, what his new colleagues—he refused to think of them as his superiors—had planned as an easily controllable weapon, to be wielded with knife-like precision, had turned into the contagious equivalent of an atomic bomb.

At first they had everything under control, and had little interest in an antiserum or a cure. But now that the slim modicum of control had been lost, their strategy had to be rethought, plans reconfigured. They couldn't count on geographical barriers to keep them safe any longer.

A cure was needed... but it had to be kept out of the wrong hands. Hence the acquisition of Dr. Albert and Captain Drake. The loss of the doctor's notes and samples had been a blow, but he had another ace or two he hadn't yet played.

Not everyone deserved a cure. Most of the world's population didn't. And wasn't that the point of this whole exercise, to cull the sheep to a manageable number? True, more would be culled than originally planned, but with a cure, enough would be left to do the grunt work.

"Sir?"

A soft voice spoke behind him. His aide, Sarah.

He turned, noting with approval how the crisp fabric of her uniform was creased just so, its fit utilitarian and just short of too attractive on her athletic build. Her white blonde hair, cut short in a style both practical and suited to her elfin features. Sarah knew how to walk the line. A good girl, with a strong military tradition in her background.

Her father had served in the same battalion with him, under his command. A good soldier who had given his life in the line of duty. He had felt an obligation to the widow and daughter, and had made sure they'd been taken care of. Thus, it seemed only natural to take Sarah under his wing when she went into the military, following in her father's footsteps.

If his condition frightened her, she never let it show.

Sarah would be kept safe from the wolves.

"Sir," Sarah repeated, "they're waiting for you downstairs."

"I'll be along shortly," he said.

Let them wait, he thought. One of these days I'll show them who's really in charge.

As if on cue a gentle chime sounded—his cell phone. He pulled it from his pocket, and his scrotum contracted when he saw the caller ID. Instantly he despised his own weakness. Fear was not to be tolerated.

Still… his mouth was dry as he took the call.

CHAPTER FOUR

As soon as JT and I walked far enough away to get out of earshot, I turned to him.

"Thank you," I said sincerely.

He nodded. "I'm sure you could have handled it on your own, but why should you have to, right?" He looked back. "Guy's a prick."

"That he is," I agreed, still breathing rapidly.

JT looked at me.

"You okay?"

"Sure, I'm fine," I said.

With perfect comic timing, the adrenaline chose that moment to rush out of my body, leaving me weak and shaking. A wave of nausea slammed into me with the suddenness of a runaway elevator. Black spots swam in front of my vision, I dropped into a crouch, and put my head down on folded arms, breathing deeply as I concentrated on not passing out or throwing up. I felt JT's hand on my shoulder again as he hunkered down next to me.

"You gonna go all 3-D yawn on me?"

"No," I managed to say. "Just a little nauseated."

I took another deep breath, and then a few more until the feeling subsided.

Better now.

I stood up on slightly shaky legs, wiping cold sweat

from my brow. I liked how JT let me use my own steam to stand, but stood close enough to help if I needed it. For a manic adrenaline junkie, he wasn't so bad.

"You do realize," he said, "that 'nauseated' actually means that you make other people sick. The correct phrasing would be 'I feel nauseous.'"

I gave him a look, briefly reconsidering my previous evaluation.

"Thanks, Encyclopedia Brown."

He grinned. "Technically that should be Dictionary Brown, but I take your point."

"Thanks," I said again, this time meaning it. "For showing up when you did. That was just so not what I needed about now."

"You gonna tell someone about Mister Fifty Shades of Asshat?"

I shook my head. "Not unless he pushes his luck a second time. Too much other stuff to worry about."

JT frowned. "Not so sure that's a good idea."

I sighed. "While I'm all about anti-harassment in the workplace, we're short on wild cards, and I'm gonna have to work with him. Besides," I added grimly, "I can pretty much take care of myself."

"Having seen you in action mode, that much I know." JT's tone was appreciative without being sleazy. "I noticed he didn't try anything when you were armed."

"Good point."

We continued walking down the hallway toward the elevator bank.

"You know him long?"

"Hell, no." I got angry all over again. "He was one of the personnel down here watching the video feed while we fought… and Mack died."

Suddenly JT sprinted toward the elevator doors, and I tensed. He ran up them and flipped over to land on his feet like Donald O'Connor in *Singing in the Rain*, with as little effort as I used to get out of bed. In the short time I'd known him, I'd gotten used to his random use of any available surface as a launching pad. The man had enough energy to fuel a rocket ship.

He resumed his place at my side as if nothing had happened.

"Hmm," he said. "That's strange. There's got to be something else going on. Because seriously, that dude acts like an ex doing the whole time-for-a-restraining-order routine." He gave me a quick up and down. "And while you are undeniably hot in a Xena-kick-my-ass-and-make-me-breakfast kind of way, if he just met you, that's not enough to warrant the vibe he's putting out."

"Kick your ass and make you breakfast?" Yes, I am easily distracted.

"You know what I mean—"

"No, I really don't."

"Classic warrior-woman fixation by your average nerd. Finding a glorious kick-ass goddess who can take out an Uruk-hai horde, looks good in a chainmail bikini, and will make you chocolate chip pancakes after a night of amazing sex."

I stared at him. He grinned back at me.

"Don't worry," he said. "I'm not your average nerd."

The elevator doors opened. He must have hit the button with his feet.

"No, I don't think you are," I agreed, stepping into the elevator. He followed, leaning casually against the back of the car as the doors slid shut.

"So what's next?"

I raised an eyebrow. "What do you mean?"

"Bad guys took your boyfriend and that dude who looked like a ferret. I assume there are plans to go after them. Any idea where they went?"

"According to the microchip in Gabriel's arm, San Diego—"

"Wait." JT held up a hand. "He's got a microchip?"

I nodded. "All the wild cards do."

"Makes sense." He nodded. "Easier to track you all in the wild."

I rolled my eyes. "Seriously?"

He shrugged. "Why wouldn't they want to keep tabs on their most valuable assets?"

"What do you mean, 'they?'"

JT looked at me. "Why don't you tell me?"

Well, crap.

"It's not that simple," I said uncomfortably.

JT nodded sagely. "It never is."

My gratitude at being rescued morphed into irritation. Funny how that works.

"So," he said. "You gonna tell me about it?"

My first instinct was to give him an unequivocal "no." Then I thought of what he'd risked to help us get here, without once asking what we were doing or why, or expecting anything in return, other than an audience for his mad parkour skills.

Well, and a safe place to ride out the zombie hurricane, I mused. Then I made a decision.

"'They' are the *Dolofonoitou Zontanous Nekrous*," I said to the best of my ability. Greek wasn't my language. "Just don't ask me to say it again."

JT cocked his head to one side, reminding me of the RCA dog or the annoying female robot in *Terminator 3*.

"*Dolofonoitou Zontanous Nekrous*," he said, the words rolling off his tongue in what could have been an imitation of Simone's flawless pronunciation. "Loosely translated, 'killers of the dead.' Not strictly correct, as far as the Greek goes, but close enough for government work."

I hate it when someone is smarter than I am.

"Uh, yeah. You can just say DZN from now on."

"So what do they do?" JT tapped his foot as if he didn't know how to stand still.

I decided to go for it.

"They're a super-secret centuries-old organization

dedicated to the detection and eradication of the living dead."

Wow. A lot of multi-syllable words in one sentence. My college education was finally paying off.

"Sort of like *SHIELD* meets *The Walking Dead*." JT nodded again as if all this made perfect sense. And maybe in this weird world it kind of did. He was quiet for a moment, other than the tapping of his foot. Then he shook his head.

"Wow," he said. "Zombies."

"Yup." My turn to nod.

"Real undead George Romero-type zombies."

"Uh-huh. Right down to the crappy diet," I confirmed.

"Right. And if they bite you?"

"You get infected, die a nasty, painful death and come back as one of them."

"Unless you're a wild card," he finished.

"That's right."

I suddenly noticed the elevator wasn't moving and none of the buttons were lit. I reached out and hit the button labeled S-1, the top floor of the facility and—more importantly—the floor with the cafeteria. I needed food in a big way, and *then* I'd go check on Lil.

"And how many wild cards are there?" JT asked.

I shook my head. "Not enough. Not nearly enough."

DELHI, INDIA

"Hello, my name is Marcy," Noopar said. "How may I be of assistance to you today?"

Noopar gave an inward sigh as she started yet another customer service call for Philatelic Inc. The stamp collecting firm was one of the smaller companies to outsource their IT to India, but they had as many IT issues as the huge global monsters, and just as many irate customers.

She used to have sympathy for her many callers. On an

intellectual level, she understood that hearing a foreign accent could be off-putting when calling from New York about a problem in a New York office. But she did her best to help, no matter how abusive some of the callers could be.

After a year at the job, working ten- to twelve-hour shifts, six days a week, in cramped conditions, her well of sympathy was drained dry. She was hungry, her head hurt, and she very much needed a bathroom break. On top of that, her co-workers in the surrounding cubicles were ill with the latest flu that was going around.

It had just hit India in the last day or so, and according to the news, it was a bad one. Already there had been fatalities, and at least a dozen people in her section had caught it, bringing it to work. The noises were disgusting enough, but now Noopar worried about catching it herself.

She didn't blame her co-workers. Calling in sick wasn't an option—employees were expected to come in first, and be sent home if they were deemed sick enough. As a result, the call center was a Petri dish of germs.

An angry voice brought her back to the present.

"I am sorry to hear about your inconvenience, sir," Noopar said, trying to remember the angry caller's complaint. "May I have your name and contact information, so I may assist you more thoroughly?"

She typed in the information given by one Chris Anderson— "That's Anderson with an 'o,' not with an 'e'!"—trying to keep up with the flow of angry words and ignore the wet hacking cough coming from Vijay's station directly across from her.

Noopar eyed the bottle of hand sanitizer next to her phone as she kept typing.

"Yes, sir. I'm sorry, sir. I believe I can help you resolve this issue—" She paused as a new spate of words blasted through her headpiece. "Yes, sir, I understand and apologize for this inconvenience and—"

A rattling cough and what sounded like liquid splatting onto a hard surface broke Noopar's already shaky focus. A foul smell rose from Vijay's workstation.

"Excuse me, sir, but may I place you on hold so I may further research this issue?" She cut off the response in mid-stream, slamming her finger on the hold button and slowly standing up to peer over the top of the partition computers.

"Vijay?"

In his early twenties, cocky, and in love with American cinema, Vjiay was both a source of annoyance and amusement. His use of American slang made her wince, especially when he tried to sneak it into the sacred customer service scripts. He was as harmless, irritating, and endearing as a hyperactive puppy.

"Vijay, what is wrong?" she gasped.

He looked up at her with yellowed, bloodshot eyes, black fluid coating his lower lip and chin. Blood oozed out of his eye sockets, nose, and ears.

"Noopar," he said in a bewildered tone. "I am not feeling well."

He fell forward, splayed hands knocking a penholder and scattering its contents over his desk, miring the pens in the black vomit already there.

"Vijay!" Noopar stared in horror as his body convulsed once, then again, before settling with ominous finality face down on the desk. She waited for him to move again.

"Vijay?" Her voice sounded small against the background buzz of dozens of voices.

The hum was suddenly broken by a scream coming from somewhere behind her. Noopar snapped around so quickly she pulled a muscle in her neck. A sharp, almost nauseating pain instantly radiated up into her head and down her left shoulder, but it barely registered as she took in what was happening.

All across the vast floor of the call center, dozens of workers were going through convulsions similar to Vijay's, while others doubled over in coughing fits, spewing up the vile-smelling black fluid. Yet more lay unmoving in the narrow corridors between rows of stations, or draped across their desks.

Another scream, and then more echoed through the building as people tried frantically to help their friends and co-workers, or make their way over the fallen to one of the exits.

Then—as Vijay liked to say—the shit really hit the fan.

Some of the people who had collapsed on the floor or at their desks began to move again. Poonam, a woman who sat only a few stations away from Noopar, used unsteady hands to push herself to her knees where she swayed back and forth for a moment, staring blankly in front of her with the pale eyes of a corpse, blood and fluid smearing her face and darkening her green cotton top. In what seemed an almost random gesture, she reached out and grabbed the leg of another worker who was trying to squeeze by her.

He gave a startled yelp as she yanked on his leg, pulling it toward her now gaping mouth. She sank her teeth into his thigh, ripping through fabric and flesh with ease.

The man—Noopar thought his name was Amil, but she wasn't sure—screamed in pain and fear, the high-pitched sound bouncing off the low ceiling. Blood gouted from the wound, most of it drenching his attacker as she went for another bite.

Noopar's mind flashed briefly on the Aghori, an obscure Hindu sect whose followers practiced cannibalism. But those corpse-like eyes told her that Poonam was something even worse.

All across the room similar scenes played out with equally deadly results. Few of the victims had the presence of mind to fight back against their former co-workers. The attacks happened quickly, and the corridors became clogged with frantic men and women climbing over one another to flee the madness. Those who managed to reach the exits crowded up against the inwardly opening doors, making it impossible to escape.

The smell of blood mingled with the stench of the horrible black vomit, and screams mixed with the now constant ringing of dozens of phones. Noopar quietly slid down behind her chair and crammed herself into the space under her desk. Perhaps if she was very quiet, no one would notice her. Maybe she would get out of the call center alive.

The hold button continued to flash for another five minutes before finally going dark.

CHAPTER FIVE

JT and I hit the cafeteria. Whatever the shortcomings of the interior design of the DZN facilities, they served decent food. Nothing fancy, but give me a good cheeseburger and crispy French fries and I'm a happy camper.

None of the other wild cards were there, so JT kept me company "in case," as he put it, "Mister Boundary Issues decides to show up." I seriously didn't expect any trouble in a roomful of people, but decided not to argue. I was too busy eating.

There were a few other people present, most of them in lab coats and a few in the inevitable black and/or camo BDUs. I'd just finished the last of my fries when Josh, Dr. Arkin's officious assistant, walked in wearing a lab coat and jeans.

A Hispanic man in his twenties, Josh had also been part of the lame-ass welcoming committee when our battered and bleeding team had tumbled out of the elevator. So I wasn't predisposed to like him. He evidently didn't think much of me either. After he filled his tray with food, he headed in our general direction, saw me sitting with JT, frowned, and turned sharply away to sit at a table on the other side of the room.

"That man does not want to talk to us," JT said, staring after Josh with a raised eyebrow.

"You noticed?

"Hard not to." He took a prodigious bite of burger and chewed happily.

"Yeah, well tough shit for him," I said grimly. "I need some answers." Shoveling the last of the fries into my mouth, I stood up and said, "I'll be right back." JT made a little "go" motion with his fingers and continued chowing down on his second burger.

I marched over to the table where Josh sat.

"Got a minute?" I plunked myself down across from him. "Good. I need to talk to you about Lil."

"I told you," he said, sounding pissy, "that Dr. Arkin does *not* have time right now."

I narrowed my eyes.

"Fine. Which is why I'm talking to you."

Josh looked up from his bowl of vegetable beef soup.

"I'm kind of busy."

"Yeah, it takes a lot of focus to eat without dribbling," I said just as a piece of barley fell off his spoon on the way to his mouth. He glared at me.

Oops. Guess it really does.

"Look," I said, trying to be patient, "Lil needs medication. I think she's bipolar, and she's been off her meds for at least four days. We need her as a functioning member of our team. Do you see the problem here?"

Josh heaved an aggrieved sigh.

"Fine. What do you want to know?"

I restrained an impulse to reach across, grab him by his thick brown hair, and shove him face-first into his soup.

"I need to know what to give her."

"It's not that simple." He sighed again, with slightly less impatience. "First of all, it depends on whether she's bipolar or schizophrenic."

"She hasn't mentioned hearing voices," I said doubtfully, "but she's definitely got a manic streak going on."

"Hmmm." Josh looked thoughtful. "That being the case, Clozaril is a possibility, but without lab monitoring it could cause a fatal drop in her white blood cells, and very quickly. Other alternatives would be Haldol and Thorazine, but those would severely impede her ability to think clearly, which could be fatal, given the situation." He paused briefly, as if rifling through a mental file cabinet. "Newer medications like Zyprexa and Seroquel are better. There's a version of Risperdal given as a shot every two weeks… or perhaps Geodon, given every month. Risperdal is stronger…"

I felt my brain glazing over.

"Lithium would work for her mood swings," he continued, "but once again she'd need monitoring, which could be difficult when she's out in the field. Straight mood stabilizers like Tegretol, Depakote, or oxcarbazepine are helpful, but wouldn't help the paranoia." He stopped and took a spoonful of soup.

I stared at him blankly.

"Right," I said. "So what do we give her?"

He rolled his eyes.

"Didn't you listen to anything I just told you?"

"Uh-huh. Narrowing it down would be helpful."

"Do you have any idea what she was on before?"

"Something like chloradine or companzie."

"Clozapine."

I nodded. "That's the one."

"That makes it easier." Josh tore a piece off his roll and dunked it in his soup. "If she was on clozapine before, the odds are good that she's only bipolar and she was most likely monitored by her doctor regularly up until the incident in Redwood Grove."

Incident. A nice sanitized way to describe a horrific slaughter.

"So look for clozapine or Clozaril," he said.

"What's the difference?"

"Clozapine is the generic, Clozaril is the more expensive name brand." He took another spoonful of soup. "Either one will do."

"Do you have any of it here?"

"In the lab?" He shook his head. "Doubtful. We have access to the pharmacies on and around campus."

Okay, that's good news. "Where's the nearest one?"

"The nearest pharmacy? It's off of Parnassus."

I did a quick mental calculation, trying to picture the layout of the nearby streets in my head.

"That's not too far away, right?"

"Not as the crow flies, but you'd have to either go back up Medical Center Way, or through the adjacent complex, none of which have been cleared."

"So you're saying it won't be easy."

"I'm telling you it's a no go," he said, looking at me as if I were riding the short bus. "And if you try it, you seriously deserve a posthumous Darwin Award."

I stood, pushing my chair back with a satisfying screech. Then I walked over, standing next to his chair, leaning forward until I was way into his personal space. I stared down at him. He gulped visibly at what he saw in my eyes.

"I'm not asking these questions for my health, or to annoy you," I said softly. "I'm asking because this is one of those life-or-death-type situations, and I need to find a solution. If this isn't a solution, fine. But if you treat me like an idiot for asking, you'll find yourself short-listed for one of those Darwin awards." I poked him in the middle of his lab-coat clad chest. "Do you get it?"

"Um. Yes. I get it."

"Good." I handed him a napkin. "Please write down those names for me."

He took a pen out of the breast pocket of his coat and scribbled stuff on the napkin.

"I'll, uh, I'll check the lab and see if we have anything in stock," he said as he wrote. "I don't think we do, but it's worth checking."

"Thanks," I said, meaning it. "I'd really appreciate that."

His relief was palpable as I moved away.

"No problem."

* * *

I rejoined JT at our table where he was finishing his meal.

"Done intimidating the natives?" He grinned up at me.

I shrugged, only slightly embarrassed.

"I wouldn't do it if they'd cooperate." I picked up my dishes and stacked them on my tray. "Time to go check on Lil. I'll see you later."

"Are you sure you don't want me to go with you?" JT asked.

"Yup," I said. "I don't know if Lil is ready for company she doesn't really know." I wasn't even sure Lil would want to see me, let alone a relative stranger, but kept that particular fear to myself. "Thanks, though."

"Let me know if you need any help, okay?"

"With what?"

"With anything." He shrugged. "But especially any kicking of douche-nozzle asses."

I laughed. "It's a deal."

CHAPTER SIX

The dorm part of the facility was laid out in a rectangle like your basic motel. Luckily the rooms were numbered, or I'd never remember which one was which. Lil's was number twenty-four, same floor as mine but on the opposite side.

So when I got off the elevator, I headed away from my room, which meant less of a chance of running into Griff. I really hated the fact that he had the power to make me uneasy like that.

Lil's door was shut when I reached it so I rapped sharply right below the 24.

No answer.

No big surprise. She hadn't said more than two words since we'd gotten off the elevator. To my knowledge, she hadn't left her room other than to use the bathroom. And given the unholy glee she normally took in zombie slaying, the fact she'd missed today's outing worried me more than anything else.

The doors didn't have locks, so I pushed it open and found Lil lying on her bed, covers pulled up so high that only the top of her head was exposed—an unkempt and unwashed mass of light brown hair tumbling over the navy blue polyester coverlet. A tray of food—chicken soup, some sort of sandwich, and an apple—sat on the bedside chest of drawers, untouched, along with a couple of white pills and a glass of apple juice.

This wasn't good.

"Lil?"

Still no answer. The Lil-shaped lump remained still, other than a slight up-and-down movement that showed she was breathing.

"Lil, I know you're awake."

There was a brief pause in the rhythm of the breathing, before it regained its too-perfect regularity. I gave a quiet sigh and sat on the edge of the bed, touching the unkempt mop of hair.

"Look, I know you're hurting." I paused, trying to pick my words carefully without even knowing what I wanted or needed to say. "I miss him too."

I heard a slight hitch in her breathing, and the covers jerked slightly. Encouraged, I continued.

"But you can't just lie here forever."

A pause.

"Why not?"

Even muffled by the covers, Lil's voice was rusty from lack of use and too much crying. It was also unusually bitter—the polar opposite of her normally sweet tone.

A dozen answers sprung to mind, but I chose the one closest to the truth.

"Because we need you," I said simply. "Mack fought until the end. He'd expect you to do the same."

"Mack *died* because of me."

The covers erupted with the suddenness and violence of Mount St. Helena as Lil sat bolt upright in bed. I suppressed a gasp at the sight of the nearly purple circles under her eyes. The formerly soft curves of her face had been replaced by haggard hollows under her cheeks. My first impulse was to wrap my arms around her in a comforting hug, but the stiff set of her shoulders told me it wouldn't be appreciated. So I settled for words instead.

"No," I said as calmly as I could muster, "he died because of those assholes in black who ambushed us."

"If I hadn't hit that man's rifle... the bullet wouldn't have hit Mack."

I shut my eyes and struggled for words. One of the goons who'd kidnapped Gabriel had been about to shoot me when Lil had charged him. If she hadn't, I'd be pushing up daisies. But the bullet had ricocheted off the metal catwalk and caught Mack under one arm. He'd bled out before we even knew he'd been hit. She'd saved my life, but Mack had died in my place.

"If you hadn't done that, Lil... I'd be dead. You can't blame yourself."

"Then maybe I should blame you." She glared at me with what looked like real hate, and my heart broke a little.

"Are you sorry I'm still alive?" I tried to keep my voice steady, but it broke on "alive," and I felt the hot sting of tears behind my eyelids.

Lil's stony expression wavered just enough for me to see the heartsick kid underneath.

"No." She shook her head, teeth digging into her lower lip to keep it from trembling. "But... but I don't want Mack to be dead." She pulled the covers around her. Fat tears rolled out of her eyes and plopped onto them, practically bouncing up before rolling down the cheap polyester fabric.

"I don't either," I said simply.

With a body-wrenching sob, Lil threw herself into my arms. I held her as she cried with a violence that would have frightened me if I hadn't understood its source all too well.

I wished I had magic words to make everything better. Hell, I wished I had the cure to the whole zombie plague, or at least a way to bring back our friends. But I didn't and I couldn't, so I settled for letting Lil cry out her sorrows as best she could.

When the storm of tears finally subsided, I handed her the box of tissues someone had thoughtfully put on her bedside table, and brushed a swatch of damp hair out of her face.

"You look like shit," I said bluntly.

Lil sniffled and blew her nose into a tissue with impressive volume.

"I feel like shit," she said.

"Let's see what we can do to fix that." I got up, went into the bathroom, and ran cold water on one of the white washcloths stacked next to the sink, wringing the excess liquid out before taking it back into the bedroom.

Lil was sitting up, wiping her eyes and nose with more tissues, long mass of hair matted and tangled around her shoulders. I sat down next to her and gently swabbed her face and the back of her neck with the damp cloth. She let me do it, leaning against me like a little kid in need of comfort. Setting the cloth aside, I just held her and brushed her hair back from her forehead with one hand, the way my mom used to do whenever I was sick.

"Think you could maybe eat something now?"

Lil nodded.

"Maybe a little."

I smiled. "Good. Let's see what we have here."

A quick dip with a finger told me the soup was tepid. The sandwich, some sort of meat and cheese, looked like a better bet. I figured whatever the pills were, they'd probably stay down better after she'd eaten.

"Here." I handed her the plate with the sandwich.

"What is it?"

"Some sort of mystery meat," I shrugged. "But my guess is turkey."

She picked it up and wrinkled her nose.

"It's either that or lukewarm soup," I said. "Your choice. But you need to eat, okay?"

Lil took a small, reluctant bite. When it didn't kill her, she took another, larger bite, and then downed the rest within minutes. If she hadn't eaten since we'd arrived, I wasn't surprised at her appetite. Being a wild card used a lot of energy—our metabolisms burned hot and fast.

I handed her the bowl of lukewarm soup. She ate it without complaint. The apple followed.

Then I held out the glass of juice and the pills. She eyed me suspiciously.

"What are these?"

"I have no idea," I answered honestly.

"Because I don't want any pills."

Ooo-kay. This did not bode well.

I scrutinized one of the tablets, holding it up to the light.

"Bayer aspirin," I said, reading the small print. "Nothing that's gonna knock you out or make you larger or smaller."

And the one that mother gives you won't do anything at all.

"I don't want them." She glowered at me, her mood dark and angry again.

"Well, unless you hurt, you don't need them," I said mildly.

"My head hurts."

"Then maybe you should take them."

Lil glared a few more seconds before reaching out and snatching the pills and the glass of juice from my hands. Popping the aspirin into her mouth, she tossed down the juice and swallowed, still looking daggers at me.

"What?" I said. "I didn't make you take them."

"I wouldn't have taken them if you hadn't come in here."

If Lil had been wearing a mood ring, it would be switching colors like a strobe light.

"And you'd still be buried under polyester blankets. Is that a good thing or a bad thing?"

She took another swallow of apple juice, ignoring my question. So I sighed and stood up.

"I'll come back later, okay?"

Lil shrugged, not looking at me.

"Whatever." Spoken like a true sullen teenager.

Turning to leave, I reached for the knob, just as someone rapped on the door. Lil dove back under the covers and I jumped back a step, startled and wary at the same time. Had Griff followed me to Lil's room? *I swear, if he has, I'm going to give him a swift kick where it counts.*

I opened the door a crack, peering out cautiously and then throwing it wide open when I recognized the tall, elegant blonde who stood there holding a large plastic pet carrier.

"Simone!"

I threw my arms around her without thinking, so relieved at her reassuring presence that I almost started crying. Even more surprising was the fact that after a few startled seconds, she set down the carrier and hugged me back. After a moment she gave me a brief tight squeeze with slender yet strong arms, and then held me back from her, hands on my shoulders.

"Ashley," she said. "You're looking well."

I shook my head. "Not so much," I said. "You, on the other hand, are looking much better than the last time I saw you."

Simone smiled ruefully. "Well, the last time you saw me, I'd almost been incinerated."

"Seeing you with your hair messed up was disturbing, I admit it."

Simone's eyebrows lifted even as she raised a hand to smooth down an imaginary stray wisp of hair from her chignon. As timelessly beautiful as Helen Mirren, she was a long-time member of the DZN and a wild card. Her knowledge of the zombie virus and familiarity with Dr. Albert's work, however, made her far too valuable to go out in the field with the rest of us.

"Did Jamie come with you?" I asked, unused to seeing Simone without her pink-haired shadow.

"She's getting settled in," Simone said. "I thought it best to keep this particular reunion as small as possible."

She glanced at the cat carrier. "They did not appreciate the helicopter ride." Then she peered around me into Lil's room.

"Is she…" She raised an eyebrow again, this time by way of inquiry.

"She's been sleeping a lot," I replied neutrally, not wanting to say too much within Lil's earshot. "And she just had a little to eat."

Simone nodded.

"Perhaps she can teach these two some dietary restraint." She indicated the carrier. "They are, if possible, even more rotund than they were before you left Redwood Grove."

An indignant meow emanated from the carrier, as if in reply to Simone's comment. It was followed shortly by another, slightly raspier meow.

"Binkey! Doodle!"

I heard the rustle of fabric and turned to see Lil throwing off her covers as she sat up straight, face alight with the first smile I'd seen from her since we'd arrived.

Simone peered past me, hoisted the carrier containing thirty-plus pounds of feline, and said, "May we come in?"

Lil nodded enthusiastically.

As soon as the door was closed, Simone set the carrier down and opened it up. Immediately two mini zeppelins, one tabby striped and the other black, launched out of their prison straight on to the bed like furry heat-seeking missiles, weaving, winding and wending their way around Lil with audible purrs. Simone and I smiled at each other as Lil buried her nose in Binkey's midnight fur, Doodle nudging her way in to rub her face up against Lil's in an ecstasy of feline affection.

"They really are fatter, aren't they?" I said to Simone.

Lil frowned up at me, Binkey's tail lashing across her face to create a momentary mustache below her nose.

"They're not fat," she said. "They're just… festively plump."

I grinned. If Lil was quoting *South Park*, there was hope.

Simone sat down on the edge of the bed and eyed her sternly.

"Lil," she said, "we need to find Gabriel and Dr. Albert. We don't have time to waste. And we need your help."

Lil didn't look up, but gave a little nod to indicate she was listening.

"There are very few wild cards, Lil. And we need every one of you if we are to accomplish our goal."

Lil buried her face in Binkey's fur, and muttered something under her breath. Simone leaned closer, putting a gentle hand on Lil's shoulder.

"What was that?"

Lil turned toward us, her expression bleak again.

"We'll *all* be dead at the end of it, won't we?"

"No, we won't!" I said without thinking, my tone fierce. "So don't go all Rez Evil Red Queen on me, okay?"

Simone looked at me, pursed her lips, and shut her eyes as if in pain, then opened them and looked at Lil.

"I'm sorry," Simone said. "Losing Kai and Mack… it hurts. And not just because they were wild cards."

"They were my friends," Lil said simply.

"Mine, too." I sat on the other side of the bed.

Lil reached out and grasped my hand.

"We'll take them down, right? The people that killed Mack?"

I nodded. "Absofuckinglutely."

Lil smiled. It was not a nice smile.

"Good," she said. "I'm in."

CHAPTER SEVEN

Simone and I left Lil curled up with her two purring companions, with promises on both sides—hers to show up to the meeting, and ours to get a litter box and cat food delivered to her room.

"Do you think she'll show up?" I asked Simone once we reached the elevator, and didn't have to worry about Lil listening in with her enhanced hearing.

"I hope so." Simone sighed heavily. "I gather she needs to be on medication."

"You know about it?"

"Gabriel updated us in one of his last reports."

Relief washed over me. I wasn't alone in this anymore.

"What did Dr. Arkin say about her condition?" Simone asked.

"I don't think she even *knows* about it," I said. "I haven't been able to talk to her about Lil since we arrived."

Simone gave me a sharp glance. The elevator arrived and we stepped in. She pressed a button, and the doors closed.

"Dr. Arkin hasn't seen her?"

"Dr. Arkin is a very busy woman," I said neutrally, in case they were good friends. "At least that's what her assistant told me."

Simone frowned. "We'll see about that."

Hmmm. Maybe not best buds. I tested the waters a little further.

"Given what happened when we arrived, I doubt Lil would agree to any kind of examination from Dr. Arkin anyway."

"I can't say that I blame her," Simone said with a sniff.

I raised an interested eyebrow. "You know her, then?"

"We've crossed paths."

I waited for more. The elevator doors opened. I followed Simone as she strode purposefully down the hall.

"I need coffee," Simone said unnecessarily. I suspected we were done with the topic of Dr. Arkin for the time being.

That was okay. I could always use more coffee.

We sat at a corner table, large cups of hot coffee in front of us. Mine was heavily laced with cream and honey. Simone's was black. Both of us sat with our backs to the wall, facing the rest of the room so we could see who was coming and going.

"Tell me about Lil's behavior," Simone said. "Gabriel's report indicates a bipolar disorder."

I took a sip of coffee. "That's what Josh thinks, too—Arkin's assistant," I clarified. "Bad mood swings. And that's putting it mildly. It's like dealing with a kid hopped up on sugar. I never know when a tantrum or a crash is gonna hit."

Simone nodded. "Then the sooner we get her back on her medication, the better. What did Josh recommend?"

"Er…" I fished the napkin out of my pants pocket and held it out to her. "These." She looked, squinted, then fished a pair of reading glasses seemingly out of thin air, nodding in satisfaction as she looked at the napkin again.

"This seems straightforward."

"Josh is going to check the lab's inventory," I said. "If they don't have it, I'll find it. And then we'll just have to convince her to take it."

"If she has a resistance to taking her medication, we

can also consider Fazaclo." Simone smiled over her coffee mug. "It's approximately the same thing, but dissolves quite easily in liquid."

"So we ask Dr. Arkin if they have any on hand, and if not, I locate the nearest pharmacy." I took a comforting gulp of sweet, cream-infused coffee. "Just make sure you write the F-one's name down."

"I will."

We sipped our coffee in silence for a few minutes. Then I asked the question I really didn't want to ask.

"How bad are things out there?"

Simone flinched. Then she took another long draught of coffee before replying.

"It's bad, Ashley."

"How bad?" I regretted the question the second the words left my mouth. I really didn't think I could handle the answer.

"Ashley!" The sound of someone squealing my name provided a welcome distraction. I turned to see Jamie, Simone's assistant, bearing down on us from across the room.

Barely topping five feet, Jamie was a symphony in black and pink, starting with her shocking pink hair, descending to a pink top covered by a black Victorian jacket that nipped in her already tiny waist. Her black pants had laces up the sides and were tucked into clunky high-heeled black boots. Tinkerbell's Goth twin, by way of Hot Topic. Not my style, but oh, how I envied the variety of her wardrobe.

She reached the table, hugging me before I had a chance to stand up.

"I'm so glad you're okay," she said, giving me a surprisingly strong squeeze with those slender arms. Her enthusiasm was a far cry from the Arctic chill I'd encountered when we'd first met in Simone's class. Jamie'd had one of the most extreme cases of hot-for-teacher I'd ever seen. At first she'd seen me as competition, but once she'd figured out that I wasn't a rival, Jamie had thawed considerably.

She plunked herself down in an empty chair.

"How are you feeling?" she asked Simone. "Are you still dizzy when you stand? Does your throat still hurt?"

"I'm fine, thank you, Jamie," Simone answered with admirable patience. "But perhaps if you're going to get yourself something to eat or drink you could bring me more coffee?"

Jamie popped back up to her feet.

"Black, right?"

"Of course." Simone smiled at her.

"I'll be right back!"

I grinned into my cup as Jamie flitted off across the cafeteria in a pink and black blur. Simone heaved a small but definite sigh of relief.

"Now where were we?" She gazed thoughtfully into the distance for a few seconds before her expression darkened. "Oh, yes. The current situation is not good, Ashley. It's almost certain that the virus has gone airborne. More than ever, a cure is imperative."

"How close were you and Dr. Albert? To a cure, I mean?"

Simone smiled ruefully.

"Close, but no cigar." She took a sip of coffee. "We're missing something. Some essential piece of data, or an unidentified ingredient. Hopefully Marianne— Dr. Arkin—can help us figure out what that missing factor might be."

"And when you say a 'cure,' what exactly do you mean? Are we talking something that can change a zombie back into a human?"

Simone shook her head.

"We can't bring the dead back to life and—" She stopped as I raised an eyebrow. "Let me rephrase that."

"Please do," I said.

"Once someone has died and reanimated, they're

beyond any cure. What we're looking at is something that will provide a resistance to the infection itself."

"Making everyone wild cards?"

Simone nodded. "Granting the immunity, if not the enhancements."

"What about someone like Gabriel?" My voice cracked when I said his name, making me sound small and vulnerable. Simone reached out, took my hands in hers, and looked me directly in the eye.

"If we can immunize people against the virus itself, I'm certain we can cure him, Ashley." She paused, and added, "We just need to get him back."

I closed my eyes, taking a deep breath as a wave of relief washed over me. Then I opened them, and sat up straight.

"What are we waiting for, then?"

"Well, first we have to—"

"Do you mind if I sit here?"

At least that's what I think he said. His accent was so thick, I couldn't be sure.

G. Funk was standing by our table holding a tray of food. Tall, lanky, clad in jeans and the same *Dr. Who* T-shirt he'd been wearing when I'd first found him hiding in his closet. Funk's townhouse had been decorated in early American geek, boasting a bedroom that combined the Bat Cave with a bachelor pad worthy of *King of the Nerds*.

"How are you doing, G?" I smiled and gestured for him to sit down. He took the chair Jamie had just vacated, and as far as I was concerned, he had earned the right to sit wherever the hell he wanted. OCD in his fastidiousness, he'd still let a bunch of dirty, tired, and desperate wild cards crash in his townhouse, and hadn't even complained when we'd tracked all sorts of dirt and gore on his carpet. His hospitality had saved our hides.

Simone smiled. "I've heard much about you, Mr. Funk."

G gave Simone a shy smile, destroying the cool hipster vibe cast by his dark sunglasses.

"I hope it's all good," he said, though it sounded more like *Oyhawpeet's awl gud.* Born in Ireland, raised in Australia. Hell of an accent.

"Absolutely." Simone smiled at him, and that's all she wrote. I heard the crash as G fell hard for Simone.

"G," I said conversationally, "have you ever seen *Excalibur*?"

"Oh, yes." He didn't even look at me when he replied. *Thought so.*

Jamie came back at that moment, carrying a tray with a bowl of soup, a glass of water, and a mug of coffee. She frowned when she saw that her seat had been confiscated. She took the one next to me without saying anything, but from the way she narrowed her eyes, I had the feeling she would have slammed the tray down if it hadn't held Simone's precious coffee.

"G, this is Jamie," I said brightly. "Jamie, this is G. He saved our asses by letting us stay in his home on our way here."

Jamie stared at him. "You're in my seat."

Whoops.

Suddenly I was really looking forward to the briefing.

BROOKLYN. NEW YORK

Chris Anderson—with an "o," not an "e"—stared in frustration at the novelty pig-shaped clock on his desk, which showed him that a full fifteen minutes had passed since he'd been placed on hold by "Marcy."

He frowned, tapping impatient fingers against the wooden desktop as generic "easy listening" music piped out of his speakerphone. His VPN connection had been down for more than two hours, and he was this *close to finalizing a deal for the Holy Grail. An inverted Jenny, printed in 1918. He'd* managed to find it before the seller—a clueless redneck who'd be at home on American Pickers—figured out exactly what he had, and took it to an auction house.

The thought of losing the Jenny after being this close had Chris's blood pressure shooting sky high.

He stopped tapping his fingers and reached into an open box of See's candy. Like the clock, the chocolate had been a gift from his sisters in California. He loved See's, but barely tasted the chocolate as he waited for the IT rep to take him off "hold" and fix the connection before he lost the deal.

A sudden commotion outside caught Chris's attention. He grabbed another piece of chocolate and stood up, wincing as his joints popped. He sat too much—one of the problems of telecommuting—and he was on the downward slope side of fifty. Things popped, crackled, and ached a little more every year.

He carefully navigated stacks of books, magazines, and boxes to get to the office window. He pushed the heavy green curtains aside and peered out. His jaw dropped, the chocolate half eaten and forgotten in his mouth.

What the hell?

His apartment was on the second floor of a five-story brownstone in a nice neighborhood; but his normally quiet street had suddenly erupted into chaos. People ran down the street, some of them bloody and wounded. Many looked terrified and others looked… well, they looked like no one was home anymore. Even through the closed windows he heard screams, moans, the sound of metal smashing into metal as cars careened into one another.

He recognized one of his neighbors, eighty-year-old Mrs. Seskin, squashed between the bumper and hood of two different cars. Her eyes were open and blood gushed out of her mouth. It seemed impossible, but she was still moving, still alive. The driver of the car that had front-ended her was folded over the wheel, not moving.

His first thought was to dash out and help Mrs. Seskin, but then he noticed some of the other people, including other neighbors, moving toward her with an odd uncoordinated *gait, like they were all learning how to walk. Even from his second-story window, Chris could see that some of them had pieces missing.*

"Oh shit, no way."

He watched with morbid fascination as a teenage girl, strips of flesh missing from her face so that the muscles of her jaw were visible, reached over the crumpled metal toward Mrs. Seskin, grabbed one of the old woman's outstretched hands, and sank her teeth into it.

Chris let the curtains fall back in front of the window.

Zombies.

Straight out of Dawn of the Dead.

Except they weren't blue and all "here's the Hare Krishna zombie" or "here's the NRA gun nut." They were real-life normal people.

Black, vomitous, fucked-up. Ripped-apart real-life people.

Chris sat back down at his desk, putting the lid back on the box of See's. If he was right about what was happening outside, he'd want to ration it.

CHAPTER EIGHT

The briefing was held in a large room on the first floor that looked like your generic corporate conference room, big rectangular table and all. I fully expected someone to pull down a screen and show us a PowerPoint presentation on the digital marketing potential of zombies.

The only constant was Colonel Paxton, holding the authority position at the far end of the table, much the same way he'd dominated the podium in Room 217, our old briefing room at Big Red. He'd arrived on the same helicopter as Simone. His *commedia dell'arte* tragedy mask of a face was set in neutral as he waited for everyone to shuffle in and sit.

Tony, Gentry, Lil, and I sat clustered at the end of the table nearest the door. Lil didn't say much to anyone, but the fact she'd actually gotten dressed and left her room was a good sign. Her hair hung in damp hanks down her back, which meant she'd also taken the effort to shower.

Nathan and Simone sat side by side, each making an effort not to look at the other, but still obviously connected. The two had a past—she'd been there when he'd been bitten by a zombie, had nursed him through his transition, and hadn't been strictly honest when he'd demanded explanations. Given Nathan's zero tolerance for bullshit, he hadn't taken it well. Still, if the sexual tension between the two of them was any indication, they might have a future together, if they didn't kill each other first.

Watching the drama unfold between them was almost like having access to a live zombie-themed soap opera channel. Jamie sitting on Simone's other side only added to the drama, although for some inexplicable reason she didn't find Nathan at all threatening.

Go figure.

The Gunsy Twins—Jones and Davis—leaned against the far wall, while Carl, the helicopter, sat glumly next to JT. I was surprised to see them both. After all, Carl had only signed up for dropping us off at UCSF. Then Red, his friend and fellow crew member, had died on our trek across San Francisco. I'd been with Red when he died and still wondered if there was something I could have done to save him.

I gave Carl a tentative smile, and was heartened when he smiled back.

As for JT, he wasn't a wild card *or* military. Even if his physical skills were off the charts compared to your average person, he was still a civilian, and I'd have thought he'd earned the right to hang out in safety, while the rest of us tried to sort out all this zombie shit.

That being said, I was happy to see him.

Dr. Arkin and Josh were there, along with my current least favorite person. Arkin and Josh sat next to each other, while Griff lounged in a chair he'd pulled away from the table, distancing himself from everyone else in the room. He stared at me from under hooded lids. I studiously ignored him.

Much the way Simone and Dr. Arkin were ignoring each other. They were an interesting contrast—Simone with her classic icy blonde film noir style, and Dr. Arkin, tall, thin, and coldly brunette. I'd once compared Simone to a Vulcan, but even if that were the case, at least she had some human ancestry mixed in there. Dr. Arkin was full on emotionless, and possibly sociopathic—too cold-blooded even to be cast as Saavik. Granted, I hadn't spent a lot of time in her company, but I was pretty sure that peeling off part of her skull would reveal a cyborg underneath.

Colonel Paxton cleared his throat, and the room fell silent.

"As you all know, the Walker's virus has breached quarantine," he said. "The flu vaccines were sent around the United States to locations conveniently close to established DZN facilities."

He picked up what looked like a remote control device and clicked it. A screen scrolled down on the wall behind him.

Okay, I was joking about the PowerPoint.

He aimed the control at the ceiling and pressed another button. Immediately the screen lit up with a photograph showing a building complex, several stories tall and all rectangles and hard edges, with lots of window banks. Those buildings were currently besieged by what looked like a shitload of zombies.

"This is the West Virginia University Medical Center, as seen from Chestnut Ridge Road." A pause. "Professor Fraser's alma mater, and home to one of the DZN's top research facilities."

He smiled ruefully, then clicked another button. The feed changed to show a several-story red-brick complex with the American flag flying out front. Smoke billowed out of several of the buildings, and the scene in front could only be described as carnage. Ambulances, fire trucks, and other emergency vehicles lay smashed in an inadvertent piece of modern sculpture.

"This is the nearby Monongalia County General Hospital, where many people suffering from Walker's sought medical care. We tried to ferry as many patients as possible to our facility, but the situation rapidly fell out of our control."

Another quick click switched us to yet another building complex, this one high-tech, with curved blue-glass frontage, the type of structure used to convey *"Hey, this is the future!"* in movies like *Gattaca* and *Lookers*.

"And this is a high-profile pharmaceuticals company down the road that offered free Walker's flu vaccines over the last month."

He hit another switch and the static photography switched to a live video feed of about a half dozen people in lab coats running full pelt up a grassy slope toward the university. A mini-swarm of zombies followed them, with several other groups of the walking dead converging from all other directions. I shuddered as a woman was culled from the human herd and ripped to pieces as we watched. Her screams seemed tinny and unreal over the speakers, but horrific nonetheless.

"Oh god… Julia…"

I looked over at Simone, whose face had gone white. Silent tears slipped down her face. Nathan covered her hand with his, and she moved closer to him.

Colonel Paxton hit the remote again. The screen now showed the interior of a room that looked much like the one we occupied, except front and center were a man and a woman, both in gore-spattered lab coats. The woman, a thirty-something brunette with petite features, looked directly up at the camera.

"Someone set off the fire alarm and most everyone evacuated. When we got outside… they were everywhere. We are certain that the Walker's virus has mutated… gone airborne." The man tried unsuccessfully to hold back tears in the background. The woman kept talking.

"We were screwed. They're slow, but there were so many…" She took a deep breath. "I'm Dr. Allison Hayward. Ben, Dr. Hodgson and I are the only doctors who made it back here. The only other survivors are Jeff Lucas and Jay Bachar, both ROTC, and three lab techs. I—" She pressed her hands against her head for a second, then looked back at the camera. "I can't remember their names. I'm sorry, I should know them, but I can't remember." Another pause.

"We have a lab full of sick people. Jeff and Jay are—" She shut her eyes for a moment. "They're putting them down. The infected. We don't have the manpower to take care of them before or after they die. So it's… it's better this way. For them and for us. They—"

The door behind her burst inward and two blood-splashed young men, both looking like they'd just started shaving that year, dove into the room, slamming the door behind them. One fumbled for the lock while the other started piling any available and movable piece of furniture in front of the door.

"Jay, Jeff… What?—" The woman, Dr. Hayward, shot them a startled glance that quickly turned to terror when the one at the door spoke.

"Someone let the lab rats loose."

Dr. Hodgson lifted his head.

"All of them?"

The other kid nodded. "All of them," he said, knocking notebooks off a bookshelf before dragging it toward the door.

"Oh, crap."

The looks of hopeless terror were clear even over the grainy video feed as another sound resonated through the speakers—the sound of meaty thuds hitting the door. Then the screen went blank.

Colonel Paxton set the remote down on the table and stared at all of us.

"That's the last transmission we had from this particular facility. It's just one example of what is happening all over the country… and is now spreading globally. In a world with jet aircraft, it only takes hours."

Simone hadn't been kidding when she said things were bad. And Paxton wasn't done spreading the bad news.

"We've had reports of sightings in the United Kingdom ranging from London to Sheffield, with the infection originating at a board meeting for a multinational company that sent representatives from India, Japan, China, South America, Romania, Poland, France, Norway… well, you get the picture."

The silence in the room testified that everyone got the picture.

Someone had to break it. Since no one else was speaking up, I jumped in.

"So we have to find the cure, right?" I said.

Colonel Paxton nodded.

"Yes."

"Which means we have to find Gabriel. And Dr. Albert," I added quickly.

"Again, that's correct, Ashley." Colonel Paxton smiled approvingly. I suppressed the urge to ask if I got a gold star.

Simone cleared her throat, dashing a quick hand across her eyes.

"We've tracked the signal in Gabriel's microchip, and it points to San Diego," she said. "Specifically at a location we thought had been shut down years ago."

"Is this a DZN lab?" I asked.

"No," Simone said with assurance. "It's an old naval base, now a national park. The underground portions were used during World War II, and the DZN was aware of it. It was part of a contingency scenario, but there were several other locations established in San Diego, all more strategically placed, that served our needs.

"So what's the plan?" Tony leaned forward, ready to rock and roll.

"We go in and extract Dr. Albert and Gabriel."

"How?" I pressed.

Colonel Paxton smiled, a scary expression on his face.

"That information will be given to you at the appropriate time, and on a need-to-know basis. Right now, considering the sabotage that was performed on the two helicopters that brought you into San Francisco, the details of our plans are considered highly confidential."

Tony frowned.

"You mean we're gonna go risk our lives, without even knowing what the fuck we're doing?"

I nudged him. "We'll know when we need to know." I dropped my voice and added, "Would you rather deal with another whirlybird crash somewhere between here and San Diego, just because the wrong person had the right information?"

Tony shut up, taking my point.

"When are we leaving?" Lil asked. She'd been silent up to now.

"Tomorrow morning," Paxton said.

"What about my cats?"

Colonel Paxton's expression didn't change, but his mental eye-roll was obvious.

"There are more important things at stake here than your pets."

Uh-oh, I thought. *Someone's IQ points just dropped sharply.*

Simone stepped forward before Lil could explode, putting a hand on Lil's shoulder as she spoke.

"Someone will look after your cats while we're gone," she said soothingly. Lil visibly relaxed under the combo of her touch and voice. Paxton started to say something, but a look from Simone shut him up.

We? I thought. *Is Simone going with us?*

Nathan frowned, coming to the same conclusion.

"You're not going," he said firmly.

Simone raised a perfectly arched eyebrow.

"Oh, indeed I am, *Mister* Smith. Captain Drake's condition is extremely unstable. Aside from Dr. Albert, I am the one person most familiar with his condition, and with the appropriate treatment."

"Dr. Albert is with Gabriel," Nathan pointed out with cold logic. "Seems to me that's already covered."

"We have no way of knowing if they're together, or if whoever took them is allowing Dr. Albert to make any more antiserum," Simone said firmly. "Dr. Arkin and I have cobbled together an antiserum derivative that may keep him stable until we can get him back to the lab. Since we can't test it, I have to be there to administer it, and tweak the concentration based on his response." She gave Nathan a look. "If we are to have any hope of bringing him back while he's still human, still sane, I need to be there."

Nathan turned to Colonel Paxton.

"Colonel, I thought the general consensus was that Professor Fraser's skill set and knowledge base was too valuable to risk her involvement in the field."

Colonel Paxton laced his fingers together.

"Captain Drake is also invaluable to our mission," he replied. "From what I've been told by Dr. Albert and Professor Fraser, as well as Dr. Arkin—" He gave her a brief nod of acknowledgement. "—Gabriel's blood likely holds at least part of the answer needed to the cure to this plague. So if that means Professor Fraser goes along… well, it's worth the risk."

Simone nodded. "Dr. Arkin has all the information needed to help synthesize the cure, and more practical experience than I. She and Dr. Albert collaborated on the Walker's vaccine, and thanks to Ashley, we have Dr. Albert's notes."

I gave a modest shrug. All I'd done was scoop up his backpack, dropped when he'd been attacked by a zombie on our way to the DZN facility. So when the men in black took Dr. Albert away, his backpack, laptop, notes, and samples of Gabriel's antiserum stayed behind.

"So if there's anyone we need to keep alive at this point," Simone continued, "it's Dr. Arkin." I could tell the admission pained her. "Jamie will stay here and assist her."

Dr. Arkin looked coldly pleased.

"*What?*" Jamie shot to her feet. "But I have to go with you!"

Simone looked at her apologetically.

"I'm sorry, Jamie, but I need you to stay here. You haven't had adequate training to go out into the field, especially into the conditions we're going to face."

"I can shoot!" Jamie said hotly.

"Not well enough," Nathan said bluntly.

Jamie glared at him.

"I'm not staying here, not when Professor Fraser needs me."

"Jamie, trust me when I say that your assistance will be much more important here," Simone said soothingly. "After all, you know my work nearly as well as I do, and no one else can decipher my handwriting."

"That's true," Dr. Arkin agreed.

Simone didn't dignify that with a response. Instead she got to her feet and put a hand on Jamie's shoulder.

"I need to know there's someone here I can trust to make sure the work we've already done is built upon, rather than replaced."

Ooh, points for a nice subtle parry and riposte. Dr. Arkin's slight frown showed that the riposte had been on target, too. What I'd give for a time machine, to go back and find out what exactly happened between the two of them.

"Besides, I won't have to worry about your safety if you're here," Simone added. I could see Jamie melt, all arguments borne away on a tide of warm fuzzies. She sat down without another word.

Well played, Simone, I thought, albeit a bit cynically.

Nathan cleared his throat.

"Fine. Now that that's settled, we'll be divided into two teams as per usual. Team A will be Ash, Lil, myself, and JT. Team B will be Simone, Tony, Gentry, and Griff."

Tony raised his hand.

"What is it," Colonel Paxton said with more than a touch of impatience.

"No offense to JT," Tony said in a tone that made it clear he didn't give a shit, "but he's not exactly a wild card." He nodded at JT. "I mean, dude, you have some wicked skills—"

JT gave a modest nod of acknowledgment.

"—but if you get gnawed on by a zom, you're dead." The way he said it, though, I could tell he wouldn't necessarily be sorry to see it happen.

If JT noticed, though, he didn't show it. He just shrugged.

"Maybe I'll turn out to be a wild card after all, and be able to leap tall buildings in a single bound."

Colonel Paxton cleared his throat.

"We've lost three wild cards in the last two weeks, along with several other key personnel. This man—" He nodded toward JT. "—has exhibited physical skills that match any of yours, even without the benefit of being a wild card. He's willing to take the chance, and we cannot afford to turn down his offer to help."

"How do we know we can trust him?" Griff said unexpectedly.

"You have *got* to be kidding," I said without thinking.

Griff shrugged. "From what I understand, he showed up miraculously when you were coming close to this facility."

"Actually, he showed up leaping across the tops of cars near Golden Gate Bridge," I corrected.

"And then he followed you all the way across San Francisco," Griff countered. He shot JT a pointed look. "Seems a bit convenient to me."

JT folded his arms and shrugged again.

"If you had no place to go," he said, "wouldn't you follow the hot chick with a katana, and the rest of the people wearing uniforms, looking like they at least had a clue?"

"Yeah, and he saved our asses by risking his own life," I said, glaring at Griff. "I'd trust him before I'd trust you, any day of the week."

Dr. Arkin spoke for the first time since we'd started the briefing.

"I can assure you, Ms. Parker, that Griff is entirely trustworthy."

"So says the woman who helped create the vaccine that brought the dead back to life," I snapped. She raised an eyebrow, and sat back in her chair.

"Go, Ash," Tony drew closer to me in an unaccustomed show of support and I thought I heard...

Did Lil just growl?

I think she did.

"There are very few people on the list who I'd trust with my life," I continued. "Especially since someone on our side brought down our 'copters and cost us the lives of five people. Five good people. JT actually risked his life to help us." I shot a scathing look across the table. "The rest of you sat on your asses and watched while our friend Mack died. So please do *not* tell me who we can or cannot trust."

There was a moment of uncomfortable silence that really needed to be filled with a slow clap. None was forthcoming, though, so Colonel Paxton cleared his throat and looked vaguely pissed.

"The decisions have already been made," he said. "We don't have time for a debate, and I will not hesitate to pull rank to move this operation forward. Do I make myself clear?"

He did. Everyone drank a big glass of "shut the fuck up." Paxton looked around the room, and nodded in satisfaction.

"Good. Be ready to leave at dawn."

CHAPTER NINE

"So…" I shot Nathan and Simone a look. "Any chance I can hit the pharmacy here before we take off?"

We stood on the enclosed catwalk that spanned the distance between the architecturally significant Center for Regenerative Medicine and the building we'd cleared. The huge elevator leading to the DZN facility was positioned smack in the middle of the walkway.

Jones and Davis had done a respectable job of clearing the undead from the loading docks around the elevator. The entrance off of Medical Center Road—the auxiliary road we'd traveled down—was blocked off by a newly erected chain-link fence, with big trucks à la the original *Dawn of the Dead* butted up against it. It would take a hell of a lot of zombies or a very determined biker gang to get through there.

It would also be a major pain in the ass to get out. Hence my conundrum.

Simone and Nathan didn't reply, so I pressed on.

"Lil and I made it to Redwood Grove and back when we got her cats. With your help," I added hastily as Nathan raised an eyebrow. "My point is, there were lots of zombies, and we made it part way on our own. With *help*, I could—"

Nathan shook his head.

"Redwood Grove is a sparsely populated area, Ash.

We're talking about San Francisco, a major medical center in the middle of a forty-nine square mile city with a minimum of eight hundred thousand full-time residents. The most densely settled large city in the state of California, and the second most densely populated major city in the United States. That means a lot more zombies than you've ever seen."

"So this would only suck more if we were in New York."

"Basically, yes," he said. "Getting in and out of that pharmacy, *any* pharmacy, is a suicide mission. It's too great of a risk—one we simply can't afford."

I slammed my hands against the catwalk railing in frustration.

"What am I supposed to do then?" My voice climbed a few decibels. "Just let Lil wander further into Crazy Town? If we can't count on her, we're down another wild card, right?"

Simone and Nathan exchanged a look.

"We have a plan," he said.

"If it ends up with pints at the Winchester, count me out."

Nathan grinned. "Hopefully there will be beer at some point, but no, that's not part of the plan."

"What is it?" I asked dubiously.

Simone put a hand on my shoulder and looked me in the eyes.

"Do you trust us, Ashley?"

I didn't hesitate.

"Yes." I simply refused to contemplate a world where either Simone or Nathan was in the enemy camp.

Simone smiled. "Good. I promise you, we'll get Lil's medicine before we leave San Francisco."

I heaved a sigh of relief. If Simone said it was so, it would happen. So I decided to switch topics.

"Do you really think we can trust Griff?" I asked.

Both Nathan and Simone snorted in derision.

Synchronized snorting. I wish I'd gotten it on tape.

"Of course not," Nathan said. "We can't afford to trust anyone, let alone someone Dr. Arkin vouches for."

"What about Colonel Paxton?"

"I would trust him with my life," Simone said. Then she gave an odd little smile and added, "Unless preserving my life meant sacrificing the rest of the world. He will do what he needs to in order to minimize loss of life and stop this plague. And if that means sacrificing anyone or anything in order to complete his mission… he will do it."

"You know, "I said, "it's probably better for morale if you just keep that to yourself."

"You're probably right," Simone said. "But I owe it to you to be honest, and I think you can handle the truth."

I nodded slowly, realizing she was right.

"Yeah. I can."

And I could. Even if I didn't like it.

RURAL BOTSWANA

The main things Eric noticed during the five-plus-hour drive from Ghanzi to the Jwana Game Park, aside from just how damned hot it was, were the rocks piled alongside the road.

And the graves. Dozens upon dozens of graves, many of them surrounded by structures made of iron bars with canvas tops, more like mini patios than any sort of burial plot.

He nudged their driver Johan, an amiable Afrikaner in his mid-thirties who handled the old Toyota 4X4 that was ferrying them through the Kalahari Desert with a reassuring competence that almost balanced the breakneck speed at which he drove. It helped that there was very little other traffic other than the occasional cow or donkey.

"What's with the rocks on the road and the fences around the graves?"

Johan was more than willing to play tour guide.

"Whole villages have been destroyed by AIDS," Johan told them. "Some villages, they had no adults left in them. The survivors used rocks to cover the dead, in order to keep the animals away."

"Why the fences though?"

"Some say they are to make certain the dead do not walk," Johan said with more than a touch of the dramatic.

Eric's wife Nancy, sprawled in the back seat with their luggage, pushed a wayward hank of damp red hair out of her face and rolled her eyes.

"Do they believe in zombies here?" she asked eagerly.

Eric shook his head. His wife thought horror movies began with Night of the Living Dead and ended with The Walking Dead. Personally he was sick to death—hah—of the current zombie craze. He'd take Sharknado or an invasion of sparkly vampires any day.

"The South Africans have the Tokoloshe," Johan said. "They are not quite zombies, but something created by shamans to take vengeance on those who might offend them. These creatures supposedly rape women and bite off the toes of sleeping people."

Nancy laughed. "So wear shoes to bed, right?"

"According to legend," Johan continued, "the only way to keep the Tokoloshe away at night is to put a brick beneath each leg of one's bed. Anyone else in the house, however, is shit out of luck."

They drove a few more minutes in companionable silence, Eric and Nancy drinking liberal amounts of water to combat the heat of more than 30 degrees centigrade. A mile or so down the road, Johan broke the silence.

"So you two are volunteering at the game park?"

Eric nodded. "We'll be working primarily at the cheetah conservation research center."

Johan nodded wisely. "Ah, for the Cat Lady."

"You know her?" Nancy leaned forward between the two front seats.

"Oh, yes," Johan said. "If you work for her, you will have

less trouble with Debswana security. Everyone at the mine knows the Cat Lady."

"Is the security that strict?"

"Oh, yes," Johan said again. "Remember that you are dealing with the richest diamond mine in Botswana. There is more than one reason they surround themselves with a game park."

"Anything else we should know?" Nancy asked.

Johan pursed his lips thoughtfully.

"The phrase 'just now' means 'I will do it later.' And 'now now' means 'I will get to it right now.' He fell silent long enough to swerve around a small but fierce dust devil speeding across the road, then continued, "And remember that superstitions are very real to the people here." He reached out a hand and tapped Eric's blue-framed sunglasses. "These? They may scare some people. That could be good though. You will keep them off guard."

Another hour passed in relative silence. Nancy dozed in the back and Eric watched the passing scenery while Johan drove. The landscape was relentlessly flat. Most of the towns they passed seemed to be abandoned.

Nancy woke up long enough to say, "I really need to pee."

Johan and Eric exchanged looks in a moment of male solidarity.

"Hon, I don't think we're gonna find any rest stops along the way."

Nancy shrugged. "Just find me something I can duck behind so I don't offend the donkeys."

"That I can do," Johan said. "A few more miles and there is another village. It's one of the dead ones, so no one will bother you."

One of the dead ones.

There was a phrase made for nightmares.

True to his word, Johan pulled off the road next to a small village consisting of clay huts topped with cone-shaped thatch roofs. No one stirred as the 4X4 came to a halt next to a cemetery with the same fenced in graves. It stretched back a few hundred feet, the back obscured by a couple of baobab trees.

Nancy hopped out of the back seat, wilting visibly as the full strength of the African sun beat down on her head. She reached back inside and grabbed her Aussie hat, then disappeared between two of the huts to do her business.

Eric opened the passenger door and stepped out to stretch his legs. They still had another hour or so on the road before they reached the game park. As hot as the interior of the car had been, it was nothing compared to the oven-like heat outside. It rose from the ground and blazed down from the sky. Sweat instantly appeared on his back and brow, then dried just as quickly. He drank more water, deeply aware that to be out here without it was almost certainly a death sentence.

Johan joined him, lighting up a cigarette as he leaned against the vehicle, seemingly impervious to the heat. Eric's gaze meandered over the cemetery. He was fascinated by the structures and wondering how far the natives who'd built it had to go to get the iron bars that walled in the individual plots. Certainly far enough to be a hassle, not to mention expensive.

They must really have wanted to protect their dead or—

Eric put a hand above his eyes to cut down the glare from the sun.

"I thought you said this place was dead." He pointed past the baobab trees into the back end of the graveyard. Unless he was seeing his first mirage, there were at least two people wandering around back there, maybe more.

Johan glanced in that direction. He frowned, and then shrugged.

"Looks like someone has moved back, perhaps."

"What are they doing?"

"Tending the graves, perhaps." He took a drag on his cigarette. At that moment Nancy screamed.

Eric took off running without a second thought. Nancy never screamed. She was the most unflappable woman he'd ever met, dealing with dangerous situations, injury and illness with a calm competence that a battlefield medic would envy.

He reached the first two huts, almost colliding with her as she pelted around the corner, her face chalk-white under its dusting of freckles. Eric grabbed her by the shoulders to steady her.

"Are you okay? Are you hurt?"

"I'm fine. We need to go."

"But—"

"Now, Eric!" Nancy dislodged his hands from her shoulders, and curled her fingers around one of his wrists in a vice-like grip, pulling him along as she headed for the car.

"What—"

Nancy shook her head. "No time!"

A guttural sound of agony ripped through the air.

Eric and Nancy skidded to a stop.

Johan squirmed on the ground next to the 4X4, three badly emaciated figures in ragged native garb kneeling next to him. They were ripping pieces out of his body with fingers that looked more like bony talons. Talons dripping with blood and pieces of Johan's flesh.

Johan howled as one of the creatures—they couldn't be human, could they?—dug a hand deep into his stomach. All Eric could think as he watched their driver's intestines being pulled out inch by agonizing inch was that special effects had nothing on real life.

A puff of wind brought a rich, foul smell of fecal matter and blood wafting on the air. Eric gagged, trying not to throw up. Then the sound of slow, relentless footsteps behind them made it easier for him to keep his gorge down.

Two more of the rotting figures approached them, eyes filmed over a milky white—corpse eyes, mouths opening and closing with never-ending hunger.

"Run," Nancy said.

She yanked on his arm and headed straight for the 4X4, evading one of the kneeling corpses as it reached for her, and dodging around the rear of the vehicle to the passenger's side. Several other walking horrors approached from the opposite side of the road, their gait slow and implacable.

Nancy threw open the front door and scrambled across the

passenger's seat to the driver's side, slamming the locks shut on the door as one of the corpses, blood and gore dripping from its mouth, staggered to its feet and splatted its hands against the window.

Eric leaped into the shotgun seat, closing the door and hitting the lock as Nancy turned the keys that were dangling in the ignition. She revved the motor, and hit the gas. The 4X4 fishtailed briefly before its tires gripped the road.

"What the fuck!" Eric said. He looked back at the rapidly receding village, where some of the figures still clustered around Johan while others staggered to the road and began following their vehicle.

"We'll go to the game preserve," Nancy said with almost unnatural calm. "The diamond mine. They'll have good security. We can ride this out."

"Ride what out?" Eric slammed his fist against the dashboard in frustration and horror. "What the fuck is going on?"

Nancy just kept driving.

CHAPTER TEN

Whupwhupwhupwhup...

Ugh, I hated that noise. It meant I was in the air, enclosed in a small, noisy, flying metal coffin that could malfunction at any moment. Planes were bad enough, but helicopters just sucked. Carl was a good pilot, but being in one made my stomach unhappy, and I so did not wanna barf again this month.

Seriously, right before the zombie plague hit I'd had a horrible case of food poisoning caused by bad sushi, then been hit with Walker's flu. Got chomped by a couple of zombies, and then topped it off by wading into all manner of blood, viscera, and tragedy. And, oh yeah, a helicopter crash.

Maybe I should buy stock in Dramamine.

I snuck a glance at Lil, sitting quietly next to a window and staring out at the passing landscape as the sun rose. It was a stark contrast to her almost manic excitement on the helicopter trip from Redwood grove to San Francisco. The circles under her eyes weren't quite as extreme as they'd been yesterday, though. Just being up and active seemed to have helped her.

At least this was a larger helicopter than the one we'd taken coming in. It had to be, in order to hold the ten of us plus the flight crew. A female mechanic had replaced poor Red. I didn't know her name, and had to stop myself from thinking of her as our token red shirt.

When we got to the roof the sky was clear, and there were two helicopters. But we all crammed into one. Both choppers took off and headed south. All smoke and mirrors.

It's not paranoia when someone's trying to kill you.

We were all in our matching SWAT chic of black BDUs, long-sleeved fire-retardant shirts, lace-up boots, and assorted Kevlar pieces to cover our vulnerable bits, although JT had made some modifications to accommodate the mobility he needed for his particular skills. He had shoes with flexible soles and a good grip on the bottom, and nothing that restricted his joints.

We also toted our weapons of choice, the trusty M4s plus the new "squirrel rifles" as Tony called them. The AM15s were stubby green autos similar to the M4, but they fired much smaller rounds—a shitload of 'em, too, courtesy of that big spinning drum thingee on the top. It was an interesting weapon, quiet as a pellet gun, no recoil or over-penetration. Yet if you had it on full auto, a tight string could cut a zombie in half like a laser.

I preferred the M4, probably because it was familiar, but the squirrel rifles were great when you had to worry about infectious splatter, or a round going through a rotting skull and into an innocent bystander.

Tony had his BAS (Big Ass Shotgun), which spent most of its time in a holster slung across his back. It was a special weapon for special occasions. Somewhat surprisingly, Tony used it wisely.

Our helicopter veered southwest toward the ocean and the Outer Sunset neighborhood. I watched through the window as zombies lurched their way up and down the streets. Outer Sunset was laid out pretty much in a grid, with numerical streets running north-south and alphabetical streets running east-west. There were no Victorian Painted Ladies out here. The neighborhood once called the Outside Lands—and didn't that just smack of Lovecraft—had been one of the last to be built on top of what were mainly sand dunes. The houses and apartments were, for the most part, painted in pastel colors, eschewing the gilt-edged purples, greens, and blues. I remembered reading somewhere that a paint job for one of the Victorians could cost upward of a hundred thousand dollars.

If I lived near the beach I'd opt for pastels too.

We headed toward 40th and Taravel. There was a Walgreen's on one of the corners that would have Lil's meds. All part of Simone and Nathan's plan to further befuddle anyone who might be aiming to sabotage us on our way to San Diego. It was a good plan, other than the fact that we couldn't let Lil know why we were there.

She'd go ballistic. Luckily we had a need-to-know cover story for our cover story.

Can you say "convoluted," children?
I thought you could.

As we flew further west, the clear weather vanished, starting with wisps of flog floating through the air before the helicopter hit a wall of gray mist. Unfortunately it wasn't quite thick enough to block the view below so I could still see that the streets were crawling with the undead. I saw a few people on rooftops, too, huddled together for warmth.

Some of them saw the helicopter flying above and waved frantically, hoping for rescue. It sucked that we couldn't help them. But if I thought about all the people we couldn't save, it would paralyze me.

So I shut my eyes, and tried not to think.

Fingers squeezed my hand. I opened my eyes and looked over at Lil, who'd crept next to me and took my hand in hers. She looked up with a shy smile.

"Hi," I said softly as she rested her head against my arm.

"Hi."

"You okay?" I asked.

She nodded. "Yeah. Are you?"

I thought about the people down below, hoping for help that wouldn't be forthcoming.

And then I lied.

"Yeah, I'm okay."

Lil shook her head. "No, you're not. But you will be, once we get Gabriel back."

I gave her a one-armed hug. "You are wise beyond your years, Padawan."

She sat quietly for a moment, still leaning against me. I felt like I had a feral kitten curled up next to me—one that wanted affection, but any false move would send it skittering away.

"It's like the animals," Lil said. "We can't save all of them, can we?"

"No," I said, giving a heartfelt sigh. "We can't."

Lil gave me a sudden squeeze and looked up at me, her expression fierce.

"You helped me get Binkey and Doodle back. I'll help you get Gabriel back."

"Hopefully he won't make as much noise as they did," Nathan commented from two seats over. He had to raise his voice to be heard over the sounds of the helicopter.

Damn. He had good hearing even for a wild card. He was right, though. Binkey and Doodle had howled enough to wake the dead when we'd tried to quietly smuggle them out of Lil's old apartment.

Lil grinned. "If he does, then it's a good thing we have you here to help us again."

"Just no more cats," Nathan said firmly. He winked at me before shutting his eyes and feigning sleep.

"Do you think G will take good care of them?" Lil bit her bottom lip and frowned. "He seems awfully…" She paused, looking for the right word.

"Anal-retentive, obsessive-compulsive, and a neat freak?"

Lil grinned. "Uh-huh."

"I think he'll be on the job," I said, and I meant it. G seemed like a man of his word, and he'd promised Simone he would look after Binkey and Doodle during our absence. That made it even more of a certainty.

"Cats are clean," he'd said, clutching a bottle of hand sanitizer. "They wash a lot." I just hoped he could handle cat box duty. Both Binkey and Doodle laid down some major paint-peelers.

My stomach gave a lurch as the helicopter suddenly dipped down toward the ground. I looked out the window and saw the Walgreen's sign. We'd reached our destination.

Like the rest of the city, the streets below were clogged with unmoving vehicles, some of them smashed in an interlocking metal mess, and others abandoned all helter-skelter. Two Muni streetcars had become jammed at opposite ends of Taravel in the block between 40th and 41st. Cars had sheared into them, creating a roadblock at either end while leaving a sizable clear space in the middle—large enough for our whirlybird to set down.

"Why are we landing?" Griff sat up from his seat in the back.

"I have an errand to run," I said coolly, ignoring the churning in my gut as the helicopter swooped in to land.

"What errand?" Lil asked. She hadn't been in on it either, for obvious reasons.

"Simone needs some… er… stuff for Gabriel's antiserum." *Stuff. Yeah. That's the ticket.* "We didn't want the bad guys to know. We'll meet you at a rendezvous point up the road."

Someday I'd get a vocabulary worthy of the situations I now found myself in. Even so, it worked. Lil nodded, and Griff shut up, at least for the moment. He kept on staring at me suspiciously, though, right up to the moment the pilot set the helicopter down.

Whatever, I didn't care what he thought.

Once we hit ground and stabilized, I scrambled for

the door, determined not to spew. My stomach thought about it for a brief moment, but thankfully everything stayed put. Tony leaped out after me, hefting Thor's Wee Hammer. Nathan and JT followed swiftly. I saw Lil staring at me in confusion through one of the windows, so I gave her a reassuring wave and blew a kiss.

She grinned and waved back.

Zombies appeared from both ends of the street and began stumbling toward the helicopter, drawn by the noise. I heard cries for help from a building across the street and my heart dropped. I looked up to see a middle-aged man leaning out of a second-story window, waving frantically. Zombies in the street below immediately zeroed in on him, moving toward the entrance to the building and fresh meat. The man's eyes widened and he vanished inside, hopefully to fortify the front door of his apartment.

Sorry, dude. And I really was. I wanted to charge in and save the day, the Mighty Mouse of zombie killing. But… I couldn't. Instead I dashed over to the entrance of the Walgreen's, along with Nathan, Tony, and JT.

Whupwhupwhupwhup…

The helicopter, in the meantime took off again, ascending to just above the grasping hands of the hungry crowd gathering below. Our ride headed off to its next destination and it was up to the four of us to accomplish our respective goals and meet them there.

Nathan looked at us. "You all clear on the plan?"

"I go get the supplies," I said.

"And I back her up." Tony gave Thor's Wee Hammer a swing.

JT grinned. "I create a distraction and lead as many zombies away from here as I can so you three have a semi-clear shot to the beach when you're finished."

"Excellent." Nathan nodded approvingly. "I'll clear whatever stragglers don't follow JT." He clapped a hand on JT's shoulder. "We'll see you at the Great Highway and Vicente when you're finished."

"That you will," JT said. He grinned at me. "I'll race you."

Then, with a whoop and a holler and no sign of fear whatsoever, he took off at a run, east on Taravel, using any and every available surface to keep his momentum going and avoid the clutching hands of hungry undead pedestrians.

"He really is crazy," I observed, watching in bemused admiration as he leapt without pause up a brick wall and onto the roof of a residential garage. He stopped there, hunkering down on the edge, and gave another ear-splitting rebel yell to attract the attention of the neighborhood zombies.

"Come on dowwwwn," he hollered gleefully. "Get your share of the tastiest piece of ass in San Francisco!" He turned and twerked with a dexterity that would have made Miley Cyrus jealous. And the crowd loved it, judging from the increased volume of moans and the outstretched hands.

Ever the showman, JT turned to one side in a classic "The Thinker" pose, flexing his biceps.

"Is there a vet around here," he yelled, "because these pythons are *sick!*"

"Dude needs help," Tony agreed.

"Or not," I commented as JT bounded across the length of the garage rooftop, where he nimbly scaled a balcony and hoisted himself up a trellis to gain access to the second story of the house. He vanished from our eyesight shortly after that, his war whoops still clearly audible.

I really hoped he'd be okay. He was on the lighter side of nuts, for sure, but he was risking his life even more than the rest of us because one scratch or bite, and he'd be screwed. I couldn't remember the exact percentage of people immune to the zombie pathogen, but the odds of becoming a wild card were only slightly more favorable than winning the lottery.

There was a muffled pop as Nathan put a round in the skull of an Asian teenage boy who hadn't been entranced by JT's award-worthy performance. It reminded me that we needed to get our asses in gear.

Minus the twerking.

CHAPTER ELEVEN

The door to the Walgreen's was ajar. A body clad in baggy khakis and a flannel shirt lay face down and prevented it from closing. I think it was a man, but the amount of flesh that had been ripped away, coupled with a neutral short haircut, made it hard to tell.

The smell was horrific, rot and blood and shit blended together in a rich bouquet of gross. Moaning sounded from inside the store, and I could hear more approaching from the streets all around. I pushed the door open and went inside.

Oh, shit.

The Walgreen's was full of the walking dead. There were at least two-dozen lurching up and down the aisles, still finishing up whatever last-minute shopping had been important enough to convince them to go out in a crisis. There were Chinese grandmas and grandpas, surfers in their flip-flops, and an assortment of the diverse population of the neighborhood. Whatever they had come here looking for, now they all craved the same meal.

In that moment, I was it.

I pulled out my swords and waded in, relatively secure in the knowledge that Tony was right behind me. Several employees wearing blue staff shirts stumbled toward me. I carved up one and left Tony to finish the cleanup in aisle two as I dashed down the cosmetics aisle toward the back of the store, heading for the sign that said "PHARMACY."

A slender female zombie in yoga pants and a form-fitting black top lurched into my path. I cut into its head with my katana, feeling the reverberation through my arms as the blade sliced through bone and brains. As I pulled the blade from its skull, hands grasped my shoulders from behind, the smell announcing another zombie looking for an easy meal. I whirled around and drove my tanto into its skull, taking out a teenage boy in a Giants hoodie, its face shredded by equal parts teeth, nails, and acne.

I hated this.

I was sick of putting down these poor dead things. They had no more control over their actions than sharks, turned into relentless eating machines. Still, I hacked, slashed, and thrust my way past the vitamin and sleep-aid aisle to the consultation window of the pharmacy. A sleepy-eyed zombie pharmacist stood at the window, reaching out for me as an older male zombie with a shock of steel gray hair lurched toward me from the cold medication aisle.

Hopping up onto the shelf of the window, I kicked the pharmacist backward, then jumped down into the pharmacy proper where I landed on my feet with flexed knees, tanto in hand. It would have been a perfect landing if I hadn't hit a patch of something nasty and slippery on the Formica floor. My right foot slid out from under me, depositing me on my ass and pulling muscles in my thigh and groin at the same time.

"Shit!" I didn't bother lowering my voice.

"You okay, Ash?" Tony poked his head over the counter.

I got to my feet, wincing as the pulled muscle let it be known it did not approve.

"Kindasorta," I said. I glanced down to see what I'd slipped in.

Blood and black vomit. Lovely. And it also meant I probably wasn't alone back there. And sure enough...

A low moan sounded from the other side of the nearest row of shelves. I sheathed my katana, transferring my tanto to my right hand as I slowly and cautiously moved toward the sound.

Something dragged along the floor, a nasty squishing noise followed by a thumping sound.

I thought of an old slumber party standard, a story called "Thump Squish," where the heroine hears something coming closer, a thump followed by a squish and drag... and it turns out to be her friend who's had her legs and arms chopped off by the psycho from the nearby insane asylum... and she's dragging herself along, the thump being the stumps of her arms as they hit the ground and the squish being the sound of her legs dragging behind.

The story creeped the hell out of me every time.

A mangled hand reached around the end of the shelf, several fingers missing. An arm clad in a blood-spattered white coat followed the preview, to reveal what had once been a pretty young Asian pharmacist. As it slowly rounded the corner, I saw that one of its feet had been gnawed off, leaving only a bloody stump. There was a thump when the good foot hit the ground, followed by a dragging swish from the stump.

Its mouth opened as its dead gaze focused on me. Black bile drooled out. It reached for me with those mutilated hands and moaned again.

"Need a hand?" Tony poked his head over the top of the counter again, like a wild card jack-in-the-box.

"Nope. Got it covered." I thrust the point of my tanto into one of those milky eyes, bracing my heel against its forehead to withdraw the blade. It crumpled to the ground and I heaved a sigh of both relief and disgust.

A hand grabbed my ankle and I gave a yelp of surprise as a *Return of the Living Dead*-type torso zombie, entrails and spine trailing out from beneath its white coat, started chewing on my boot.

"Gah!"

This one had been male, and I fully expected it to say "Bra-a-a-ains!" I jerked my foot out of its mouth and stomped down on its head with the heel of my boot. As cinematic as it would have been to have my heel crunch through its skull and splatter brain matter across the floor, I only succeeded in denting it a little bit. So I dispatched it with a quick thrust through the skull.

Gross. It had left tooth marks and zombie drool on my boot.

I stayed still for a moment and listened for any more pharmaceutically inclined zombies. Tony was happily dispatching the former customers across the store, but I couldn't detect any more signs of… er… life in the pharmacy itself.

Keeping my tanto in one hand, I pulled a slip of paper out of my pants pocket and took a quick look at the list of medications. Thank goodness Simone's handwriting was more legible than mine.

It took me about five minutes to find what I needed. The medications were shelved in alphabetical order, which made things refreshingly easy for once. I'd been afraid they'd be stored by type or classification, never daring to hope it would be as easy as ABC. Opening the main compartment of my knapsack, I dumped in plenty of the meds, insuring we'd have enough psychotropics to keep Lil's problem in check, even if we got stranded somewhere.

I also tossed in a couple of bottles of ibuprofen, just 'cause I foresaw a lot of headaches and body aches in the near future. We each already carried a mini-first aid kit in our gear, but it never hurt to be prepared.

The muffled pop of rifle fire sounded from the front of the store.

"Ash, Tony, we need to move out." Nathan's strong voice carried into the pharmacy itself. I fastened my knapsack securely and leaped back over the counter, wincing at the pain in my thigh and groin muscles.

Tony caught my expression, and pointed at the connecting door. "It's only locked from the inside," he said.

I shrugged, not willing to admit I hadn't noticed it. Instead I shot him a cocky look.

"Haven't you ever heard of a shortcut?"

To my surprise, I was rewarded with a grin. It was a faint shadow of his old one, when he'd be exchanging movie quotes with Kai, but a grin nonetheless.

It'll do, zombie pig. It'll do.

CHAPTER TWELVE

We made our way back through gore-splattered aisles, taking down the few strays that'd escaped Tony's attention while I shopped for drugs. Nathan waited at the front entrance, fancy firearm at the ready, all "poised for Action Man" as he coolly took aim and eliminated zombies coming in from all sides.

"I thought the plan was for you to lure them away," I said when Tony and I joined him outside the store. There were still a hell of a lot of zombies honing in on us—at least twenty or so. More corpses littered the streets, bullet holes in their heads a testament to Nathan's marksmanship.

"Oh, a lot of them followed JT," he said, targeting a young male zombie in sweat pants, a tie-dyed shirt, and those hideous white man's dreadlocks that always seemed to end up on skinny, pasty blonds with an aversion to bathing.

Bap.

One shot and down it went.

"There were a hell of a lot more before he took off," Nathan continued. "And some of them followed the helicopter." He took out what had been a cute little Cantonese girl in flowered pajamas drenched in blood. I winced as she… it went down.

"Ready to make a run for it?" Nathan slung his firearm over one shoulder and unhooked a Halligan bar from a loop on his belt. Without waiting for an answer, he took off at a run down 40th Avenue, heading south, leaving Tony and me to follow. He straight-armed an older male zombie with mad scientist hair bristling out in all directions, straggly soup-strainer beard and mustache holding bits of its last gory meal.

We caught up and jogged at a steady clip down a block, turning right toward the ocean on Ulloa Avenue. It was a gentle downhill slope to the sea. The houses were, for the most part, well tended, big wheels and basketball hoops in the driveways proclaiming them family homes with kids. Unlike Taravel, this street was entirely residential. The only business was an elementary school on our left. There was no sign of life in the schoolyard, and thankfully no zombies or corpses either.

By this point in the disaster, most people had either fled, holed up as best they could, or died. I could still hear the occasional screams and shouts—and maybe more of JT's war whoops off in the distance—but the last two days had changed San Francisco from a city in chaos to an apocalyptic landscape of blood, smoke, and death.

I looked up at a two-story house on my right just in time to see a curtain twitch shut as if someone had been looking out, but didn't want to be seen. The front door of the house stood behind a sturdy wrought-iron gate and fence, the yard bordered by a high cement wall. Maybe whoever was inside would be safe, at least for a while.

I wished whoever was in there a silent good thought and kept jogging after Nathan and Tony, who quickly outpaced me with their longer legs. We wove around the occasional vehicle left askew across the sidewalk or plowed into a fence, fenders and front ends crumpled beyond repair. We cut over a few blocks early onto Vicente, where we encountered another Muni train that had collided with a PG&E repair truck, making the street more or less impassable.

The smell of anti-freeze and gasoline mingled with

the scent of necrosis. I would have been a happy camper if I'd never had occasion to become so damned intimate with that particular odor.

There still were plenty of zombies wandering the streets, but they were pretty spread out, so we ran past them with as little contact as possible. A good shove took less time than a sword thrust or a headshot.

Others scratched and pounded for entrance at various houses, peeling off and honing in on us as we ran by, more accessible prey catching their single-minded attention. Good. It might keep whoever cowered inside safe for that much longer—long enough to shore up their defenses.

I didn't want to think about their long-term survival odds—or anyone else's, if we couldn't stop this contagion. For the umpteenth time I swore to myself that I was going to kick Dr. Albert's ass from here to eternity after we rescued him and he finished perfecting the cure.

HARAJUKU, JAPAN

Ayako stopped texting and took another obsessive look at the bite on her forearm. Beneath her ruined lace sleeve, the jagged semi-circle of punctures on her skin was an angry red, tinged with black. The wound throbbed, and the heat from it had been steadily spreading like a lava flow. Her whole body was wracked with fever, and her head ached as if her brain was a desperate trapped rat trying to claw its way out of her skull.

It hurt even to text, so she gave up on her uncooperative cell phone, got up off the boutique floor, and walked over to the window where Natsuki stood gazing down from the deserted fashion boutique that was their temporary refuge and prison.

Ayako laid her head on her friend's shoulder, looking like an orphaned waif in her innocent Girly Girl outfit—frilly dress, lace jacket, white stockings, and glossy black shoes. Natsuki sported a more adventurous look, one part steampunk and two parts Napoleonic wars, with a black, brass-buttoned military long coat, belted tunic, breeches, and knee-high boots.

"Anything?" Natsuki asked, still staring down on Takeshita Street.

Ayako shook her head, instantly regretting it as the movement sent daggers of pain through her skull.

"No luck. I have bars, but no one's answering." She sighed. "Do you think it's… you don't think…" She trailed off and bit her lip, afraid to finish her thought.

Natsuki answered anyway.

"I don't know," she said. "It might be happening all over." Her voice quavered as she continued. "Look at them all—it's everybody."

In the street below, the usual Takenoko-zoku menagerie paraded under festive arches sporting happy Miyazaki cartoon characters, past the shops and galleries and fast-food eateries toward Harajuku Station. There were dark-eyed Goth-Loli girls wearing black patent leather, twee Tim Burton stripes, and cobweb lacework with wild, candy-colored decoras, their artfully mismatched outfits garlanded with little dolls and toys. They moved alongside too-cool-for-school crews of '50s Rockers, Hip-Hoppers, CyberPunks, and angelic, rustic Mori Girls dressed in simple earthy homespun like children of the forest.

There went the Noir Chic Kimono set, here came Sugar Hearts, Pastel Goths, and Glitter Courtesans. Spiky haired, angular Cosplay Heroes and spunky spritely Animaidens, and even the Kawakowaii Girls—a.k.a. the Scary Cutes, dressed up in school uniforms, adorable except for their habitual vampire or demon or zombie makeup.

Now everyone was a Scary Cute.

Ayako and Natsuki recognized most of them. These were their friends, rivals, idols and followers. The two girls had no idea what kind of disaster had taken place, or how the two of them had managed to escape, when all the rest had turned into a crowd of corpses, ambling with halting, spasmodic steps. Some had bloodstained mouths, and many showed nasty open wounds or were missing fingers, limbs, or pieces of their faces.

Ayako stared, hypnotized by the gruesome spectacle. Colors and shapes shifted, melted into one another as her fever continued to spike. Overwhelmed by terror, she bolted from the window with a wordless cry, falling onto her makeshift pallet of piled coats and woolen shawls, sobbing and shaking uncontrollably.

Somewhere off in the distance, sirens howled. Unseen helicopters pounded the air, and occasionally there was the muffled boom of an explosion that rattled the windows.

Ayako lay trembling and moaning in an increasingly inarticulate delirium. Her friend knelt by her side, gently singing a lullaby and shepherding damp strands of hair away from her fevered forehead.

"S-s-so cold."

Natsuki took off her coat and covered Ayako with it.

After what felt like hours, the quivering incoherent muttering subsided, and Ayako lay deathly still. Natsuki watched her intently for a long, drawn-out minute. She bit her lip, hesitated, then gingerly reached out to touch her friend's neck.

"Ayako-chan? Are you awake?"

No response.

She felt for a pulse.

There was nothing.

But wait... was that a faint, fluttering heartbeat, or were her hopeful fingertips just being fooled? She leaned in closer and listened carefully for sounds of Ayako's breathing, gasping in relief when she felt the faint, wet ghost of an exhalation.

Natsuki maintained her watch as the sky outside began slowly bronzing toward evening. Periodically she would try calling or texting someone... anyone. But her cell phone was useless.

They were alone.

Clang!

Natsuki jumped, startled, when she heard the noise—a sharp, deliberate-sounding impact from downstairs. Was it rescue? Or…

She looked toward the stairs. It was dark in the shop. She held her breath, straining to hear more. There was a sound that might have been a footstep, then maybe another. Then a series of mysterious metallic clacks. She leaned in close and whispered in her friend's ear.

"Ayako-chan, I think there's someone here. Stay quiet and I'll go check it out."

If the younger girl heard her, she gave no trace of it. Natsuki risked one last whisper.

"I'll be right back."

She stood, pins and needles in her legs, and looked around for something she could use to defend herself. Nothing. So she fished the keychain flashlight out of her purse, took a moment to compose herself and then, with a small, determined nod, crept down the stairs using the small beam to guide her.

At the base of the stairs Natsuki paused, brow furrowed. She heard odd, unpleasant chalkboard-scratching sounds, and it was even darker than she had expected. The power was still out, but surely there should be light from the floor-length windows that faced the street.

She took a cautious step away from the stairs, pointing her little flashlight toward the window… and found herself face-to-face with a crowd of the dead, clawing at the glass with ruined fingers, leaving dark smears in their wake.

Natsuki recoiled at the sight, and stumbled backward. But even as part of her wanted to run screaming back upstairs, the rational part of her mind realized that the store windows were holding. The monsters were kept outside, at least for the time being.

A sharp metallic noise sounded from inside the room.

She froze, and slowly turned, side-to-side, her heart beating so fast that her chest ached. In the half-light the clothing racks, *display tables, and mannequins formed a maze. She made her way as quietly as she could toward the source of the noise, somewhere at the front of the store. The sound of the clawing grew more frantic as she approached.*

But there was another sound, too, like ragged breathing.

She drew closer, and cautiously peered around a clothing rack. Someone was there, near the entrance, kneeling on the floor. It was a boy about Ayako's age, wearing a replica of the CyberSamurai armor from the series RoboMech Paladins. *On the floor at his side lay an actual katana. The blade gleamed bright, except for the dark streaks of blood.*

Natsuki recognized him.

"Tet-T-Tetsuo?"

The boy raised his head and turned to look up at her. His face was haunted, his eyes lost in a distant stare. Then they focused.

"Natsuki-san?" he said. "You're... alive?"

The breath she'd been holding expelled in a relieved rush.

"Tetsuo! I'm so glad to see you!"

"Stay back!" he barked, thrusting his head up as she started toward him.

She flinched and stopped. Tetsuo dropped his head again.

"It's the American disease," he said, his voice softer. "It's called Walker's. It changes us into... them. They can't be killed, Natsuki. I tried... I cut two of them in half, but they kept coming after me. They're everywhere now. There's nothing we can do. It's... it's the end of the world."

"Tetsuo?"

"I won't let them get me," he continued. "I won't be one of those things. I'm going to stay human... stay... human..." *He leaned forward and his entire body clenched, a horrible rattling sound emanating from his throat.*

Natsuki took a step in stunned silence, and another until she stood in front of him.

"Tetsuo?" Her eyes widened in shock.

His hands were locked around the hilt of a smaller wakizashi blade. He had thrust it just below his armored cuirass, burying it deep into his own stomach, and was striving to pull it across his abdomen. His face screwed up in a rictus of agony and the veins in his neck rose taut like steel cables as he dragged the blade a few jerky, brutal inches at a time, and then gave one final thrust upward.

Natsuki realized she was standing in an expanding pool of his blood and lurched back, slamming against the glass wall, oblivious to the scraping, moaning pack on the other side. Her strength broke down at last, and she sank down to the floor, sobbing uncontrollably.

CHAPTER THIRTEEN

We crossed the eight blocks to the Great Highway with almost suspicious ease, proving I'd been living in a combination horror-and-spy movie that made it impossible to accept anything going right. Not without expecting a really big other shoe to drop as soon as I started to relax.

Fine. Then I won't relax.

A loud cry caught my ears.

"Do you hear that?" I asked as the three of us reached the strip of grass, pickleweed, and bike path that separated the neighborhood from the Great Highway and Ocean Beach.

"Probably peacocks from the zoo," Nathan shrugged. "It's only a few blocks away."

The whoop sounded again, this time closer. I shielded my eyes from the glare of the fog-diffused sun and scanned the surrounding terrain and houses back across the street. Then I grinned.

"It's a peacock alright. But not from the zoo." I pointed to where JT waved from atop one of the houses facing 48th, the last street before the bike path and the Great Highway. He looked as manically cheerful as ever, and as relaxed as if he were out for a Sunday stroll.

Taking a running start, JT leaped from the roof of the three-story house he was on to the next roof over, moving quickly to the red-brick building at the end of the block. There he dropped down onto a balcony and propelled himself without hesitation onto a very tall lamppost planted next to the building. He slid down it like a fireman on a pole, making it look as easy as a kid on a jungle gym as he landed feet first on the ground.

I snuck a sideways glance at Nathan, who wore one of his rare grins as he watched JT do his stuff. He shook his head.

"He's either gonna get himself killed, or outlast us all," he muttered.

Even Tony wore an expression of unwilling admiration. He wasn't predisposed to like JT, who he thought was too cocky, too much... well, too much like Kai in a way. Kai's death was way too fresh for Tony to be able to feel anything but resentment. But to a kid of Tony's age and with his pop-culture worship, seeing someone make like Spider-Man had to be cool.

It was impossible not to admire him.

A few houses down there were several zombies in wetsuits, looking as if sharks with very small bite radiuses had attacked them. They saw JT land and immediately headed in his direction. Diehard surfers, so to speak, their boards trailed after them, still attached to their ankles by leashes.

Another zombie in a bike helmet and ripped nylon shorts headed toward him from the other end of the block. He ignored them all, leaping onto the nearest car, bounding across it to the next, and then onto an ancient RV parked right next to the bike path. Finally he dropped onto the pickleweed a mere ten feet away, then jogged up to us, barely even winded after his rooftop journey.

He looked very pleased with himself.

"Main pack of them is over by the zoo," he said nonchalantly. "Most of them didn't see me head back this way and I saw another bunch heading after the 'copter."

"How far did you go?" I asked him curiously.

"Sloat and 39th. There were already a lot wandering around the parking lot next to the zoo and banging on the fences there." He shook his head. "I am pretty sure I saw a lion wandering around outside of its cage."

Yikes.

"Which," JT continued, "begs the question—can this zombie bug pass to animals?"

"Not as far as we know," Nathan said.

"Good. Because if that changes any time soon, we are all screwed." He continued as we set off across the tangled mass of smashed autos covering the Great Highway, "I mean, can you imagine zombie cats, or even worse, zombie birds? They would totally fuck you up." He bounced across the hood of a '70s model Cadillac, skidded off the top of a black Hummer, and hit the roof of a Honda Civic. Hands tinted necrotic gray-green reached out the open windows, fingers clutching fruitlessly at prey it couldn't hope to catch.

Nathan, Tony, and I made our way much slower, weaving in and out between the stalled cars, cautious of possible undead occupants, of which there were more than a few. I couldn't stop myself from wondering how they died. Had some of the cars' occupants already had Walker's? Had they died and come back "like *that*," before anyone else was aware what had happened... stuck in gridlocked traffic in what were now metal tombs.

Lost in my bleak musings, it took me totally by surprise when a middle-aged male zombie in a truly hideous Hawaiian shirt popped out of the driver's window of a brown Smart car. We're talking a bright yellow pattern with different tropical drinks in neon colors stamped all over it. The zombie grabbed me by my sword arm and yanked me toward the car window and its gaping mouth. It needed Listerine in the worst possible way.

I reacted instinctively by slamming my free hand against the car right above the open window. I stopped, and we were at a stalemate—it couldn't pull me in any further, and

I couldn't use my weapons. So I decided to compromise.

Shoving my Kevlar-protected right forearm into its mouth so it would stop yanking me downward, I grabbed my tanto with the left hand, but couldn't go through the eye socket—its face was bent over my arm as it tried to figure out how to chew its way through the hard shell to the tasty center. I had a clear shot at an ear, though, and drove in the point of my tanto as hard as I could, wincing at the added stink of the black goo that oozed out.

Still, it did the job. The poor fat bastard's mouth opened and its grip on my right arm relaxed as it slid back into the car.

Aloha, zombie.

The enormity of our task hit me like a big, fat, rotting bludgeon of reality. How could we ever hope to contain this? It was out, it was airborne, and it was spreading beyond any possible hope of quarantine. What good would a cure do for all the people who'd already died? We couldn't turn zombies back into living, breathing human beings. I mean, once someone had chunks ripped out of their flesh and things started rotting, there was no way to come back from that.

Then I thought of the people trapped in their houses, ones on the run trying to find a safe refuge. And what about the people in places where Walker's hadn't hit yet? If there was a cure, they'd stand a chance. They might not become wild cards, but they could fight without fear of infection.

We could beat this.

Wow, I thought as I crossed the last lane of zombie-infested traffic. *Way to talk myself in and out of the pit of despair, and in record time.*

HARAJUKU, JAPAN

Upstairs, Ayako's body remained silent and unmoving on her makeshift sickbed. Then, without warning, her hand began to twitch. A few moments later, her body shuddered and arched, then settled again.

Her eyes opened.

Stiffly, haltingly, the girl arose, and began slowly moving toward the stairs. She descended them like a sleepwalker, silently, slowly winding her way around the shop's maze toward where Natsuki stood, slumped against the glass wall, facing the horde outside. Ayako reached out for her, and at that moment Natsuki turned to face her.

Ayako screamed.

Natsuki's eyes were clouded over. Her jugular had been torn open. She opened her mouth and a gutteral moan emerged as she lunged.

Ayako threw up her forearm to defend herself, and Natsuki's teeth sunk deep into her flesh. Shrieking in pain, Ayako lashed out with her free hand and connected. The thing that had been Natsuki flew back and into the window, striking it so hard it cracked. The zombies outside grew even more agitated, whipped into a frenzy.

Breathing heavily, Ayako sensed movement behind her. She wheeled around just as an armored figure—with a sword in his gut—blundered through the nearest clothing rack, shattering the bar and scattering blouses and hangers. Ayako ducked his clutching hands with a nimbleness that surprised her, and somersaulted out of his reach.

She came up out of her roll into what she imagined a fighting stance would be. Her left arm was bleeding, but her mind was clear.

A piece of the broken clothing rack lay by her feet. Ayako had never picked up a sword, but she had played badminton. She stooped, grabbed the bar, and gave a wicked swing as she stood, clocking Natsuki in mid-charge and sending her flying into a mannequin. Then she whirled around with a two-hand grip that smashed into Tetsuo, only to have the bar rebound off armor and pinwheel out of her hands.

Tetsuo reached out and seized her throat with both hands, lifting her kicking feet off the ground as he pulled her face *toward his waiting teeth. Ayako managed to interpose one hand and force his snapping jaws back with a strength she couldn't explain. With the other hand, she reached down and fumbled for the hilt that was sticking out under the bottom of his chest plate. With a twist and a sickening sound, she pulled the wakizashi blade free and brought it swiftly up through his chin.*

The armored monster became a corpse once again, crashing to the ground like a fallen statue.

Meanwhile, the Natsuki-thing stumbled to its feet and came after her from behind. Ayako snapped a vicious kick into its face, knocking it off its feet. She quickly retrieved the short sword and, as the female zombie rose, thrust the blade into its heart.

No effect.

So she pulled the blade out and shoved it through the ear, instead.

Ayako didn't cry after the fight. She was shaky, but strangely exhilarated, and suddenly ravenous, too.

She tore designer T-shirts into bandages for her wounds, and traded her sweet little shoes and flimsy lace jacket for Natsuki's cavalier boots and long black military duster. She kept her frilly red velvet dress, but added Tetsuo's cuirass.

Finally, she strapped on his wakizashi and katana, and moved toward the door.

CHAPTER FOURTEEN

We reached the other side of the Great Highway, fog curling up around the sand dunes on the gentle breeze. The water was the same uniform gray as the sky. It looked like a soundstage, and the sound of water dripping was a constant backdrop to the other, more ominous noises still coming from the streets we'd left behind. It could only have been creepier if it were night, instead of morning.

I took a brief pause to wipe the zombie drool off my forearm onto a patch of pampas grass, then followed the three men down between two dunes toward the large square storm drain that marked the Vicente Street opening to the beach.

Sand drifts partially covered stretches of hardscrabble rock, and the remnants of cement rubble marked the ocean's relentless ability to wear almost anything away over time. Rusted pieces of pipe stuck up seemingly at random, and I wondered what they'd been a part of before the waves had torn them from their moorings.

Mighty poetic thinking, all things considered. I'd always sucked at poetry. Hated it and all the symbolic metaphorical crap therein, but I guess something about the end of the world brought out the latent poet in me. Maybe I'd start wearing berets, smoking skinny French cigarettes, and spouting existentialist bullshit when this was over. Hell, I was already wearing black, right?

I tripped on a rock, barely catching myself before I pitched face forward the rest of the way down the slope. Maybe the Universe was warning me away from the life of a beatnik. Whatever it was, I focused on navigating the uneven slope without breaking my neck.

From the point it emerged out of the pickleweed and pampas grass to the two-level housing platform at the other end, the storm drain was about twenty feet long. It consisted of two large cement-covered pipes with large rectangular concrete slabs covering them every few feet or so. The entire thing was covered with colorful graffiti and artwork.

Stairs led from the beach to the platform, where steel-pipe fencing and a padlocked gate discouraged people from climbing up. If the discarded beer bottles littering the platform were anything to go by, it didn't work.

JT couldn't help himself from leaping from concrete rectangle to rectangle with total disregard for the drops that lay in between, scaling the platform in less time than it took Tony, Nathan, and me to navigate the slope and hop down onto the sand.

Nathan paused, holding up a hand for silence.

The fog was noticeably denser on the beach and visibility pretty much sucked, the sand vanishing into the mist after a few hundred feet. It was even thicker over the ocean, the water and sky merging together in a wall of pale gray. Both beautiful and eerie.

The sound of the surf didn't quite cover up the sounds of moans coming from the streets above, but it did its best, the booming of waves hitting hard on the beach. The fog was thick enough to hide a ghost ship full of vengeful pirate leper zombies. Although I suppose technically those would be revenants. In a world where the dead really did walk, it was probably best to get it right.

The tide was at a midpoint. I could see the high water mark at the edge of the pampas grass—detritus, driftwood, and bits of shells indicating the demarcation point. Water still lapped at the base of the storm drain as waves rolled in, and then receded.

JT swung over the fence separating the lower and upper level of the platform, and landed with a thud. Nathan shot him a glare. JT gave an apologetic shrug and Nathan cocked his head to one side as he listened. I couldn't tell if he actually heard something beyond the chorus of the damned, or was just being cautious, but he'd survived more situations and more years than the rest of us, so I trusted his judgment.

Finally he relaxed ever so slightly and nodded.

"Okay," he said quietly, "I think we're good. JT, can you see any action on the beach from where you're standing?"

JT shook his head.

"Nope. Maybe one of you super-visioned types might have better luck seeing through the fog."

Nathan nodded at me.

"Ash, wanna give it a try?"

"Sure." I clambered across the pipes to the stairs, climbed those, and carefully grasped the gate, preferring a more traditional approach. "We can see further, and more clearly," I said to JT, "but it doesn't mean we have x-ray vision."

"And here I wore my special Superman undies for nothing."

Snorting, I grabbed the top pipe of the gate to hoist myself up. It was slippery under my palms, damp from the mist, but also a little sticky. I didn't think about it until I'd hopped down onto the platform and my foot made a slight sloshing noise, as if I'd stepped in a puddle. I looked down, and saw that the puddle was tinged with red.

I glanced quickly around the rest of the platform's surface. The telltale signs of Walkers were spattered all around—droplets of blood, black bile, and on the circular metal access cover, bits of flesh as if something had been trying to pound its way in. The story it told didn't promise a happy ending.

"Shit." My voice was flat.

JT looked at me inquiringly.

"Don't touch anything," I told him. "There's blood, and it might be infected."

"What is it?" Nathan asked.

"Nothing now," I said, "but looks like something happened here. I think someone tried to get into the storm drain to hide, but couldn't get the cover up and—"

An even worse thought sprung into my head. I quickly climbed back over the railing onto the top of the stairs, jumping the five feet down into soft sand. I landed in a crouch and ran over to the base of the storm drain, splashing ankle deep in the surf.

The original mouths of the pipes were inside and under the platform, now covered with metal plates riveting them to the cement walls. Two smaller black pipes like sink faucets protruded from the wall above them. Some enterprising idiot had tried to pry sections of the metal plates open. He or she had succeeded in making an opening large enough for someone to squeeze inside.

Faded graffiti marked the dank walls, making me wonder why on earth someone would want to mark a sewer pipe as his or her territory. The only way in or out was through the access cover up top, and the metal ladder that hugged one wall below it. Thick steel bars enclosed the front, creating a sort of cage with concrete sides. Maybe a very skinny adolescent could squeeze through those bars, but they were meant to keep people out.

They also did a very effective job of keeping people in.

We all float down here.

I stared at the two waterlogged corpses now occupying the space. Both had been teenagers, a boy and a girl. The girl's long, dark brown hair splayed out in the water on the floor, some clinging like seaweed to her swollen face, body flush up against the bars. Crabs skittered around her jeans-and-hoodie-clad body, warring with ravens and seagulls now picking at her flesh. The boy lay next to the ladder, one arm still looped around one of the lower rungs. I could see the bite marks on that arm where his shirt sleeve fell away from his bicep.

Nathan joined me.

"They must have been caught on the beach," I said dully. "Climbed in here from the top to get away. The zombies wouldn't be able to pull that metal cover up."

He nodded. "They probably thought if they could wait it out and hide long enough, the zombies would go away."

Tony looked bewildered.

"But… the zombies did go away. There aren't any down here so why didn't they climb out?"

I looked at the way the boy clung to the ladder, even in death. The kid had probably held on as long as he could before either exhaustion or hypothermia got the best of him.

"The tide came in," I said softly. "The zombies wouldn't go away as long as the kids were alive, so they had a choice—go out and get torn to pieces, or hope the tide didn't rise too high."

I can hold my breath for a long, long time, I thought, and then I shivered.

"By the time they figured out they were gonna drown, there had to have been zombies all over the top. They probably couldn't have moved the cover back off even if they'd had the guts to try. They didn't stand a chance."

Tony stared at the bodies for a long moment.

"That really sucks," he finally said.

I wondered if he was picturing the same grim scenario as me, the two huddled on the ladder, trying to keep their heads above water and resist the numbness brought on by the frigid water as it slowly rose around them. Did the girl finally give up, let go and slip under the water? Or had she fought until the last minute to stay alive, same as the boy?

Tony was right, though. Either way it sucked.

"Why didn't they come back?" JT looked at the bodies with a clinical compassion.

"It doesn't look like she's been bit," I replied. "But the kid over there definitely took one for the team."

"The rate of infection varies," Nathan added. "The bite doesn't look too deep, so there's a good chance he drowned before succumbing to the virus."

"So at least she didn't have to see her boyfriend turn," I said, almost to myself as I thought about my own experience with Matt.

Just then the boy's hand twitched, the fingers clutching the rung in a brief spasm before releasing it. JT drew in his breath with a sharp inhale, and then let it out again in a sigh.

"Ah," he said.

Slowly the boy's corpse lifted its head, swiveling it around until its dead eyes stared straight at us. Its mouth opened as it gave the inevitable moan. A hermit crab scuttled out of its lips and plopped to the ground. The newly minted zombie got to its feet, every movement yielding grotesque squishing noises from its waterlogged flesh and clothing. The ravens and gulls scattered as the figure staggered over to the girl's still lifeless form. The crabs stayed where they were.

I wondered what it took to scare a crab.

After a cursory examination, the zombie moved away from the corpse. Guess the meat wasn't fresh enough—too cold maybe. Instead it lurched over to the bars and reached toward us, moaning plaintively. For a brief instant I understood why someone would want to believe there was still a spar of humanity inside of these empty, rotting shells. It sounded so damn sad, and so lonely, and I suddenly couldn't separate the poor kid from the soulless monster he had become.

I remembered a commercial where an old lamp had been put out on the curb in the cold night, with sad music playing. The one where the narrator said, "it's just a lamp, people!" Anthropomorphizing was ingrained in human nature, be it with animals, insects, plants, or inanimate objects.

And yeah, I'd felt bad for the lamp too.

I unslung my squirrel rifle, sighted down the barrel, and pulled the trigger. There was a soft popping sound and a small hole appeared in the center of the kid's forehead. It crumpled to the ground next to the girl, one arm landing improbably to drape over her waist.

"It's just a lamp, people," I said softly, and stepped back.

INCIARTE TAR PIT. SIERRA DE PERIJÁ. VENEZUELA

"What are we going to do?" Ana stood perfectly still, the smell of tar thick in her nostrils, afraid any movement would suck her down further in the viscous goo.

"I don't know." Jonathan Rivera, her boss and mentor at ConocoPhillips, stayed equally still at her side, both of them mired knee deep, unable to move any further. Moans filled the air along the shore, the sound both plaintive and terrifying. She and Jonathan were about ten feet out from the shore. Only fear had enabled them to get that far into the mire without being stuck.

"There has to be something we can do," Ana said, trying desperately to keep her voice from breaking. "There's got to be a way out of here, right?"

"Ana…" Jonathan stopped as the volume of the moaning increased, the sound chilling even in the harsh light of day.

Ana shuddered.

Not seven feet away were hideous parodies of humanity— men and women with chunks missing from their bodies, milky corneas framed by yellow, bloodied whites. They stunk, the reek of rotting flesh warring with the acrid odor of tar.

Greedy hands reached out toward them, fingers clutching for the prey that was beyond their reach. What made it worse was Ana recognized many of them as others from their team. People she'd worked with for the last few days.

Ana had always been fascinated by tar pits, going into the field of paleontology based on a visit to the La Brea museum as a child. They formed when natural asphalt seeped upward from cracks in the sediment above oil-bearing rocks. Rainwater collected on the surface, making the pits look like harmless waterholes, luring thirsty animals to their doom. If they weren't engulfed immediately through their struggles, they would starve to death. Predators looking for an easy meal became stuck as well, adding to the rich collection of fossils first found in the La Brea pits, and more recently in the Menes in Inciarte, Venezuela.

Jonathan and Ana were working at the site where the fossilized remains of a saber-tooth tiger had been discovered in 2008, and many other fossils had since been extracted. It was a paleontologist's wet dream, and the opportunity to be a part of the operation. It was the chance of a lifetime for Ana, especially with the added bonus of being at Jonathan's side as his assistant.

Only now that dream had turned into a nightmare, as it seemed that Ana and Jonathan might become part of the fossil collection.

They'd arrived later than usual because Jonathan was feeling under the weather, having caught the bug that was going around the site—not to mention the small hotel where they were staying. A few of the local workers had been sick enough the day before that they should have gone home, but most of them elected to stay.

Ana had considered insisting that Jonathan stay back at the hotel, but he had seemed better after a cup of coffee and several packets of Thera-Flu, so they set off for the site. When they'd arrived, they'd found it strangely empty, the normal eager bustle and noise of the workers conspicuously absent. Hammers and chisels lay discarded on the ground along with buckets, dustpans, and broken plaster of paris molds vying for space with clipboards, pads of paper, pencils and measuring tapes.

It was only after she'd gotten out of the jeep that Ana had spotted a severed human leg, foot still shod in a work boot, lying on the ground near the large canvas tent that served as a makeshift cafeteria and break area. The calf—what was left of it—was muscular and hairy. The thing had been gnawed to the bone in some places.

Jonathan had gotten out of the vehicle.

Ana stared at the bite marks, but it wasn't until the first of the creatures had staggered out from the tent's interior that she realized those bites were human.

One of the workers—Ana thought his name was Pedro—had a chisel sticking out of his stomach. Black fluid, as viscous as the tar, oozed from the point of penetration. He reached for her, taking lumbering steps that brought him dangerously close. Ana grabbed the protruding end of the chisel, shoving with all of her weight behind it, sending the thing into another monstrosity that was coming up from behind.

Jonathan gave a yell as more of the creatures appeared.

"Get back in the car!" he hollered, breaking into a hacking cough as the words left his mouth. Ana turned to obey, but found her path blocked off by a half dozen of the things clustered around them. One of them, a former young intern, with shapely legs, looked as if she'd been wading with piranhas. She grabbed Ana's arm, uncoordinated fingers scrabbling on her long-sleeved cotton shirt. Ana had shrieked, slapped the thing's hand away, and run in the opposite direction, Jonathan close at her heels.

They had barreled right through the safety of the worksite with its wooden walkways and railing, tripping over the grids of twine. The creatures followed relentlessly, their numbers cutting off any escape, until she and Jonathan found themselves faced with the choice of stepping further into the unprotected pit itself, or being torn to pieces.

Now they stood, unable to go any further as the zombies slowly trudged after them, sinking into the tar beneath the water's surface until they too were trapped.

One of them, intestines spilling out over its khaki shirt and pants, kept reaching, bending toward them until its upper half finally collapsed into the ooze, arms still outstretched, fingers clutching as it tried to pull itself forward. It kept moving long after it should have suffocated.

"What are they?" Ana whispered. She prayed desperately for someone, anyone to come and rescue them. She didn't want to die like this.

Jonathan coughed again, eyes jaundiced and bright red from his illness and the fumes from the tar. Suddenly his eyes rolled up in his head and he buckled over, folding in on himself. Ana cried out and grabbed him before his body could hit the tar. She nearly keeled over herself. Only the goo holding her legs in place stabilized her enough to take Jonathan's weight and remain upright.

Maybe I should just let us both go down, Ana thought. Surely death by suffocation would be kinder than the slow torture of starvation. And yet she couldn't give up. Couldn't believe it was inevitable that she and Jonathan would share the same as those unfortunate animals from so many centuries past.

Jonathan's bulk grew heavier by the moment, until Ana realized she'd either have to release him, or they'd both go down. Her arms trembled with fatigue and she prepared herself to make the choice of letting him die, just so she could have a few more hours of life.

"Please wake up, Jon, please wake up, please don't be dead," Ana intoned the words over and over like a prayer.

Just as her muscles couldn't take any more, Jonathan emitted a sudden groan, and stirred in her grasp.

"Oh, thank God!" Ana gave a laugh of relief, despite the hopelessness of their situation. At least she wouldn't be alone.

Then Jonathan lifted his head and stared at her with dead eyes. He groaned again, wrapping his hands around her body and pulling her close. As his teeth sunk into her neck, Ana realized the choice had been made for her.

She only hoped she didn't come back.

CHAPTER FIFTEEN

Our little group was quiet as we made our way south along the edge of the beach, sticking close to the water to hide our presence as much as possible from the zombies above. The hard-packed sand was easier to walk on, too, and we needed to keep our pace brisk.

Even JT was subdued after witnessing the sad little drama we'd left behind us in the storm drain. As for me, I wouldn't want to talk even if it'd been safe to do so. Scream to the heavens, maybe, just to get some of the sorrow and horror out of my head.

The kid I'd killed had already been dead, but both he and his girlfriend had suffered a drawn-out, terrifying fate. And let's face it—I would always empathize with the damn lamp. Moisture from the fog mingled with a slow but steady stream of tears trickling down my face. I didn't bother trying to wipe them away. They'd dry up eventually, and none of my companions would judge me.

We passed a long stretch of sandy slope to our left. I could see some sort of structure up top, and yet more abandoned cars. The strident cries of peacocks mingled with the moans of the damned. JT nodded in that direction.

"The zoo is up there, across the Great Highway," he said quietly. Which meant there were a bunch of zombies up there, as well. There were bound to be some that had found their way to the beach.

Nathan picked up his pace even more, motioning for the rest of us to do the same. I didn't need to be told twice. Even as we hurried further south, I saw human silhouettes in the fog moving slowly in our direction. One missed its step on a steeper part of the sandy slope, tumbling down the rest of the way like a Raggedy Ann doll. It landed in a tangle of disjointed limbs about twenty feet behind us, getting slowly to its feet and emitting a low moan as it realized food was near.

Nathan quickly dispatched it with a round to the head, but it was too late. Others answered the moan and more forms emerged from the fog.

"Move it, people," Nathan growled.

We started jogging down the beach—not my choice of exercise on a good day, let alone lugging however many pounds of gear I was carrying. My M4 and squirrel rifle slapped against my back and shoulders as I jogged. Luckily my thigh and groin seemed to have recovered, thanks to the wild card perk of accelerated healing.

I wondered how soldiers dealt with all their deadly accessories efficiently and without getting the shit beaten out of them by their own gear. Maybe it just took practice. Well, I wasn't going to be finished with my on-the-job training any time soon, so I had plenty of time to get good at it.

And with that totally depressing thought I sucked it up. Even with the crappy visibility, I could see the beach narrowing, the coastline bulging out with an artificial stretch of boulders and slabs of concrete added to stave off erosion. Directly ahead of us it narrowed down to a few feet between the water's edge on our right and a very steep rise to our left, made up of rocks topped by a lip of crumbling asphalt.

Waves crashed onto shore, curls of white foam rolling in to splash against the rocks before receding. I did not like the looks of it.

JT's brow furrowed.

"You'll wanna watch it going around that outcropping. Winter surf makes for sneaker waves, although they're not as bad here as they are on some of the other beaches."

Great. Sneaker waves. The idea of getting washed out to sea bothered me more than going *mano a mano* with the undead. I mean, zombies could be stopped—a bullet to the head did the job. The ocean, on the other hand, wouldn't pay attention if I said, "Please don't drown me or smash me against these rocks." And I couldn't put a bullet in its brain pan, either.

I thought of those kids we'd found, and gave an involuntary shudder.

The tide was definitely rising. Each set of waves seemed to encroach just a little bit further onto the few feet of sand still visible. One out of every five or so sent foamy water hissing over our feet. It wasn't too bad, though, until we got to the outcropping. Waves slapped against the rocks, water swirling in and around the crevices and hiding the sand.

The water receded, leaving a foot or two of wet sand. There were rocks sunken in depressions, making little hidden land mines. I noted their locations as best I could before the incoming waves covered them up again.

"Next time the water goes out, we run for it," Nathan said.

Moans echoed through the fog. I glanced back and sure enough, slumped figures slowly emerged out of the mist, mangled features and misshapen limbs becoming visible as they slowly but steadily made their way toward us. Creepy as hell.

Eat your heart out, John Carpenter.

More sets of waves rushed in, coming in quick succession, each one a little higher than the previous one as we waited impatiently for a chance to go. What looked like the last big set splashed high up against the rocks.

JT raised an eyebrow.

"I'll see you on the other side," he said. Then, as

nimble as a spider monkey, he scrambled up and across the rocks and out of sight.

"Come on, tide," I muttered as the zombies grew closer. It was probably just my imagination, but their pace seemed to pick up when they caught sight of us. Nathan kept a cool eye on them, taking out the front two with calm efficiency. Then again, he pretty much did everything with calm efficiency. It may have been his only setting.

Finally the water receded with a hissing sound, far and fast enough to leave a damp spit of sand.

"Now!" Nathan waved Tony and me ahead, taking one more shot and felling one more zombie before following behind us. We ran for it, darting around and leaping over the now partially submerged rocks as we raced the waves.

We made it to the next recession in the beach, the coastline curving back in to form a little cove. JT was already there, examining the next rocky barrier with a clinical eye. The three of us trotted up next to him.

There was a good thirty-foot stretch where the tide had already reached the edge, leaving no visible ground. The murky water left no way of knowing how deep it was. It could be a few inches, or a few feet. A twisted ankle waiting to happen—a broken one if the misstep was really bad, and a quick trip out to sea if a sneaker wave decided to pay a visit.

Climbing over the rocks, however, didn't look much better. The ones near the bottom were already wet, covered with nasty slippery green moss, and the ones above it weren't much better.

"This sucks," I said.

Tony nodded, looking glumly at the water and the rocks.

"It's, like, a total Scully-versus-Cherry moment."

We all looked at him.

Scully versus Cherry? It sounded like *X-Files* porn to me.

"You know," Tony explained, "the whirlpool and the monster in the cliffs that that Greek dude had to get by, and like, he had to decide which one was a better choice."

"Scylla versus Charybdis," JT said, pronouncing them with ease.

Show off.

Tony nodded.

"Yeah, those. Manny and I used to call them Scully and Cherry. Drove our English teacher crazy." He grinned to himself at the memory, a flash of genuine happiness before his face clouded back over. His friend Manny had died in Redwood Grove during the initial zombie outbreak.

"Not a bad analogy," Nathan said. "Question is, which one do we choose?"

Just then a larger than normal wave crashed against the rocks nearest to us, sending spray in our direction as the water roiled up around the cliffs and lapped at our toes.

Sneaker wave.

We looked at each other.

"Cherry?" I said.

"Cherry," Nathan replied.

CHAPTER SIXTEEN

We stowed our weapons in their respective slings and sheaths to leave our hands free for climbing. JT led the way, finding footholds and handholds with ease as he made his way about five feet above the slick, moss-covered rocks.

"There isn't a sole around with enough traction to deal with this shit," he said. We followed as best we could, Nathan bringing up the rear again.

I found myself falling behind, however, tentative in finding my footholds and handgrips, slipping on what seemed like every damn rock I stepped on. I found myself taking a slightly lower and slower route than the menfolk in part due to a lifelong fear of heights. I was *so* not going to take up mountaineering in the near future.

My foot slipped on one of those damned mossy patches, making my stomach lurch. I reached out with my right hand for stability, grasping at an outcropping only to have my hand slip into a slimy crevice. Something moved in there and I shrieked in surprise, sounding embarrassingly shrill.

"You okay?" Nathan paused about five feet above and ten feet ahead of me.

"I'm fine," I said, really hating my shaky voice. "I think there was a crab or something."

"Well then, get your ass up here where it's dry," he replied unsympathetically.

"Indy, *euwww*," Tony whined. "I can't save you. There are icky bugs!"

"Fuck you, Tony," I responded.

He laughed, which just pissed me off even more.

A wave crashed onto the rocks, soaking my legs and making me aware just how far down I was in comparison with the rest of my team. I was really feeling the weight of my gear about now. And it smelled bad on the rocks, rot and brine mingling in an unpleasant olfactory experience. You'd think I'd be used to it by now, but somehow it never got any better.

A flash of metal caught my eye, a stake sticking in one of the larger crevices. It looked like one of those things fishermen used to anchor their poles in the sand when fishing off the beach, a sand spike or something like that. I wondered what happened to the fisherman who'd put it there, and then decided I really didn't want to know. It made a good handgrip, though, as I navigated a particularly slippery patch of rocks.

Suddenly the stake punctured something that felt like a balloon, releasing the rich smell of shit as it did so. I gagged just as a hand reached up from the crevice and clutched at my wrist, fingers blue and bloated like rotting sausages. I yelped, causing Tony to snigger again.

"What's wrong, Willie? Another bug?"

JT popped his head down and took a look.

"Nope, Ashley's got a new boyfriend."

I would so kick both of their asses later.

I yanked my arm back, fingers still clinging to my wrist as I pulled up the probable owner of the sand spike, who was still clad in yellow waterproof slicker, the hood pulled over its head, thankfully obscuring the features. Using my other hand to hold onto the rocks, I tried to shake off Zombie Fisherman's grip, but damned if it wasn't tenacious.

To quote my dad, the smell was enough to drop a buzzard off a shitwagon.

Bracing my feet as best I could, I reached across with my other hand and pried its fingers off my wrist, wincing at the feel of spongy flesh. Its moan was bubbly, almost like a kid making noise under water. Then I took hold of the stake again and yanked as hard as I could without losing my balance and falling backward into the ocean. It came loose with a squelching sound, upping the gross factor even more.

Readjusting my grip for leverage, I drove it down again, this time into the zombie's head. Stopped by the tough fabric of the slicker's hood, the point barely penetrated the skull, but it was enough to push the zombie back into the crevice. I leaned my full weight onto the stake, driving it home with a crunching pop.

Ugh. Gross and—

"Ash! Look out!"

I looked out toward the ocean, just in time to see another set of waves roaring in. Except these were piling into one another to form one big, fat, nasty uber wave.

Well, crap.

I heard Nathan yell my name again right before the wave hit. I held onto the sound of his voice along with the sand spike as cold water hit me with the force of Thor's Not-So-Wee-Hammer, smashing me against the unyielding surface of the rocks before trying to suck me back into the sea in the backwash.

I clung to the spike for all I was worth, hoping against hope it was anchored firmly in its former owner, and that the zombie was wedged securely enough in the crevice to hold my weight. The water receded, and I risked a glance backward only to see another wall of water heading my way.

Oh, joy. An entire set of Ashley-killing waves was out there.

The next wave hit and I gasped, cold water going up my nose and into my mouth. I choked and sputtered for what seemed like an endless amount of time, the ocean sapping my strength and my body heat. I clung to the stake, willing my fingers to keep their grip no matter how numb they got, shutting my eyes against the salt water and trying to hold my breath.

Finally, the water receded again, leaving me soaked and shivering, but still clinging to the rocks like a soggy Kevlar limpet. I stayed where I was for a moment, just breathing and glad to be alive before opening my eyes and peering up at Nathan. He looked relieved and furious in equal parts.

"Get your ass up here *now*, before another set like that rolls in," he growled.

I nodded, still spitting salt water out of my mouth and snorting it out my nose like a walrus. My hand still grasped the sand spike, fingers cramping from the force of my grip. Saying a silent *thank you* to the poor twice-dead fisherman, I used it to hoist myself up, gratefully accepting the hand Nathan held out to me so I could climb up out of reach of the waves.

CHAPTER SEVENTEEN

We reached the end of the rocks, dropping down onto hard-packed sand and what looked like a reassuringly wide expanse of beach. The fog was still pretty thick ahead of us, but what path I could see was clear, and the pack that had been trailing us hadn't made it past the place where I'd nearly met a watery death.

When I hit the sand, I shook myself like a wet dog, various weapons rattling against one another and my Kevlar. I'd need to do some major cleaning on them as soon as I had a chance. My boots squished with each step. Nothing says fun and chafing like wet socks and underwear.

"How much further?" I asked, hauling myself to my feet.

"Maybe half a mile to the stairs leading up to Fort Funston," Nathan said.

"What's at Fort Funston?"

"Nice open space up top for the helicopter to land."

"You can also hang glide off the cliffs there," JT added.

"Very helpful," I said. "Because I'm in such a hurry to throw myself off a cliff." I turned back to Nathan. "The 'copter should already be waiting, right?"

"Yup. So we'd better hurry before the zombies beat us there."

* * *

We jogged at a steady pace along the deserted stretch. Fort Funston had been a heavy caliber gun battery, built before WWII so the soldiers housed in the bunkers there could watch the sea and defend against enemy attacks. The remnants of old armaments and gun emplacements littered the beach and the cliffs above, making it look like something out of *Planet of the Apes*. I expected to see the torso of Lady Liberty sticking up out of the sand at any moment, and was fully prepared to drop to my knees and do my best "God... damn you all to *hell*" if it happened.

We passed another sewer runoff, this one decorated with paintings and mosaics of dogs, including a doggie Buddha. JT nodded at it as we jogged by.

"Temple of the Dogs. My ex and I used to bring her pooch here. Yappy little shit of a chihuahua. Not missing either of them."

A little further down the beach, Nathan moved up away from the water to a sandy trail that cut sharply to the left. I looked up at a seemingly endless pathway, rising in a curving trail up the cliff. A rope rail ran between thick cylindrical wooden posts.

"You've got to be kidding me," I groaned, feeling every soggy pound of my waterlogged clothing and gear.

"Stop whining," Nathan said unsympathetically.

"I'm not whining. I'm bitching."

"Whatever. Suck it up and get the hell up those stairs. We have work to do."

Sucking it up, sir. But he was right. My discomfort was nothing compared to what was happening around the world... or what Gabriel might be going through. I was still alive enough to be out of breath and cranky—which was more than a lot of people could say.

I jogged steadily up the stairs from hell—uneven wooden logs half buried in the sand—ignoring the burning in my lungs and the aching in my leg muscles. By the time we reached the plateau, I was ready to collapse.

Only the sight of a drinking fountain prevented me from giving in to my burning calf muscles and collapsing face first onto the ground. That, and the nearby porta-johns.

I really had to pee.

The two choppers were there, too. Several of our team and a few people I didn't recognize were gathered beside them. I didn't see Lil or Griff, but Simone was there, posture tense as she scanned our little group. Her face lit up with relief when she saw Nathan. Just a flash before she resumed her usual expression of detached interest.

Somehow Simone managed to look elegant in BDUs. I had a feeling she'd look good in just about anything— even prison orange. Not that we'd ever have an occasion to put that theory to the test.

"Why are there two 'copters?" JT asked. He looked as fresh as if we'd been out for a casual stroll. I eyed him resentfully.

"Redundancy," Nathan replied brusquely. He jogged over toward the aircraft—and Simone—without another word.

JT raised an eyebrow and looked at me.

"And that means…?"

"You're the walking dictionary," I said by way of avoiding the question.

He raised his eyebrow even higher and nodded.

"Okay, I can play," he said. "Same reason we ditched the second 'copter back at UCSF. One's a decoy, to throw the bad guys off our track, yes?"

Damn, he's good, I thought, but kept my mouth shut and my expression neutral.

He grinned. "Thought so." He looked like he had something else to say, and I held up a hand.

"Er… hold that thought. Gotta pee," I said, and escaped toward the fountain and the porta-johns.

I passed the Gunsy Twins standing in front of the helicopters as they kept a keen watch on the surrounding terrain—trails leading off into the hills, and a large parking lot, surprisingly empty of cars. A long driveway led out to the main road. One of the Twins—Davis, I think—gave me a small salute and what passed for a smile on his expressionless face. I wiggled my fingers in return.

"Ash!"

Lil came bounding toward me from the porta-johns. I gave her a tired but sincere smile as she threw her arms around me in a hug before releasing me almost immediately with a nose-wrinkled grimace.

"You're soaked," she said. "And you smell gross."

"Slipped on a rock," I said evasively. Lil handled danger to herself without fear, but she tended to flip out, even after the fact, if someone she cared about got injured or even came close. Kai's death hadn't helped.

I saw motion out of the corner of my eye, and a few scattered figures lurched slowly toward us from the other side of the parking lot. Jones and Davis made quick work of them, but more were headed our way up the long driveway leading from the main road.

Time to do my business, I thought wearily.

I picked up my pace to the fountain, stepping over and around a number of aluminum dog dishes that littered the ground. As I bent over to get a sip of water, I accidentally kicked an empty dish set on the ground under a low faucet. It clattered against the pavement and the resulting clatter brought a moan from somewhere nearby. I whirled around but didn't see anything. It sounded again—a muffled hollow echo accompanied it, like a kid pretending to be a ghost.

The porta-johns.

Crap.

No pun intended, but I still had to use the bathroom.

Marching over to the cluster of glorified outhouses, I banged on the door to the first one, and something banged back, dead palms slapping against the hard plastic. *Damn, what a shitty coffin.* The little sign said

"OCCUPIED" and I planned on leaving it that way.

The next one showed the green "VACANT." I raised my hand to knock, but the door swung out before I made contact. I jumped back just in time to avoid getting smacked. My adrenalin spiked, and my hand tightened around the grip of my tanto as I prepared to dispatch—

Griff.

"I'm sorry, was I taking too long?" he inquired.

I caught my breath and growled—an involuntary rumble deep in my throat. I'd come *that* close to stabbing him. Part of me wished I'd at least grazed him, and given him a good scare. But as much as he deserved it, killing a fellow human being wasn't on my agenda for the day.

Even so, I didn't trust him.

"I've heard of friendly fire," Griff continued in that obnoxiously amused tone of his, "but friendly thrusts? Shouldn't those be—"

"Oh, just shut the fuck up," I said, pushing past him. I banged on the next door down. Nothing banged back, so I went inside, making sure to lock it behind me. It smelled less offensive on the inside than its neighbor had from the outside, but I still took a quick peek down the hole. As I did so, a truly gross scene from a Norwegian zombie movie played through my mind.

I did my business, and got out of there in record time.

As soon as I emerged, Nathan waved impatiently for me to join them. I quickly rinsed my hands in the faucet by the dog bowls, glancing out over the cliff as glimpses of the sun burned through the fog.

It was eerily beautiful, eucalyptus and cypress trees sharing ground with the crumbling walls of the old battery. Trails wound around the tree-studded hills, and I could see why this would be a paradise for dogs and their owners. I wondered if it ever would be again, or if Dr. Albert's plague had screwed it up for good.

Nathan called my name as the helicopter rotors started *whupwhupwhupping* in rotation. One of the helicopters took off, heading toward North Island and following the original plan, but without any of the wild cards on board. Instead it had members of the Zombie Tactical Squad, people Simone trusted beyond a shadow of a doubt, and who could handle themselves if anything went wrong, like another helicopter malfunction.

Nathan climbed aboard the remaining chopper, which I suspected came from a source other than the DZN. I had a feeling Simone or Nathan had called in a last-minute favor to put yet one more layer of smoke and mirrors between us and our unknown enemies. I walked toward it, my limbs suddenly leaden even as the wind from the rotors whipped my still-wet hair about my face. The resulting sting was surprisingly painful.

Our new ride was slightly roomier than the one that we'd started out with that morning. It had two rows of two seats facing front, currently occupied by Simone, Nathan, Carl, and the same female mechanic who'd flown with us to Walgreen's. Eight more seats ran parallel down the length of the helicopter, four on either side. Lil, Gentry, JT, and Griff were on one side, while the Gunsy twins and Tony occupied the other. I took the remaining seat in the very back and curled up as tightly as I could, trying to ignore how wet and cold I was.

I wondered if anything in my pack had survived without being soaked.

Oh, crap, what if Lil's meds got wet? Were they in watertight containers? They had to be, right?

My shivering increased, but I was so tired I could barely keep my eyes open. I started to drop off to sleep, only to have another shiverfest wrack my body, waking me up again, although I didn't open my eyes.

I felt someone near me, and then something warm and dry was draped over my lap. My hand touched the surface of a blanket. Scratchy, but warm. I smiled drowsily at whoever put it there.

"Thanks," I said sleepily.

"Any time."

My smile froze as I recognized Griff's voice. I deliberately kept my eyes shut until I heard him moving away from me. When I opened them, he was sitting a few seats ahead of me on the other side, an odd little smile on his face. Lil and JT stared in my direction, as vigilant as Foo Dogs standing guard in Imperial China.

I couldn't imagine what Griff's motivation had been, and my brain was just too tired to wrap itself around the puzzle. Finally, I gave up trying. The bottom line was that I was finally getting warm again, and needed sleep more than I needed to think.

So I slept.

CHAPTER EIGHTEEN

I sat down in the back of Room 217 in Patterson Hall, hoping against hope that the cute but douchey teaching assistant wouldn't notice that I'd been late yet again. Last thing I needed was another public humiliation—something else to make me stand out as a twenty-nine-year-old student on campus filled with kids ten years my junior.

Kids who were just waiting to steal my husband.

No wait. He was already gone.

No big loss. I had Matt now, my hunky younger boyfriend.

But Matt's dead.

I looked down to the front of the hall, admiring the cute TA. His mint gold hair gleamed against the black of his shirt and Kevlar vest. The look suited his features. He seemed like an angel who'd gone a few rounds with Rocky, a once broken nose set slightly crooked, throwing off otherwise regular features.

Gabriel.

Gabriel was the hunky TA, and also my boyfriend. I still had him, even if he was a douche at times.

I smiled down at him, wondering idly why he was wearing his SWAT gear to teach in, instead of his usual jeans and button-down shirt. Very sexy, mind you, with just a hint of "Oh, are you wearing handcuffs, officer?"

I kind of hoped he was.

But should he really be wearing something like that to class?

Appropriate or not, it was going over well with the students.

Not that any of them looked that great—not even the bevy of coach-carrying blondes in the front row, hanging on his every word. Half of them looked sick, snuffling and coughing, and the other half...

Huh.

The other half looked dead.

Yup, zombies.

In class.

Shouldn't I be doing something about them?

Gabriel looked up and saw me dithering in the back of the room. I braced myself for the inevitable snarky comment, but he smiled up at me, his denim-blue eyes warm and affectionate. He dropped the book he held on the floor. It landed with a loud, echoing thunk, *much louder than seemed possible, but it didn't seem to bother him. He walked eagerly up the center aisle toward me, the initial warmth in his eyes darkening to something just as welcoming, but more primal.*

I waited where I was instead of running toward him, afraid if I moved he'd vanish. He kept smiling as he neared me, but his face didn't look quite right. His skin seemed unusually sallow, almost green in places. Faint hollows under his eyes grew darker with each step, and the startling blue of his corneas began filming over until they were the bluish white of curdled skim milk. Pieces of skin curled off his cheekbones in strips, and the bright gold of his hair became dull and matted, patches of skull showing through.

I knew I should do something—kill him or run—but I couldn't move. Didn't want *to move. It was still Gabriel. Wasn't it? So I stayed rooted in place until he stood in front of me, still smiling although now his teeth were coated with blood and black fluid. His hands clutched my shoulders as the rest of the students lurched to their feet, staggering slowly toward us.*

"I've missed you, Ash," he said, voice clogged with unspeakable gore. "Have you missed me?"

He lowered his face to kiss me, those gore-stained lips closing over mine before I could scream.

* * *

I jerked awake, a scream choking in my throat to stop it from ripping through the confines of the helicopter. My eyes flew open and I sat up straight, heart pounding.

Jeez Louise. I looked around. No zombies, no Gabriel. No one seemed to have noticed my nightmare, for which I was very grateful.

"You okay?" Griff opened his eyes and looked at me.

Oh, hell.

He wasn't wearing his usual smirk, but I wasn't about to give him any more ammunition.

"Yup, just dandy."

"Looked like one hell of a bad dream."

If I didn't know better, I'd have sworn he looked concerned.

"Last time I was in one of these things, it crashed," I said. "Not a fan of flying."

He nodded and closed his eyes.

I stared at him for a moment before pulling the blanket—the one he'd given me—back up around my shoulders. So far he'd tried to flirt with me, assault me, and tucked me in like a kid at naptime. I *so* did not get him. Then again, I didn't want him, so that was okay.

Tony snored next to me, sounding like a muffled chainsaw under the noise of the rotors. I wondered how long we'd been in the air, and pondered the ability of humans to sleep under the most stressful of circumstances.

Someone wake up Hicks, indeed.

I twisted around in my seat and looked out the window at the landscape passing below us. I could see the ocean off to the right, with rolling green fields, vineyards, and buildings directly below. A few curvy roads meandering through the landscape. I didn't see any people, although I saw a few horses and cows grazing in wide-open areas. I was guessing we were flying over Paso Robles or thereabouts.

We stopped to refuel at an isolated private airport somewhere north of Santa Barbara and everyone but the mechanic and the Gunsy Twins stayed inside the helicopter. The mechanic refueled while the snipers kept watch.

A long winding drive led from the tarmac up to a two-story house. There was no overt sign of life, but I saw a shadow cross in front of one of the windows. No one living or dead emerged from the house. Even if it were the owner of the airport, the sight of Jones and Davis with their fancy-schmancy firearms would deter him from storming out and demanding payment.

I shut my eyes again, trying not to see Gabriel's rotting face, and wondering if my dream was fear or premonition. What if he was really too far gone to bring back? If he didn't have his antiserum, his options really sucked. So we had to find him before he was forced to choose.

I felt the weight of someone staring at me, and immediately suspected Griff. I raised my lids to half-mast and looked in his direction. His eyes were closed, however, so maybe I'd imagined it.

My eyes drooped again, body and mind demanding more sleep. I knew I needed it, but I was reluctant to chance it—run the risk of another horror show sponsored by my subconscious and my innermost fears.

What if it's not just your fears, my subconscious whispered in my ear. *What if you're just facing what you already know? What if you're just seeing the future?*

Sorry, I growled back mentally. *I don't believe in psychic powers.*

But how can you be sure?

"Go play with my inner child and shut the hell up," I muttered under my breath. My subconscious settled into a smug silence, having made its point.

Asshole subconscious.

I closed my eyes and fell into an uneasy doze.

At least it was dream free.

"The village looks alive enough to me," the warlord muttered impatiently as he looked down on his next target, a remote native settlement somewhere in the highlands of Congo-Kinshasa.

His lieutenant N'kruma—not quite nineteen years old, but already wise enough not to contradict his leader—kept silent.

The warlord, Joshua Gideon Coli, had been preparing to raid an illegal mining encampment in the next gorge over. But then this tempting morsel had presented itself. A pair of unfortunate locals had been caught the day before. They claimed to be refugees, and told crazy stories about a horrible outbreak of blood-fever. Whole villages were fast in the grip of demons, and everyone for miles was dead.

Coli had listened to their ravings and regarded them with lizard-lidded eyes before he grew restless and ordered his soldiers to cut off their lips, and then prepare stakes to impale them.

But in their ravings he saw opportunity. From the description of their village, it sounded ripe for the picking. Their stories had been fabrications, designed to frighten him away. And now he allowed himself a grim smile of satisfaction. The huts below them were clearly still occupied, and its inhabitants were milling about without care.

Bushmeat.

He handed over the battered set of binoculars to his taciturn aide-de-camp and gave the order to move in. Coli's soldiers rose to their feet, three hundred strong, extinguished their tasteless Chinese cigarettes, and fanned out, AK-47s at the ready.

The soldiers were overwhelmingly orphans. Ugandans, Sudanese, Rwandans, and more than a dozen other ethnic groups. Most had become orphans when they were forced to kill the other members of their own families. None were uniformed, nearly all were barefoot, and most were under the age of sixteen—many just half that age. More than a few were female, and they conducted a variety of duties in addition to soldiering.

The troops knew the drill. The youngest would lead the sweep, marching out in front to clear any land mines or booby traps, and to draw gunfire from any armed resistance. The older soldiers would follow behind, and then Coli's army would draw the net around the target village, rounding up the locals without exception. Once the men of the village had given up the hiding places of their foodstores and valuables, they would be swiftly dispatched—along with the elderly.

The older soldiers would be given free reign over the mothers and unmarried older girls for an hour or two, depending on how generous their warlord felt.

Ultimately the smaller children would be the only survivors, and if they did what they were told they would be brought into the fold of Coli's orphan army. Otherwise they would be used to show the proper way to cut throats, and be buried in the latrines. This is how for more than a decade Coli had managed to raise a guerilla army, ransack the hinterlands of three countries, and fight off government militias, Marxist rebels, and rival war bands.

As he watched his soldier children saunter down the hill toward their victims, something struck him as being… not right. The closer they drew to the villagers, the more the hairs on the back of Coli's neck rose. Things were unnaturally quiet. He could hear a few sporadic pops as his troops shot a few villagers to get their attention, yet there were none of the usual screams or panicked attempts to flee.

What the hell is going on down there? he wondered.

A whole crowd of locals assembled, but they all seemed to be drunk, or on drugs, staggering toward the ragtag army without fear. One marched right up to a young soldier and embraced him. So did two more villagers.

What the fuck is this?

And then the screaming began—but not from the villagers. Instead, it was his soldiers who were crying out in confusion, alarm, and pain. What was meant to be a methodical harvest suddenly deteriorated into a riot of confusion and terror. Frenzied shrieks and wild, uncoordinated bursts of gunfire ripped through the air. Infuriated at the break in discipline, the warlord barked harsh orders to his captains.

"Fils de putes! *Get down there and tell your squads to do their jobs, or so help me I'll pour petrol down your throats and set your heads on fire!"*

The captains immediately scrambled down the hill toward the howling fray. Coli shook his head and cursed long and spectacularly in three languages while pacing back and forth along the hilltop. What a bloody mess. His whole day would be ruined, unless...

He stepped away from the ridge, and pulled a cigar from the pocket of his fatigue jacket, along with a Zippo. He'd been saving the precious Cuban for a special occasion, and resented wasting it on this fiasco. But c'est le guerre. He had to do something to salve the pain.

As he flicked the lighter to life, someone called his name.

"General?" N'kruma said, softly. "Coli?" he continued, his voice rising slightly.

The warlord slowly turned in surprise. He had never seen the hardened soldier show fear before. Now, however, N'kruma stood staring down the hill in shocked silence, his arms limp at his sides, his AK-47 dangling just as uselessly. He looked every bit a scared young boy, instead of the rapist and killer that he was.

"They're coming, Coli."

Coli unslung his own prized weapon, a squat black French bullpup assault rifle, and strode over to gaze past his lieutenant. What he saw made no sense at all. The villagers were approaching—at least those who weren't bent over screaming, flailing soldiers. And they weren't alone.

At the forefront were many of the young people who had been his first wave, all dripping fresh blood from wounds so severe it seemed impossible that they were still walking.

"Nique ta mere..." The warlord muttered the words around his still unlit cigar. Paralyzed, he stared into the horrible vacant eyes of his own child soldiers. He had seen horrible things in them before—fear, anguish, hate, despair, lust, and death agonies—but nothing as terrible as what he saw now, this relentless empty stare reflected in every face before him.

Survival instinct kicked in at last and he squeezed off a burst. Bodies went flying back as the bullets tossed them like bundles of torn bloody rags. N'kruma followed suit, and they continued spraying across the line of advance, mowing the enemy down until their clips were spent.

But the waves of soldiers and villagers were not spent. They continued to make their way up the hill, and those who had been gunned down simply rose up again, moving forward again, even with their bodies ripped open.

Switching out his ammo clip, Coli heard a high-pitched keening and realized it was coming from his lieutenant. The warlord retreated back a pace as N'kruma continued to shake and wail and fire his weapon in ever-frantic arcs, until his former comrades reached him at last and pulled him down into their arms.

His screams ended abruptly with a wet, tearing sound.

Coli tried to take another step back, and lost his footing. The big man crashed to the ground, his cigar and ammo clip tumbling out of reach. He swung the weapon like a club for a moment, then threw it at them in a frenzied attempt to turn and crawl away to freedom.

He screamed as the first bites landed on the backs of his legs. Coli's army was following him again, and just as always, they would follow him to the bitter end.

CHAPTER NINETEEN

The sound of voices in my headset pulled me out of my sleep, and I heard more nearby. They were muffled by the rotors, but every other word or so was discernable. I heard "Los Angeles" and "FUBAR" very clearly.

Opening my eyes, I found the rest of my teammates looking down at the landscape below, with varying degrees of horror and sorrow on their faces. Even Griff's expression was grim, his lips compressed in a tight line. I didn't get how bad it was, though, until I turned around and looked for myself.

San Francisco had been a mess when we'd arrived, but the outbreak had been in its beginning stages. The two days we'd spent in relative isolation at the DZN lab had been enough time for the zombie virus to well and truly take hold. The chaos we'd experienced had been horrible, but now as I looked at the patchwork quilt of burning buildings, multiple-car pileups, people running and screaming, and a staggering number of zombies... well, it made what we'd experienced in San Francisco seem like a walk in a park. A zombie-infested park, but nothing compared to the live Hieronymus Bosch painting that had replaced Santa Monica, Brentwood, and the rest of West LA.

The 405 Freeway was a river of unmoving metal. People struggled to move between and over the stalled cars, trampling one another in their desperation to get out of what had become a cement-walled death trap. The on and off ramps were clogged with panicked masses, packed like cows in a slaughterhouse chute. Many were picked up by zombies clustered around the exits.

My mother's family was from Southern California, so we'd spent many holidays visiting various relatives scattered throughout LA and San Diego. I wasn't particularly close with them, and had fallen out of contact as I grew older, but the thought of them down in that mess, and what Mom must be going through not knowing if they were okay…

Hell, she didn't even know if I was okay at this point.

I swallowed hard and looked at Gentry.

"How… how long has it been this bad down here?"

"First sightings were early yesterday morning. It got bad really fast. They haven't been able to do much in the way of evacuation." He dragged a hand across his forehead and down his face.

"I know a lot of people in Los Angeles." I turned to find Griff staring down at the carnage, tension clearly visible in the set of his jaw.

"Good friends?"

He shook his head.

"No. But still, I wouldn't have wished this on any of them." The distant look on his face made me wonder if there was more to his feelings than he was letting on. Like maybe he really cared about someone in the hell below.

I turned back to Gentry.

"Are they going to try to set up a quarantine?"

Gentry shrugged, but the gesture was anything but nonchalant. It looked as if it hurt him.

"They're trying, but how can you quarantine every single road in and out of Los Angeles County? Santa Barbara, Oxnard, Ventura, Thousand Oaks, Santa Clarita, Riverside, San Bernardino—" He ticked them off with his fingers. "—all already infected."

"Will they…" I swallowed again, afraid to ask the next question, but really needing to know the answer. "Are they going to use nukes?"

He didn't answer, and my heart sank.

"You have got to be shitting me," JT muttered.

Tony crossed his arms and snorted.

"Dude, we almost got nuked from orbit back in Redwood Grove, when they first thought this shit was gonna spread."

"Yeah," I added, "but that was when they thought they could contain the whole thing in one small area where collateral damage would be minimal." It was more or less a quote from Colonel Paxton. "If they took out a big city, with a large population, it'd be a PR disaster. No way the President would okay it. Right, Gentry?"

Again with the disconcerting silence.

"Um, Gentry?" I prompted. "We could use some reassurance right about now."

"I don't know," Gentry finally replied. "This thing is hemorrhaging from every point of origin we've discovered so far. Reports are coming in from all over the globe—from major population centers to obscure little ass-end-of-nowhere type places. There's no telling what the powers that be might do at this point."

So much for reassurance.

Things fell quiet again for a while as we all watched the grim scenario playing out below us. Smoke, fire, twisted wreckages of metal and flesh, and everywhere were zombies dragging down those who couldn't flee fast enough. Some were torn to pieces, and others nibbled on just enough to insure that they'd come back to swell the ranks of the walking dead. They didn't move quickly—didn't scramble up walls and buildings like badly done CGI army ants. They didn't have to. Their slow, implacable momentum began as a small trickle, then grew into an unstoppable tsunami, taking everything down in its path.

"Maybe nukes are the answer after all," Lil said in a small voice. She stared out the window, her face pale and strained.

"No." I shook my head. "Don't ever say that."

She turned toward me, expression fierce even as tears welled up in her eyes.

"Why not?" She clenched her fists. "It's hopeless. No matter what we do, it's just going to keep spreading."

I stood up, nearly tripping over my blanket as it puddled around my feet. I caught my balance before I went sprawling headlong across the aisle, and knelt in front of Lil's seat.

"We have to keep trying," I said, taking her hands in mine. "And if we find a cure, we can still stop this."

"But things will never be the way they were," she said softly.

"That's true," I admitted, as much to myself as to Lil. "But if we can stop things from getting worse... that's still something."

JT leaned over and patted her on the arm.

"She's right, kid," he said. "You can't think about all the things you can't fix. You have to focus on the things you can."

Tony snorted. "Get your inspirational bumper stickers here, dudes."

JT shrugged, undaunted. "Shit gets put on bumper stickers for a reason. Sometimes that reason is because it's true."

"And sometimes it's just shit," Griff said softly, looking straight at me.

I glared at both Griff and Tony as Lil's face blanched even further. I gave her hands a squeeze.

"JT's right," I said, with more force than necessary. "We focus on the stuff we *can* fix. And right now that means getting Gabriel and Dr. Crazy Pants back from the bad guys so we can find a cure. Got it?"

An urgent squawk sounded from the com system. I

snapped my head around so suddenly I pulled a muscle in my neck. Nathan and Simone were sitting bolt upright in their seats, both looking grim but not surprised.

This was *so* not good.

"We are going down. Repeat, we are going down!"

"Is that the other 'copter?" Lil's eyes widened like a panicked horse.

I swallowed hard.

"I think so." Talk about shitty timing, and even shittier déjà vu.

A burst of unintelligible static flooded the headsets, followed by a loud explosion that blasted into our ears, piercing my head like an auditory knife to the brain.

Shit, shit, shit!

I grabbed my headset and pulled it off, throwing it away from me as if it would somehow change the fate of the other helicopter. Even if they'd survived the crash, they'd gone down in the middle of hell.

Lil started crying. I hugged her as best I could from my awkward position in front of her.

"We're going to crash, too," she choked out between sobs.

"No, we're not," I said as firmly as my own terror would allow. Lil needed me to be strong, so I had to hold it together no matter how badly I wanted to curl up in a fetal ball.

"Redundancy," JT said. I glanced up to find him nodding as if he'd just figured something out.

I nodded back. "Yeah," I said. "We've taken as many precautions as possible to conceal our destination, but we could still be tracked via satellite."

Griff smiled. "Then those two—" He nodded toward Simone and Nathan. "—are banking on the hope that this one hasn't been tampered with." He stopped and stared. "Hope they're right."

* * *

We flew down the coast, following the line of the I-5 Freeway until it curved east, and then followed the toll road down through Laguna Niguel until it hooked back up to the 5 above San Juan Capistrano and San Clemente.

The toll road, usually lightly traveled, was as jam-packed as the 5, but traffic seemed to be moving, albeit at a glacial pace. I didn't see any zombies yet, but it was only a matter of time before the spread reached the bedroom communities.

JT switched seats with me so I could sit next to Lil, who curled up against me despite my still-damp clothing. He also retrieved the blanket and handed it to me. It was Griff, however, who helped me tuck it around Lil when I spread it out over the two of us. I muttered a quick "thank you" to both of them. Then I put my headgear back on, even though part of me was really into blissful ignorance about now.

We passed over the San Onofre nuclear power plant, the two mound shaped reactors looking for all the world like a pair of breasts. My dad called them "nuclear hooters," which he'd say whenever we drove past it. My mom had giggled every time.

A new and scary thought popped into the horror show inside my head. What was going to happen to the reactors around the world? They had to be kept cooled, right? If they had to be evacuated, there weren't exactly "off" switches workers could hit on the way out. Remembering what had happened at Fukushima, I multiplied it by… well, however many nuclear reactors there were, scattered around the world.

Seeing my expression, Gentry reached across and tapped me on the leg.

"Don't worry," he said, nodding back in the direction of San Onofre. "DZN has core personnel and military backup in and around most facilities, to make sure the reactors aren't compromised. At least not by zombies."

I let out a breath I hadn't realized I was holding.

"So when did you add mind-reading to your wild card skills?" I asked.

Gentry gave me a rueful grin.

"Let's just say you'd make a lousy poker player."

CHAPTER TWENTY

San Diego, one of the most beautiful cities in the country, lay under the same pall of smoke and chaos as Los Angeles, but on a smaller scale. It lacked the urban sprawl of L.A. and the surrounding counties, but it packed enough people into a relatively small area to make for plenty of zombie fodder.

We'd flown down the coast, past all the little seaside towns from Oceanside to Del Mar and La Jolla, cutting inland once we hit Mission Bay. I recognized Mission Valley as we passed over I-8 before jigging south along the 163, a scenic freeway marked by graceful bridges and tons of trees.

We were headed for Balboa Park, home to museums, theaters, the world famous San Diego Zoo and, evidently, yet another DZN base hidden somewhere among its acreage. My money was on the Air and Space Museum or the Fleet Science Center.

The helicopter dipped low as we approached our destination, the late afternoon winter sun hitting the bridge that led to the iconic California Tower, originally built for the Panama-California Exposition more than a century ago. Hundreds of zombies staggered down across the bridge and into the park like gormless, rotting tourists, bumping aimlessly against statues, architectural treasures, and yet more abandoned vehicles.

Where the hell are we going to set down in this mess?

My unspoken question was quickly answered as Carl maneuvered the helicopter over an open courtyard garden and the parking lot behind it. In a graceful swoop worthy of Roy Scheider, he took the helicopter into a canyon tucked behind the parking lot and set down in the middle of a large dirt clearing.

The canyon was flanked by palm fronds, giant ferns, and ancient looking trees, some with above-ground root systems that looked like petrified tentacles. Cthulhu meets Jurassic Park. I expected to see velociraptors emerging from the shadows.

The mood was somber as we disembarked, everyone moving quickly to gather their gear before the helicopter's landing drew too much attention from the zombies up top. Carl and the mechanic immediately set to pulling down low-hanging branches and palm fronds to camouflage the helicopter from anyone who might fly over. Definitely justifiable paranoia.

I could see several figures moving slowly around up there, but our landing area was concealed by plenty of thick foliage. If we moved quickly, we might be able to motor before an intrepid zombie spotted us and started the moaning chorus.

A wooden staircase at the far end of the canyon led up to the parking lot, tall palm trees flanking it like ragged sentries. Up top were small cream-colored buildings with curved red-shingled roofs.

Something white caught my eye—a set of earbuds on the dusty ground. They were attached to a blood-spattered iPod. A plastic water bottle lay crumpled against one of the Lovecraftian tangles, dark patches in the dirt telling the story of what probably happened to the iPod's owner.

I glanced over at Lil, who was staring off into the distance. I put a hand on her shoulder.

"You okay?" I spoke in an undertone.

She nodded. "Just thinking about the zoo," she said softly. "It's huge, isn't it?"

Uh-oh.

"Yeah, it's pretty big," I said cautiously. "With a ton of people who are committed to taking care of the animals during all sorts of emergencies."

Lil nodded again.

"Yeah, you're probably right."

A plaintive moan drifted our way from the bottom of the wooden staircase. We all looked back to see a lone female zombie in sweats, tennis shoes, and T-shirt staring at us with a dead yet hungry gaze. It had nasty wounds on its arms and legs, one ankle nearly gnawed through, and I'd bet dollars to donuts it was missing an iPod. It lurched unsteadily in our direction, moaning again. A ragged chorus responded from the parking lot above.

A small pop sounded, and a hole appeared in the jogger's head. It slumped to the ground, but already other zombies were appearing on the platform at the top of the wooden stairs.

"Time to move," Nathan said quietly to everyone gathered round. "Hand-to-hand weapons to keep the noise down." He nodded at Davis and Jones. "Except you two, of course." He unhooked his Halligan bar from his belt as Simone pulled an identical tool from a duffel bag.

Awww, how cute. Matching weapons. I had the sense to keep the observation to myself.

"Where are we headed?" I asked.

"It's not too far," Nathan replied. "Just stick together and follow Simone. She knows the way."

Simone took point, moving up the slope to the east like some sort of magic ninja, her feet barely making any sound on the leaf-covered ground. The Gunsy Twins and Nathan moved with similar efficiency. JT moved quickly, refraining from swinging off the many low-hanging branches. He seemed to be taking the situation more seriously, instead of treating everything like an obstacle course for him to conquer.

I unsheathed my blades, and fell in behind the rest of the group, taking Tail-End Charlie just so I could keep an eye on Lil and not have Griff at my back. Compared to Simone, I felt like a clumsy puppy chasing after a sleek greyhound, feet landing on every stray branch. It made me feel slightly better to hear Tony, Lil, and Gentry crunching through the carpet of dead leaves, and downright happy when the catlike Griff tripped on one of the tentacle-like roots along the way.

And like a cat, he pretended nothing had happened.

Near the top, we reached a green fence separating us from a cement path, which led down into the canyon and up a flight of stairs that ended behind a row of the cream-colored buildings. The ever-present moans of the undead drifted toward us along with the all-too-familiar smell of necrosis.

I'd kill for some Febreze about now.

Simone nimbly hopped over the fence and ascended the stairs, the rest of us close behind. She stopped at a strip of walkway that was still below the rest of the park, several of the buildings hiding us from sight.

"Try to stay together," she said quietly. "If you fall behind, just remember to head left through the International Cottages to the Organ Pavilion. You can't miss it."

Organ Pavilion? My eyebrows shot up. Not the obvious choice.

"Once there," Simone continued, "go straight to the door at the end of the right colonnade. Someone will be there to let us in."

"What's a colonnade?" Tony asked, saving me the trouble.

"It's a row of columns placed at regular intervals, usually supporting a roof," JT said without missing a beat.

Tony looked at him without love.

"Like, shouldn't you be on *Jeopardy*, dude?"

"Tried out, didn't make it," JT admitted in a cheerful

undertone. "Totally blew it in the sports categories. I hate sports."

Simone shushed them with a look, and hefted her Halligan bar.

"We need to move quickly and quietly," she said. "Let's go." With that, she took off at a sprint. I couldn't help but notice the way Nathan's gaze followed her.

Who knows? If we survived, maybe they'd figure their shit out.

CHAPTER TWENTY-ONE

Simone led us up a walkway between two of the International Cottages, and to the edge of a large grass clearing littered with food stands, barbecue grills, and overturned tables, rotting food and body parts scattered all over the formerly green lawn. A large banner reading "Ethnic Food Fair" stretched between two trees.

I'd been here many years ago during this same event, and still remembered all of the participants in their festive national costume. I'd dragged my indulgent parents into each and every one of the houses with their cheerful blue-painted shutters, and insisted on sampling food from every country.

Now the words "Ethnic Food Fair" took on a new and more literal meaning as zombies of all ages and nationalities in dirndls, lederhosen, kimonos, kilts, saris, and assorted other national garb gnawed on body parts or wandered around in search of food. It was like a ride at Disneyland, as imagined by George Romero.

It's a dead world, after all…

That's enough of that, I told my brain firmly before that particular brain worm took hold.

There were muffled pops again as the Gunsy Twins started doing their job culling the herd. Zombies dropped as the rest of us broke from cover and plowed through the crowd as best we could. Those of us with immunity focused on keeping the zombies off of the helicopter crew. Gentry, Simone, and Nathan were a few yards ahead, while off to my left Lil wielded her pickaxe with gleeful abandon, splattering blood and black fluid in her wake. Tony swung Thor's Wee Hammer with less glee but equal effectiveness, while JT effortlessly bounded on and over anything in his way.

I raised my katana as a zombie in traditional Greek costume reached for me, arms raised as though it were about to start line dancing.

"Sorry, Zorba," I said, slicing through its neck.

I heard a snort.

"Life is what you do while you're waiting to die."

I turned to see Griff right behind me, facing off against a female zombie wearing an orange sari.

"Life is where the time goes by," I shot back.

He grinned, looking genuinely amused for the first time since I'd met him as he nonchalantly bashed his opponent right in the middle of its bindi. I had to admire his aim.

"Raised on show tunes, were you?" he said.

I shrugged, but before I could answer, a shit-ton of ethnically diverse zombies headed my way. At the forefront was a swarm of formerly adorable Chinese toddlers in blood-stained folk-dance gear. They staggered unsteadily on chubby little legs, almost the way normal toddlers do when first learning to walk—like little Godzillas stomping through Tokyo. A little girl zombie reached towards me with chubby arms, as if asking me to pick it up.

This was so wrong on every possible level.

"Empty shells," I muttered, reminding myself of a near-fatal lesson I'd learned in Golden Gate Park. Steeling myself, I raised my katana, but before I could cut off its head, Griff swung his crowbar and knocked it backward into the other toddlers. They toppled over like fat little bowling pins, tripping up a couple of adults who looked like refugees from Riverdance.

Griff turned to me. "Keep moving," he said, his expression unreadable. "Just take out the ones you have to for now, not the ones that'll give you more nightmares."

I nodded tersely, and kept moving. I couldn't bring myself to thank him, but as much as I hated to admit it, he was right.

That's when it hit me.

This was so much worse than the swarm we'd defeated in Redwood Grove, I didn't even know how to parse it. I mean, we weren't just talking about Balboa Park. We weren't even talking about San Diego, Southern California, or the entire frigging state. This shit, as Tony liked to say, had gotten real, and on a global scale.

Taking out a few dozen zombies in brightly colored costumes wasn't going to make a whole hell of a lot of difference. This zombie United Nations was only the tip of the proverbial iceberg.

So I kept running, not bothering with my katana any more. I knocked zombies out of my way by hip-checking them or kicking them hard in the kneecaps. Maybe they didn't feel any pain, but the laws of physics still applied.

Clearing the International Cottages, we emerged onto an asphalt road littered with cars. A huge parking lot stretched out before us down a slope while hedges and trees lined the sidewalk to our left and hugged the back of a large square structure a few hundred yards away.

Simone darted across the road between the stalled vehicles, heading toward the sidewalk beyond. Nathan was right behind her. The rest of us followed, ducklings trailing their mother.

Undead hands reached out of car windows, clutching at us as we wove in between the front ends and bumpers. Zombies staggered toward us from the parking lots;

tourists who'd come to spend the day at Balboa Park, but were now on permanent vacation in hell.

Carl gave a yell of fear and disgust as a female zombie in a full-skirted yellow dress and a little sweater, all retro with a matte black Bettie Page 'do, reached out from between two cars and grabbed his left arm. It yanked him hand first toward its open mouth, which still bore the remnants of bright red lipstick, now smeared with black vomit and blood.

Not gonna happen.

I vaulted clumsily over the hood of the car nearest me, shoving my Kevlar-covered right forearm into Retro Zombie's gaping mouth before it could chomp down on Carl's fingers. I then shoved the point of my tanto into its eye socket, grimacing at the smell and the inevitable gross squishing noise upon entry and withdrawal.

"Thanks." Carl gave me a shaky grin and pulled his arm free. We checked to make sure none of the splatter had hit him.

"Gotta keep the pilot alive, right?"

What looked like the matching Daddy-O Ken to Bettie Page Barbie lurched towards us, hipster bowling shirt covered in gore. I smacked Carl on the shoulder and we caught up with the rest of the team at the base of what looked like Hollywood's idea of a Greek temple, complete with ornate columns. Benches filled in about two-thirds of a brick courtyard in front.

"There." Simone pointed toward a small wrought-iron gate. "Follow me."

The moment Simone dashed up the stairs and onto the walkway, all of the zoms in the vicinity turned to follow, as if on autopilot. Some staggered straight up to the walkway, clutching fingers trying to reach us over the raised edge. Others unsteadily navigated the stairs. The Gunsy Twins took up positions on either side of the walkway, taking out the slowly moving targets one headshot at a time. They were joined by Nathan and Gentry.

Simone rapped hard on the iron grill and shouted, "Appel!" The sounds brought a renewed chorus of moans from all around us. Our guys continued to cull the herd, but more zombies appeared from all directions—more than they could possibly put down. Soon the pavilion courtyard was thick with them, and it quickly became apparent that we were boxed in.

If we didn't get in soon, we were toast.

"Now would be a good time to get the damn door open," Nathan growled as he took out three zombies closing in on us. The rest of us stood in a cluster, hand-held weapons ready. I dropped my knapsack in front of the gate.

Simone slammed an open palm against the metal again, three times in quick succession.

"Appel!"

"Maybe you should try 'friend' in Elvish," JT suggested helpfully.

Tony gave a surprised snort of laughter, then looked pissed at himself for doing so.

Pop. Pop.

Two more shots, two more zombies crumpling to the ground a scant fifteen feet away from us. The ones behind stumbled over their fallen comrades, but kept moving toward us. Simone kept hammering at the gate and yelling.

The rest of us drew into a tighter knot. Almost unconsciously I moved slightly in front of Lil, determined to protect her even as Griff stepped out in front of the two of us like a knight in Kevlar armor.

I bristled. I mean, *seriously*. Like I needed protecting.

Then I looked at Lil, and almost laughed. Her expression mirrored my thoughts.

She grinned up at me with one of her instant mood shifts, looking for all the world like the what you got if the death goddess Kali got it on with a Care Bear. If it was time to die, we'd do it together. Although I really hoped it wasn't that time yet.

I really needed to see that she got her meds.

Simone slammed her open palm against the gate again, yelling as she did so.

"Appel!" *Slam.*

"Eric!" *Slam.*

"Appel!" *Slam.*

"Open the gate!"

Slamslamslam!

"I can't open the gate with all of you leaning on it." An unfamiliar male voice sounded from behind the gate, sounding like an especially cantankerous Wizard of Oz.

"Everyone step back," Nathan ordered. We all did, except the female mechanic—who seemed frozen in place as she stared at the incoming zombies.

Yup, definitely a red shirt.

Simone grasped her arm and gently but firmly pulled her to the side. Iron hinges creaked as someone pushed the gate open at a glacial pace.

"Pay no attention to the man behind the curtain," I muttered, keeping an eye on the ever-growing crowd of zombies. An especially tall teenage boy in a basketball jersey pushed its way to the edge, wriggling like a worm as it pulled itself up onto the walkway onto its stomach. I stepped forward and chopped its head off, using one foot to shove its corpse back into the crowd below. Opportunistic hands reached for me, grasping my boot hard enough to pull me off balance.

Motherfu—

I twisted as I fell, but still hit the cement hard, taking the impact on my right hip and shoulder. My knapsack prevented serious thwackage to my head, but the fall rattled me enough to lose my grip on both of my blades.

Greedy hands grabbed my legs and pulled me toward the edge of the walkway.

CHAPTER TWENTY-TWO

I twisted, kicking against the fingers clutching my ankles, and reached for my katana—but it had bounced out of my reach, along with my tanto. My fingers scrabbled for purchase on the cement as greedy hands pulled me toward the edge of the walkway. Lil screamed my name and grabbed me by one arm as another hard tug yanked my legs over the side, teeth sinking into my boots trying to get to the flesh beneath.

More hands clutched at my calves and thighs, their grip hurting even through the Kevlar. Lil's grip on my wrist slipped even as my butt started sliding off the edge. I heard her scream again, the sound mingling with the rising moans of the zombies below, all anxious for a piece of me.

I so did not want to become an appetizer for a bunch of tourists.

Hands reached under my armpits and yanked me back onto the walkway, my tailbone hitting the edge with a painful thwack. Someone else—Gentry, I think—bashed the butt end of his M4 into the heads of the zombies who had front row seating. The hands and teeth clutching and biting at my feet and legs loosened, then let go as whoever had me in a death grip around my waist fell backward onto the cement. I heard a huff of air as I landed on top of my savior, the back of my head smacking into something hard.

"Are you okay?" Lil crouched next to me. I looked up at her, adrenaline coursing through my body as I processed just how close to death I'd just come.

"Yeah," I said. "I think so."

Swiveling my head around, I found myself face to face with Griff. He was grimacing in pain, no doubt from my skull colliding with his nose, which currently dripped blood.

"Thanks," I said, meaning it.

"My pleasure," he replied, shifting slightly underneath my weight in a way that managed to add an unmistakable subtext to his words. Before I could call him on it, he stood up, hoisting me to my feet with his arms still wrapped around my body. He held onto me for a few seconds longer than necessary, then let me go.

Tony and JT immediately stepped between us.

The sound of the gate slamming against the wall saved me from having to say anything else to Griff. We all turned to find a tall man in his late forties or early fifties, wearing jeans and an oversized khaki shirt, glaring at us from the shadows inside the building. He had a thick tangle of black hair liberally shot with silver, all pulled back into an unkempt ponytail, and a bushy mustache and beard worthy of a member of ZZ Top.

"Get inside," he barked unceremoniously.

Red Shirt was the first in, followed by Carl. I grabbed my knapsack and swords, then followed. The Gunsy Twins were the last to enter, still firing shots into the crowd of zombies shuffling toward us on the walkway. Our grumpy savior hustled them inside, grabbing the gate and pulling it shut after them. It closed with a decisive clang. Then, even as undead fingers clutched the iron bars, he slammed an inside door closed, this one made of solid wood. The chorus of moans faded down into white noise.

We found ourselves inside what had to be the organ housing. It was an organized chaos, wood walls filled with pipes of various shapes and sizes, including a large one that wrapped around itself like a giant tuba. Cords held the pipes in place. The whole effect reminded me of a church as imagined by Dr. Seuss.

"Follow me," Appel barked, walking swiftly through the organ's innards. He stopped suddenly, glaring at us. "But don't touch anything." He resumed his rapid passage up a staircase. "Some of these pipes weigh a hundred and fifty pounds," he said as we passed by some that resembled anacondas. "They have brass tongues inside that determine the tones."

Lil and I exchanged incredulous looks. We were getting the grand tour, when all I really wanted was a damn bathroom. If he kept talking, I'd happily pee in one of the larger pipes, and see what *that* did for the tone.

We followed him into a labyrinth of yet more pipes, chimes, and drums, and lots of wood. JT ran his hand over the chimes, earning a glare from our obviously reluctant host.

"I said, don't touch anything!"

"Sorry," JT responded, looking anything but sorry as he eyed the drums with longing.

"This accesses the motor that opens and closes the door separating the organ from the audience," our guide continued pedantically. "It has to be clean, so the parts keep working."

"That's all very fascinating," Simone said with an admirable lack of sarcasm, "but now is not the time for a tour. We have more imperative matters to deal with."

Our guide gave a harrumph that managed to combine irritation and displeasure. He stopped in front of a small door that would have looked at home in the Shire, barely large enough for a normal person to fit through. "This goes into the air chest, the heart of the organ. I'll ask you again not to—"

"Not to touch anything," Tony said with bored disdain. "Got the message, Mariner."

Appel ignored the *Waterworld* reference and turned to the rest of us.

"There isn't a lot of room in the antechamber or the air chamber, so you'll need to be patient and come in one or two at a time, at the most. This is the heart of the organ, and should we all survive what is going on above us…" He paused and patted the door, expression suddenly vulnerable. "I want this heart to keep beating."

With that one sentiment he made it impossible to hate him.

"So don't touch anything!"

But he was still irritating.

Red Shirt and Carl went in first, then Lil and I followed. The antechamber seemed a mix of a church confessional and a pump house or pipe factory, while the air chamber itself looked almost like a sauna—all wood interior with a bewildering array of what looked like bellows, chains, and other steampunky workings.

At the far side of the air chamber was an open hatch in the floor. Appel gestured impatiently.

"Down here, quickly."

Red Shirt and Carl went down the hatch without hesitation. I peered after them at a ladder that led down into shadows. Awfully low tech compared to the *Spy Versus Spy* elevator at the SF facility.

"What, no transporter?"

Appel gave me a blank look.

I shut up and climbed down the ladder. If the gods were kind, there would be a bathroom at the bottom.

The base of the ladder deposited me in a large cement room with a low ceiling, lit by several florescent strips set at regular intervals above. At the far end of the room was a metal door. Iron cots were lined up against one wall, while tables and chairs that would have been at home in a '60s school cafeteria were shoved up against the opposite side. Boxes with various acronyms and symbols were stacked on either side of the ladder.

A ragtag group of a dozen or so people sat at the tables or huddled on the cots. A mixture of age, gender, and race, the one thing they shared in common was a similar, shell-shocked expression.

One of them, an attractive brunette in her thirties, stood up from one of the tables and glared at me. She had a horizontal furrow between her brows, what my mom would call an "I want" line. She wore an attractive blue-green dress with a demure neckline and a knee-length hem that wouldn't have been out of place at a church social.

She put one hand on the shoulder of a young, pre-teen girl still sitting next to her. Based on the strong resemblance, I guessed that they were mother and daughter.

"Are you here to get us out?" the woman demanded.

"Not until I use a bathroom," I said shortly. "After that, we'll talk."

She nodded and pointed toward the metal entryway. "Third door on your left."

I nodded my thanks and hurried toward it before anyone else could talk to me. Some things couldn't wait, and this was one of them.

The door creaked as I pulled it toward me, the sound of hinges in desperate need of WD-40.

The hallway beyond the door was the very definition of "stark." Cement walls and floor, lit by low-wattage bare bulbs. The place was in dire need of a makeover. Something along the lines of *Dr. Strangelove's Lab Improvement*. Hell, even some tacky shag carpeting or Nagel prints on the walls would have been an improvement.

There was, at least, a bathroom, third door on the left, as promised. Two stalls, a urinal and a sink. A rusty paper towel dispenser sagged on the wall. The words "cold" and "dank" sprung to mind. Whatever, there was toilet paper and the toilet flushed. If I could get a cup of coffee, I'd declare my life complete.

Dropping my equipment next to the door, I made use of the facilities. Then I gave myself a quick once-over in the bathroom mirror, which was a dinged-up sheet of polished stainless steel. I looked as pathetic as I felt, all hollowed-out eyes, sand and dried blood on my face, tendrils of hair plastered to my forehead.

Ugh.

I took my helmet off and splashed water liberally over my face and hair in an attempt to make myself feel just a little less gross. I also freed my hair from its tight braid, relishing the sensation of my scalp loosening as I shook the heavy mass free and massaged my fingers through the strands. A headache I hadn't even realized I had started to fade away. I decided to leave my hair down for a while, at least until it was zombie fightin' time again.

Retrieving my knapsack and firearms, I stepped into the hallway and nearly dropped everything again when I ran smack into Griff. Remembering the last time, I immediately backed away a few steps and braced myself, eying him warily.

He gestured toward my hair.

"Nice look for you."

"Did you follow me?"

He looked at me, his nose still dripping blood.

"In that you were headed to a bathroom and I needed to take care of this—" He gestured to his nose. "Yes."

"Ah," I said. "Sorry about that." There was a moment of semi-awkward silence, at least on my part. Griff seemed perfectly at ease, and I suddenly felt like I needed to get over myself.

"About the whole life-saving thing…" I said. "Well, thanks." That felt inadequate, though, so I added, "I guess I owe you one."

Griff gave me one of his half-smiles.

"And I fully intend to collect."

So much for the high ground.

"I'll buy you a drink," I said.

"Not what I had in mind." He gave me a look that was at least a 5.0 on the smolder scale, even with blood trickling down his face. Too bad for him I was mostly immune.

Mostly.

I mean, having someone save your life kind of tipped the scales just a little bit in their favor, right?

"Fine," I said. "Two drinks. Or I'll save your life. Whichever comes first."

Griff gave an imperceptible nod combined with a subtle grin.

"Fair enough. And if I save your life again… I get to choose my own reward." The look he gave me made it clear what his idea of reward would be.

I raised an eyebrow.

"You know, that's just not going to happen."

He grinned. "We'll see."

"Cold day in hell," I said.

Griff just smiled. "The dead are walking the earth, love," he said. "Snowballs in hell can't be that far behind."

With that he vanished into the bathroom, taking the last word with him.

Damn.

CHAPTER TWENTY-THREE

Back in the main room, I spotted Simone across the room, talking to Appel and Nathan. Lil, Carl, the Gunsy Twins, and Red Shirt were seated around one of the tables while Tony and Gentry stacked their gear on a pile nearby. JT bounced over to me as I added my knapsack and weapons to the pile, keeping my tanto close at hand.

"You okay?" He tilted his head toward the back door. "I saw Griff headed your way."

"Everything's fine," I said. "He was a perfect gentleman. More or less."

"Cool. But just so you know, if you hadn't come back in the next two minutes I was going after you."

I laughed. "Good thing I didn't have stomach issues, or we both would have been embarrassed."

"I never get embarrassed."

Somehow I believed him.

I hooked my arm through his and we strolled over to the table the wild cards had appropriated. I sat down on a rickety folding chair next to Lil, who had her pickaxe on the table in front of her, gore and all.

"Um… yuck?"

Lil looked at me, then at her pickaxe. She shrugged. "Nothing that'll hurt us."

I raised an eyebrow. "We're not the only ones here."

"So? They're not sitting at our table."

My other eyebrow shot up to join its twin. Before I could say anything, however, Tony plunked himself down across from us and gave Lil a look.

"Lil, you're being a total bitch."

Then Gentry sat down next to Tony and gave Lil the Hairy Eyeball.

"And unhygienic," he added.

Lil pouted, but took her pickaxe off the table and tucked it under her chair instead.

"We're all pretty unhygienic," I pointed out in the interest of fairness. "Shouldn't we be hosing ourselves off in some semi-toxic chemicals about now?"

Gentry nodded. "All things being created equal, yeah. But this isn't a modern DZN facility, so we can't." He shook his head and added grimly, "Besides, if this thing is airborne, a little bit of splatter is the least of our worries."

"Are there at least showers?"

"I think so," he said.

"I hope so," I said. "Right now, if I had to choose between food and a hot shower, I think the shower might win."

"Speaking of eating," JT said, dragging a chair up next to mine, "is there anything by way of food?"

Gentry nodded. "Professor Fraser is taking care of that right now."

I glanced across the room where Simone was deep in conversation with an increasingly cranky looking Appel.

"He doesn't look very happy about it."

Gentry gave a small shrug. "He's been pretty much on his own down here for the last ten years. I guess he doesn't adapt too well to company."

Once more my eyebrows went up. They were getting quite a workout today.

"I'm sorry," I said, not sorry at all, "but this isn't exactly an isolated outpost in deepest Siberia. This is in the middle of one of the most popular tourist destinations in California. You'd think he'd be used to company."

"Not down here," Gentry said. "From what I can gather, this facility has been a one-man operation for the last twenty years."

"It's only twenty years old?" I looked around, taking in the pitted concrete walls and "been here since the dawn of time" ambience.

"Hardly," said a voice over my shoulder. I jumped a little as Simone spoke behind me. She put a hand on my shoulder by way of apology, and continued, "This facility was built as a safe house during the 1915 Panama-California Exposition. There were rumors that a small outbreak had occurred in Panama during the building of the Canal, and the DZN feared the possibility of infection during the celebration."

Everyone in the room focused their attention on her. *Once a teacher, always a teacher.*

"Thankfully, nothing came of their fears, and the safe house was expanded into a small research facility. It was fully manned up through the end of the Cold War. When the USSR broke up, that reduced the threat of a Soviet-engineered outbreak, and smaller facilities like this one were deemed redundant. Nevertheless, they were kept as safe houses with minimal staff. In this case—" She gestured across the room, toward Eric Appel. "—just him."

I glanced around at the civilians.

"He saved these people?"

"Damn straight he did."

I looked up to find the woman in the blue-green dress standing at the end of the table, glaring at me with eyes the same color as her dress. The young girl stood behind her, arms wrapped around the woman's waist. She didn't look so good, but considering what she'd been through, that wasn't surprising.

"He saved us," she continued, patting the girl on one hand. "He called out to us, then pulled us in here—as many people as he could when things went to hell."

I looked at the half dozen or so people scattered around the room.

"I guess not a lot of people listened to him."

The woman shook her head.

"No. But it happened so fast…" She paused, biting her lip. "Most people thought it was a film shoot or reality show. What else could it be? No one believed they were in danger until—" She stopped, angrily swiping away the tears that welled up. "Until it was too late."

"I'm sorry," I said, and meant it. She had to have lost someone up above who hadn't believed in time.

"So you're here to get us out, right?" she continued. "I mean, now that you've used the bathroom and all."

I tried a smile on for size. It didn't fit very well, and I was just too worn out to come up with a quick and easy answer, especially since I had no idea *why* we were actually here in Balboa Park instead of kicking ass and getting Gabriel back.

"Um, not exactly."

The woman's frown grew more pronounced, and several of the nearby civilians began muttering restlessly. The girl, in the meantime, stared at me with large jade-green eyes set deeply into shadowed sockets.

"Then why *are* you here?" she asked.

Luckily for me, Simone was there.

"We're here to find a cure," she said calmly.

"A cure for what?" The girl looked at Simone with those big haunted eyes. "Can you bring my dad back? He was eaten, you know."

Simone knelt down in front of the girl.

"No, sweetheart, we can't bring your father back," she said softly. "I'm sorry—truly I am. But we can cure the disease that killed him."

I looked at the girl's mother.

"I know that's not good enough," I said. "But that's all that we have right now."

She was silent for a few moments, and it was

impossible to read all of the emotions that passed across her face. Then she seemed to come to a decision.

"Okay." She nodded. "Let us know what we can do to help."

I held out my hand. "Ashley."

She shook it. "Aimee. That's A-I-M double E."

I nodded. "One of those weird-ass spellings. I got it."

Aimee grinned, just a little bit. Not a full-on smile, but enough for the moment. She patted the girl on the head.

"And this is Grace."

"Amazing Grace, huh?" The girl gave me a shy tip of her head and ducked back behind her mother. "Glad to meet you both," I said.

Aimee squeezed her daughter's hand.

"Let's go help Mr. Appel, doll," she said, making an obvious effort to keep things together. "Okay?" They went over to Appel, and then the three of them went through the door at the far end of the room.

Simone pulled up a chair at the end of our table.

"Is there coffee?" I asked hopefully.

Simone nodded. "There will be. Appel... Eric, that is, said he'd get some."

"And food?"

"Lots of freeze-dried things. MREs and such."

I grimaced. "They really weren't expecting to use this place, were they?"

She shook her head. "Not really. North Island and Cabrillo Point were both deemed more tactically important, so money and resources were funneled into them, leaving this place and its personnel to make do with scraps. Whoever facilitated the takeover of Cabrillo Point knew what they were doing. And that means there has to be someone from the DZN involved."

"So why aren't we at North Island then?" Lil sat up in her seat, looking as ornery as I'd ever seen her. "I mean, if they have all the stuff we need, why are we wasting our time here?"

Simone sighed heavily.

"Whoever burned the lab at Big Red and brought your helicopters down are no doubt privy to the benefits of North Island. It was the logical place for us to go from a tactical standpoint, to gather manpower and firearms. It's geographically positioned to give us access to Cabrillo Point from the water."

She paused, looked directly at Lil.

"And North Island is where the other helicopter was headed when it went down."

Lil flinched, and some of the orneriness evaporated.

"That could have been us," she said. Simone nodded, sorrow and sympathy in her expression as she continued.

"Now you all understand why we couldn't go there, and why we had all of the cloak-and-dagger machinations with the helicopters. We don't know who we can actually trust. Not in the organization, or in the military—not any more. So we've had to go elsewhere for help."

Tony looked thoughtful.

"So if all of the resources are on North Island, then how are we gonna get what we need to deal with the assholes that snatched Gabriel?"

Simone smiled. "There are always options, Tony, if one knows where to find them, how to contact them, and has the wherewithal to pay the price."

"Cryptic but upbeat." Nathan appeared at the end of the table. "Very true to form, Simone." He carried a tray of cups and, if my super sense of smell didn't fail me, a carafe of coffee. I always knew I liked him for a good reason.

"I'll take that as a compliment, Nathan," Simone replied graciously as he set the tray down in the middle of the table. "Coffee? How kind." She and I both reached for the carafe at the same time. I won, but made up for it by pouring a cup for her before filling one for myself. There was powdered creamer and packets of sugar.

Not exactly honey and cream, but I wasn't about to complain. I stirred in two packets of the sugar and one of the creamer, took a sip, and sighed with bliss.

Lil wrinkled her nose. She wasn't much of a coffee drinker.

Nathan caught her expression and grinned.

"There's also tea and hot chocolate on the way out, for those with more sensitive taste buds."

Lil's expression immediately brightened. Which by itself was a good thing, but her mercurial mood shifts were not. I needed to start getting her the meds before they got totally out of hand and—

"Maybe I should go help in the kitchen," I said, pushing back my chair and getting to my feet.

"Um, or maybe you should consider your last ten or so hours, and give it a rest?" JT looked at me askance.

"No," I said firmly. "I think some gentle movement might do me some good. Help keep the muscles from tightening up. Right?" I gave Simone a significant look, but she was too busy sipping her coffee in closed-eyed bliss to notice.

Nathan cocked his head to one side, glanced from me to Lil, who was thankfully oblivious to it all, and gave a small knowing nod.

"Definitely the best thing for you, Ash," he said. "Just don't overdo it."

I smiled gratefully.

Jones raised his hand. "If you're bringing cocoa, I'll take one."

Davis nodded. "Me, too."

"You got it." I grinned. *Gotta love a couple of eagle-eyed killing machines who want their cups of cocoa.* "You want marshmallows with that?" They grinned back.

Picking up my cup, I took a gulp of coffee before grabbing my knapsack from the pile of gear and heading into the kitchen. Another cement-walled room lit by stark bare bulbs in the ceiling, it boasted a stainless steel double-sided sink, an ancient six-burner stove-and-oven combo, and a large refrigerator and freezer unit that could hide a body or two. Storage cupboards and more boxes lined up along the walls. A closed metal door was dead-bolted shut on the other side of the room.

Aimee and Grace were bustling about, opening cans of soup and dumping them into a couple of mega-sized saucepans on the stove, while Appel pulled plastic bowls out of one of the cupboards and deposited them on the counter with as much clatter as possible.

"Can I help?" I said with as much perk as I could summon.

Appel gave me a sour look before ignoring me in favor of a drawer full of utensils. I shrugged and turned to Aimee.

"We have some requests for hot chocolate," I said, "so I thought I'd help."

She offered me the ghost of a smile.

"Boil up some water in the teakettle, and go to it."

I filled a white enamel teakettle with water from the tap and put it on one of the burners to heat. While I waited for the water to boil, I snagged a few packets of powdered hot chocolate and emptied them into some white mugs lined up on the counter. Then I dug into my knapsack for the stuff Simone said would dissolve easily in liquid. Zocalo or something. How pharmacists and physicians remembered these names was beyond me.

Ah, there we go. Fazaclo.

The pills came in little individual blister packets. I figured one was enough to start, especially since I had no idea of what the side effects might be, and didn't want to do anything that could hurt Lil. I felt guilty enough sneaking her the meds—totally not something I'd do under normal circumstances. But nothing was normal now, so I pushed one of the pills through the thin foil and dumped it into one of the mugs, on top of the powdered hot chocolate.

"Any spoons?" I asked as I put the meds back in my knapsack and zipped it up.

"Um. Yeah." Aimee's flat tone made me look up. She was staring at me as if she'd caught me giving her daughter drugs.

Er… okay, couldn't quite blame her.

"Look," I said, "I know what this looks like and—"

She cut me off.

"Is it one of your people?"

"I… well… Yes. It's—"

"Then it's none of my business."

"But—"

Aimee held up a 'talk to the hand' hand.

"Seriously. Don't bother. I really don't want to know." She turned away from me, the set of her shoulders managing to imply a door being slammed in my face. Grace continued to stir soup, happily unaware of the subtext in the air.

Well, crap. I mean, I knew it really didn't matter what Aimee thought of me, given the big picture. Yet her disapproval still hurt, especially given the circumstances. Then again, she wasn't interested in hearing my side of things. So, well…

Fuck it.

Tightening my jaw, I grabbed the teapot off the stove, topped off all the mugs with hot water and stirred, being careful to save Lil's mug for last. I kept the spoon in it so I wouldn't accidentally slip the wrong person a shot of psychotropic meds.

Wouldn't that *be fun?*

CHAPTER TWENTY-FOUR

Griff had joined the rest of the team at our table, co-opting my chair. He was talking to Lil, that lazy smile on his face as he said something that made her laugh.

Uh-oh. I didn't like the way this looked at all. Lil was too young and too naïve. All of her former distrust seemed to have vanished in the face of his undeniable charisma. I looked to the rest of the team for help.

Tony was too busy scowling at JT, while Gentry looked like he really needed a few hours of sleep. As for Nathan and Simone, they were caught up in staring—or possibly glaring—into each other's eyes. So I'd just have to play it cool, and hand out hot chocolate.

Plastering a bright smile on my face, I set the mug in front of Lil, plucking the spoon out at the last moment.

"Here ya go!"

She smiled up at me.

"That looks good," Griff said.

"Here, you can have this one!" Lil started to push her mug in front of him.

Really?

I immediately plucked another mug from the tray and plunked it down in front of Griff, sloshing a little bit of liquid on the table.

"Here ya go." I nudged Lil's mug back in front of her. She gave me a look that was half confusion and half irritation, but didn't argue. I ignored the look and handed out the rest of the hot chocolate. Davis and Jones took theirs with as close to blissful expressions as I'd yet seen on their perpetually stoic faces.

I tried not to watch too obviously as Lil took the first sip of her hot chocolate. She didn't seem to notice anything wrong—no wrinkle of the nose or anything to indicate it tasted funny. I felt my shoulders relax just a bit as she took a big swallow.

Dumping my knapsack by my feet, I took a seat at the end of the table, refilling my cup with more coffee. Sure, I needed sleep, but at this point the siren song of coffee sang louder than the dubious lullaby from the uncomfortable-looking cots across the room.

Aimee and Appel appeared from the kitchen bearing trays loaded with bowls and cutlery. I jumped to my feet to help, but Aimee shrugged me away when I tried to take the tray from her.

"I've got this," she said.

Right.

Chastened, I sat back down. Appel plonked a bowl of soup in front of me, followed by a spoon and a napkin. I tried not to drool at the fragrance of Campbell's very best chicken noodle soup.

"Thanks," I said, not expecting any answer.

"You're welcome."

I nearly dropped my spoon, and looked up just in time to see him give me a cranky yet approving nod before he moved onto the next table. After Aimee's palpable disapproval, it felt pretty good.

Polishing off the soup, I sipped my coffee and shut my eyes, listening to the gentle hum of voices and pretending just for a little while that I was at a coffee house, and that there were no zombies trying to eat us.

"So how did you become a wild card?"

The sudden question—coming from Tony of all people, and in a fairly aggressive tone of voice—cut through any other conversation at the table. I opened my eyes and saw him staring at Griff with an expression that matched his voice.

Griff raised an insolent eyebrow.

"Why does it matter?"

"You're part of our team now, right?" Tony pressed.

"I've been fighting at your side," Griff responded, and I thought I detected a crack in the veneer. "Fighting for the same things you are."

"Well, when we formed our team, we had to tell each other how we got bit. How we became wild cards." Tony paused, his jaw tightening. "I thought it was stupid when we did it."

And indeed he had been a right little sullen asshat at the time.

"But it makes sense now," he continued. "We shared our origin stories." I hid a grin at that. "We all knew where everyone else came from. What we all went through.

"So if you're part of this team, I wanna know how you got here."

He was totally right. We'd started out with a team of strangers who shared one commonality—we'd all been through hell and survived. That common ground to start had made up for some major personality conflicts. Griff was a stranger, one we were expected to take on good faith in a world where that meant very little. Points to Tony for the adult insight.

Nathan and Simone both looked at him as if seeing him for the first time.

Griff leaned back in his chair, and then gave a small but decisive nod.

"I was in jail," he said bluntly. "I was offered a choice between being a guinea pig for a new vaccine, or spending the better part of my glory days behind bars." He shrugged, and gave me a sideways look. "Would've been a waste to have me off the market."

I snorted.

"What were you in for?" JT gave Griff a guileless smile. "No, wait, let me guess. Sexual assault?"

"Please. Not my style." Griff actually looked offended. Either he had incredibly selective memory or he was totally full of shit.

"What was it then?" I couldn't resist jumping in, just to see if he showed any embarrassment.

"Assault and battery, with a little manslaughter tossed in." Griff shrugged. "Accidents happen."

JT looked as cynical as I'd ever seen him.

"Which was the accident? The assault, or the battery?"

Griff looked at him with dislike.

"The manslaughter."

"Do tell."

"Actually, I thought we were talking about my—" He nodded toward Tony. "—origin story."

"Fair enough," JT said. "Although personally I'd like to know if one of my teammates might 'accidentally' slaughter me." A brief flash in Griff's eyes said that it might be a possibility, but then he smiled and continued.

"Along with a half dozen other 'volunteers,' I was given different versions of what they called the Walker's vaccine, one after the other. The last one made me sick—it felt like white-hot poison running through the veins. I felt my body rotting from the inside out."

Everyone in the room was silent now, hanging on his every word. Not even JT had anything snarky to add at this point.

"I wanted to die—begged them to kill me." He paused, then continued. "No such luck. They just kept pumping me full of electrolytes and whatever else was needed to keep my body from shutting down. What they *wouldn't* give me was anything for the pain." He took a long drink of hot chocolate as if it were a shot of whiskey. "I went through three days like that. And I was the lucky one.

"My fellow volunteers went through the same hell, and died, their internal organs liquefied and leaking out their bodies." He gave a small smile. "And then they came back.

"So six of us went in to be tested. Five died horribly, and then proved there's life after death. I survived." He finished his hot chocolate. "I'll never be afraid of death again."

Anyway, we delivered the bomb.

Tony broke the silence.

"So you never got bit, huh?"

Griff looked at him for a moment. "No. Is that what I need to join your special little club? Get a chunk of me ripped out by one of those things?"

Lil glared at Tony, and shook her head.

"No. You don't," she said. "You're one of us now."

I forced myself to keep my mouth shut.

Just drink your hot chocolate, I thought.

CHAPTER TWENTY-FIVE

Gradually conversations started up again around the room, accompanied by the sound of utensils clinking on dishes.

The headache I'd felt in the bathroom made its presence known again. I rubbed my forehead and massaged my scalp, trying to ease the pressure.

"You too?" Gentry gave me a tired grin from across the table. "I'd kill for a couple of aspirin about now." He rubbed his neck. "I think I pulled something out there."

"How about some ibuprofen?"

He eyed me hopefully. "You carrying?"

"Oh, yeah, baby," I cooed. "I've got the good stuff." I pulled my knapsack out and rummaged around in it, pulling out several bottles and boxes and setting them on the table in search of some of the ibuprofen I'd snagged from Walgreen's. How much crap did I have in there anyway?

Finally I located some painkillers. I pulled them out and set them down on the table in triumph.

"Here ya go!" Then I noticed the silence as everyone watched Lil examine one of the boxes, pulling out a foil packet with one pill missing. She looked at it, head cocked to one side.

Then she looked at me.

"You drugged my chocolate, didn't you?" Her voice was eerily calm.

My face said it all.

"Lil—"

"I trusted you." She picked up her mug, looked at it. "I *trusted* you!"

In a move so sudden no one could have predicted it, she threw the mug at me, the now lukewarm cocoa spraying me in the face right before the mug itself would have hit my nose, had I not gotten a hand up in time to block it.

The impact hurt, but not nearly as much as the blazing hate in Lil's eyes as she glared at me. Then she shoved back her chair and got to her feet, staring at Nathan and Tony.

"You knew about it too."

"Lil," I tried again, "your doctor prescribed this for a reason. You need it." I looked at her pleadingly. "And we need you."

"Yeah? Well, I don't need you any more!" She glared around the table at all of us. "None of you!" With that, she grabbed her gear off the pile by the wall and stormed off through the metal door.

The room was dead silent, so to speak. Gentry, JT, Simone, and Nathan all looked sympathetic, while Tony glared into his soup bowl. And Griff? Let's just say I'd hate to play poker with the man if I had to wager anything important.

Picking up a napkin, I wiped the hot chocolate off my face and neck, closing my eyes and feeling the headache pound in my skull. Then I opened them, picked up the bottle of ibuprofen and dumped four pills into my hand.

"Here," I said, tossing the bottle to Gentry, who caught it in one deft move. Then I downed the pills with a slug of coffee.

Nathan reached across the table and put a hand on my shoulder.

"Ash, give her some time." I gave him a tired smile.

"I don't think that'll help about now," I answered. "You saw her face. She hates me."

"Well, it's your own damned fault." Aimee glared at me from across the room.

Oh, gee—thanks for that.

Nathan turned and stared at her. Boy, I wouldn't have wanted to be the recipient of that look.

Aimee, however, just glared back. Brave soul.

"Lil," Nathan said, "is bipolar. She is also one of the few people immune to this virus. She's behaving erratically, and she doesn't think she needs her meds." He stood up. "We need her. So why don't you tell me how you think Ashley was wrong to try and fix this."

Aimee opened her mouth… and then shut it again.

Nathan wasn't finished yet. "Ash has been nothing but ethical and fucking heroic since this shit storm began. So are we done with the uninformed judgmental bullshit?"

Aimee turned to me.

"I'm sorry. I had no idea."

I shrugged wearily "I didn't either. I—"

Suddenly it was too much. Lil hated me. On top of Kaitlyn's death, and Kai's, and Mack's… losing Gabriel… it was just too damn much.

I burst into tears.

Crap. Defeated, I put my head down on the table and cried.

Arms wrapped around me.

"It's okay," a voice murmured. Simone.

"No, it's not," I sobbed.

"Yes, it is… Shhhh…" Hands rubbed my back, my hair, and several voices continued to tell me things would be okay. One of them sounded suspiciously like Aimee.

I opened my eyes and sat up. Sure enough, there she was, right beside me.

"You don't really mean it," I said.

Aimee looked at me, then back at her daughter, who sat across the room eating her soup.

"I want to believe that it is."

"So do I." I heaved a sigh. "But it's not okay. And it's

not going to be for a long time."

She looked as if she wanted to argue, then just nodded her agreement.

"I need to go find Lil," I said, sitting up. I grabbed a handful of napkins and blew my nose.

"She's not going to listen to you," Simone said. "Certainly not now, and maybe not for a long time."

"I know," I said tiredly. "But I have to try." I started to get to my feet, but Nathan held my shoulder with one hand, and kept me in my chair.

"No, you don't," Nathan said. "Leave her alone for a little while."

"So what do I do?" I hated the uncertain tone in my voice.

"Just wait a little bit," Nathan said. "Let her calm down."

I nodded. As much as I hated to admit it, he was right.

"Maybe you should let someone else talk to her first," Simone said gently.

I drained the dregs from my cup, and gave her a watery smile. JT refilled it, and I nodded my thanks.

"No, I need to be the one to talk to her." Simone started to speak, and I held up my hand. "Maybe someone else can go with me, but I'm the one she has a problem with."

Simone shook her head.

"Ashley, she's not going to be rational. Her condition, when untreated, results in exactly the kind of erratic behavior and increasing paranoia Lil's been exhibiting over the past few days."

I stayed silent.

Simone sighed.

"Fine. Then take someone else with you. She's already unstable, and she might even try and hurt you again." She looked me straight in the eye. "I don't think she'd be able to forgive herself for that."

I flinched. The mug was bad enough, but the thought she might try something else...

This just sucks.

Tony cleared his throat.

"No, it's best if it's not you... or Nathan," Simone said, and she placed a hand over Tony's. "Lil sees you both as the enemy right now, because you helped Ashley get the medicine. Best if it's someone neutral."

"I could go."

We all turned to stare. Griff was studying his bowl of soup as if it contained the meaning of life.

Was he serious?

"She doesn't know you." Tony spoke up before I had the chance, his tone hostile. "What makes you think you could make a difference?"

Griff looked up. "Exactly. She doesn't know me. So there's no reason for her to feel betrayed by me is there?"

Tony opened his mouth and then shut it again. Simone and Nathan exchanged looks, ending with a nod.

"Not the worst idea I've ever heard," Nathan said.

JT raised his hand.

"Um, actually it kind of is." He folded his arms across his chest and cocked his head to one side. "I'll go."

"You were on the same mission, Spider-Man," Griff said coldly. "What makes you think the girl will trust you?"

I spoke before JT could answer.

"He has a point," I said. Both JT and Tony started to protest and I held up a hand. "Look, Lil knows Griff and I haven't exactly... gotten along. If I'm the enemy, she might see him as a friend. She seemed to be heading that way already, before my epic fail with her meds."

"Sorry about that, Ash," Gentry said.

"Not your fault," I assured him. "I'm tired and I wasn't thinking." I turned my attention back to JT. "Griff saved my life less than an hour ago. I'm willing to chance it, at least long enough to sort things out with Lil."

"Kind of you," Griff murmured.

"Fair enough," JT said. "But I still don't trust him. So how about I tag along, and stay out of sight? That way, if you're right—" He glanced at Griff. "—maybe Mr. Manslaughter here can actually help out." He turned back to me.

"And if I'm right, you'll have backup."

Griff gave an indifferent shrug. "Works for me."

"Fine," I said. I looked at Simone. "So how long do we wait?"

Aimee spoke up. "As the mother of a pre-adolescent, I'd recommend about half an hour. Long enough for her to get in a good sulk, but not so long she'll start feeling offended that you haven't come after her." She glanced at her daughter, still oblivious to all the drama. "It's an art, really."

"Okay, Guru Mom," I said, "any ideas where she might have gone back there?"

"Grace always runs off to her tree fort or her room, depending on the weather. She wants to be surrounded by the stuff that makes her happy."

I laughed, albeit a bit sadly.

"Lil loves animals. Got any petting zoos back there?" Then it hit me.

Oh, shit…

"Even more important," I said slowly, "are there any back doors in and out of this place?"

CHAPTER TWENTY-SIX

Led by Appel, Griff, JT, and I moved rapidly down the dimly lit corridor past the bathrooms, a series of storage areas, and some very basic medical facilities. Nothing fancy, and certainly nothing that would interest an angry nineteen-year-old.

As it turned out, there were three "back doors" to the facility.

"One's right there through the kitchen," Appel told us. "It's locked tight at both ends. Comes out under a fountain in the back of the House of Hospitality. You'd have to know where it is to get in from the outside, and either have a key or some major firepower."

"What about the other ones?" I asked.

"There's a utility passage, at the very end of the corridors. It's not easy to find, so she probably didn't go out that way," he said. "Your best bet is down this way." He pointed. "It's dark, and difficult to negotiate, but if she can find it, she can get out." With that, he headed back towards the main room, leaving us to our search.

The corridor was easy enough to locate—narrow, as Appel had indicated, and dark enough that JT needed a flashlight to navigate. Judging from the accumulated grime, it hadn't been used in a while. Until now.

"She definitely went this way," I said, looking at the Lil-sized footprints on the dusty floor. Encouraged, I picked up my pace to a slow trot, despite feeling all of the aches and pains of the last twenty-four hours. Every second that passed meant a greater chance that Lil had reached the other end, and was headed for the San Diego Zoo, no doubt with some crazy plan to free all the animals.

"Dammit," I growled as the corridor stretched on into darkness, with no end in sight. There weren't any doors to break up the grimy stretch of concrete. "Does this thing even go anywhere?"

JT patted me on the back. He'd placed himself between me and Griff, who moved swiftly and silently ahead of us, and behaved himself.

"We'll get there," JT said.

And he was right. About five minutes later the corridor dead-ended into a chamber with a metal ladder on the opposite wall. Lil's footprints led right to the ladder. I ran over and clutched the bottom rung.

Up above about twenty feet there was a grate, through which darkening blue sky could be seen. Even from a distance, I could tell that it had been pushed aside, and only partially shoved back into place.

I sagged in despair, only my grip on the ladder keeping me standing.

"She's out," I said dully. "She's on her way to the zoo, and it's nearly dark. How the hell are we going to find her?"

"I'll go look for her," JT said, coming over beside me.

I shook my head. "No, I can't just stay here. And you'll need backup, especially since you can't see in the dark as well as a wild card."

"But I can move faster than you can," JT insisted. "And I've got pretty damn fine night vision. I'm young and spry, remember? I'll go up top, get up high, and see if I can spot her. She probably hasn't gotten too far."

"We'll wait here for five minutes," Griff said. "And then we're heading up top, too."

"Five minutes," JT nodded. "I can totally work with that." With that, he scaled the ladder like a circus acrobat, shoved the grate aside far enough to scramble past, pushed it back into place and vanished.

As soon as he was gone, I started pacing like one of the caged animals Lil wanted to free, my boots crunching in years of accumulated grit.

"She'll be fine," Griff said, leaning against the wall and watching me pace.

"How do you know that?" I snapped. "She's a wild card, but she's not invulnerable. She's also not rational right now, which means she could see a swarm of fifty zoms and think she could take them all."

"She may not be rational, but she's not stupid," he countered. "She's on a mission, so she's going to focus on that, right?"

My pace slowed ever so slightly as I took in the logic of his words.

"And as much as I hate to admit it," he added, "if anyone is going to be able to spot her before she gets too far, it's the kid from District B13."

I had no idea what he was talking about, so I just kept pacing, and looked at my watch. Except I wasn't wearing one, so I looked at my wrist with its Kevlar armor and wondered how much time had passed.

"It hasn't been five minutes," Griff said. He held out an iPhone. "See?"

I was about to reply when an explosion sounded somewhere in the distance, followed by gunfire. But this wasn't outside—it came from back where the rest were waiting.

"What the hell?" Griff shoved his phone back in his pocket.

I ran to the chamber entrance. More gunfire, punctuated by screams. The tone changed from terror to pain, the pitch rising in a keening wail.

I looked up at the grate. And then I thought of Aimee

and Grace, who had no way to defend themselves.

I made my choice quickly, even though it hurt my heart to make it.

I looked at Griff.

"We have to go back."

He nodded, reaching into his vest pocket this time.

I ran over to the ladder and stared up, willing JT to reappear with Lil in tow, so I didn't have to play *Sophie's Choice*. No such luck though.

"Don't worry," Griff said softly, putting a hand on my shoulder. "I'll find her."

I nodded. Then it sank in.

"You mean *we'll* find her," I said.

"No, love," Griff said. "I'll find her." The reassuring hand tightened. I started to turn toward him just as something sharp stabbed into my right arm, between the plates of Kevlar.

"What the fu—"

Things started going fuzzy. I felt myself go limp, Griff catching me before I hit the ground.

"Trust me," he whispered as he scooped me up in his arms. "You'll thank me for this later."

No, I thought as my world spiraled down into a pinpoint of black. *I'll kill you for this.*

MECCA, SAUDI ARABIA

"La 'ilaha 'illa Allah. Muhammadur-Rasul Allah." The *mechanical drone blared from the public address system in the Al-Masjid al-Haram mosque.*

There is no god but Allah. Muhammad is the Messenger of Allah.

Aziz tried yet again to adjust the hang of his ihram. The outfit was nothing more than a pair of sheets of humble white homespun cloth—one forming a simple kilt secured with a sash, and the other draped over his shoulders. It didn't suit the

Moroccan youth or his lanky teenage frame.

Around him, the mass of pilgrims walked in solemn orbits around the imposing black cube of the Kaaba shrine, the geographic center of the Muslim universe and the holiest shrine in Islam. The pilgrims came from everywhere around the globe, able to speak dozens of languages. But here they spoke Arabic, the sounds of their litanies and prayers reverberating throughout the open courtyard in a susurrating chorus.

Unfortunately many had differing attitudes toward how frequently one should bathe, so the hot desert air around Aziz's face was as fierce as an open oven, and thick with the ripe smell of unwashed human flesh.

Aziz knew he should be feeling the exhilaration of the umrah, and of the closeness to this sacred spot, but instead he felt annoyance and rising anxiety. The anxiety came from the troubling news and wild rumors burning across the globe via the Internet. The source of his annoyance, however, was more immediate—his fellow pilgrim Omar, an elderly local who had taken it upon himself to mentor his new young friend.

"In the Jahiliyyah, the days of ignorance before the coming of the Prophet, blessings be upon him and peace," Omar said, continuing his endless diatribe, "all the tribes and sects of Araby would come here to Mecca for the Hajj, even the Christians. It's true!" He stretched out a leathery hand and gestured grandly to the great black curtained shrine.

"In those days, the Kaaba was a nest of idolatry, with a graven image for every god of every tribe within a thousand leagues—hundreds of them!"

Aziz nodded without comment. His mind was more focused on heading over to the Kentucky Fried Chicken next door, when the time came to break his fast. He fussed with his drape again, and tried to check his cell phone, without angering the old Arab. Just a decade ago, bringing a camera phone into the shrine would have been an unthinkable blasphemy. Today the mosque embraced technology, and was on a 24/7 Hajjcam livefeed.

Enamored with the sound of his own lecture, Omar didn't notice Aziz's distraction.

"But then Prophet Muhammad, peace be upon him, cast out all the idols and restored the shrine that Father Ibrahim and Ismail, peace be unto them, had rebuilt. This was the very shrine built by the first man, Prophet Sayyidina Adam, peace be upon him, which had been destroyed by the Great Flood in the time of the Prophet Noah ibn Lamik, peace be upon—"

"Shit!"

Aziz's involuntary cry startled the pilgrims near him. Many of them gasped.

Omar's eyes blazed as he turned to the youth in shock and anger.

"God have mercy on your parents' ears!" he said. "What devil provoked such an outburst?"

Aziz held up his cell phone.

"It's all over!" he replied, his voice shaking. "The zombie outbreak is everywhere! Riyadh, Jeddah… they're even here in Mecca now. Fuck! We've got to get the hell out of here!"

Faces went pale, and the neat prayer lines began to dissolve. Murmuring grew in volume until it became hard to hear.

Omar, however, stiffened in outrage.

"Leave this place? Ridiculous! Where could you be safer?" He pushed through the distressed worshippers to the corner of the Kaaba itself, and raised his voice as loud as he could. "Do you truly think the Preserver, the Subduer, the Source of Peace and Safety would forsake us here?

"Zombies?" he continued. "Ha! The Holy Qur'an tells us they are subject to the will of the Master of the Day of Judgment!"

It was Aziz's turn to stare in shock.

"What? Are you kidding?"

Omar nodded solemnly. "In the name of Allah, the Beneficent, the Merciful," he said loudly, "in the 54th Sura, Surat Al-Qamar, the Sura of the Moon, Almighty God the Resurrector tells us the Hour has drawn near and the moon has split. If they see a sign they turn away, saying 'There is no end to this witchcraft!' They have denied the truth and followed their whims and desires, but everything has its time. News has come to them which contains a threat: consummate wisdom—

but warnings are profitless. Turn away from them then!

"On the Day the Summoner calls them to something unspeakably terrible, they will emerge from their graves with downcast eyes, like swarming locusts, necks outstretched, eyes transfixed, rushing headlong to the Summoner. The disbelievers will say, 'This is a pitiless day!'"

All of the pilgrims within earshot raised their arms and voices to heaven.

"Allàhu Akbar!" they called, again and again a chorus of triumph that sounded—at least to Aziz—increasingly desperate.

Higher pitched, almost like screams.

Wait, *he thought.* Those *are screams!*

Waves of panic passed through the crowd as an unseen commotion rippled toward the shrine. Suddenly the sea of white-clad pilgrims broke before an onslaught of red-stained ones. Men, women, and children tried to escape, but there was no place to go in the crush of bodies.

"My brothers and sisters! I beg you! Be calm! Don't—" Omar's plea was cut off as a man, naked and bloodied, emerged from the Kaaba's black curtains and seized him from behind. Omar tried to scream as the thing bit him on the cheek, and began gnawing away.

Aziz wheeled from the sight and bolted for an exit. All around him men and women fled in terror, many falling to the ground to be trampled to death, or worse. His eyes wet with fear, Aziz kept running as fast as he could, not even daring to stop and help the fallen. As he ran, he heard the recording on the mosque's loudspeaker was now repeating in a broken loop.

"La 'ilaha 'illa—,"

"La 'ilaha 'illa—,"

There is no god…

There is no god.

CHAPTER TWENTY-SEVEN

I swam back to consciousness slowly, head and heart pounding with equal fury. Nothing says 'special' like waking up to a headache and a panic attack at the same time. I was also so thirsty I would have killed for a sip of water.

I tried taking in some deep breaths, but the air was warm and stale and I couldn't get a decent lungful of oxygen. My arm hurt where that bastard Griff had injected me with some sort of knockout drug.

I would so kill his ass when I found him.

I tried sitting up, thinking that might help, but my head immediately smacked into a hard surface. When I reached out, my hands met unyielding metal. I could barely move my legs and arms, and the air became staler with each frantic inhalation I drew.

Ohgodohgodohgod… That bastard had left me to die in some sort of airless coffin. Visions of Edgar Allen Poe filled my head, along with those horrible drawings of cholera victims who'd been buried alive. I so didn't want to die that way.

I slammed my hands on the surface above me, hyperventilating as I tried to punch my way through. All I achieved were sore hands, a lurching stomach, and my head pounding even worse than it had when I woke up.

Okay. Calm down.

Through sheer force of will, I made myself stop panicking. I lay still for a few moments and focused on breathing. Once I calmed down, I noticed there was a little bit of air coming from my right, so I turned my head in that direction and pulled as much fresh air as possible into my lungs until the spinning in my head and pounding in my brain both stopped.

When it felt as if I could move without my head exploding, I reached out my hands again, but slowly this time, feeling my way around the perimeter of my prison. It wasn't a box, it wasn't a coffin… in fact, I seemed to be sharing it with some blankets. My fingers found a latch near my left hip. I tugged at it and was rewarded with a click as a hatch opened upward. Immediately the darkness was slightly less complete as my vision adjusted enough to see shapes, and then some detail.

I very carefully swung my legs out over the edge, ducked my head so I wouldn't hit the top lip of the hatch, and peered out into a cement-walled room lined with storage bins piled about four feet off the ground, looking a lot like the overhead compartments on airplanes. At least Griff had tucked me into one with blankets instead of, say, cutlery. I'd make sure to thank him for his consideration after I knocked his teeth in.

As the muzziness in my brain started to clear, it occurred to me the last sounds I'd heard had been gunfire and screaming. My friends and teammates needed my help. So I lowered myself to the floor as carefully as I could. Nevertheless, the impact as my feet hit unyielding concrete sent bolts of pain through my head. My stomach gave a lurch, but I managed to keep everything inside.

What the hell had that bastard shot me up with?

And how long had I been out?

I was gonna go all Benihana on his ass with my katana when I—

Then it hit me. A quick pat down confirmed that not

only was my katana gone, but I was also missing my M4 and my squirrel gun. Griff had either overlooked or decided to leave me with my tanto and my Ruger. The arming equivalent of a pity fuck.

He's a dead man.

I leaned over, hands resting on my knees, and took a few deep, steadying breaths, letting the oxygen rush through my body and clear out the cobwebs left by the sedative. After what could have been five or fifteen minutes—I couldn't really tell—I finally felt like I could make it down the hall without rebounding off the walls.

Pulling out my tanto, I walked unsteadily over the door, turning the knob and shoving. It opened easily, and I found myself in a hallway. There were a few bare bulbs, and when I looked at the floor, I saw multiple footprints in the dust, confirming that it was the same one we had followed earlier. I stood there for a minute, just listening. No gunfire, no explosions, no screams. Just... moans, and the distinct sound of flesh being ripped apart.

Somehow zombies had breached the facility.

I clutched my tanto and reminded myself of how many zombies I'd killed with it, then set forth back down the hall, hoping against hope that Lil would be back, or, at the very least Simone, Nathan and the rest would be holding their own.

The smell of cordite and copper grew stronger as I neared the bathrooms. I paused as I reached the door leading into the main room of the facility. I put my ear to the door and listened, my heart sinking as the moans of zombies grew louder.

This could not be good.

I slowly pushed the door open. The hot copper tang of blood, combined with the stench of necrosis and shit nearly overwhelmed me as I stepped inside the room. My heart, already in my throat, sunk down into my toes.

The room was an abattoir, blood and viscera smeared and scattered on the floor, tabletops, and cots. The only movement came from the dozen or so zombies crouching over bodies or bumping about the room aimlessly, their smorgasbord now cold and unappetizing.

A few were too badly mutilated to do more than crawl or twitch on the ground. I killed those with my tanto before the rest even noticed my presence. Then it was like someone lit a huge neon sign above my head, saying "Live meat! Tasty treat!"

Maybe it was because I was fueled with righteous rage, but despite my headache and nausea, not one of the zoms could touch me. I would have loved having my katana for this, but I made do with the tanto, punching the tip of the blade in and out of eye sockets with an efficiency that bordered on robotic. Fingers clutched at me. My feet kicked spent brass as I dodged them and did my job.

After I'd dispatched the last one, I took a closer look at the victims, and recognized some of the civilians who'd taken refuge here, the poor bastards. Then I came face to face with an undead Gunsy Twin, either David or Jones— I'd never been able to tell them apart. The right side of his jaw was missing so that his teeth now showed through.

He reached for me.

I swallowed and put my blade through his brain.

More began to stir around the room, as the virus took effect. I tried to blur out the features and narrow my vision to the kill point, because I didn't know what I might do if faced with Simone, Tony, Nathan, or Gentry. Any hesitation would result in my death.

No, I needed to stay alive.

Someone had to pay.

I had no idea how long it took, but suddenly I realized I was the only person who was moving. Only then did I let myself really look at the fallen. I steeled myself for the worst, moving from corpse to corpse with dread in my heart. It wasn't too long, however, before it became apparent none of the wild cards were among the fallen. Neither were Carl and Red Shirt. In fact, the only members of our team in the room were the Gunsy Twins.

Damn. They'd saved our asses several times, at the risk of their own.

It finally caught up with them. They deserved something better than…

And then I noticed something odd. The one lying next to the table had a bullet wound in his forehead, as well as others around his body. His corpse was the only one showing any signs of ballistic trauma. He was also the only person in the room who hadn't turned.

Looking closer, I spotted something about half an inch long sticking out of his shoulder. I knelt by the corpse and carefully pulled the thing out. It was a mini dart of some sort, lodged between Kevlar plates. It hadn't penetrated his skin.

I immediately searched the other Gunsy Twin, the one who'd turned—I'm pretty sure it was Davis. He had another of the same type of dart sticking out of his neck, embedded deep in the flesh. A quick examination of a half dozen other bodies turned up nothing.

A scenario began to come together in my head.

Odds were that these darts had been treated with the same kind of stuff Griff had used on me. Davis and Jones had presented the most immediate threat, and they'd been taken out of the picture. But the dart that hit Jones hadn't struck home, and someone had been forced to use good old-fashioned bullets. He'd been gnawed on after the fact, but he hadn't turned.

But why weren't Carl and Red Shirt among the fallen?

Whoever had breached our refuge had taken Simone, Nathan, Gentry, and Tony—probably knowing they were wild cards. Which meant someone had ratted us out. My money was on Griff.

Continuing my head count, I discovered that Aimee, Grace, and Appel weren't there, either.

Curiouser and curiouser. Could they have been in on it?

But why would Appel bother to save all those civilians, only to let them be slaughtered? It didn't add up and the whole conundrum made my head hurt worse than it already had.

A moan from the kitchen caught my ear. I strode toward the door as another zombie—formerly an older man in his Sunday best—moved toward me, arms outstretched. I dispatched it quickly and moved through the doorway, spotting an open door on the other side of the room. The other back door—the one that was impossible to find... unless you knew what to look for.

More moans echoed from that corridor, and I crossed to the door. Slamming it shut, I threw the bolt lock on it. The one *someone* had unlatched earlier. If it had stayed locked, everyone who'd taken refuge here would have been safe.

I swore to myself that if it *was* Griff, I'd kill him a piece at a time.

Hell, whoever it was, I'd kill them very slowly without any regrets.

At least that's what I told myself.

CHAPTER TWENTY-EIGHT

I went back into the main room, trying not to gag on the richly concentrated odors of death. The stench seemed heavier now, probably because I wasn't focused on killing.

Exhaustion and dehydration hit me like a double fist to the head. Little fireflies swam in my vision and the room started to spin. I sank to the ground, head between my legs as I fought my body's desire to give in to unconsciousness. I took deep breaths through my mouth, trying to filter out the smells.

Now was not a good time to remember that smell was particulate.

When the spinning subsided enough to let me stand up without falling back down, I went back into the kitchen and found some bottled water. I drank a sixteen-ounce bottle down in two gulps, twisting the cap off a second and sipping it while I considered my options.

Part of me... most of me... desperately wanted to find Lil and make sure she was safe, but the more pragmatic part of my brain knew I needed to prioritize the original mission—to get Gabriel and Dr. Albert back. Most likely my fellow wild cards had been taken to where they were being held, so it looked like I'd be making my way to Cabrillo Point.

All I needed was to figure out where it was, and how I was going to get there. From one of my childhood family trips, I had a vague recollection that it was out on a peninsula past Point Loma, one of the more expensive neighborhoods in San Diego. I'd need transportation.

First, however, I needed to get out of the facility without being swarmed by zombies, or ambushed by our unknown enemies. That meant the way we'd come in and the exit via the kitchen were both out. The "back door" Lil had used was probably also a no-go, since Griff knew where it was. That just left the one option—the exit Appel had described as "not easy to find."

No surprise there.

Whoever was responsible for the assault, they had scavenged most of the weapons and gear, but they must've been in a hurry because I spotted my knapsack under the table where I'd dropped it, hidden by one of the corpses. I gingerly pulled it out, trying not to look at the corpses of my teammates. I winced at the nasty sound made by the canvas as it separated from a tacky pool of blood.

Moving to a table that was free of bodies and blood, I performed a quick inventory. Thanks to Griff, I was pretty much down to bare bones. He'd taken my radio—not that I had anyone I could call now—my M4, and the squirrel rifle. Most of all I mourned the absence of my katana. On the plus side, without all the gear banging around, I'd be able to move quickly and quietly.

I still couldn't figure out why Griff had taken the rifles and sword, but left me my pistol and tanto, but I'd given up trying to figure him out. As far as that prick was concerned, all that mattered was finding him and—to use one of my dad's favorite phrases—turning his asshole into a turtleneck.

Rifling through my remaining goodies, I tossed the extra M4 magazines—they wouldn't be much use without the rifle—and the extra drum mags, too. Those I emptied first, since the .22 rounds would fit the Ruger.

Nathan would be proud—and surprised—that I'd

retained something from his firearms lecture.

Finding a stray hair elastic in the mix, I braided my hair and folded it double, securing it with the band to keep it out of my face. Then I sheathed my tanto and strapped it into its usual cross-shoulder position.

Even if I made it out, I'd need transportation. Too bad I didn't know how to fly a helicopter. The roads would be FUBAR, though probably not as bad as San Francisco had been. I needed a vehicle, preferably one with working GPS. Finding an available car was a big "if," though, since I hadn't learned hotwiring in my spare time. I needed keys—preferably ones with a remote.

I tried not to feel like a grave robber as I reluctantly started patting down corpses and pulling out keys. I was on my fourth corpse when a creaking noise came from somewhere above. I had the Ruger out of its holster with a speed that would have done Quick Draw McGraw proud, and aimed it at the top of the access ladder as the hatch slowly opened.

"Stay where you are," I ordered as a pair of feet in Doc Martens appeared on the top rung of the ladder. "I'm armed, I'm really pissed off and I will not hesitate to shoot."

"It's Appel," came the muffled reply from up top. "I'm coming down."

The feet descended another rung, but I wasn't buying it. At this point, I didn't know whom I could trust.

"I said, stay where you are!" I fired a warning shot about a foot away from his Doc Martens. It pinged off the cement wall. Not a lot of stopping power, but he didn't know that.

The feet froze in place.

"I've got Aimee and her daughter up here. Grace is hurt. She's bleeding badly. I need to get them down there now—to the first aid kit."

Shit.

But it could be a ploy. "Aimee, are you up there?" I called.

"Yes." I heard a muffled sob. "Please… we need to get Grace some help. They got her in the leg."

Those bastards shot a child? I took a deep breath. Okay, it still might be bullshit, but I'd take that chance. I moved over behind a pile of boxes, just in case, keeping my pistol trained on the ladder.

"Okay, come down."

Appel descended first, slowly, as if the movement hurt. He stopped partway down and reached up as Aimee handed a semi-conscious Grace down to him. Grace had a makeshift bandage tied around her lower right leg, but it fell as she was jostled by the movement, and she gave a little whimper.

I gasped when I saw the unmistakable imprint of human teeth that had sunk in deep and taken away a chunk of flesh. Her patent-leather shoe was soaked with blood, and the wound itself had already started to turn black.

Oh, god—poor Grace. Poor Aimee. I closed my eyes for a moment, my heart hurting so badly I could barely breathe.

Opening my eyes again, I holstered the Ruger and ran over to help Appel as he laboriously carried a semi-conscious Grace the rest of the way down the ladder. Aimee followed swiftly, her face white with shock and fear, her daughter's blood splattered over her dress and hands.

"What happened?" I asked as we set Grace down on one of the empty cots. She whimpered again, her skin tone sallow. A little bit of black fluid oozed out of one of her nostrils.

Appel didn't answer, and turned to Aimee.

"Get me the first aid kit." She nodded and vanished into the kitchen. Then he looked at me.

"The bastards got in through the entrance in the back of the House of Hospitality," he said. "They opened the door, and let the zombies in." He turned back to Grace, gently removing the bandage from her leg as he continued, "As soon as the first ones came through the door, I knew we'd been breached. I told Aimee to bring Grace and follow me up to the air chamber. We could lock the hatch from above."

"What about everyone else?" I gestured around the room at the carnage.

A brief flash of guilt passed over his face, only to be replaced by a stony façade.

"There wasn't enough room for everyone," he said quietly. "And not enough time to get them up the ladder. As it was…" He shook his head and gently brushed Grace's hair back from her forehead. That simple gesture spoke volumes of the person he really was, beneath the bad temper. "One of them managed to take a bite out of Grace," he said. "Your people started firing on the zombies. Last thing I saw before I closed the hatch were men with guns. They came in from the kitchen, and started firing on your people."

"Were they wearing black?" I asked.

He thought for a moment, then nodded.

"Yes. Yes, they were."

Bastards. By itself, what they wore didn't mean anything—hell, *I* was wearing black. But there wasn't any doubt in my mind.

Aimee returned with a large white box, a ubiquitous red cross stamped on the front. She set it on the cot next to the one on which Grace lay, fear for her daughter clearly etched on her face. I wanted to tell her everything would be okay, but I couldn't. I knew all too well what fate awaited this sweet little girl unless, by some miracle, she was a wild card.

That brief hope died when Grace started coughing—thick, rasping coughs that turned into a liquid choking sound, as if she was drowning from within. Appel immediately lifted her upper body from the cot, just in time for Grace to expel a mouthful of black, foul-smelling fluid. More blood trickled from her nose.

The choking turned into feeble crying.

Aimee moved to comfort her, but Appel shook his head and motioned her back.

"Don't touch her. She's infected."

"Are you crazy?" Aimee once again reached for her daughter, but I grabbed her arm, holding tight when she tried to yank away.

"He's right," I said, facing her furious glare without flinching. "If you get any of her blood or vomit in an open wound, even a scrape, you'll die too."

Aimee leaned in close.

"My husband is dead," she said, biting off each word for emphasis. "Ripped to pieces in front of us. So if you think I'm going to let my daughter suffer without the comfort of her mother's touch, you're crazy. Now let go of my arm."

I stared at her for a beat, saw the determination and anguish in her eyes, and slowly let go of her. She immediately pushed past Appel and sat on the cot, cradling Grace in her arms.

Appel dug into the first aid kit, pulling out antiseptic, antibiotic ointment, and bandages. He quickly and deftly cleaned the wound, wincing when Grace thrashed. I knew how much pain she was in. I wished I could take it away from her.

Aimee stroked Grace's hair, murmuring soothingly to her, tears running unheeded down her face as Appel slathered the wound with ointment before wrapping clean bandages around it. His own willingless to risk infection made me admire him even more.

He then turned to me. "You've had more experience with this than I have," he said. "Is there anything else I can do for her?" His expression told me he already knew the answer, but hoped against hope he was wrong.

"Make her comfortable," I said softly. "If you have anything that will knock her out, spare her the pain. It—" I stopped and swallowed, unable to continue.

"You said you were looking for a cure," Aimee said softly.

I nodded. "We're trying to find it. The people who did this... they're trying to stop us."

"If you find it... can you help her?" She stared at me with fierce hope, but my expression told her all she didn't want to know.

She bowed her head and took a deep breath.

"How long?"

As if in answer, Grace's body began to convulse and more black fluid gushed out of her mouth. I shook my head wordlessly, unable to speak as tears welled up in my eyes.

Thankfully it didn't last long. Grace heaved one last shuddering breath before her body went limp. Appel took a blanket from another cot and draped it gently over her body and face.

I hated what I had to say next.

"She's going to come back."

Aimee looked at me without comprehension.

"What do you mean?"

"This thing... this virus, I mean. It brings you back after it kills you."

For a brief second, a terrible hope flashed in Aimee's eyes. Then it dimmed.

"You mean back as one of those things, don't you?" she said dully. "A zombie."

I nodded.

"Yeah. And she won't know who you are. You'll just—" Oh, I hated this world. "You'll be food to her. And that's how it spreads."

Aimee looked down at her daughter's corpse.

"How long?" she asked again.

At that moment, Grace's corpse twitched beneath the blanket.

I looked at Appel. "Take her out of here, now."

Aimee put her hand on my arm.

"No. I'm staying with her to the end."

"Are you sure?" I gestured around the room. "Look at

them. You've seen what I had to do in here. It's the only way. So if you can't handle it, you need to leave."

She nodded.

Another twitch under the blanket as Grace began to wake up.

"I want to be here." Aimee took a deep breath. "I *need* to be here." Appel put a comforting hand on her shoulder.

The blanket slid down as Grace sat up, her beautiful green eyes now milky white in a sea of red-streaked yellow. Her mouth opened and closed, teeth clacking like a malevolent nutcracker.

I took my tanto, and drove it home. Then I bowed my head over Grace's body, and cried alongside her mother.

CHAPTER TWENTY-NINE

Appel set a mug of soup in front of me. I looked up and gave him a shadow of a smile.

"Thanks."

He nodded and put another one in front of Aimee, who stared at it blankly for a few seconds before reaching out and cradling it between her hands.

We were both sitting at the table where I'd spread out my gear. Grace's body was covered up with the blanket over on the cot and all the other bodies had been stacked on one side of the room as neatly as possible, with blankets over them as well. They stank—the whole room did—but we didn't have the strength to move them into one of the rooms down the hall.

I took a sip of the soup—Campbell's chicken noodle again, which was fine by me.

"I need to get out of here," I said.

"Won't be easy," Appel said, sitting across from me with his own mug of soup. "Those things are all over the place now. Last time I checked up top, they were piled up against the doors and pouring in like army ants from all directions."

"What about the kitchen exit?" I asked.

He shook his head. "I can hear them against the outer hatch. The assholes that did this got them all riled up."

"I could try the route Lil took," I thought out loud.

"But that fucker Griff must've told them about it." I looked at Appel. "What about the other back door you mentioned? The one that you said was harder to find?"

"The one at the end of the utility corridors." Appel nodded. "It's a bit tricky getting there, and you'll likely come up in the middle of a bunch of zombies. The entire park is thick with them."

"That's a chance I'll have to take," I said, wondering if I had a hope in hell of making it on my own, and then dismissing the thought as unimportant. I had to try. "I need you to help me. So show me how to get out of here. Can you draw me a map?"

Appel shook his head.

"It won't work. You'll be ripped to pieces."

"Damn it!" I slammed my fist on the table. Appel flinched, but Aimee just stared into her soup. "I don't have a choice! If I don't get my people back, this shit's going to keep spreading until there's nothing left!"

Aimee slowly raised her head and spoke, her words so soft they were almost lost.

"Do you really think a cure is possible?"

"Yes." I reached over and took her hand in mine. "The people who did this, they know it is. And they don't want us to find it. Maybe they want to control it, maybe they want everyone to die. I don't know. But I do know this—that it's the only chance we have to stop it, or even slow it down."

"Would it help if we could draw the zombies away from you?" Aimee's expression sharpened.

"Y-e-es," I said with hesitation. "But it would take a helluva distraction to take their attention away from live prey."

She stood up. "The organ," she said. "I can play the organ, and draw them to the pavilion while you get out the back way."

I nodded slowly. "That might work."

Appel shook his head. "That means opening the door."

"What do you mean?" I looked from one to the other. "What door?"

"The organ console is wheeled out onto the pavilion stage when it's played," Appel said. "If it rains, we leave it inside, but we still have to open the door."

Aimee shrugged. "You can activate the door hydraulics, and then get back into the air chamber. That way you'd be safe."

"I am not leaving you out there by yourself," Appel growled.

"What are you people not telling me?" I asked tersely.

"When the door is open, the console is exposed," he said. "It means she'll be on stage out in the open and unprotected."

"Fine," Aimee snapped. "So I play for a little while and then we shut the door again."

It was Appel's turn to slam a hand on the table. This time Aimee jumped, eyes wide.

"No! The hydraulics aren't working properly!" He turned back to me. "I can open it by myself, but it takes two or more stagehands to get it closed, and it takes a good ten minutes to do so."

"Those things move slowly—they'll take a while to get onto the stage." She gave me a brittle smile. "Long enough for you to get free and clear, right?""But not long enough for *you* to get back inside," I said. It wasn't a question.

Aimee's silence and Appel's glower were answer enough.

"Forget it," I said. "Not acceptable."

Aimee stood so quickly that her chair flew back with a crash. She looked me straight in the eye.

"You do *not* get to decide what is acceptable for me," she said. Appel started to protest and she rounded on him. "*You either*. My life is over, do you understand? My husband is gone. My daughter is gone." Suddenly the anger vanished. "My world is gone," she finished quietly. "And if doing this will help save a few people, and help you catch the bastards that let those things in here, then I'm going to do it."

The anger flared back up. She glared at Appel.

"And you're going to help me."

He and I looked at each other. I saw the sorrow in his eyes, no doubt reflected in mine, as well. He gave a heavy sigh and nodded.

"Very well."

I could tell just how much it hurt him to say those words.

"And you." My turn on the receiving end of that glare. "Make. This. Count."

"I will."

And I would. Or I'd die trying.

CHAPTER THIRTY

Appel hadn't been joking when he told me how cramped the utility corridors were. I had to make my way in a perpetual crouch, with my hair collecting cobwebs from the ductwork overhead.

Who the hell did they get to service this place, Oompa Loompas?

My thigh muscles hated me about now, and my claustrophobia was kicking in big time. Each footstep stirred up clouds of dust and turned my flashlight beam into a temporary whiteout.

Okay, I told myself. *The dust means no one's been this way in a damned long time. One less thing to worry about. So just keep moving and stop being such a baby.*

I reached the end of the passageway, checked the hastily scrawled map Appel had given me, then shone the light up and over to the left. And *voila*! My beam found what I was looking for—a set of rebar ladder rungs like big rusty staples, jutting out from the concrete wall. They led up past the ducts and piping and into the darkness overhead. I tried to follow the rungs with my beam, but it didn't reach very far; either the batteries were getting weak or the blackness up there was that much thicker.

Thanks for that thought, brain.

I started to climb, moving as quickly as I could. I had to be in position when the organ started.

The rungs led up into a shaft that was even more cramped for space than the corridors I'd just left, and even thicker cobwebs. Ignoring thoughts of Shelob and every spider movie I'd ever seen, I brushed them aside and climbed that much faster, anxious to reach my destination. As the ladder kept going and going, it started to feel as if the "up" was a lot farther than the "down" had been.

The flashlight finally caught something up ahead—a circle of riveted metal and a rusted handle. A hatch like you'd see in those old submarine movies, with the emphasis on "old." For a moment, as I clung to the ladder in the tiny—and possibly spidery—hole, I wondered if the gears in the handle would even turn, then pushed the thought aside.

It *would* turn.

It had to.

All I had to do was be patient, and wait for the music to start.

Empty seconds stretched into empty minutes, and my subconscious tried to fill the time in with whatever it could. It had plenty of fodder to choose from. Rage at Griff, frantic worry for my friends, doubts about what lay ahead. These warred with sorrow for Aimee, about to play the organ for the last time, and the tremendous weight of guilt that I'd agreed to let her do it. She was going to die and so, most likely, was Appel.

The thoughts became too much, worse than the waiting itself, smothering me even faster than the close confines of the shaft. I took a deep breath, tuned it all out, and tried desperately to focus.

Cabrillo Point. That's all that matters now.

Cabrillo Point… and Gabriel.

How the hell am I going to get there?

I'd found a total of three remotes. All I had to do was

push the button and follow the chirp, right? After all, I had super hearing.

Not so much.

Balboa Park had at least a half dozen parking lots spread out over the grounds. If the cars were in any of the lots directly behind the pavilion, I was kind of screwed, because the area was already swarming with the undead. No, I'd have to keep to the underbrush and range out further, keep my fingers crossed that the car owners had parked in one of the auxiliary lots.

Thunder rumbled outside, sounding close by, then changed in tone and pitch and became music. A small involuntary smile curved my lips as I recognized *Toccata and Fugue in D Minor*, one of the few organ pieces I knew, thanks to many childhood viewings of *Fantasia* and *Twenty Thousand Leagues Under the Sea*. Captain Nemo going down with the *Nautilus*.

Aimee had a flare for the dramatic.

I gripped the hatch's locking wheel and strained against it. It gave an inch, then more, the grating of metal blending in with the music until it finally broke loose, spinning freely. I felt more than heard the bolts retracting until the wheel finally stopped and I could lift the hatch an inch or two.

Organ music flooded in immediately, almost deafening to my wild card ears. I steeled myself against the auditory assault and peeked out into a small concrete chamber, oblong and utterly plain.

There was a basketball-size opening in the left wall halfway up, and a spillway in the opposite wall at floor level, but my attention was drawn to a metal grate. Beams of sunlight danced on the concrete wall, along with ominous shadows.

There was someone standing on that grate. In fact, several someones. Or possibly somethings.

Well, crap.

If they were some of the crew that raided the facility,

my odds of getting out unnoticed were slim to none. If they were zombies, at least I could put them down without them shooting at me. For the first time in my life I really hoped I was about to have an encounter of the undead kind.

I raised the hatch enough to slip out into the chamber, drew my pistol and crept forward. Halfway across I had my answer—the uber stinky fluids dripping through the grate and pooling beneath.

I edged closer to get a better look. There were three zombies, just standing there with their heads swiveling this way and that, as if not sure what to make of the new sound echoing around them. After a few moments, they staggered away in the direction of the pavilion.

Guess they figured it out.

I didn't waste any time. I stood up straight and lifted the grating out of its well, sliding it aside just far enough to let me pull myself out before sliding it back into place. Any noise I made was covered by the thundering organ music.

I stayed low to the ground as I surveyed the area, then scuttled over to some shrubbery next to a large lily pond. A few hundred feet away was the Botanical building, similar to the Conservatory of Flowers in Golden Gate Park. On my right was the Timken Museum of Art. There were agitated zombies everywhere, milling around restlessly and bumping into each other. The only positive was that the organ music was doing its job, drawing their communal attention skyward towards the pavilion.

My cover wasn't great, though, and it was only a matter of time before I was noticed. So I needed to get behind the Botanical building to the access road where I'd have the advantage of lots of trees.

I waited for my moment, unholstering the Ruger. There was a moment when the crowd in front of me thinned out, all of their attention away from me, and I ran, keeping low to the ground with as little excess movement as possible. I made it to the next stand of shrubs and froze, scanning the area to see if I'd been noticed.

So far, so good.

I saw another opening and took it, making it to a small knot of trees right past the little art museum. This time, however, when I did my spot check, there were faces turned my way—a well-gnawed tourist with a camera around his neck, and a young female zombie with way too many tattoos.

Someone should've told her how bad those tats would look when she was dead.

Their mouths gaped open and I could only imagine the hungry moans that would've started up had the soaring music not drowned it out. I drew a bead and fired two quick shots. There was no report at all—just the sight of Tourist Zombie's left eye popping as it dropped like a sack of potatoes. Tats, sporting a perforated forehead, swayed for a few seconds before slowly crumpling to the ground.

I held my breath to see if their fall would alert the others, but the rest of the zoms just picked their way around the bodies, still fixated on the pavilion.

I repeated this strategy several times—run and hide, run and hide—dropping enough zombies to warrant a change of magazines. Before long I was much closer to the access road. One more quick sprint and I'd be into the trees and hopefully out of sight.

A figure stepped into the open directly ahead, taking me by surprise. I slid to a stop and brought the pistol up, focusing on the front sight, centered on the forehead… only to pull the shot when recognition suddenly sank in.

"JT?"

The figure was gone as quickly as it appeared, melting back into the greenery. But it had been him… hadn't it?

A coldness gripped the back of my mind as I ran even faster and burst into the grove of trees.

CHAPTER THIRTY-ONE

It was gloomy in the grove, shaded from the sunlight, and it took my eyes a moment to adjust. But then I saw him standing a few yards away, head slightly bowed.

"JT!"

My heart leapt as he lifted his head to look straight at me, and I saw that his skin color was normal. My relief quickly turned into concern, and then I went on high alert as I noticed the shiner over one eye, the swollen lip, and the fact that he wasn't bouncing around like a Super Ball. He stood there, arms behind his back.

Damn.

I brought the Ruger up again, trained it, not on JT but on the murky shadow behind him.

"Hey, Ash," JT said in his normal voice. Distance had rendered the organ music a little less deafening. "Met some assholes when I was looking for Lil."

"Let him go," I said, half surprised to hear my own voice.

The shadow stepped closer to JT, transmogrifying into a man in black paramilitary gear.

I knew it. Fucking men in black.

"I knew Griff was blowing smoke." The man smirked. "She's dead, my ass. Figured we should stick around and make sure." He looked me up and down in a way that made me long for a hot shower. "And here you are."

The Ruger made a spitting sound and a round grazed the man's cheek. "The next one's in your eye," I growled. "I said, let him go."

The man gritted his teeth, reached up to touch the wound in his cheek.

"Do it," he said.

Do it?

JT's eyes widened.

"Ash, watch—"

Not until that first blow caught me just behind the left ear did it even occur to me I'd been outflanked. The world erupted in colors.

I staggered forward, somehow staying on my feet, only to be hit twice more in approximately the same place and driven to my knees. I rolled with it and came up in a fighting stance, trying to get my senses in order, focus my eyes back to single instead of double vision, and stop the ringing in my ears. I'd dropped the pistol somewhere so I went for my tanto, but it was gone as well, leaving me with an empty sheath.

My vision cleared enough to see someone new standing in front of me, also decked out in tactical black, only this guy was stockier and bald, with a truly scruffy-looking beard that looked like a plant in desperate need of watering. He was holding my blade, appraising it.

"Fucking wild cards," he said in a raspy voice somewhere between Aldo Ray and Harvey Fierstein. "You think you're all that, dontcha?"

He tossed the knife away to one side, then motioned me up.

"C'mon, girly. Let's see what you've got."

I bunched myself and lunged at him with furious intent, but it became quickly obvious I was screwed. Most of my practical experience was with weapons, not hand-to-hand, and against opponents that were slow, erratic and more than a little dead.

None of which described this guy at all.

He was fast—really fast, despite his size. He slipped my attack with just a sidestep and a twist of his shoulders. And where that next punch came from I still have no idea. It stopped me in my tracks, splitting both lips at the same time, and then a roundhouse kick dug into my side and I felt a couple of ribs crack. The bastard bobbed and weaved, dancing like a butterfly and stinging like a fucking bee, hitting me three more times from three different directions before blasting me with another kick that left me sprawled in the dirt and spitting blood.

Everything hurt. I felt like I'd been dumped in a cement mixer with a load of gravel and spun around a few times. The last time I'd hurt this badly had been when the Walker's virus had raged through my body. I was vaguely aware that the music had changed, Bach replaced by the hauntingly beautiful hymn "Amazing Grace."

Suddenly the asshole was right behind me, leaning over me, pulling my arms behind my back with a jerk that nearly dislocated both shoulders.

"I expected better," he whispered in my ear as he slipped a plastic zip tie around my wrists and cinched it tight.

"Sykes, what are you doing!" the first mook called to him. "You've had your fun, now cap her already. The old man wants her dead—"

"I don't give a shit what he wants," Sykes barked back. "We don't work for him, remember? I don't trust that half-dead fuck or his infected lapdog. And if Miss Hot Shit wild card here means something to him, well maybe there's value in that… maybe something we can keep back for ourselves in case this shit goes sideways."

The organ music suddenly stuttered and stopped completely. The silence that followed made my chest ache.

Sykes walked around in front of me and admired his handiwork.

"I've always wanted to fuck a superhero, but I guess you'll do." He shook his head in mock sadness. "Yessir,

I really did expect better…" Then he hit me again, just for kicks.

And that was just one too many.

It all came bubbling up at once—losing Gabriel, losing my friends, Griff's betrayal, Aimee's sacrifice… And now I was going to go out on my knees in front of this douchebag. My blood started to boil. I wouldn't have been surprised if steam started pouring from my ears.

No. I wouldn't waste the sacrifice Aimee was giving me, or the memory of her daughter.

I began to strain against the zip tie, shaking with rage as the plastic bit into my wrists and cut off the circulation. But I wouldn't let that stop me, not even when my vision darkened and my heartbeats started pounding in my ears.

Fuck it.

It's just plastic.

"Aw, isn't that cute," the raspy voice chuckled. "Save your strength, bitch. Those are industrial ties, they're rated for—"

Pop.

My arms were suddenly free and I lunged blindly, swinging for the last place I'd seen him clearly, putting everything I had into the blow. I took him by surprise and the punch landed flush, just above his sternum. Hell, it might've gone all the way through him if his flak vest hadn't taken the brunt of the impact. But there was still enough left to knock him off his feet.

He hit the ground in a heap and slid a few more feet after that. As tempted as I was to savor the sight of him lying in the dirt, groaning and gasping for breath, I didn't dare give him a chance to recover.

So I went after him, still riding the adrenaline rush as I lifted him off the ground like a rag doll, and flung him at the nearest tree. Sykes hit about six feet up the trunk with a crunch, hanging there for a brief moment before tumbling to the ground.

"Hope that makes up for your disappointment," I snarled.

I turned back toward Asshole Number Two. He stood there slack-jawed at what he'd just seen. Our eyes met and I smiled. Whatever he saw in my eyes was enough to snap him out of his stupor and he fumbled for the firearm that was hanging on a sling at his side.

As I lunged for him, JT suddenly came to life, shoving backward into the guy and grappling with him as best he could. Then he did a little jump, bringing his legs up and through his own bound arms so they were no longer secured behind him. His feet continued up and over into a perfect somersault, and somehow he planted a heel in his captor's face along the way, the old manic grin back on his face.

It was an impressive bit of Gymkata. Kurt Thomas would've been proud.

Striding forward, I caught the stunned mercenary by the throat.

"No bluffs this time," I told him through clenched teeth and blood, my rage still burning nice and hot. "You give me answers, or I crush your windpipe. Understood?"

The man gave a weak nod.

"Who is this 'old man' who wants me dead?" I asked. He kept silent. "Who are you working for!" Nothing. I tightened my grip for emphasis. "I won't ask again. Got it?"

"Get down!"

JT suddenly hit me with a body block, bowling me over a split-second before a barrage of incoming rounds arrived, like a swarm of angry bees erupting right where I'd been standing. They hit the creep I'd been interrogating instead.

JT and I didn't stick around to see if he survived. We scrambled for cover, beating a hasty retreat, zigzagging through the trees with JT leading the way.

"Two more," he called back as more rounds zipped over our heads. "They fanned out just before you showed up."

Well, hell, I thought. Nathan or Gabriel would have known better than to assume there were only two of them. *Rookie move, Parker.*

The gunfire tapered off, but JT and I kept moving, using the vegetation for cover, pausing only to check for pursuers before starting off again, still zigzagging.

Serpentine, serpentine!

I giggled quietly and inappropriately, wishing my dad was there doing his Peter Falk impression.

"That was a pretty awesome stunt you pulled back there," JT said, slowing down a little so I could keep pace with him. "I didn't know you were that strong."

"Neither did I," I admitted. "Fucker made me mad."

"Hulk smash," JT grinned, then took off at a sprint again as more "bees" buzzed past us. He pulled ahead into another thick tangle, vanishing from sight.

"Damn it," I panted. "Wait up! We need to stay together!"

I picked up my pace and plowed through the trees after him. I emerged into daylight again almost immediately, momentarily blinded by the sun just long enough to trip on a stray root and start to fall face forward, hair coming out of its braid and into my eyes.

Strong arms caught me and kept me from doing a face plant, holding onto me as I regained my balance and tightening as I tried to push away. I cocked back a fist, ready to kick more ass.

"Whoa there, baby sister," said a reedy voice I didn't recognize, with a hint of a southern accent. "What's your hurry, darlin'? We're all friends here."

That brought me up short just before I let fly. I got my first good look at the man who was holding me. Older, early sixties maybe, with a wind-burned face and limp silver hair down to his shoulders, he reminded me of Sam Elliott in *Road House*. He wore a heavy flannel shirt under a leather vest, the latter adorned with several patches. They were a little too close to my face for me to focus on them.

I could, however, see the patches on the other men a few feet away, all leaning on large Harley Davidsons. One of them, a bear of a man with a long goatee, was standing with his arm around JT's shoulders like they were old friends. The slightly panicked look on JT's face and the fact his feet were dangling off the ground said otherwise.

There were seven of them in total, each wearing a leather vest that matched my new pal's. They were dressed in jeans and heavy boots, with bandanas and sunglasses. I rapidly considered my next move, deciding I'd try and reason with them before resorting to more violence, although I fully expected that to be the outcome.

Before I could utter a word, however, two more commandos in black burst out of the trees behind us. They looked as stunned as I'd been to see the bikers, briefly letting the barrels of their submachine guns lower before raising them again.

"Welcome to the party, boys," one of the bikers said calmly. "But you may have to go for more beer. I don't think we brought enough for everyone."

"Give us the girl," said one of the commandos in a no-nonsense tone. "That's all we want. There doesn't have to be any trouble."

"Oh, I think there does," Silver Hair sighed. He reached up and turned my face from side to side, examining my bruises and busted lips. "Looks like you already had your chance. Sloppy work." He shook his head. "Nah, I think we'll handle it from here. You just run along, okay?"

The two exchanged knowing looks.

"You gonna back that up, pappy?" one of them said, making a little gesture with his weapon.

The old man seemed unconcerned.

"Oh, I don't know. I imagine we'll come up with something. What do you think, Bird?"

"Sounds about right," came a response from *behind* the commandos as two more bikers stepped out of the trees, each with a hand tucked inside his vest as if reaching for something.

Wait, more of them?

No, those two looked familiar. I glanced around and found two of the Harleys unattended. I don't know what was more impressive—that they'd moved so fast, or that they'd done it completely unnoticed, like ninja bikers.

Surrounded now, the commandos started to fidget and I wasn't sure what they might do next. I hoped it didn't include spraying all of us in a hail of bullets.

"Gentlemen."

One of the other bikers spoke up, his voice soft yet commanding. Clean-shaven except for a little chin fuzz, he wore a watchcap with a flaming skull insignia on the front. And though he wasn't as large as some of the others, something about him said "leader." He just sat there, leaning on his bike with his arms folded across his chest, waiting until he knew he had the mooks' attention before continuing.

"Do the math," he said simply. "Walk away." The two bikers behind them punctuated their leader's words with the ominous sound of something metallic being ratcheted.

The commandos exchanged nervous looks again.

"You win," one of them said. "Keep the bitch. Take turns for all I care." He looked directly at me and gave an ugly grin. "At least we would've done you quick." He mimed putting a bullet in his head.

With that lovely sentiment, the two cautiously backed away into the trees and out of sight. A few beats later one of the bikers—Bird, I think—disappeared after them.

Well, that was interesting.

I exchanged a quick look with JT and saw the same mixture of admiration and confusion. Were these enemies or allies?

Hell, I was more than impressed. I was nervous. But I hid my anxiety behind a tough façade. I leaned in to the older biker.

"You gonna let me go," I whispered, "or do I have to make you?"

Silver Hair cackled at that. He held out his arms to release me, and bowed graciously in doing so.

"As you wish."

I gave a crooked grin. "Thank you, Farm Boy."

That got a laugh from the other bikers, as well as JT. He looked up at his captor.

"How about letting me touch terra firma again, boss?" The hulk obligingly set JT down, giving him a pat on the head as he did so.

Now what?

We sized one another up for a moment or two and then Bird re-emerged from the trees.

"They're leaving, all right," he reported. "Didn't even stop for their wounded." He looked at me with admiration and added, "She really did a number on two of 'em." Then he went back to his bike.

"So what now?" I asked. Because, well, I really wanted to know. Was this the point where things got all rapey?

The leader swung a leg over his bike and put his sunglasses on.

"I guess we get moving." He glanced back at me. "Cabrillo Point, right?"

Whoa. Talk about a kick in the figurative nuts.

"Who *are* you people?"

The leader grinned. "Just passing through, y'know? We were down at the border, visiting friends when the shit went down. We're working our way back home to Tacoma. Then we get a call about a damsel in distress…" He took out his smartphone, keyed in something and held it out to show a picture of me in my zombie fighting gear.

"How… who…" I stopped, totally flummoxed.

"Looks like you've got a guardian angel."

"Who?"

He shrugged. "Someone who knew who we are, and where we were."

"You're military?"

"Ex, most of us. But we stay connected. You never know when there'll be a need." He grinned again. "Sometimes you get the army, and sometimes you get the reserves."

I gave a crooked grin. "And sometimes you get a motorcycle gang?"

"Club," one of the other men corrected. He was older, like Silver Hair, but bigger. "Not a gang. We're a club."

JT raised an eyebrow. "And the difference is?"

"We follow the rules," the leader said. "Most of the time. None of that *Sons of Anarchy* bullshit. No meth, no coke."

"Unless it's diet," another one cackled.

"No guns?" I asked.

"Oh, we carry," the leader said. "Legally. But Cali doesn't recognize out-of-state permits, and none of us are stationed here."

"So you totally bluffed those assholes into backing down?" I looked over at the two bikers who'd snuck around behind them. They grinned at me and one pulled out what looked like a pistol. He cocked the hammer, making that ominous sound again, and flame shot out from the muzzle.

"Let me get this straight," I said. "You faked out a couple of mercs, and now you're gonna get me and JT from here to Cabrillo Point on unprotected bikes through a buttload of zombies, without guns?"

The leader gave me a sly smile. "We may be unarmed now, but that doesn't mean we plan on staying that way. Bear, what did you find?"

The goateed hulk nodded, looking down at a small tablet computer that all but disappeared in his hand. "I've got two hits in the area that might have what we need."

"Heads up," one of the others announced, "we're getting popular." He motioned up the road to where some of the zombies had stopped to look our way. "Better move, and soon."

As the bikers mounted up, I grabbed JT's arm.

"JT…" I swallowed, then forged ahead. "Did you ever find Lil?"

My heart sank when I saw his expression. My throat constricted as I choked back tears I couldn't afford to shed.

"I'm sorry, Ash," he said. "Those assholes ambushed me before I had time to even start looking for her."

I nodded, unable to speak. Who else was I going to lose?

JT put a sympathetic hand on my shoulder. "She might have made it to the zoo."

"Yeah, maybe," I managed.

But I didn't really believe it.

The leader kick-started his bike, and the others followed suit. The engines rumbled deep and low, which was good—they wouldn't attract too much attention, at least no more than necessary. He looked back, and noticed that I was still standing there.

"Waiting for something?"

I sent a silent salute to Aimee and Appel and then gave one last look towards the zoo.

I'm sorry, Lil.

"No," I said, wiping my eyes. "Not any more."

I slid onto the back of his bike.

CHAPTER THIRTY-TWO

The back streets of San Diego were surprisingly dead.

Deserted, that is. There were zombies to be seen, mind you, but at random intervals and mostly easy to ignore. Whatever larger crowds might have been attracted by the sound of our bikes, they never had the chance to get near us. These guys were experts at getting in and out of places quickly and efficiently. Their leader was my current chauffeur.

"Are we anywhere near the bridge to North Island?" I asked, yelling into his ear to be heard above the throaty rumble of the engine. "I mean, there's a naval base there, right?"

"There is," he said with an exaggerated nod. "But if that was an option, your friend would've called them, instead of us. Either the base is no longer viable, or someone thinks they can't be trusted. But then you already knew that, didn't you?"

Damn.

"Just making sure you're not blowing smoke up my ass," I admitted. "Trust doesn't come very easily these days, y'know?"

He laughed. "Yeah, I can't argue with that."

Their club was called Veterans Allegiance, and their names were stitched on their vests amid the other military or patriotic patches. The leader was Dragon, and the silver-haired gentleman who'd groped me earlier was Viper. The two ninjas were Dirty Bird—the one with the beard—and Rooster.

Zilla was the older of the two big dudes, while Bear was the one with the goatee. The last one, Cheeky, had been keeping an eye on the zombies before we'd bailed out of Balboa Park. I'd wondered what he'd done to get the shitty end of the nickname stick, but after he shot me a couple of leering glances, I had a pretty good idea.

We hit a rough patch on the way down the hill, and it hurt like a bitch. With the adrenaline rush gone, I was feeling every bit of that ass-kicking I'd gotten from Sykes. My side hurt with each breath I took, my lips felt like they'd been turned inside out, and my left eye was all but swollen shut. The pounding in my head was the worst, and every bump in the road made it worse.

I wrapped my arms around Dragon's waist, laid my head against his back and closed my eyes, trying to will the pain away. Then we hit a particularly nasty bump in the road, and the pain went away as things went black.

I came to lying on the ground, JT kneeling by my side with an uncharacteristically concerned look on his battered face. The biker named Rooster was there as well, leaning over me as he buttoned my shirt up the front. Which meant my shirt had been unbuttoned at some point between my passing out and waking up.

"What the hell?"

"It's okay, Ash," JT said quickly. "Guy's an army medic, not an asshole. He'll take care of you."

"Gee, thanks, kid," the biker said.

I relaxed, relieved I didn't have to defend my honor when I felt like hammered shit.

Rooster finished buttoning my shirt.

"You have a couple of busted ribs," he said, very matter-of-fact, "but I imagine you already knew that. I wrapped 'em as best I could. It'll feel a little tight at first, but we need to keep them immobilized as much as possible."

He leaned over with a small flashlight and shined it into my eyes once, then twice.

"You may have a slight concussion, as well. But I doubt either one will be giving you a problem for very long. You seem to heal remarkably fast, Ms. Parker. I was gonna stitch up your lips, too, and that split over your cheekbone, but they're already knitting on their own. You oughta tell me how that works."

"It's a long story," I grunted as JT helped me up into a sitting position. I looked around, and saw that we were parked in the middle of what looked like a country lane, with trees and weeds flanking the road. "Where the hell are we?"

"Mission Hills," Rooster said, standing up. "Above the airport. We've found our first target. Time to suit up." He grabbed his med kit and returned to his bike.

The other bikers were suited up and prepared for battle. To a man they'd donned leather chaps and heavy leather jackets with reinforced skid panels in the arms and back, along with equally heavy gloves. They looked like a squad of Arnolds from *Terminator 2*. Zilla had further accessorized with a couple loops of log chain and a fist-sized padlock draped across one shoulder.

JT nudged me and nodded in the biker's direction.

"He'd make a much better Ghost Rider than Nicolas Cage, dontcha think?"

I snorted. "Who wouldn't?" He and Cheeky helped me to my feet and over to the edge of the road, where Dragon was standing with his foot on a guardrail, peering through a pair of binoculars.

Beyond that guardrail the ground dropped away precipitously, so much it made me dizzy just to look. The wall of the canyon was mostly loose rock and scrub, bare in some places and overgrown in others. On our side, the slope was almost vertical. On the other side of the canyon, however, it was terraced in places.

We were looking down on a cul-de-sac of small bungalows that sprouted from the hillside like mushrooms from a stump. I counted six in this particular cluster, all in the same faux-rustic style. Very nice, from the look of it, probably quite pricey.

I borrowed Dragon's binoculars for a closer look. Signs of violence were everywhere—blood spattered on the sidewalks, on the broken windows of cars, running down the side panels. I could make out red drag marks on the stoop of one house. Then I saw an overturned Big Wheel on the sidewalk, and stopped looking.

"That one," Dragon said, directing my attention to the house at the back of the drive. "It belongs to a Richard McCamey. He dabbles in real estate, mostly to cover his backroom gun dealings."

"*Alleged* gun dealings," Rooster interjected.

Dragon gave a derisive snort. "Yeah, the guy's got some hella-good lawyers. But at least he deals in quality stuff. No Lorcins or Hi-Points."

I had no idea what that meant, and decided I didn't care.

"And judging from the quantities he's been moving lately," Dragon continued, "even if he bugged out when things went down, no way he'd have taken everything with him."

I dared another look with the binoculars, careful not to hit the swollen eye.

"Windows are intact, everything's closed up. What if he's still in there?"

Dragon put on his sunglasses and grinned.

"We ask him to share. Nicely, of course." He headed for his bike, and the others followed suit. JT and I started to follow, but Dragon held up a hand. "You two stay here and rest up." I opened my mouth to argue, but he gave me a stern look. "And don't give me no shit about it either. This is our dance."

Silver Hair—Viper—gave Cheeky a smack on the shoulder.

"You stay, too, and keep an eye on 'em. Make sure they stay put."

Cheeky's eyes bugged out of his head cartoon-style, which got quite a laugh from the other bikers.

"Aw, c'mon, Don!" he railed. "That's not fair! How long do I have to keep putting up with this bullshit."

"Until you're not the FNG anymore." The older man laughed. "So get used to it." The rest of the gang started up their bikes, drowning out Cheeky's sputtering tirade as they pulled away and rumbled off down the road. The sound of their engines faded into the distance, rolling around the canyon like echoes of distant thunder.

JT and I went back to the guardrail, watching until we could pick out the bikes on the far side of the canyon, coming up the road to the housing addition, finally turning into the cul-de-sac itself and parking in front of the McCamey house.

There were four or five zombies already in the driveway and others emerged from open doors and around the sides of houses, drawn by the sound of the bikes. Despite this, the bikers shut off their engines and dismounted so casually they might have been going to a barbecue.

Dragon and Viper headed directly for the house, Viper kicking in the front door while the others fanned out across the cul-de-sac and met the dead head-on. I watched and admired.

Rooster was the most explosive, throwing elbows to the forehead that dropped two zeds in their tracks. He finished them off with a steel-toed boot. Dirty Bird favored some sort of wire garrote held between his fists. In one smooth movement he would brush past a zom, loop the wire round its neck, then give the line a pull and watch the head pop off cleanly.

"I want one of those," JT said as he watched Bird in action. "Don't you?"

"No thanks," I said. "I'll stick to my katana."

Or would, if Griff hadn't stolen it.

Bear's approach was less complicated. He used his bulk to bowl down the zombies in his path like ninepins, leaving the actual coup de grâce to Zilla, who used his chain like a steel whip, working the big mace-like padlock on the end and looking like he was having the time of his life. Even with the distance I thought I could hear him laughing.

"Goddammit... it ain't right..." Cheeky muttered under his breath, still sulking at being left out of the action.

"Dude," JT whispered to him, "on your left."

Cheeky and I turned just in time to see two figures round the bend in the road, shuffling toward us—a young black male, barely out of his teens, with an arm missing and rib bones jutting from his torso, and the other so chewed up that its gender and ethnicity were hard to determine. It staggered toward us with an unblinking stare.

Cheeky gave JT a smack on the shoulder.

"I owe ya, man." Then he drew a claw hammer from his belt and headed out with a smile.

"Interesting guy," JT observed.

I nodded. "And so easy to shop for."

We turned back to the battle of the cul-de-sac, but it was already over. There were no more active zoms in sight. As we watched, Dragon and Viper exited the house with several duffle bags, which they strapped to their bikes. Dragon looked up our way and gave a little salute before hopping on his bike and leading the way.

They rejoined us within five minutes, looking pleased with themselves. Viper opened up one of the duffle bags and started handing out handguns and ammo like some sort of Santa on steroids.

"Who wants the 1911s?" he asked. Dragon, Bird and Zilla raised their hands and got two matching guns each. "Rooster, here's your .40 S&Ws. Try not to drop 'em."

Rooster flipped him off amiably, taking his goodies.

Viper continued to rummage in his bag. "Lessee… Bear, here's your .44 magnum, but you say 'make my day' one more time, and I'm switching it out for a water pistol."

Bear waited until he had the guns firmly in hand before growling, "Make my day," in a very respectable Dirty Harry impersonation.

"Got anything in that black bag for me?" Cheeky asked hopefully.

Viper grinned again. "Would a Kel-Tec shotgun make you click your heels, Dorothy?"

"There's no place like home, goddammit!" Cheeky took the shotgun, looking as happy as Ralphie had been getting his official Red Ryder.

It's the little things in life, y'know?

Dragon cocked his head to one side. "Miss Parker, you have much experience with pistols?"

I gestured to my empty holster. "This used to contain a Ruger."

He nodded and handed me a canvas shoulder pouch.

"There's two Glocks in there with plenty of ammo. You shouldn't have any problems—nine mil is pretty low recoil, and there's no outside controls to mess with. The safety's in the trigger. Just don't touch it till you want to shoot something."

Schweet…

He handed JT a similar bag and then turned back to me as if in an afterthought.

"Oh, yeah, one more thing. Turns out McCamey was a bit of a collector. Had some nice, high-priced items in there." He went back to his bike and fished something out of one of the other bags, pulling out a highly polished katana and scabbard. "I understand you like to play with these. It ain't no Hattori Hanzo, but it'll do, dontcha think?" I stared wordlessly as he slid the blade back in its scabbard and set it in my hands.

It was way beyond the utilitarian blade I'd lost—like

comparing a print to an original work of art. I was so stunned I could only manage a half-assed stammer by way of thanks, but I think he got the message.

"Let's ride, people." Dragon strode back to his bike.

"Hey!" I said suddenly. He stopped and turned back to me. "What about McCamey? Was he in there?"

Dragon grinned. "Part of him was."

An anxious sea of Japanese sararimen and office ladies eyed the morning commuter train hungrily as it pulled into Kawasaki Station. When its doors slid open they rushed inside like samurai storming a castle. It took 3.75 seconds for the train to fill to capacity, and then the neatly uniformed, white-gloved station attendants nicknamed oshiya—"pushers"—began to politely shove additional commuters into the car, until no physical space remained, and the train sped on toward downtown Tokyo.

Another minor ocean of commuters lay in wait at Shinagawa Station as the same train pulled up, seven minutes and fifty-six seconds later. The train squealed to an ear-piercing stop and as the doors opened, the screech of the brakes was matched by the screams on the platform as the train disgorged a red, ragged tsunami wave of freshly-minted undead...

On Rapa Nui, the most remote island left on earth, Rano and Tikaroa picked their way among the tide pools, fishing spears in hand as they hunted for eels, sea snails, and crabs. On the cliffs above them, a line of monolithic heads stared balefully out upon the Pacific.

Rano failed in his pursuit of a little rock octopus, swearing colorfully in Spanish as it escaped, darting into open water. He shook his head as he watched it go. Another movement caught his eye further out in the waves. A dark spot moving slowly toward shore. Maybe a marine turtle?

A face broke through the waves, then, as impossible as it

seemed, a man's entire head. Rano held up a hand to shade his eyes, making sure what he saw wasn't a trick of the sun's strong reflection. But there was indeed a man coming up from out of the ocean. He wore a Chilean sailor's uniform, but Rano couldn't see any ship on the horizon.

"Tika?" he said softly. "There's a man walking in from the sea."

His brother didn't look up, still fixated on his own prey in the water below.

A moment later, a second figure surfaced, then a third. And then another.

"Que milagro," Rano murmured.

The boy hurried down the beach to greet them.

On an isolated stretch of the so-called demilitarized zone between North and South Korea, the situation had been building, until it had reached the breaking point. In his office at the border station, Republic of Korea Commander Kyo hung up the phone receiver and looked up at his subordinates.

"It's happening. Here. Now." As if on cue, sounds of gunfire erupted outside, startling the hardened soldiers. It was coming from the line. From the North. Of course.

At his command, the ROK troops scrambled from the barracks to join their fellows already at the border. But the firefight wasn't what they were expecting. Their own men were at their regular positions, simply staring at the DPRK troops in disbelief. The North Koreans were indeed engaged in a full-on firefight—but against their own troops; a moaning, shambling, advancing horde of North Korean soldiers, thousands of them, all torn and bloodied, all dead.

"Cease fire!" the Northern captain barked. He turned and marched alone up to within arm's reach of the checkpoint gate, halted and saluted to Kyo. "I formally request political asylum for myself and my unit."

Kyo approached the fence, stopping at the same distance as his counterpart.

"What you request is impossible."

The North Korean officer furrowed his brow and tried again. "We are prepared to immediately surrender our weapons."

Kyo shook his head.

"Keep them—you'll need them."

The North Korean gave up any further pretense at protocol or formality. He lunged for the fence, grabbing it with both hands and pressing his face hard against the chain links. He stared directly into Kyo's eyes, his voice low and desperate.

"Please—we're dead if you don't."

Kyo was struck by how much the Northerner resembled him—they could be cousins, or brothers. He closed in and leaned hard into the fence himself, so that the two men were nearly head to head.

"You don't understand—we can't..." His voice cracked. "They're coming for us, too." Kyo turned and pointed behind him, to the south, where from out of the mists, another army of dead soldiers was advancing toward them.

In Detroit, firefighters responding to a factory fire were shocked to see a ring of charred and smoldering bodies emerging slowly from out of the flames, moving to surround them...

During a Sunday morning Holy Mass with seminarians and novices in St. Peter's Basilica, the visibly ill Pope faltered while elevating the Host. He dropped the body of Christ and suddenly turned on the Cardinal-bishop of Ostia, tearing out his throat before biting three members of the Swiss Guard who rushed to his aid.

An armed standoff between gangsters and the Metropolitan Police Service, following a botched bank robbery in London's East End, was unexpectedly resolved when a fresh swarm overran the neighborhood, causing criminals and police to join forces.

CHAPTER THIRTY-THREE

We left the Mission Hills area and came down out of the canyons, back into the emptiness of a city holding its breath. I wondered how many people were still hiding in the shadows, holed up behind closed doors and boarded-up windows. How long they'd be able to hold out without help.

I knew it wouldn't be long enough.

I was riding with Rooster this time, a San Diego native who knew his way around the city without the help of Siri or Google Maps. JT was perched behind Zilla.

We made it to the Pacific Highway and found long sections of road improbably empty and easy to navigate. The interchanges, however, were snarled with the same kind of metal log-jam we'd encountered in San Francisco, forcing us back onto surface streets to avoid the wreckage and clusters of zombies.

Along the way, the zombies provided us a chance to do some target practicing with our new toys. I decided I liked the Glocks. They were just as shootable as Dragon had promised. And from the back of the bike, I could fire with both hands at the same time. How cool was that?

We entered a light industrial area with lots of warehouses and a maze of narrow streets, parking lots, back alleys, and chain-link fences. Rooster slowed noticeably, keeping the engine quieter with a low throttle. The other bikers peeled off one by one, heading off down different streets.

I leaned forward and tapped him on the shoulder.

"What's up?"

"They're checking out the area," he said over the low rumble of his bike. Then he eased his bike to a stop in front of a chained gate with a sign reading "Sidd's Auto Repair and Detailing." Zilla and JT pulled up next to us, the rest of the club joining us shortly thereafter.

Beyond the gate was a small shop set into the corner of a much larger metal warehouse, one wall lined with eight garage doors.

"See that double-fenced area in the back, with the razor wire on top?" I nodded as he continued. "They rent that area out to the local police as an impound lot." He grinned. "Pretty fucking ingenious. I mean, if you want to hide something, do it with the police in plain view. Who's gonna think twice about it?"

"So these Sidd's guys are dealing guns, too?" JT asked.

Rooster shook his head. "Nah. This is a terror cell. Or at least the seeds for one."

My jaw dropped.

"In San Diego? Are you sure? Who is it?"

He shrugged. "Heck if I know. Take your pick. Christian zealots, Muslim extremists, maybe people who like to graze their cattle on government land."

Viper laughed. "We've got it all, darlin'. Iranians, Albanians, Pomeranians…"

"Do you think they're still in there?" JT shielded his eyes, looking for movement in the locked business compound.

"Nah," Rooster said. "Revolutionaries aren't the bravest bunch. If they survived, they bugged out long ago. Let's just hope they left some stuff behind."

Dragon shut off his engine and dismounted, and the others followed suit, looking around warily.

"It's nice and open here," Dragon said. "If we can get

back outside quick enough, we've got several avenues available." He paused as a low moan drifted down the street. Several blocks away a lone figure had staggered into the middle of the lane and looked our way.

"Ms. Parker," Dragon said without looking at me, "do you think you and your friend can hold the gate for us? We're gonna see a lot more company than we did in Mission Hills."

"No problem," I said. "This is what I do." I glanced at JT. "What *we* do, I should say."

"Damn straight." JT cracked his knuckles and flashed his manic grin.

"I'll stay with them." Cheeky gave me a nod, racking the pump on his stubby Kel-Tec. "We'll hold the line, no problem. Just get it done so we can get out of here."

Bird was already at the gate, where he quickly picked the lock and unwound the heavy chain holding it shut. The gate swung wide open and the bikers drove through, leaving me, JT, and Cheeky to hold the fort.

There were now three zombies up the street, both moaning and staggering our way. Cheeky scratched one cheek thoughtfully.

"How are either of you at distance shooting?" he asked. "I can hose 'em once they get up close, but maybe we should keep 'em thinned out, dontcha think?"

"Good plan," I agreed. I drew one of my Glocks and took a nice wide stance, trying to remember everything Gabriel and Nathan had taught me as I aimed and fired.

Nothing.

Damn. I missed my M4 and even more, I missed Gabriel and his sharpshooting abilities. Hell, I just missed Gabriel.

The zoms were still a block away, so I raised the muzzle a little more and fired again. One of them twitched when the round hit a shoulder. *Ah, better.* Another adjustment, another round fired. This time the head jerked to the side and the figure crumpled to the ground.

JT nodded, took out his own Glock and mimicked my stance. He fired just once. A second figure took one or two more steps, and then dropped in its tracks.

"Nobody likes a show-off," I muttered.

Attracted by the ruckus, more walking dead emerged from a doorway on the right side of the street, and another crawled out from behind a parked car on the left. I knew how quickly the odds could shift against us, and got down to business. The Glocks barked with precision, and more bodies littered the street. But even as JT and I put them down, more seemed to come out of the woodwork.

Cheeky was going to get his chance to get up close and personal.

Gunfire rang out from behind us, somewhere in back of the warehouses. I hoped it was our guys, and not some crazy terror cell.

I dropped another magazine and reloaded, drew my second gun and began firing with both hands now, feeling like some badass in a John Woo movie. Both JT and I hit our targets with decent regularity, but some slipped past our fire, growing close enough for Cheeky to cut them to shreds with his shotgun.

More and more flowed in from all directions, however—their numbers continuing to grow. Cheeky had to stop and reload his shotgun, and in the time that took we suddenly found a dozen zombies less than ten feet away.

"Shit," I said, backing up toward the gate. I took down one of the closest with a shot to the head, but it was becoming obvious that we were going to have to retreat behind the gate, or become entrees on the buffet.

Then I heard the low rumble of an engine behind me, followed by the roar of an automatic weapon a split second later. It was so close that my eardrums felt like they were bleeding, as the front line of zombies shredded before my eyes.

I looked behind me to find Zilla sitting astride his bike, a large belt-fed machine gun balanced across the handlebars, blasting away. The rest of the bikers, similarly armed, joined in the fun with a devastating barrage, reminding me of the scene in *Predator* when all the testosterone-drenched soldiers defoliated a section of jungle.

The gunfire stopped suddenly, leaving a ringing in my ears.

"Get on!" someone shouted, although it sounded far away.

I didn't have to think twice. I jumped on behind the nearest biker, who turned out to be Bird. At the same time JT hopped behind Zilla, and then we were roaring out into the street past a forest of groping hands, somehow making it through to a clear stretch of road, burning our way through the industrial district until we'd made it back to the Pacific Highway.

Heading west, we reached a nice open stretch, no zombies in sight, and eased to a stop, parking in the middle of the passing lane. A quick head count confirmed that everyone had made it out alive and unscathed.

Damn, these guys were good.

"So," I said wryly. "Do we have any ammo left? Or did we just burn through everything you guys snagged?"

"Not hardly," Bear said. He motioned to a bunch of ammo boxes strapped to his bike. "I don't know who was backing those turds, but they were well stocked. Check this out..." He pulled back a tarp on the far side of his bike to show a case labeled "Airtronic RPG-7," whatever that meant. "It comes with its own rocket-propelled grenades," Bear said, as proud as if he'd given birth to the thing. "Sweet, huh?"

"Errrr... sure," I said, trying to match his enthusiasm and failing miserably. "It's a honey." I walked over to one of the machine guns. "These look like fun."

"Don't bother, kiddo," Rooster said. "That thing probably weighs more than you do."

"Oh yeah?" Thus challenged, I flashed him a grin and hefted it one-handed.

He gave a snort. "I stand corrected," he said.

I held it up for a closer look, trying to ignore a painful twinge in my ribs.

"Shee-it," Cheeky said. "Remind me not to arm-wrestle you, sweetheart."

Normally I'd deliver a smackdown for the "sweetheart," but all things considered, I decided to let it slide.

Ouch. My ribs gave another, more painful twinge.

I put the monster down—I didn't want them to know just how much I still hurt.

Viper strode over and handed me a short assault-style rifle, very much like my old M4.

"Baby sister, this is for you." He winked and added, "Those other things, they're for us."

I raised an eyebrow. "What? Are you guys gonna start a war or something?"

"Not a war," Dragon answered. "But a distraction? Definitely. It worked for you in Balboa Park, didn't it? But I think you're gonna need a little more than organ music this time."

I heaved a sigh.

"Listen, I appreciate the thought, guys, I really do. But you don't know what you're getting into. Hell, I hardly know what *I'm* getting into, at this point. I don't know how to get there, or get inside once I *do* get there."

"Well," Dragon said, "for starters, we know that there's more to Cabrillo Point than what's in the National Park brochures. We'll assume that whoever's holed up there is gonna have some firepower, and that you'll need help getting past that."

"As to how you're gonna get inside—" Rooster dismounted and sauntered over to me. "—we might be able to help you with that." Pulling out a smartphone, he punched in a code, displaying the same photo of me that Dragon had shown at Balboa Park. "When we got the call to come look for you, we got this photo and an encrypted file, as well. This was inside."

The screen changed to a schematic of some sort.

"Far as we can tell, it's a floor plan to the facility you're looking for." He fiddled with the phone and zoomed in on part of the screen. "The best way to break in is already marked out." He held the phone out.

I stared at him, then took the phone. This was just too convenient. I could almost see the words "It's a trap!" in big neon letters, blazing above my head. And yet, what other options did I have? I made my decision.

"This diversion—what exactly do you have in mind?"

"Oh, I don't know," Dragon mused. "Knocking on the front door always seems to work pretty well. But let's not get ahead of ourselves. First things first."

"And that would be?"

He grinned. "We've gotta find you a boat, so you can go kill Bill."

CHAPTER THIRTY-FOUR

"We're gonna need a bigger boat."

JT looked a little green around the gills as our rubber craft lurched up over another swell.

"Farewell and adieu… ye fair Spanish bikers," I intoned, slightly off key. JT shut his eyes, as if in pain, and leaned back against the inflated rim.

We'd snagged a *Zodiac* rubber raiding craft at the San Diego Yacht Club—the Veterans Allegiance seemed to have a source for everything a girl could want. I'd driven some speedboats up at my parents' place in Lake County, so operating the thing wasn't as much an issue as it could have been. But it didn't make for the smoothest of rides.

"Just make sure when you near the point," Dragon had said, "you cut the engine and use the oars. We don't know what kind of surveillance they'll have where you're going in. Better safe than sorry, right?"

Right.

I felt surprisingly good, all things considered, enjoying the mist of salt spray on my skin, but then my injuries were healing up faster than JT's. And while he hadn't sustained nearly as nasty a beating as I had, he'd spent enough time as a punching bag that I wasn't surprised he was feeling a bit punk. He also was not a fan of open water. Even Super Parkour Man had his phobias.

I thoughtfully resisted the urge to start humming the theme from *Jaws*.

"You want some painkillers?" I asked.

"Nah. Just get me to dry land, and give me some three-story buildings to play on—then I'll be fine."

I grinned and kept steering us toward the Point. Dragon had pulled up a fancy map program on his phone, with a satellite view of the installation. I'm pretty sure it wasn't legal. He'd shown me exactly where my point of entry would be.

So I was scanning the shore, despite the fact that it was late afternoon, and we were losing the light with every passing minute. To make it more fun, a fog had come in that could give San Francisco a run for its money, and the bay was surprisingly choppy—it looked like a storm was coming in off the ocean.

San Diego Bay was a regular obstacle course as various craft just drifted aimlessly in the water, bobbing all around in the swells, moving with the current, and apparently abandoned. I saw a few boats with random blood smears, and more than one undead mariner on board.

Other boats were manned by the living, all headed out towards the open sea. Some of the people were armed, but luckily no one seemed interested in messing with us. At least not yet.

"So how did you get into the leaping tall buildings at a single bound stuff?"

JT gave a faint grin.

"Parkour? It seemed like a natural progression from the circus."

"You were studying to be a clown?" I raised an eyebrow.

JT snorted. "Hardly. I fucking hate clowns. Mimes, too. Nope, I was into high wire and trapeze. I was going to that school across the street from Golden Gate Park, right next to G's apartment complex. You remember?"

I nodded. We'd passed it on the way into UCSF.

"Anyway, I was dicking around one day, doing the

Donald O'Connor run up the wall routine, and someone asked if I'd tried free running. I looked into it, and I've never looked back."

He stopped as we hit a particularly large swell, and I began to edge toward the shore.

"What's the plan when we get there?" JT sat upright now, looking a little more lively now that the possibility of dry land was in his near future.

"Dragon and the boys are going to create a diversion, to give us an opportunity to sneak in. He said when we got close that we should wait for the signal."

"What's the signal?"

"He said we'd know it when we heard it." I grinned. "Big badaboom."

As we motored along the shoreline, closing in on the position, I could see a trail curving up from the water line. There were no signs of zombies, which was both a relief and a worry. A relief in that we'd have a break from fighting our way through them, and a worry because it meant someone else had cleared them out. Whoever had done that, they weren't likely to be friendly.

A sudden *whupwhupwhup* of helicopter rotors made both of us shoot panicked looks skyward. A black whirlybird flew in our direction, coming from somewhere on the Point.

"No reason for them to look at us, right?" JT said nervously. "It's not like we're the only boat on the water."

"No, but we're probably the only people dressed like SWAT ninjas in a military sneaky snake stealth boat."

JT winced. "Good point."

The helicopter flew overhead. I resisted the temptation to look up.

"These are *not* the droids you're looking for," JT muttered. I would have laughed if I hadn't been holding my breath.

Then the helicopter swung past us, heading further out over the bay. My breath whooshed out in a sigh of relief.

"Looks like they didn't see us."

With the kind of timing that usually only happens in Michael Bay movies, the helicopter turned and headed back in our direction. A man in black leaned out of the open door, tracking us with his rifle.

"Shit, shit, shit!"

"We could swim for it," JT said.

"With all the gear we've got on?" I shook my head. "We'd sink as soon as we'd hit the water."

We were so screwed.

Then the helicopter exploded.

JT slammed into me, knocking me face down in the bottom of the boat and covering me with his body as bits and pieces of flaming metal—and possibly body parts—rained down around us. By some miracle, none of them hit us, or the boat.

Yup, definitely a Michael Bay film.

We both raised our heads and stared at the still-flaming debris littering the surface around us. As if on cue, more explosions came from the Point, and the sound of gunfire.

Team America, fuck yeah.

JT cocked his head to one side.

"I'm gonna go out on a limb and say that that's our signal."

I made a noise that was a cross between a laugh and a sob.

"Can't stop the signal, Mal."

CHAPTER THIRTY-FIVE

Seals lolled about on both the sandy beach and the rocks, seemingly immune to the carnage in the bay. Several snapped and barked as we came aground, but none seemed motivated to do more than galumph a few feet out of the way. Good thing 'cause being foiled by seals at this point would've been downright embarrassing.

JT and I hopped out of the boat and dragged it further up onto the sand, further annoying the local seal population. We grabbed the goody bags Viper had given us and made sure our weapons were locked and loaded. I touched the hilt of my new katana just to reassure myself that it was still there. What did it say about me that I couldn't wait to try it out?

I kept it sheathed, though, opting to carry one of the Glocks. I figured if we did run into trouble, it was more likely to be the kind toting firearms, and I'd yet to figure out how to parry bullets. JT had a Glock, as well. I don't know how much target practice he'd logged, but I trusted him to get the hell out of the way and let me take point.

The light was fading fast as we climbed the rocks, trekking about fifty or so feet to a dirt trail that—according to the schematics—led up to the Cabrillo Point lighthouse. We didn't need or want to go that far, though. Our destination was only a short distance up the trail, to one of the old gun escarpments.

"Look for tracks," I said softly as we jogged up the path. JT had regained some of his usual ebullience, and there was a distinct spring in his step now that he was back on terra firma. He wasn't quite as Tigger bouncy-trouncy as usual, but a nature trail wasn't exactly the best place for free running.

We rounded a bend and found ourselves in front of a pair of pitted metal doors set into the hillside itself, tracks running out from under them. Back during WWII, a big damn gun had been rolled out on these tracks to help defend San Diego from the possibility of invasion by sea. Although to my shady knowledge of history, San Diego had never actually been invaded.

"This is it," I said quietly. I pulled on one of the metal handles set into the doors and was rewarded by a surprisingly squeak-free movement as it opened toward me, revealing the dark tunnel beyond.

JT peeked inside.

"Got a flashlight?"

"I don't need one."

JT shot me an exasperated look.

"It's great that you're all that and a bag of super-powered chips, miss wild card. But some of us can't see in the dark. Guess I'll just have to follow you and feel my way along."

I raised an eyebrow.

"Remind me to keep you and Cheeky separated in the future. How about you just put a hand on my shoulder?"

"I'll take what I can get." He put his left hand on my right shoulder, and we cautiously entered the tunnel, following the tracks, boots crunching softly on the gravel.

The temperature dropped a good ten degrees once we got more than a few feet in, a little more than uncomfortably chilly. There was a little ambient light from what remained of daylight, revealing that whatever had been mounted inside was long gone, leaving just the empty tracks and a low-hanging ceiling hewed out of the rocks and fortified with cement.

"Creepy," JT said. I had to agree with him, although it was also cool in an old haunted-mine sort of way. Under normal circumstances—without the possibility of running into armed enemies—I might have enjoyed exploring it.

The further we went, the darker it got—it wasn't exactly pitch black in the tunnel, but it was close. JT's hand stayed firmly on my shoulder as I led us slowly down the tunnel, the rock ceiling dipping uncomfortably low in places. I ducked under a particularly low-hanging outcropping.

"Watch your—"

"Shit!"

I winced at the meaty thwack sound JT's head had made colliding with the outcropping.

"—head," I finished lamely.

"Yeah, thanks for that. As a seeing eye wild card you need work." After a few more minutes of slow progress, he asked, "Do we know where this ends up?"

"As far as I could tell from the schematic, this should lead to the lower level of the facility," I said. "It wasn't clear on what it was we'd find there, though."

"No handy dandy map to the dungeons?"

"I think they call them 'holding chambers' these days."

"Well, la-di-fucking-dah."

We both laughed, then immediately stopped as the sound echoed up and down the tunnel, bouncing off the walls.

Just as the silence returned, a low, ominous rumble shook the tunnel. Little pieces of rock crumbled off the walls, hitting the ground with small clattering sounds. I was suddenly very aware of just how old this place was, and how easy it would be for the whole thing to collapse.

"Earthquake?"

"Or the boys having more fun," I said. "Either way, let's keep moving."

As we moved further along, both the temperature and the angle of the ground rose a little bit. We reached a bend, the tunnel curving sharply to the left. Here it became more of a corridor, the rock walls giving way to cement, dim lights flickering from weak bulbs enclosed in little metal cages, spaced out at regular intervals along the ceiling. It wasn't much, but enough that JT could navigate on his own.

Neither of us spoke as we continued along. The odds of running into someone increased with each step we took, and the element of surprise was pretty much the only thing we had going for us.

After another ten minutes or so, the corridor came to an abrupt end. It dead-ended into another metal door painted the same dull gray as the walls, rounded rivets bordering the edges and a wheel in the middle, like something you'd see on a battleship.

JT took hold of it, muttering, "Leftie loosie, righty tighty," and gave it a yank to the left. Sure enough, the wheel creaked reluctantly, but it turned. When it stopped, he pushed the door open a few inches.

The creak made me wince. We waited for a minute, listening for the sounds of footsteps or voices, but heard nothing.

Good.

JT gave the door another push, wide enough to peek through the gap into yet another corridor. Another few inches and I stepped cautiously through, leading with my Glock… just in case.

This corridor stretched off left and right about fifty feet on either side before making sharp L-turns going in the same direction. The floor was dusty, as if it hadn't seen any use in a while. JT and I looked at each other dubiously.

"We'll make better time if we separate," I said, my voice low. "Just try and stay out of sight, and if you see anyone from our team, get them out back through the tunnel."

JT shook his head. "Splitting up's a bad idea."

"I think it's worth the risk," I argued quietly. "We need to get them out of here as quickly as possible."

"But if we separate, you won't have backup."

I bristled. "Neither will you."

He shrugged. "I usually don't need it. Last time was an exception."

"Hey, the only reason I got caught was because they used you as bait."

"And I'm truly sorry for that, but I'm not gonna let myself get caught off guard again."

I held his gaze. "Neither am I."

He nodded slowly. "Fair enough. But if you do need me... holler." He looked around appraisingly. "I think I can get some speed going in this place. I'll take left, you take right?"

"Sounds good." I started off down the hall, then stopped and turned back. "JT... no twerking."

"I promise nothing."

He flashed his manic grin and vanished in the opposite direction.

CHAPTER THIRTY-SIX

When I reached the corner, I took it cautiously, Glock leading the way. This hallway was empty, too, but there were metal doors spaced out every ten feet or so. The doors had small windows with bars set into them, like old-fashioned prison cells. About a hundred feet down, the hall turned yet another corner.

How big is this place?

I moved slowly and quietly, pausing to peer into the cells. Each had a utilitarian cot, but other than that, they were empty. As I neared the next turn in the hallway, I heard something, and stopped short. Then I inched up to the turn, heart hammering my chest so loudly it almost drowned out the voices coming from a cell around the corner. Stealing a glance, I saw a door about twenty feet away. It was partially open, and I could smell the hot copper odor of fresh blood, along with the sharp tang of sweat and unwashed flesh.

"Sooo good. Fresh and tasty."

"Please... stop. No more." The voice was so twisted with pain, I couldn't tell if it was a man or a woman.

"Shhh... just relax. It's just a little piece."

"Nononononononooo!" The rising wail of agony in that cry got me moving again. Switching the Glock to my left hand, I unsheathed the katana and crept toward the cell. Whoever was inside was far too occupied to hear me approach. They also didn't hear my horrified intake of breath when I reached the door and looked.

The room was splattered with gore, looking like a modern art major had taken a can of red paint and Jackson Pollocked the place. Several dead and naked bodies, missing large amounts of flesh, lay in one corner, crumpled as if tossed aside. The smell they gave off was truly foul.

Two more people, also stripped of clothing, were strapped to cots by their wrists and ankles, more restraining straps around their waists, necks, and across the thighs. Both were bleeding from gaping wounds all over their bodies. I recognized them both—Carl and Red Shirt. Carl was dead, his eyes staring sightlessly off into the distance, a frozen scream testifying to the horror and pain of his death.

Red Shirt was still alive, screaming in agony as someone slowly and methodically carved a piece of flesh from her thigh with a wicked sharp blade, the kind my dad used to gut fish.

That someone was Jake, a man who had been bitten and then trapped in a cabin with his wife and daughter during the outbreak in Redwood Grove. Like Gabriel, he was a half-deader, which meant he was partially immune to the virus, but still needed to eat human flesh in order to stay alive. His sanity went on permanent vacation after he'd eaten his wife and child.

I wanted to feel sorry for him. He hadn't asked to be turned into a monster. But something about him repulsed me on a visceral level. There was no fixing that kind of crazy.

Jake had the same placid smile on his face he'd had when we'd caught up to him in a swank cabin above Redwood Grove. He'd lost all concept of right or wrong, and was feeding off of several women, only one of whom made it out alive. He'd gone missing during the fire that nearly killed Simone, and most of me had hoped he'd died.

Red Shirt's scream broke in the middle, dissolving into gulping, hopeless sobs.

I gripped my katana with my right hand and pushed the door further open with my left so I could slip inside. One quick cut and it would be over.

I froze as Jake suddenly turned. His gaze fell on the door and slipped past it as he held out the piece of flesh to someone out of my sight line.

"Want a bite?"

"No," the unseen speaker said, voice so low and guttural that at first I couldn't identify it.

"Awww, come on! You have to eat, right? And she's sooooo fresh and tasty!" The cajoling in Jake's voice was horrible, a parody of a mother trying to get a fussy child to eat its vegetables. He wiggled the thing, blood dripping between his fingers. "It's wa-ah-fer-thin!"

"Get that the fuck away from me!"

My heart stopped.

Jake giggled and tossed the divot of flesh toward the speaker. It landed with a splat on the ground, right in front of a pair of black combat boots, the type that I wore... that all of our team wore. There was a metal cuff around one ankle, attached to a chain.

Oh no no no no... please no.

My gaze traveled slowly up those boots to unwashed black BDUs crusted in gore and dirt, then to a black thermal, equally filthy. Slowly, reluctantly, I forced myself to look at the hollow-cheeked, jaundiced face above the shirt—denim-blue eyes sunken into the sockets. His mint-gold hair was lank and dull against his scalp. His wrists were shackled against the wall.

"Gabriel?"

I said his name before I could stop myself.

Both of them looked at me, Gabriel's head snapping around so quickly I could hear his neck crack. The horror in his eyes broke my heart.

"Oh my god, Gabriel..."

"Hey!" Jake's smile widened with genuine pleasure, like a host greeting a new guest to his party. "Ashley, right? You're here for dinner, and right on time!" He approached me, bloody hand outstretched.

I extended the point of the katana toward him.

"You want to back the fuck away, Jake."

He shrugged and stopped.

"Sure, whatever. Just hurry up or it'll get cold." He grinned over at Red Shirt, still sobbing hopelessly as she lay there, waiting for more pain and death. "Don't want it to get cold, right?"

Giving him as wide a berth as possible, I cautiously stepped further into the abattoir and moved toward Gabriel, my heart pounding in my ears.

"Stay away from me," he rasped.

"I'm here to get you out," I said as gently and calmly as I could under the circumstances.

"Just get out of here." His voice became a thick growl, somehow less than human. The smell of sweat and despair rose from his body.

"Gabriel…"

"No!" He shook his head fiercely.

"I'm here to help, Gabriel."

"*No!*"

I held out my free hand pleadingly, my focus on the man I was pretty sure I loved.

Bad mistake.

Jake barreled into me, knocking me sideways into the wall. My head hit the concrete with a dull crack. The last thing I heard was Gabriel yelling my name as the lights went out.

CHAPTER THIRTY-SEVEN

"I'm sorry… so sorry."

A voice whispered in my ear as my consciousness tried to swim up to the surface against a tide of pain and dizziness.

"I'm so sorry, Ash… so sorry."

My eyes fluttered open as I recognized Gabriel's voice. His face was right above mine, looking blessedly normal.

I smiled up at him through the throbbing in my skull.

"Sorry… so sorry."

Why are you sorry? I wanted to ask, but I couldn't get my voice to work. I couldn't move my arms or legs either.

Something shiny moved into my line of sight. A sharp blade, glinting in the fluorescent lights.

Gabriel looked down at me sadly. "I'm really sorry… so sorry…"

He lowered the knife and sliced into my forearm.

I jerked awake just as the knife bit into my flesh, the pain excruciating. A scream ripped through my throat. The blade cut deeper, then leveled out, oh so slowly moving down my arm until it finally dipped up and out, taking a piece of me with it. I felt the warmth of my own blood running out of the wound, cold air stinging the raw meat left behind.

"Sorry, so sorry," a voice whispered.

Not Gabriel, my pain-fogged mind told me. *Thank god...*

Jake crouched next to me, tears streaming down his face as he shoved the piece of me into his mouth, rocking back and forth and muttering the same words he'd said when I'd found him eating the remains of his wife and child.

I tried to sit up, but as in my dream, I couldn't move my arms and legs. They were secured tightly to one of the cots, another strap around my waist making sure I wasn't going anywhere. I also became aware that my Kevlar armor was gone, as were the rest of my clothes.

Naked, tied to a cot and being snacked on by a crazy man. My day had officially reached its nadir.

I thrashed for a moment, the metal frame creaking loudly as I tried to wriggle out of it, but Jake—crazy as he was—had done the job well. Maybe if I wasn't so sick and dizzy with pain I could have broken at least one of the restraints, but for now I wasn't going anywhere.

Jake abruptly stopped rocking and a smile curved his mouth, the tears drying up as if he'd turned off an internal faucet. He turned and crooked a finger in a "come here" gesture.

"Your turn," he said brightly.

"Fuck off."

If I craned my head, I could see Gabriel a few feet away from the foot of my cot, hands bunched into fists as he glared at Jake. If it was possible, he looked even worse than he had before Jake had bushwhacked me. Sweat poured down his face, and his body shook as if racked with chills.

"Don't be stupid." Jake frowned. "You need to eat, and this one's even better than the last. She didn't have much staying power. But this one—" he patted my bare thigh, "she's really tasty."

I suddenly realized Red Shirt's sobs had stopped. Turning my head to the side, I saw the cot on which she was lying, still strapped down, and most certainly dead.

"I will fucking *kill* you, you crazy son of a bitch!" I thrashed against the restraints again, rocking the entire cot back and forth in my effort to get free.

Jake grinned down at me.

"And she's stronger, too. She'll stay fresh for a *long* time." He slid the blade into my skin again, the other arm this time, slicing through skin, fat, and some muscle, taking his time.

I will not scream, I will not scream, I will not scream...

I screamed.

"Stop it, God damn you!"

Chains rattled as Gabriel lunged toward him, only to be brought up short by his shackles. He grunted in pain as the metal dug into his wrists and ankle.

Jake shook his head sadly.

"You need to stop that. You'll hurt yourself."

"Stop hurting her," Gabriel growled.

Jake sighed. "Look. I've told you. They don't feel it. They're not like us." He punched the knife tip in and out of my left thigh so quickly I didn't register the pain until a few seconds after he'd withdrawn it.

Then it hurt like hell. I managed to hold back all but a small whimper.

"I will kill you, you son of a bitch..."

Jake giggled. "Sure! Maybe a piece of you will go down the wrong pipe. It could happen." He held up the last filet of Ashley he'd sliced off, and let it slide down his throat like an oyster. His eyes closed in bliss.

"Seriously, Gabe, this is quality meat here."

The knife dipped down toward my stomach.

This can't be happening, I thought. I did not survive all the shit the world had thrown at me, just to end up as steak tartare for a nut job.

Then that sharp blade cut into me an inch or two to the left of my naval. The pain was excruciating. I didn't even try and hold back the screams. They were the only release I had.

When Jake finished with his latest slice, he cocked his head in Gabriel's direction.

"Seriously. You need to eat. They told me to get you to eat. And if you *don't* eat, that means no more fresh meat for me, unless I find it myself." He looked down at me with what I can only describe as a fond expression. "It was really nice of you to find me instead, Ashley. That's probably going to make you my favorite meal ever."

"If I eat… will you let her go?" Gabriel got to his feet slowly.

"Gabriel, no!" The words wrenched themselves from my throat, which was already raw from screaming.

"You want me to let her go?" Jake looked at him indignantly. "I mean… are you crazy? That last one was plain old ahi. *This* one is *otoro*. You just… seriously, check it out."

Jake slowly approached Gabriel, holding out the strip of flesh he'd just carved from my stomach, like someone trying to tempt a feral cat.

"Just smell this," Jake whispered. "Soooo good."

He held it up to Gabriel's nose.

I watched as Gabriel, almost against his will, inhaled. His eyes shut for a moment, his expression that of a connoisseur smelling a particularly good wine.

Jake smiled happily. "I know, right?"

Then he stepped just a little bit closer.

"Now you gotta taste it."

Jake brought my flesh up to Gabriel's mouth and touched it to his lips, all the while talking in a singsong voice, as if to a child, "Tasty tasty tasty treat, open up, it's fun to eat!"

He rubbed the meat—I had to think of it that way, or I'd go crazy—around Gabriel's mouth, smearing blood on his lips and chin. Gabriel jerked his head to one side, then the other. His hands strained against the metal holding him to the wall. Jake giggled and then popped the piece of flesh into Gabriel's mouth.

No no no…

Gabriel's mouth went slack. His tongue crept out to taste the blood. His eyes opened, blazing with a feral desire that terrified me.

Spit it out, I thought. *Oh god, please spit it out...*

Gabriel swallowed.

"Good, huh?"

Jake and I both watched the rapturous expression on Gabriel's face as he savored the taste sensation of human flesh. It might have been my imagination, but I could have sworn his color improved almost immediately.

"More." Gabriel looked at Jake, then over at me. The feral hunger in his eyes terrified me. Blood and saliva trickled from the sides of his mouth. "I want more."

Jake beamed. "Sure! Hang on, I'll throw another shrimp on the barbie." He raised the knife and headed back in my direction.

"No." Gabriel licked his lips again. "I want... I want to do it myself."

Jake looked as though he was going to cry, a proud father watching his son catch his first big fish.

"Sure. Okay!" Pulling a key out of a blood-encrusted jeans pocket, he eagerly unlocked the shackles holding Gabriel's arms to the wall. They fell off his wrists with a metallic clank. He then handed Gabriel the key so he could undo the ankle shackle himself.

He did so clumsily, rubbing his wrists to restore circulation.

I wondered how long he'd been chained up in here with Jake trying to change his diet from vegan to cannibal. It didn't take him long to recover his balance, and he moved with terrifying purpose across the room to where I lay strapped on to the cot.

Jake dipped a finger into the raw wound he'd just inflicted and popped the tip into his mouth, licking the blood with a rapturous expression. Then he set the knife on top of my bare and bloody stomach, grinned and stepped away with a little bow.

"You're never gonna want to go back after this."

I gazed pleadingly up at Gabriel as he put both hands on my thighs, running them up to my hips, his eyes glazed with a lust that had nothing to do with sex and yet everything to do with my naked flesh. He leaned down and nuzzled the curve of my neck, inhaling deeply.

"Oh, Ash," he said thickly, "you smell so nice…"

And my brains are spicy. The thought bubbled up out of nowhere and I gave a choked laugh that turned into a sob. Tears trickled from my eyes as Gabriel continued to touch me in an obscene parody of a lover's embrace. He ran his tongue down to my collarbone, nipping softly at my skin as he continued along my right arm to the wound in my forearm. He gave a small groan of ecstasy as he very gently licked the blood dripping in rivulets.

"Gabriel… you don't want to do this," I whispered.

"Shhhh…" He put a finger up to my mouth, rubbing the ball of his thumb along my jawline. His other hand wandered back down to my stomach, where it found the waiting knife. His fingers curled around the handle, then tightened.

My insides churned as he lifted it, looking from the blade to me as if deciding where to cut first.

"Hurry up," Jake urged. "I'm hungry!"

"Shut up," Gabriel snapped. "I don't want to rush this." He placed the blade against the front of my right thigh, the edge resting lightly against my skin. I tried not to anticipate how much it would hurt when he cut into me, but despite my efforts to control my fear, my breath came in increasingly shallow gasps as I began to hyperventilate.

I gave an involuntary shriek of pain as the blade suddenly bit into me.

Jake giggled.

"Nice one! It's great when they're still lively, right?"

Gabriel nodded as he sliced the blade just a little bit deeper. I gasped at the white-hot agony, trying not to scream again if only to deny Jake that satisfaction. He stepped in closer, hovering behind Gabriel's shoulder, craning his neck to get a good look.

"Come on already," he begged, practically dancing up and down as strings of drool dribbled from his mouth to his chin. "I'm ready for filet mignon!"

Gabriel gave a smile absolutely devoid of humor before his face hardened and he growled.

"Here you go."

He turned and plunged the knife into Jake's stomach.

CHAPTER THIRTY-EIGHT

Jake's eyes went wide with shock. He held out one hand, the other clutching the wound as blood spurted out between his fingers. His breath left him in a drawn-out exhale that reminded me of Romero in *Escape from New York*. Which was kind of ironic since I'd always thought that was just bad method acting.

He crumpled to his knees, staring up at Gabriel with an expression of total betrayal. Gabriel smiled and, in a move so quick I could barely follow it, slashed the blade along Jake's throat. Then he turned back to me and sliced the same blade through the restraints holding my wrists and ankles. Dropping the knife on my chest, he strode over to a pile of clothes against one wall. Scooping them up, he tossed them next to the cot, my boots tumbling to one side and landing with a quiet thud on the concrete.

I struggled to a sitting position and swung my legs over the edge of the cot. The blood rushed to my head and I fought the inevitable wave of nausea that seemed to be a daily occurrence for me these days.

"Is… is there any water?" It hurt to talk. I felt like someone had taken a grater to my throat. I tasted blood where I'd bitten the inside of my mouth to try to stop the screams.

"Get dressed and get out of here, Ash." He wiped one

hand across his mouth, then again, as if trying to scrub something away.

"Gabriel, what—" I reached for my clothes, trying to untangle pants from the shirt. Pieces of Kevlar fell out of the bundle, along with my underwear. My skin crawled with the thought that Jake had touched them, pulled them off of my unconscious form. If I'd had my choice, I'd have burned them on the spot. But since I didn't particularly want to run around naked, I opted to buck up and get over it.

Gritting my teeth, I pulled on the underwear, then shoved my legs into the BDUs, hissing in pain as the pants scraped against the cut on my thigh and the open wound on my stomach. Shirt and Kevlar followed, fabric sinking into the wounds on my forearms. Oh, it hurt like a son of a bitch—I might as well have lit a match and shoved the flame in there.

"Here." Gabriel dumped my weapons on the cot next to me, then retreated to the far side of the room, watching me.

As I pulled my socks on and laced the boots, I stared up at him, a mixture of hope and fear rising in my chest. His color definitely looked better and the madness, that horrible hunger, was gone from his eyes.

Gabriel—my Gabriel—was back. I got to my feet and started toward him. He shot his hand up to stop me, his expression fierce.

"Stay away from me."

"Gabriel, I've been through hell to find you," I said, trying to control my hurt. Don't I at least get a hug?" My attempt at a joking tone failed miserably. All I managed was to sound totally pathetic.

He shook his head, violently this time.

"You need to stay back, Ash."

"Why?"

"They've been trying to get me to eat human flesh ever since they brought me here," he said. "Bastard wouldn't let me take any more antiserum. I'm…" He stopped, swallowed. "I've been so hungry, Ash. I could feel the disease spreading through me. Knew what I'd become if I didn't give in."

He paused, shut his eyes for a moment.

"I couldn't watch Jake torture you," he said softly. "He would have eaten you alive, bit by bit, and I would have had to watch. The only way I could stop him was to let him think I'd given in. Make him believe I'd join him. And the only thing that would convince him was taking that first bite."

His eyes reopened, raw hunger shining from them. I forced myself not to flinch and stayed where I was. He licked his lips, an unconscious and disturbing gesture.

"It took everything I had not to cut another piece out of you."

"But you didn't," I said. I held his gaze, even though it took everything I had not to recoil in horror. "You controlled it. That has to count for something."

His expression flashed between revulsion and desire as he replied with a whisper. "I can still taste you."

This is so the wrong place to hear him say that.

"You can control this, Gabriel. You can be cured. Simone and Dr. Albert helped you before, and there's no reason to believe they can't do something for you now." I was rewarded with a sliver of hope in his eyes. It wasn't much, but it was better than the bleak despair. "So come with me."

I reached out to him. He started to reach back… but then his hand dropped to his side, the despair returning. Gabriel shook his head slowly, back and forth without stopping.

"Ash, you need to leave now."

"Fine," I said shortly. "You're coming with me."

The head-shaking became almost violent.

"I can't!"

Enough is enough. I strode forward and grabbed him

by the shirt, trying not to grimace at the feel of crusted filth on the fabric.

"You are going with me," I growled, staring up into those hunger-glazed eyes. "I need you. The rest of the team needs you. And stop shaking your head!" Something snapped inside and I slammed him against the wall hard enough to cause his head to snap back and hit the concrete.

Rage joined the hunger in his eyes. Growling, he reached for me with both hands. I knocked them out of the way and punched him in the jaw once, then again, setting my knuckles on fire with pain and leaving him momentarily dazed. I took a few steps back and waited, poised to defend myself and wallop the shit out of him if necessary.

Gabriel stepped forward, stumbled, and then regained his balance. He looked at me, his expression wiped clean of anything but rueful admiration.

"Damn. That hurts," he said, rubbing his jaw with one hand.

"Good," I snapped. "I need you to focus. We have to get our people out of here, and I can't do it alone. So you need to pull yourself together and control this shit! And then maybe—just maybe—Simone can help you!"

He heaved a long drawn-out sigh, his back straightening.

"Okay. What the hell are our people doing here?"

"You didn't know?"

"No. I've been stuck in here the last few days with—" He gave a terse nod toward Jake's corpse.

Which was now moving.

"Son of a bitch," I muttered. I grabbed my katana off the cot. Jake, now a full-fledged zombie instead of a half-dead crazy pants cannibal, lurched to his feet and gave a plaintive moan as he saw me. I drew my sword and cut his head off in one smooth move. Very *Yojimbo* versus *El Zombiachi*.

As I geared up, sheathing the katana and pulling out

the two Glocks, I gave Gabriel a brief rundown of events since he'd been kidnapped. I gave a Glock to Gabriel, along with some spare clips, and kept the other one in hand. His face tightened in pain when I told him about losing Mack and the Gunsy twins, but he kept quiet until I'd finished.

Then all he said was, "Let's go."

CHAPTER THIRTY-NINE

We left the room, Gabriel in front. He peered cautiously around the corner first, moving unsteadily—a stark contrast to his normal confident and competent grace. I wondered how long it had been since he'd had a real meal and decided not to ask.

"Any ideas where they'd be?" I asked quietly as we moved down the corridor in the direction I'd been heading.

"I only saw a little of the layout when they brought us here," Gabriel answered just as quietly. "Dr. Albert and I were separated pretty much right from the start. They let him take some blood samples, but then they put me in a little cell by myself. That bastard tried to convince me it was my duty as a patriot to join them. Wanted me to be like him."

His face tightened with disgust.

"I told him no fucking way. Spit in his face." He gave a little laugh. "That's when he had them put me in with Jake."

"Who?" I asked. "Who put you in with Jake? Who wanted you to be like him?"

"Same bastard who had us kidnapped."

"We've been trying to figure out who the hell that is since they ambushed us at UCSF."

Gabriel stopped in his tracks so suddenly that I ran into him. He turned, putting his hands on my shoulders as he stared down at me.

"You don't know?"

I shook my head wordlessly.

Gabriel opened his mouth to answer, but froze when we heard the distinctive *ch-chak* sound of rounds being cycled into chambers.

A door was open down the hallway behind us, and a half dozen armed men in black paramilitary gear stepped out, all with their weapons aimed our way. Even worse, I recognized two of them as the ones who'd been chased off by the biker boys.

Shit.

We both raised our hands without being told. I didn't even lift my Glock. We were outnumbered and out-armed.

The two men from the park stepped forward, snatching the Glocks out of our hands. One took my blades out of their sheaths and tossed them to the ground with a clatter. Then they pushed us in front of them.

I felt the barrel of a rifle nudging my back.

"Not necessary," I said in measured tones.

"Totally necessary, bitch," the one behind me said. He poked the barrel into my back again, harder this time. "Go on. Try something. I'd love to get some payback for Sykes and Jacobs." He did it again, hard enough to leave a bruise. Gabriel growled softly under his breath, a low rumble that only my ears picked up. Silently willing him to stay calm, I took a deep breath and kept walking.

Now is not the time

They marched us through the doors at the end of the corridor, which led into an octagonal-shaped room that looked for all the world like a cross between the lobby for an '80s doctor's office, and a men's club. Dark leather couches and chairs were combined with metal and glass tables. Silver-framed Nagel and Olivia prints warred with fox hunting scenes framed in wood on dove-gray walls.

People in uniform, civvies, lab coats, and more mooks in black paramilitary garb hurried back and forth across the room, vanishing through other doors with an air of barely contained panic.

Good.

We crossed the lobby to a set of dark wood-panel doors. One of the paramilitary assholes rapped hard. After a beat, the doors opened inward, and Gabriel and I were escorted into a space more like a conference room, though dimly lit. Thanks to my wild card vision I didn't have any trouble seeing details.

A long wooden conference table occupied the middle, surrounded by cushy Aeron chairs, some of them occupied. Multiple video screens ringed the walls, with a large one dominating the room at the far end. Some of the screens—including the large one—were dark, but many of them were live, and a couple were manned. As far as I could tell at a glance, about half showed various points of the facility, both inside and out.

I recognized the lighthouse, as well as the visitor's center. Another screen showed the guard's gatehouse and main entrance to the park, zombies crowded up against the lock gates, hands reaching through the bars. Smoke was rising from various locations, and there were a lot of armed soldiers looking really pissed off.

No doubt the work of my very own cuddly sons of anarchy. The boys were nowhere to be seen, though, and I hoped that meant they were just out of sight, and not out of commission.

One screen provided an interior view of the cell Gabriel and I had just escaped. Which meant these assholes had watched while Jake carved slices from living, screaming people—myself included. Another showed a lab and, unless I was mistaken, the backside of Dr. Albert, ginger hair and all. Yet another showed a cell with a single occupant sleeping soundly under a mound of covers, no distinguishing features visible. None of them appeared to show a view of the tunnel JT and I had come through, or the corridor where we'd separated.

Which meant JT might still be free and clear.

I finally dragged my gaze from the screens to the people sitting at the table, a baker's dozen or so. I recognized most of them, having seen them on the news or *The Daily Show*. One had been a well-known presidential candidate—hell, I'd voted for him. Mostly men, a mix of politicians, industry movers and shakers, and even a popular talk show host who looked as though someone had poured buckets of mashed potatoes into a suit and called it a man. There was a female politician, as well, known for her firebrand speeches and crazy eyes.

The entire group stared at Gabriel and me. I tried not to look at Crazy Eyes. Frankly, she creeped me out.

They crossed all of the lines between political parties, ideological groups, and even religions. I stared back at them, trying to soak in the fact that these people were the brains and money behind Walker's. Finally I just shook my head.

"You have got to be kidding me. You people nearly took our country over the fiscal cliff because you couldn't agree on a national budget, but you can cross the friggin' aisle to launch a zombie apocalypse?" I shot a look at Crazy Eyes. "You don't even *believe* in vaccinations. So what the fuck, people?"

The talk show host sputtered in wordless indignation, reminding me of a walrus without the cute factor, while Crazy Eyes and the rest broke out into indignant, chaotic babbling. One voice, however, managed to cut through the rest—a deep, almost harsh male voice that sounded horribly familiar.

"Well, well, Miss Parker," he said. "Still ready with the smart-ass quips, I see." The voice came from a chair at the far end of the table, one of those tall-backed "king of the boardroom" numbers, its back and occupant facing the other direction.

"And still disrespectful of your betters." The chair spun, and its occupant swung into view.

Oh, crap.

CHAPTER FORTY

Adrenaline coursed through me and my heart pounded in my ears as I stared at General Heald, the iron-jawed, craggy faced asshole most likely to be played by Charlton Heston in the movie.

He had tried to blackmail me into joining the DZN by threatening my boyfriend with vivisection. His plan had backfired when he'd become infected—through nobody's fault but his own, but that didn't stop him from blaming me.

His presence explained a lot.

"*You're* a wild card?"

"Not quite, Miss Parker." He picked something out of a dish on the table, holding it up as if contemplating it. But he really just wanted me to get a good look at it. It was a human finger.

Heald was a half-deader.

I am well and truly screwed.

He grinned at me, a truly unpleasant expression that had humor in it, but the type of humor bullies show to someone they think is weaker than them.

"What? Nothing to say?" he asked.

I stared at him, fists clenched.

"What do you want me to say?" I managed to keep my voice calm—refusing to give him the satisfaction of showing fear.

"Honestly?" he said. "I just want you to die." He shook his

head in mock bewilderment. "But that's been far more difficult to accomplish than I would have thought. You're either very lucky, or part cockroach. Too bad you're not a patriot."

"Oh, fuck you, Goldfinger," I shot back. "We've been saving lives the entire time—no matter what shit was thrown against us. My team and I stopped the first outbreak. That's what you wanted us to do in the first place, wasn't it?"

"You know, General," the presidential candidate said, rising out of his chair, "I think Miss Parker deserves an explanation. As she said, she's been fighting for our country, and yet she doesn't understand the big picture."

"I voted for you," I said, apropos of nothing. "Right now, I am seriously regretting that decision."

He nodded solemnly. "I can see why you might be upset."

I didn't even try to suppress my snort of derision. He continued anyway.

"Our environment is suffering," he said earnestly. "Humanity has lost its ability to coexist with Gaia—"

Gaia? Give me a break.

"—and our population far exceeds the available resources. The planet is being corrupted to the brink of destruction. Entire species are going extinct, and our polar icecaps are melting."

A few of the group nodded their agreement, while others frowned or looked bored. Maybe the ideological lines hadn't blurred as much as I'd assumed. Guess unleashing the zombocalypse wouldn't have them joining hands and singing "Kumbaya."

"Without something radical to reduce our population," he continued, his voice rich and confident, "we were looking at global famine. Something had to be done, or we'd face pure anarchy—not in the distant future, but within our lifetimes." He paused, looking at me as if for agreement.

"So you thought the best way to save the world was to unleash the walking dead," I replied. "*Riiight*... Makes perfect sense."

Heald made a growling noise that caused the hair to

rise on the back of my neck, but my former candidate of choice held up his hand.

"Let me continue." He took a step toward me. "You're with the *Dolofonoitou Zontanous Nekrous*. You know that this virus—or whatever it is—has been around for centuries. Had nature been allowed to run its proper course, this could have happened on its own. And if it hadn't been zombies, it would have been another super bug, resistant to antibiotics. Mother Nature isn't kind, Miss Parker."

"Maybe not," I snapped, "but you people have turned her into a homicidal psychopath."

He sighed and shook his head.

"Look. You just don't understand. Resources are limited. After the world's population is managed—"

"A very polite way to describe genocide," I interjected.

His jaw tightened, but he continued doggedly.

"—we can then manage these resources. Distribute them fairly and insure everyone has what they need."

"Naturally you folks will be the ones who decide what's fair." I didn't bother trying to hide my disgust.

"Not only us," the talk show host interjected. I was surprised it had taken so long for him to weigh in. He wasn't big on letting other people talk. "We're just the first group, and the most organized. Then again, we are Americans." He stuck his chest out with pride, a patriotic puffer pigeon. I grimaced and turned back to my former favorite politician.

"How, exactly, do you intend to guarantee that you and your special buddies aren't going to get sick like everyone else? In case you missed the memo, this shit has gone airborne!"

He bristled. "We weren't expecting it to mutate so quickly, if at all, which is why it's so important that we develop the cure."

"Oh, give me a—" I stopped, and shook my head in disgust. "Seriously, did you ever consider that it might be better to develop a cure *before* you set this thing loose?

And why the hell did someone try to burn down the lab at Big Red? What do you think Professor Fraser and Dr. Albert were working on?"

"Dr. Albert and his original lab partner, Dr. Arkin, have more than enough data to develop the cure," Heald said coldly. "They'll do their jobs as long as they're provided with what they need. Professor Fraser, on the other hand?" He shook his head. "She can't be trusted."

"Yeah, she's got a pesky little thing called a conscience."

"Exactly. She's only alive now because we need as many wild cards as possible, to provide a broad spectrum of blood samples." The general eyed me with distaste. "I thought he could do without yours."

"You go to—"

Suddenly the doors opened to admit a bunch of familiar figures, all under armed escort.

"Simone!" I said. The exclamation burst out of me, my relief getting the better of me. Gentry grinned, while Tony made a surreptitious Chang Sing hand salute, which I returned. Nathan gave me a nod, and Simone's face brightened visibly when she saw me with Gabriel.

"Ashley, how—"

"Time enough later for a reunion," Heald interrupted. "It's time to…"

Then Griff sauntered in as if he owned the place.

Heald's voice faded into the background as my vision clouded with red, the entire world shrinking down to the man who'd betrayed us.

I lunged for him, but before I got more than a couple of steps, my guard slammed the stock of his rifle against my back, clubbing me to the floor on my hands and knees. There was a rumble of protest from my teammates, Nathan letting loose with an impressive string of epitaphs.

I gave a low growl and delivered a vicious donkey kick to the side of the guard's right kneecap, the resulting popping sound and scream of pain bringing a smile to my face. I followed up with a foot sweep, knocking his legs out from under him. I'd have leapt on top of him and punched his face in if several pairs of hands hadn't seized me from behind, and dragged me to my feet.

They pulled my arms back until I thought they'd pop out of their sockets. The man I'd injured held his knee and glared up at me, involuntary tears of pain running down his face.

"Bitch!"

I smiled down at him despite the pain.

"Totally necessary."

Then I turned my attention back to Griff, who leaned nonchalantly against the wall a few feet away from me, his expression unreadable as he looked straight at me.

"I am so going to kill you," I promised.

Heald gave a bark of laughter.

"Tell me again why you saved her life?" He shook his head in disgust. Then he picked up something from next to his chair, and tossed it on the table with a loud clatter.

My katana. The one I'd been using since Redwood Grove.

My expression must have given away my confusion, because Heald laughed again.

"Our friend here showed me this as proof that you'd been killed." He looked at Griff with irritation. "I should have known better than to take you at your word when a pretty woman is involved. Always thinking with your dick. That's what got you in trouble in the first place."

Griff gave a small smile.

"Hey, it's not often that I get to sleep with someone who won't die if the condom breaks."

Um. Euww?

"You were supposed to kill her." Heald glared at him.

"Messing with her head was one thing," Griff replied. "But killing her? Not down with that. Besides," he added with a shrug, "I like her."

Heald leaned forward and glared.

"All you had to do is what you *love* to do—be a good little vector, and spread the virus." Simone looked up sharply at that, staring at Griff as Heald continued,

"There's something appropriately Biblical about the sins of the flesh leading to the consumption of the flesh. But you couldn't even accomplish that."

"Guess I fucked up," Griff replied calmly. He shrugged. "I don't like doing someone else's dirty work."

Heald gestured to Gabriel.

"You're almost as much a disappointment as Captain Drake here. And both of you falling short of your duties because of this—" He looked at me with utter contempt. "—this *worthless* little whore."

I ignored him and continued to give Griff the death stare.

"So you're the one who sold us out, and got all those innocent people killed at the Organ Pavilion."

Griff's eyes flashed with an indefinable emotion.

"No, my job was easy. I was supposed to mess with your head, keep you off balance so you couldn't do your job. I did that. Then I was supposed to kill you, or at least make sure you died." He shrugged again. "I didn't."

"You're trying to tell me you didn't rat us out?"

Heald started chuckling from his seat at the end of the table.

"No, Miss Parker. Griff didn't 'rat you out.' That honor goes to someone else entirely." He turned and addressed someone behind him. "Sarah, if you'd be so kind? And make sure to turn the speaker up."

"Yes, sir."

An attractive young black woman in dress uniform emerged from the shadows behind Heald's chair, went over to a control console, and tapped away on the keyboard.

"Now that, *Miss* Parker, is someone who knows her place as a woman, and her duty as a patriot," he said, smiling broadly as a face appeared on the large screen, pink hair clashing with a bright red T-shirt.

I didn't bother with a snappy retort.

Holy shit...

I heard Simone's gasp of shocked disbelief.

"Jamie?"

CHAPTER FORTY-ONE

Jamie's expression brightened visibly when she heard Simone's voice.

"Simone? Is that you?"

"Y... yes, Jamie. I'm here."

"You're safe then! Ashley got you out!"

"What?" Heald sat up in his chair.

Jamie ignored him. "Ash, you there?"

"Um... over here. I'd wave, but..." The man holding me tightened his grip.

Jamie looked in my direction and beamed.

"You got the schematics!"

I stared in disbelief. "Um... yeah, I did."

"Awesome!" Jamie smiled. "You're getting Simone out of there, right?"

"Well—" I looked at Simone, who seemed to be in a state of shock.

"What the hell is going on?" Heald looked as if he might burst a blood vessel, his voice cutting through the room like a butcher knife.

Jamie looked at him and frowned.

"You told me she'd be safe. After the fire, you said if I fed you info, you'd leave Simone alone." Her voice went hard. "Well, you lied, didn't you? You didn't think I'd find out that you'd brought the 'copter down?" Jamie shook her head. "It's a good thing I didn't know they'd switched helicopters." Her expression suddenly shifted to genuine hurt, and she looked toward Simone. "Simone... Why didn't you tell me about that? Don't you trust me?"

Oh, fuck me gently with a chainsaw. She's a bunny boiler.

Simone looked as though she wanted to weep, but she composed herself before she replied.

"I didn't know myself, Jamie," she said. "Nathan arranged it."

Jamie nodded. "Got it," she said, as if everything suddenly made sense.

"We had an agreement!" Heald roared. The others sitting around the table looked at him with varying degrees of distaste.

"You broke it when you tried to bring the 'copter down," Jamie replied coldly. "I feed you info, you leave Professor Fraser alone. Pretty simple, right? You were supposed to leave her alone when you raided the pavilion. You didn't. So I sent Ash in to take care of things."

Heald slammed his fists on the tabletop in a move so sudden and violent it made everyone jump, myself included.

"It's always you, isn't it, Miss Parker?" He glared at me with a hatred that burned. "*You* did this to me!" With one hand, he swept the dish off the table. It shattered against a wall, barely missing a prominent televangelist. Bits of meat scattered, and blood dribbled down the wall to the ground.

Heald got to his feet. The room was silent as he stalked over to where Gabriel and I stood. He planted himself right in front of me, practically nose to nose as he spoke in a quiet tone much scarier than his ranting.

"Maybe I should thank you for my change of diet," he said, his breath rank with the smell of partially digested carrion. "And for my change of perspective." He smiled. "Darwin had it right. Nature decides in the long run. The sheep are meant to be ruled by the wolves. And the wolves decide who is worthy to be kept in the herd."

I'd had enough.

"Oh, for crissake, you couldn't just go beat a drum in the woods somewhere?"

His hand cracked across my face, hard. I tasted blood and Gabriel made a lunge in his direction. Hands seized him before he could do any damage.

"And you," Heald looked at Gabriel with a mixture of disappointment and disgust. "You were a good soldier. One of the best. But you're weak."

"Why?" I glared at Heald. "Because he wouldn't switch diets?"

Heald smiled. "Oh, he did. But only to save you. And you, Miss Parker, aren't worth the price he'll have to pay."

"What do you mean?"

"Look at him." He gestured toward Gabriel, whose skin had yellowed again, beads of sweat popping out on his brow as if he was a junkie in need of a fix. "He's tasted it. If he doesn't eat more, he'll continue to rot inside."

Gabriel flinched at his words.

"You're lying," I said hotly.

"Am I?" Heald's smile broadened. "His body craves human flesh now, because it knows what will keep him alive, from turning into a walking pus bag. He saved you, but not himself. One of these days he won't be able to stop himself."

"He's right, Ash." Gabriel's voice was raspy, almost broken.

"No, he's not!" I struggled against the hands holding me, wanting nothing more than to touch him, make him believe me by sheer force of will.

"Damn straight I'm right!" Heald turned back to Gabriel. "You *will* kill her one day, soldier. Make no mistake about that. There's no turning back now."

"We don't know that!" Simone's voice cut sharply through the room.

"He's always responded to the antiserum," she continued. "That means there is still a chance of stopping the progression."

Heald tilted his head to one side as if considering her words.

"Too bad we'll never know."

With that he drew a pistol holstered at his side, aimed it at Simone and pulled the trigger. A hole appeared in her chest and she reeled back with a surprised "oh!" before crumpling to the ground. Nathan gave an inarticulate yell and knelt by her side as a banshee wail of pain emanated from the speakers.

The room was silent with shock. Even Crazy Eyes looked horrified, and Heald's aide Sarah looked at him as if he'd suddenly sprouted two heads. Jamie stared down at the scene, mouth open, expression beyond aghast.

Heald lowered his sidearm and looked up at the screen.

"And fuck you too, you little traitor!"

Jamie fixed Heald with a deadly stare, even as tears streamed down her face.

"You shouldn't have done that," she said.

The screen went black.

CHAPTER FORTY-TWO

The shit hit the fan.

As the cabal at the table started muttering amongst themselves, the sound of a not-too-distant explosion caught everyone's attention. Then, Crazy Eyes pointed at one of the screens, and we all watched as a trail of light arced into the gates at the park entrance, still crowded with the undead.

Another muted explosion went off and the gates blew apart, along with some of the zombies. There were plenty more behind them, though, and those started pouring in past the gatehouse, overwhelming the stunned soldiers who'd been guarding it.

A soldier, a young kid who still sported adolescent acne on his chin and forehead, stuck his head into the room.

"Sir, those damn bikers are back! They've blown the gates and the zeds are coming in! There are hundreds of them, sir!" This was enough to bring the occupants of the table to their feet in a panic. The former candidate grabbed Heald by one arm.

"We need to evacuate!"

Heald shook him off impatiently.

"We're safe down here."

The man shook his head.

"We need to get out of here while we still can. Those things are going to overrun the place and if we don't move now, we won't be able to get to the helicopters!"

The others agreed, and they all began pushing their way toward the doors. But Heald crossed the room ahead of them, and stood in their way.

"I'm telling you, you're safe in here," he snapped. "If you go out there, you'll only get in the way while my men are trying to do their jobs."

"You're the only one who'll be safe if those things get in here," the talk-show celeb replied, pushing his way past Heald and out the doors. He was closely followed by several of his compatriots.

"He's right," Crazy Eyes yelled. "You're safe 'cause those godless creatures can tell you're halfway to being one of them. You're a freak of nature!"

Heald's eyes narrowed.

"You're all sheep," he said contemptuously. "Go ahead, leave. The wolves will bring you down soon enough. And I don't need you anymore."

At that moment, another soldier, this one in black commando garb and a visor pulled down over his head, shoved his way into the room, holding someone by the scruff of her shirt.

"Caught this one wandering the halls, sir!"

My head snapped in the direction of the voice just as its owner shoved his prisoner forward, her face obscured by a thick fall of brown hair. Almost afraid to breathe, I looked over at Griff, who gave a little nod.

"Lil!"

She looked up, those wide green eyes flashing fire from behind the curtain of hair as she saw me. I couldn't tell if she was happy or pissed off, but it didn't matter. The soldier shoved her away from him, and both of them pulled out pistols. They began to fire around the room. Bullets ricocheted off the walls and blew out video screens.

Members of the cabal gave panicked screams and scattered in all directions. The resulting chaos made it almost too easy for me to bring my heel hard down the instep of the guard who was holding me, yank my arms out of his grip, and hurl him against the wall with enough force to stun him. The men holding Gabriel released him to go for their weapons, but he turned on them with a feral snarl and smashed their heads together with an ugly cracking sound.

Tony and Gentry easily disarmed and incapacitated their guards. Gentry snagged one of the firearms and proceeded to calmly take out anyone wearing a uniform, while JT stripped off his disguising helmet and hurled it with unerring accuracy at the guy whose knee I'd dislocated. The asshole was pulling his pistol, and the helmet bounced off his wrist, giving me time to deliver another kick—this one to his jaw.

Say goodnight, Gracie.

I dashed over to Nathan, still crouched down by Simone. He'd stripped off his black T-shirt, exposing a network of scars over his back and torso, and was using it as compression against Simone's wound, trying to stop the bleeding.

"Nathan?" I couldn't bring myself to ask.

"Still alive," he answered without looking at me. "We need to get her out of here."

"Copter?"

He shook his head. "They'll be overrun in no time, if they aren't already."

I looked up at the screens that hadn't been shot out. Nathan was right. Most of the outside was already crawling with the walking dead. I saw several of the cabal members running across a parking lot, headed toward a helicopter, only to be pulled down by zombies converging from all sides.

On another screen, the talk show host pounded on the glass doors of the gift shop, zombies approaching him from behind. Frightened people stared from the inside while he was torn to pieces, his blood splattering the doors as rotting fists started hammering and pushing on the glass. The doors gave way as I watched.

On yet another screen, people pushed to get on board a pair of helicopters, rotors already spinning. Crazy Eyes was one of them, clawing with as much vigor as a hungry zombie to get to the front of the throng and climb up into one of the aircraft. She made it inside just before soldiers started shoving people back.

The helicopters rose into the sky.

It was slaughter, pure and simple, but I couldn't bring myself to feel sorry for any of the people caught in the carnage. They'd drawn a really fucked up line in the sand, and chosen the wrong side.

"Ash, look out!"

I looked up in time to see Gentry smash a rifle stock against the jaw of a soldier preparing to shoot me from across the room. His finger pressed the trigger as he was hit, and the shot went wild, hitting Heald's aide Sarah. She dropped without a sound, the shot a perfect bulls-eye in the center of her forehead.

Heald looked at his fallen aide, his expression one of shock. Then he swiveled his head in my direction, the grief wiped out by homicidal rage.

"You!" he hissed, a world of hate in that one word. "I should have shot you like a dog before you got lucky and survived the infection. Would have saved me a shitload of trouble."

He raised his pistol and took aim.

"At least I can fix that."

I dove to the side as he fired, the wind of the bullet whistling by my ear. I hit the ground hard, the impact forcing my breath out of my lungs. I rolled over onto my back and found myself staring down the barrel of Heald's pistol. I saw my death in that black hole and in Heald's eyes.

"Good riddance, Miss Parker," he said, and he pulled the trigger.

CHAPTER FORTY-THREE

As Heald's gun went off with a sharp crack, a snarling figure tackled him from the side, propelling him into the table with bone-crunching impact and making the shot go wild. Gabriel's hands wrapped around Heald's throat, smashing the back of his head into the table once, twice and—

Another sharp report echoed in the room. I scrambled to my feet in time to see Gabriel stiffen and then slump over Heald, his grip loosening and then slipping from the general's throat.

Oh, god, no.

Heald grunted and shoved Gabriel's limp body off of his own. My eyes widened in horror as I saw blood seeping out from a hole in Gabriel's stomach, the edges of his shirt scorched around the point of entry.

"Oh, no…" I whispered.

Heald whirled toward me and pulled the trigger again. I spun so that the bullet grazed my left arm, the Kevlar arm guard stopping it from hitting flesh. With my right arm, I grabbed my katana from the table where Heald had tossed it. I brought the edge down on his wrist and chopped right through skin, bone, and sinew. The gun flew to the side with a clatter. His hand fell to the floor with an anticlimatic plop.

Heald howled with pain, blood spurting from his wrist.

"You bi—"

I cut off his last word by cutting off his head.

My entire world narrowed down to Gabriel, who lay on the table in a spreading pool. Tossing my katana next to him, I knelt beside him as blood pumped out of the wound, welling up with each heartbeat.

"Don't move," I commanded, looking for something to use as a compress. "We'll get you to Dr. Albert. He'll fix—"

Gabriel turned his head and looked at me with those denim-blue eyes. He gave a little smile, reached out with one hand toward my face. The hand dropped as he gave one last wavering sigh.

And then… everything stopped.

The sounds of gunfire and screams faded out as I stared at Gabriel's lifeless face, his eyes staring blankly up at nothing, his features relaxed, all the tension and strain leached out of them.

Death cannot stop true love, I thought. *All it can do is delay it for a while…*

I stayed at his side, one hand resting on top of his, the other smoothing the hair back from his forehead. Someone came up to me and said my name. I ignored them as I stared down at Gabriel's beautiful, peaceful face, waiting for him to wake up and talk to me. I didn't care if he was an asshole, either. He could rag on me for being late to class, or whatever he wanted, as long as he woke up.

As long as he wasn't really gone.

"Ash…"

Gabriel's hand twitched beneath mine.

"Shhh!" I waved them back. "Wait."

I continued to stroke Gabriel's hair as his hand twitched again, his fingers intertwining with mine.

Then his head turned and he stared at me with the milky-white, soulless gaze of the walking dead. His mouth opened and he reached out to pull me down toward that gaping maw, his grip tightening implacably around my fingers.

I shut my eyes and gave a long shuddering breath, an eerie echo of Gabriel's last moment. Then I picked up my katana in a reverse grip and brought the point down into his right eye.

And that was it.

I stood up slowly, an icy numbness spreading from inside my chest to the rest of me. I felt hollow, the world suddenly distant and unimportant. I heard noises, people saying my name, but I didn't care. They didn't matter. Nothing mattered any more. Everything I'd fought for was gone.

"Ash," someone repeated, "we have to get out of here. Place has been breached."

I felt a hand on my shoulder. I turned to see JT standing next to me, Lil at his side. I looked around the room to see that the only people still standing were the wild cards, including Griff. Nathan had Simone cradled in his arms. Everyone else was unconscious, dead, or gone.

Something buzzed in one of my vest pockets. I fumbled for a moment and then pulled out Rooster's smartphone.

Hey, little sister. Time to go. Meet us at North Island.

Viper.

I slowly came back to life and looked at JT.

"We need to get everyone out of here the way we came in," I said.

Simone's eyes fluttered open and she whispered something that only Nathan heard. He looked up.

"We need to get Dr. Albert, and as many blood samples as we can."

JT nodded. "I saw the lab on my way here. We'll hit it on our way out."

Simone whispered something else. Nathan's expression tightened and he turned his head toward Griff.

"I don't like it… but she says you need to go with us."

Griff shrugged.

"Got nowhere else to go."

Nobody looked happy about it, but no one argued either. I was too numb to care. I followed my team through the now empty lobby as the familiar unsteady gait of the living dead could be heard shuffling through the halls.

We hit the lab, and retrieved Dr. Albert, whose main response was irritation at the interruption of his research. From there, JT traced the way back to the tunnel, and then let someone else with better night vision take the lead until we emerged onto the trail.

Zombies were stumbling down the path from above. Rather than engage them, we picked up our pace until we reached the *Zodiac*, still resting above the tide in the little cove and surrounded by territorial seals. Gentry and Tony shooed them away, dragging the boat down to the water. Nathan placed Simone in first, and the rest of us followed.

Gentry took the helm. I handed over the phone to JT, curled up next to Simone and shut my eyes, wondering if I'd ever feel anything but this terrible hollow numbness.

Part of me didn't care.

Still, when Lil's hand crept into mine, I took it and didn't let go until we'd reached North Island.

CHAPTER FORTY-FOUR

The cafeteria was unusually crowded as I stood in line to get some food for Lil. She was in one of her downswings, and was holed up in her room. Hopefully she'd agree to eat something.

It'd been a week since we'd returned to the DZN facility in San Francisco. The *Zodiac* had gotten us safely to North Island, where military personnel and the Veteran's Allegiance boys greeted us. The minute we'd landed, Rooster had taken charge of Simone's care, rushing her off to the base's hospital, Nathan close behind.

If the bullet had been an inch further in any direction, and if Nathan had not kept up compression to slow the bleeding, not even the accelerated healing abilities of a wild card would have saved her.

I'd required some cleanup, as well, to prevent my wounds from becoming septic. The treatment didn't hurt quite as much as the original damage Jake had caused, but it was a close second.

We'd left for San Francisco the next day, after saying farewell to the bikers. I owed these guys a debt that I could never repay. We all did. So I hugged each and every one of them, and didn't even squawk when Cheeky gave my butt an extra squeeze when it was his turn.

"Stay strong, little sister," Viper said. "You'll get through this."

I wasn't so sure, but I didn't say so.

Once back in San Francisco, Dr. Albert holed up with Dr. Arkin, with Simone's help from the sidelines. It quickly became clear why she'd insisted that we bring Griff back with us. His condition was unique as a vector and a wild card. As such, he was irreplaceable. Hopes ran high that a retrovirus might be created based on Griff's particular immunity, combined with the properties that made Gabriel responsive to the antiserum. It wouldn't necessarily cure anyone, but it might help their systems fight off the infection.

If we could slow down the spread of the plague, we might prevent it from becoming an extinction event.

Then there had been Jamie. Poor obsessed Jamie who'd betrayed us to keep Simone safe. I wouldn't have survived if she hadn't stepped in and helped me, but I wasn't under any illusions about her reasons for doing so.

She'd been gone when we returned to San Francisco. No one knew when she'd left or where she went. Simone was devastated, but Nathan told me privately he thought it was for the best.

I heard Tony's voice coming up behind me as he and JT got in line.

"Dude," he said, "J.J. Abrams totally needs to be hung up by his nutsack for the *Star Trek* reboot."

"Don't I know it," JT agreed. "There can be no forgiveness for totally fucking around with the original space-time continuum, Spock or no Spock."

They fist bumped, Tony looking the most animated I'd seen him since Kai's death. He'd gotten over his knee-jerk distrust of JT, with reluctant admiration morphing into friendship. The two of them spent a lot of time with G as well, hanging out in the cafeteria and bonding over comics and other forms of geekdom, arguing endlessly over which Doctor Who was the best. Sometimes Gentry joined them but he couldn't quite achieve the same level of enthusiasm.

He was, however, interested in learning more about parkour, as was Tony. I thought maybe I'd give it a try myself down the line, but right now I couldn't summon up the energy.

I didn't have the energy or interest for much of anything these days, other than taking care of Lil, whether she wanted me to or not. The affection she had shown me after Gabriel's death ebbed and flowed, depending on her mood of the moment. The bad guys had given her tranquilizers at the Cabrillo Point facility, but Lil being Lil, she'd held them under her tongue and spat them out. So when JT had stumbled across her in a cell, she'd pretended to be asleep, and had almost broken his nose before realizing who he was.

She was taking her meds now, but the betrayal she'd felt for me had left its mark, even though a part of her realized I'd been doing it for her own good. I learned not to take her mood swings personally.

It helped that I was still numb, my feelings encased in a bubble that distanced me from everything and everyone. Nothing seemed quite real. When I interacted with people, I made all the right and polite responses, but my emotions were so muted that I felt like a cardboard cutout of myself. Even talking with my parents, making sure they were safe, hadn't felt the way I'd hoped it would.

In a way, that was fine by me. I didn't really want to feel, because I knew once I did it would hurt so badly I might not want to live.

Lil still needed me, though. That gave me purpose, even if sometimes it was just to scoop out the litter box. So for now, I'd focus on her. As long as she needed me, I could stay in this safe zone of emotional null.

For her sake.

I took my tray, balancing it carefully as I threaded my way past the tables and people toward the door.

Just before I reached it, I noticed a woman, mid- to late-thirties, with short brown hair, dressed in scrubs and a loose black T-shirt. She was sitting at a table by herself, staring blankly into a bowl of soup. She held her spoon in a loose grip as if she'd forgotten it was there. I glanced down, and caught my breath.

She had deep indentations, now healing with shiny scar tissue, which went up and down both arms. Jake's one surviving victim from Redwood Grove. The last time I'd seen her, she was covered with raw, seeping wounds. It was a wonder she was still alive, and a minor miracle that she'd retained even a semblance of sanity.

I hesitated, then decided to take the plunge. I sat down across from her. She looked at me without interest. I pulled my sleeves up, revealing the divots Jake had sliced out of my forearms.

"Got a real nice one on my stomach, too."

Her face shadowed with understanding and pain. She reached out wordlessly, putting a hand on mine and squeezing gently.

"You, too?"

"Yeah." I nodded. "Same guy."

She swallowed hard.

"I'm sorry."

"I am too," I said. "No one should have to go through that."

"I still dream about it sometimes… about him." Her face contorted with the memory.

"Do you want to talk about it?"

She looked at me for a moment, and then nodded again, slowly.

"Yes. Yes I do," she said. "I can talk to you about it. You'll understand. And if I don't… if I keep it inside me, it will eat me alive."

She took a deep breath, and then continued.

"When they set up the military barricades, I had to get home, back to Redwood Grove. So I took a back way, to sneak around them." Her eyes were distant as she remembered. "When I got home, there were bodies everywhere, but they wouldn't stay dead. I panicked, locked myself out of my car, so I ran—made it to a friend's house a few blocks away, Janet. We got in her car, tried to drive up to the college, but there were a bunch of those things on the road, and Janet got scared. Turned the car around and drove up into the mountains.

"We found the house up there, the one where—" She swallowed, the muscles in her face twitching. "That man… Jake was there. He invited us in. Said we'd be safe." She looked up at me, eyes wide. "He waited until we were sleeping. I think he drugged our food or drinks. We woke up fastened to tables… we couldn't move. He fed us enough to keep us alive.

"Sometimes he remembered to stop the bleeding after he'd—" She stopped. Her fingers clutched convulsively.

"He ate us, you know," she said simply. "Ate us. Little bits at a time. He'd apologize, even cry a little. Say he was sorry over and over again. But he wouldn't stop. No matter how much Janet or I screamed."

"I know."

She shook her head as if to clear it.

"Yes, I imagine you do."

I put my other hand on top of hers.

"You'll be glad to know that he's dead," I said. "*Really* dead. He can't hurt you or anyone else again."

She gave a convulsive shudder and shut her eyes.

"Thank God," she whispered. She opened them again. "I'm sorry, I'm forgetting my manners. I'm Betty."

"I'm Ashley," I replied. "If you ever want to talk again, just ask for me." I got to my feet, wanting to get Lil her soup before it got cold. Then suddenly my brain did a somersault, and I turned back.

Betty's Beads.

"Why did you sneak past the quarantine?"

She looked at me and smiled sadly.

"I needed to get home to my daughter. But I never did find her."

I let my breath out in one long exhale. Put the tray down and took Betty by the hand, practically lifting her out of her chair.

"Come with me," I said. "I've got someone you'll want to meet."

CHAPTER FORTY-FIVE

A few minutes later we stood outside Lil's room. I rapped on the door.

"Hey," I said, my pulse racing. "It's Ash."

No answer, so I opened the door and pushed it open, sticking my head inside. Lil was in her usual position on the bed, curled up in a little ball under the covers, with only the top of her head sticking out. Binkey and Doodle were on sentry duty on top of her.

"Hey," I said again, "I've got someone who wants to see you."

"Go away," she said, voice muffled by the bedclothes.

Betty stuck her head into the room.

"What cute cats," she said. "They remind me of…" And then she stopped.

"Lily?" She stepped into the room.

The covers slipped off of Lil's head and shoulders as she slowly sat up, an expression of almost painful hope on her face.

"Mom?"

Betty nodded, her face and throat working convulsively as she stared at her daughter.

"Mommy?"

Betty tried to speak, but the words wouldn't come. A sob burst forth as she held her arms out. With a wordless cry, Lil catapulted out of bed, causing the cats to scatter as she threw herself into her mother's arms and began to cry in huge, wrenching sobs that wracked her entire body.

Tears stung my own eyes as I backed out of the room, shutting the door behind me with a quiet click. I stood in the hallway for a moment, then slowly walked away from her room, trying to ignore the hollow feeling inside as I realized Lil would no longer need me.

I walked aimlessly for a little while, ignoring the people I passed, most of whom I didn't recognize anyway. Without any forethought, I made my way up to the main level and from there, to the main elevator that went to the glassed-in crosswalk.

Once up top, I wandered over and up the stairwell that led to the rooftop where the helicopter had taken Gabriel and Dr. Albert away. I sat down in the middle of the makeshift helipad, wrapping my arms around my knees and hugging them close to my body. I stared straight ahead at the cement wall in front of me, my eyes focusing on a zigzagging crack in the cement that looked as if it had been left by Zorro. Then I put my head down on my knees and cried.

I cried until my head hurt and my throat was raw from the loud, keening sobs that ripped their way out of me. I cried for Kai, for Mack, the Gunsy Twins, Carl, and Red Shirt, whose name I'd never bothered to learn. For Aimee and her daughter. I cried for my old boyfriend Matt and my roommate, for everyone who'd suffered because of misguided altruism, greed, and arrogance.

Mostly, though, I cried for Gabriel and for myself, and for the chance we'd never have to find out what the two of us could have had together. I cried until my eyes were swollen and my head throbbed. Until the tears finally stopped coming, dissolving into the occasional hitching sob until even those died off, leaving me hollowed out to my very core.

Then I wiped my eyes and nose as best as I could with my shirtsleeves, then wrapped my arms back around my knees. I don't know how long I sat there like that. Long enough for the sun to fade down into the horizon, a cold wind picking up and biting through my clothes. I didn't care, though. I barely even noticed it. If I was lucky, I'd catch a chill and have it turn into pneumonia and die.

Not fucking likely, thanks to my sturdy immune system. But I could hope.

I heard the sound of footsteps coming up the stairs and out onto the rooftop, crunching across the asphalt as they came toward me. I stayed where I was, still hugging my knees and staring at the mark of Zorro. Griff sat down next to me and silently handed me a bottle of water. I took it without saying anything, unscrewed the lid and took a sip.

We sat in a strangely compatible silence for a while longer. Griff reminded me of a cat, the kind that did exactly what it wanted, when it wanted, its sense of loyalty predicated by its needs from moment to moment. I still wasn't sure if he should be considered a hero or a villain in all of this. Arguments could be made on either side, I suppose.

He'd saved my life, but let the rest of the team get taken without trying to help. He'd gone after Lil and brought her back alive, because he'd promised me he would. And he'd come through for all of us in the end.

"Thank you for finding Lil." My voice cracked as I broke the silence between us, throat still raw from the tears. I took another sip of water before continuing. "I really didn't think I'd see her again."

He shrugged.

"Told you I would."

"You told me a lot of things," I reminded him. "Some of them kind of creepy."

His mouth curved in a rueful smile.

"Just following orders. If it's worth anything, I regret a lot of it."

"Not all of it?"

He gave me a sideways glance.

"You can be a real bitch sometimes, you know. Figure you deserved at least some of it."

I snorted. "'Officer, she was asking for it.' Is that it?"

"No." He was silent for a moment, and then he continued. "I like you," he said simply. "You're smart, brave, and you don't give up."

I nodded, accepting his words at face value.

"Plus you've got great tits."

The outrageousness of that comment startled a little snort of laughter out of me.

"I'm not going to sleep with you, if that's what you're getting at."

"Not asking you to."

"Good."

We lapsed back into silence, staring up at the night sky as we listened to the sounds of a dying city rise up to the rooftop. Maybe it could still be saved, once the doctors had perfected the retrovirus, and we got it out to whatever percentage of the population still lived. It would be dangerous, but hell, that's what wild cards were for, right?

Maybe I was still needed after all.

EPILOGUE

INTERNATIONAL SPACE STATION

The whole of the bright blue, cloud-dappled Earth gleamed in the eyes of Commander Jess Lowry as she stood in a ring of windows in the cupola of the International Space Station.

From their vantage point, circling the globe every hour and a half, days and nights seemed to fly past every forty-five minutes with a burst of sunrise and then a plunge into darkness. Normally she loved the night side—a miniature clockwork wonderland, filled with a glittering, shimmering glaze of electric diamond dust tracing out lattices of firefly pinpoints and luminescent trails stretching across entire continents in bright points of copper, gold, yellow, and white.

All that was gone now.

Her eyes darkened as she kept her vigil over the new night sky. The once-bright landforms were dead, and the Earth hung limply in space like a badly bruised corpse, ugly black holes where Rio and New York and Tokyo used to shine. She suppressed a shudder as she remembered the screams coming over the station's comlink, from Houston's mission control room.

There was a sound behind her, as Flight Engineer Nikolai Mironoff zipped down the main tube like an arrow, effortlessly threading through a cluttered gauntlet of laptop stations, instrument panels, plastic tubing, and other bits of random equipment without hitting any of the potential snares. He *floated into sight and pulled himself to a halt alongside her.*

"Kakie novosti?" she asked, still staring out the cupola's borosilicate viewports.

"Nothing we don't already know" the Russian replied. "Power levels on both starboard and port arrays are holding steady. I have shut down all non-essential modules and transferred everything on our checklists to Zvezda."

She turned to him. "Good. The Soyuz ready to go?"

The cosmonaut hesitated, and she knew he didn't trust the obsolescent spacecraft for a re-entry. Yet they had no choice in the matter. It was either risk an orbital drop in the battered old Soviet workhorse, or stay on board while their oxygen and power levels raced to see which was exhausted first.

"It's ready to take us straight to hell right now," he replied. "But maybe—if we are very, very lucky—maybe it will get us through the upper atmosphere before it all falls to pieces."

"Thanks, Nikolai." Jess gave him a weary smile and returned her gaze to the outside.

"A mote of dust suspended in a sunbeam..." she sighed.

"Shto eta?"

"Something Carl Sagan said once, about the earth being a pale blue dot. On it everyone you love, everyone you know, everyone you ever heard of, every human being who ever was, lived out their lives. Every saint and sinner in the history of our species lived there, on a mote of dust suspended in a sunbeam." She gave Nikolai a rueful smile. "Now I wonder if there's anyone left down there at all."

"If that chertovskiy Soyuz doesn't kill us on impact, there will be. We'll be the new Adám i Jéva. We'll repopulate the planet, you and I."

She played along.

"Where shall we touch down then? Any ideas where to set up the new Eden?"

Nikolai peered out at the uninviting ball floating before them, scowling slightly at the slim prospects before making a small flourish with one hand.

"Ladies choice, of course."

"Let me think about that."

He nodded, and took watch alongside her.

She reached for the hi-resolution handheld imager—a combination telescope and camera—and tore it off its velcro tether. The planet continued its slow, relentless turning, cycling through light and dark while she pored over the whole world laid out before them, scanning for possible landing areas.

There was a spot of shimmering haze at the northern tip of the Persian Gulf. That was the Kuwaiti oil fields on fire.

In the North Atlantic she could see the wake of a large vessel—an aircraft carrier perhaps, though she had no way to tell if it was American or Russian, or even if it was still under the control of human beings.

Australia's east coast glowed from wildfires, raging out of control.

On the highest settings of her imager, tiny pinpricks of light from various spots on the California coast caught her attention. But what were they? Campfires? Burning rubble? Were they signs of life? Or just more signs of death?

She kept searching, while the world kept spinning.

ACKNOWLEDGEMENTS

I hate writing acknowledgements as much as I love the people I want to thank! There are just so many of 'em, though, and I hate to forget anyone. So apologies in advance if your name is not listed here. It's not because I don't love and appreciate you! It's because the brain... it melts... *it melts*!!

First up, those epically awesome Titan folks: Nick Landau, Vivien Cheung, Katy Wild, Alice Nightingale, Natalie Laverick, Miranda Jewess, Charlotte Couldrey, Tim Whale, Selina Juneja, Julia Lloyd, Ella Bowman, Hannah Dennis, Chris McLane, Martin Stiff, and my usual extra helping of love to Tom Green and Katherine Carroll, who make publicity fun for me! Love me the Titan crew, especially my Dark Editorial Overlord, Steve Saffel, who is not just a wonderful editor, but a truly supportive friend.

Research can be time-consuming and frustrating, but with the help of Facebook and my eclectically knowledgeable friends and family, it was fun and relatively easy this time around. In no particular order but with equal gratitude: Elizabeth Buxton, James Jackson, Aaron Sikes, Eric Bar, Nancy Vandermay, Kate Laity, Aud Fredstie, Maddie Karathanas, Jonathan Stern, Richard Hartman, Jonathan Brett Kennedy, James Jackson, Peter Indiana Allison, Michael Beach, Marcy

Meyer, Pamela Cale, Ernie Williams, and oh, I know there are more... You know who you are!

I am continually blown away by the generosity of my friends. Sending waves of thanks and love to John Hornor Jacobs for the Redneck Legolas art; my cousin Steffan Fredsti for the katanas and cousinly support; Anne Stevenson for Titania; Aimee Hix for Motivational Penguin and Dana's Delights; and Jane Thorne-Gutierrez for chocolate, band-aids and the Magic Amethyst. Huge thanks to the Veteran's Allegiance for their willingness and enthusiasm to appear in my book!

Owen and Julie, your time and counseling when my sanity was cracking were invaluable (not to mention the bacon chutney). Further sanity points were awarded to me by Maureen A., Maureen Z., Aldyth, Brad, and James. Thank you. And Jen, you helped keep my world together when it fell apart. Thanks for being the Danny to my Sgt. Angel (or vice versa, if you insist!).

Endless appreciation to Jess Lourey for her unfailing 'you can do it' feedback when I was at my lowest ebb, and heartfelt thanks to Cynthia Gentry for those writing dates! Loren Rhoads, those talks over coffee always inspire. Special thanks to Joe McKinney and Craig DiLouie for taking the time to read (I owes ya drinks!), and a huge hug and thank you to my favorite Perpetual Writing Machine Jonathan Maberry for his encouragement, as well as inspiration by example.

My family has always supported my writing (thanks, Mom and Bill!), and while my sister Lisa wouldn't have been caught dead being a cheerleader in high school, she's been great at cheering me on through my struggles to finish this book. And most of all, thanks and love to Hell Ocho, T. Chris "Cookie" Martindale, and David Fitzgerald... I could not have written this book without the three of you.

ABOUT THE AUTHOR

Dana Fredsti is an ex B-movie actress with a background in theatrical combat (a skill she utilized in *Army of Darkness* as a sword-fighting Deadite and fight captain). She's addicted to bad movies and any book or film, good or bad, which include zombies. She is the author of the Ashley Parker series, touted as Buffy meets *The Walking Dead*, as well as the cozy noir mystery *Murder for Hire: the Peruvian Pigeon*, and co-author of *What Women Really Want in Bed*. She guest blogs frequently and has made numerous podcast and radio appearances. She lives in San Francisco with her boyfriend, their dog Pogeen, and a small horde of felines.